UNCHAINED
MEMORIES

By the Author

Where the Light Glows

Unchained Memories

Visit us at www.boldstrokesbooks.com

UNCHAINED MEMORIES

by

Dena Blake

2017

ISBN 13: 978-1-62639-993-8

This Trade Paperback Original Is Published By
Bold Strokes Books, Inc.
P.O. Box 249
Valley Falls, NY 12185

First Edition: September 2017

Credits
Editor: Shelley Thrasher
Production Design: Stacia Seaman
Cover Design by Sheri (graphicartist2020@hotmail.com)

Acknowledgments

Thank you to Radclyffe and Sandy Lowe for letting me do what I love. Seeing it in print is a dream come true. My editor extraordinaire, Shelley Thrasher, will never know just how grateful I am to her for making me look like I can form a well-written sentence. Thanks to Kris Bryant and Lisa Moreau for coaching me through the ins and outs of the publishing process and never letting me miss something important. The BSB family is truly fantastic.

Thanks to Robyn for catching all those words I can't seem to ever get right, and for asking all the right questions. To Kate for never failing to tell me your thoughts about my writing as well as the world around me. I hope those conversations never stop coming. To my kids, Wes and Haley, for giving me true-life writing material for this book. Some things you just can't make up. To my family for being the most awesome support system a girl could ever want.

Last, but never least, to all of you who will read this book, thank you for taking a chance on me.

For Wes and Haley. I'm so proud of the adults you've become. I love you more than I can ever put into words.

CHAPTER ONE

I bet there'll be a sequel to that one." Jamie twisted in the passenger seat and made a goofy face at Jillian.

"Not," they both said in unison.

"What's not to like? You had aliens, zombies, and teenagers?" Ken asked.

"Right," Jillian blurted as she laughed. "I think it was the teenagers that threw it over the top." Jillian and Jamie had spent the entire movie doing what sisters do, whispering in each other's ears, making fun of the plot and the characters.

Jamie twisted to face her again. "*Plus* the aliens...and the zombies." She choked on her words as she sucked in a breath and laughed.

Jillian pulled up Rotten Tomatoes on her phone. "It got a green splat on the Tomatometer." Which it totally deserved. The movie had been unrealistic and hokey. It was their fault for letting Ken choose the day's entertainment. The last few times Jillian was in town, she and Jamie had chosen the movie so, in all fairness, he was due a turn. Jamie fully admitted Ken was a great husband and father, but he had a uniquely odd sense of entertainment. Jillian just hoped it didn't rub off on their daughter, Abby, who was too busy with her friends to spend any time with them lately.

"Whatever. Abby would've loved it," Ken said, still trying to convince them of its cult merit. "She'll probably go see it with her friends."

Jamie's eyes widened. "Never. That's a make-out movie if I've ever seen one."

"Are you letting her date now?" Jillian's voice rose. She hadn't realized Abby was that old.

"Not yet, but she's almost fifteen. It won't be long," Jamie said as she scrunched her face.

"Fine. I'll pick something better next time." Ken squeezed Jamie's hand.

Jillian couldn't hold her laughter. "Oh my gosh, how sweet is that? He actually thinks we're going to let him choose again."

"That's my husband, always the optimist." Jamie leaned across the console and gave Ken a quick kiss on the cheek. Jillian's heart swelled at how well her sister and brother-in-law fit together. They were the perfect couple, balancing each other in everything they did. She couldn't remember ever seeing them fight.

Ken had been such a good sport about their teasing. He'd even began slinging one-liners from the movie as they got closer to home. He was in the middle of one when "Oh, shit!" came out of his mouth.

Jillian had only seen the truck coming toward them from the corner of her eye. Then everything slowed. Jillian heard the metal crunching before she felt the impact. The jolt sent her phone flying from her hand. She heard the ear-splitting pop as the air bag hit Jamie in the face and the back of her head hit the headrest. Jillian went flying next as the air bag punched her in the side. Pain in her arm, now her face as she catapulted into the side of the driver's seat. She was going to be sick. This roller-coaster ride needed to end. Now. The car scraped the pavement as it launched across the beltway and tumbled into the ditch. All sound was gone. Only ringing in her ears remained. The car wobbled back and forth as it came to a stop. Jillian wiped the moisture from her eyes. It was thick, sticky almost. It was hard to see. Pain shot through her nose when she tried to suck in a breath.

"Jamie," she said. No answer from her sister. "Jamie!" Again, no answer. She tried to pull herself forward. The passenger seat was empty. She reached forward, felt Ken slumped against the driver's door, his head resting forward on the air bag.

"Ken, where's Jamie?" She heard a gurgle, an attempt to speak. She had to find Jamie. A metallic taste in her mouth overwhelmed her. Her stomach lurched as she found the door handle and pushed out of the car. *Oh God.* Her head spun. Her face throbbed. She braced herself against the side of the car and took a breath before she scanned the road, looking for Jamie. *There she is.* She lay on her side crumpled in the grass not far from the car. Jillian stumbled over and fell to the ground next to her.

She put her hand on her shoulder and shook. "Jamie," she said.

No response. She rolled her onto her back. Her chest wasn't moving. *She's not breathing.* CPR instructions flew through Jillian's head. She knew how to do that. Her heart hammered as she took Jamie's face in her hands and put her mouth over it. *Breathe, Jamie, breathe.* Then the paramedic was there, pushing her out of the way. She watched him pump her chest and try to breathe life into her sister.

Another paramedic's voice came through the constant ringing in her ears. "Miss, please look at me. I need to see your eyes." He was talking to her. She pulled her gaze from Jamie, and the paramedic flashed a light in her eyes. She blinked and veered her gaze back to Jamie. The paramedic had stopped CPR. A wave of helplessness shot through her when he looked back at Jillian and shook his head.

Her vision narrowed. Her limbs felt heavy and her world swayed. *Nooooo!* She shot up and tried to push past him to Jamie. Her head spun again. She took a few steps and stumbled. Everything went black.

CHAPTER TWO

Tires screeched and a horn blared loudly as Jillian pulled into traffic on the two-lane road. All she could see in the rearview mirror were arms flailing wildly and an open mouth she knew was spouting some very choice words into the windshield right now.

Abby twisted in her seat to look back. "What's wrong with her?"

"I guess I cut her off when I pulled out. They drive differently here than they do in New York." She glanced in the rearview mirror again. "She has no reason to be upset." Jillian had put on her blinker, and the other driver was going way too fast for this road.

"She's acting crazy." Abby pulled the headphones from her bag and slid them over her ears.

The woman was right on her ass. Jillian took a right at the next light onto the four-lane road, trying to lose her, but the woman didn't let up. She pulled to the right, hoping she would pass, but the woman pulled to the right also. She could still hear the woman screaming out the window, "Pull over. I want to talk to you." Jillian knew better than to pull over. She'd reported too many stories on road-rage victims. Confronting someone like this could end up getting both her and Abby killed. She had to lose this lunatic before they got to where they were going. She didn't want to draw any more attention to herself than necessary, and she definitely didn't want to end up dead on her first day back home. She gunned the engine, slipping between two cars to her left, then swerved into the left-turn lane, barely making the light. She circled around, went back the other way, and headed to the house where she and Abby would be staying for the near future.

Jillian squinted, thinking she'd made a mistake, but she'd already passed the house three times, and from the numbers tacked above the porch, there was no mistake about it. Fifteen-thirty-two Sycamore. She sighed. It looked exactly the same as the day she'd left. The over-the-top gingerbread ornamentation her mother loved, the single tower in front hovering above the open porch. Bay windows at each end of the house. This was it, all right. It even still had the sunflower flourish on the front façade and decorative shingle siding she remembered. The only difference was the porch railing. It no longer had the elaborate decorations of the Queen Anne style. That particular piece of history must have been removed during the renovation.

The place was huge—one, two, three stories, she counted—but it wasn't quite as large as it was in her memories. She guessed that was a creation of her childhood mind. After giving it a more thorough look, she decided the house was just as she remembered. Large and looming. Somehow, in her absence, she'd forgotten just how frightening it actually was. Maybe it was because she'd put this place out of her mind the day she and her sister had boarded that flight to New York.

Now she was right back where she'd started, in her hometown of Norman, Oklahoma. Among people who wouldn't recognize her the way she was dressed now. No fancy clothes, no high heels, barely a stitch of makeup. Even a new nose. Not a single shred of Jillian McIntyre was left. She was plain old JJ Davis now. Taking on the false persona every time she left New York had been her sister, Jamie's, idea. In a small town like Norman, Jillian knew if she showed up as herself, she might possibly be recognized. JJ Davis, however, went virtually unnoticed. With her thrift-store wardrobe and minimal amount of makeup, she blended right in. Right into the woodwork, that is. Changing her look hadn't been difficult since the accident. Her broken nose had made it much easier, but pulling off a mild-mannered personality was a completely different story.

Jillian McIntyre hadn't planned to abandon her broadcasting career to move back to Oklahoma, and she hadn't counted on raising an angry, pubescent teen either. Nevertheless, years ago, when her sister had drawn up her will, she'd made Jillian promise only one thing. If anything ever happened to her and Ken, she was to make sure her niece, Abby, was brought up in a household with two loving parents. Now she had to find one of those loving parents, and this was the only way she knew how to accomplish that.

When she'd gone to the Department of Human Services office, Jillian had almost blown the whole thing. She knew she'd talked too much. Patience was a virtue she no longer retained. Fame and fortune can change a person in many ways. Jillian was no exception. When she wanted something done, she wanted it done now. Her assistant had created the alias, but she'd failed to create a work history and financial records. Essentially, JJ Davis didn't exist except for the Social Security number she'd stolen from some child who'd died at birth and the phony driver's license she carried. No way would she be approved for aid. The Department of Human Services would do a thorough background and financial check before assigning her to the group home. They would never believe she was an out-of-work schoolteacher trying to raise her sister's kid. What a farce that was, in more ways than one. She'd had to tell the supervisor, Maxine Freeman, the same story she'd told Abby to get her to buy in on the trip. That she was doing an investigative report on the benefits of outside-funded housing assistance to bring more light to the needs of the system and to possibly obtain them more funding. Due to the nose reconstruction after the accident, Maxine hadn't recognized her and was a little skeptical at first. When Jillian had mentioned the possibility of filming her for a spot on the final TV show, she could see the excitement in Maxine's eyes. After that, she was all in.

In addition to the nose reconstruction, Jillian had dyed her hair blond and chosen to wear brown contacts to disguise the unique color of her eyes. She looked enough like her sister to pass as her. Jamie had a teaching degree, so there would be no questions. Thankfully, only her initials were listed on her credentials. She would now be JJ Davis. Her only concern now was that two people thought she was here on assignment. Which one of them would be likely to let the cat out of the bag first?

She'd waited in Maxine's office long enough to overhear a very important phone conversation. The new tenants at Heartstrings House, the group home Jillian funded and also needed to access, were going to be delayed a month. That would give her more than enough time to accomplish what she came for.

Jillian felt a little guilty taking someone else's slot. She certainly didn't need it, but she'd promised herself when she'd left the DHS office this morning. She would donate double—no, she would donate triple the amount it cost each week to support her and her niece and make sure it got back into the system somehow. She hated doing it this way, but the only way she could get anywhere near Abby's father without scaring him off was to pretend she needed help. Which, ironically, was true in many ways.

Jillian held the steering wheel, her hands shaking. Knowing she was about to see him again threw her into a tizzy. Blake Mathews, her sister's first love. Would he still be the same? Would he recognize her? Would he even remember Jamie? Would his sister, Amelia, still be around? Those were only a few of the many questions racing through her head. She adjusted the rearview mirror to look at her reflection and chuckled. It had been so many years ago, and from what Jamie had told her, Blake had never had a clue she was pregnant. Glancing over at Abby, she let her gaze leave the road momentarily again. Fifteen years ago, to be exact. Abby returned her look with a spiteful glare. She had Jamie's startling eyes, just like her own. When she chose to share it, her smile was as warm as Jillian remembered her father's to be.

She pulled the old Honda up to the curb and moved the shift knob into park. Glancing at her watch, she slid it off her wrist and tucked it into the side pocket of her bag. A Rolex was much too expensive for someone like JJ Davis to be sporting, but it was the only thing she'd brought with her. She needed something to remind her of Jillian McIntyre's existence.

"We're here," she said, receiving no response from Abby. She reached over and pulled the headphone from her ear. "Hey, we're here."

"Great." The resentment in her crystal blue eyes came through loud and clear. "Looks like paradise."

Jillian let out a slow sigh. She hadn't wanted to uproot Abby from her home in New York, but under the circumstances, she had no other choice. The loss of her parents had been devastating, and leaving her behind while she investigated Blake wasn't an option.

"Who's that?" Abby pulled the lever on the seat and bolted straight up.

Jillian glanced up at the doorway, and her heart stopped. She squeezed her eyes shut. The young man standing on the porch was surely something she'd conjured up from the past. She opened her eyes and he was still there. Tall and lanky, his forehead sprayed with auburn hair, he looked to be only about seventeen. She'd driven straight through, but she didn't think she was that exhausted. She pinched her leg. She must have fallen asleep. The boy threw them a wave, and she pinched harder. This had to be a dream, or maybe she was dead.

The front door opened, and a man with hair the color of dark-red Oklahoma clay stepped out next to the teenager. Dressed in khaki pants and a blue-and-white, long-sleeve, button-down shirt, he slid one hand into his pocket and placed the other on the porch beam as though he were a model posing for a shoot.

Jillian's mouth dropped open. This wasn't possible. It was Blake. Then and now.

The men started toward the car, and Jillian couldn't move. He was older, but he hadn't changed. Even now, Blake Mathews was still the most handsome man she'd ever seen. He was her sister's first everything.

Her plan seemed feasible when she'd run it through her head the hundred times on the drive over here, but now she was having second thoughts. What if Blake didn't understand what had happened so many years before? What if he didn't care? She looked at Abby, still planted in the front seat, flipping through her CD case. What if he didn't want anything to do with Abby? *Damn it, Jamie. I can't believe you did this to me.* Jillian took in a deep breath to steady herself. It was too late to think about any of that now.

As Blake came around the front of the car toward her, the young man rounded the back of the old brown Honda CRV and yanked at the hatch.

"Blake Mathews," he said, pulling the driver's door open and holding out his hand.

"Good morning, Mr. Mathews." She hesitated before swinging her legs out and taking his hand. "I'm JJ Davis, and this is my niece, Abigale Davis."

"Abby." The fifteen-year-old corrected her.

"Nice to meet you, ladies." He peeked in and gave Abby a subtle smile. "And please, call me Blake."

Jillian rounded the car and stopped by the teenager taking the bags from the back. Still caught by the resemblance, she couldn't form a sentence.

"This is my son, David."

Son? She darted her gaze to Abby and then back to David. Abby was fifteen, and this young man looked to be at least seventeen, maybe older. She stared back at Blake. He couldn't possibly have a son.

"You have a son?"

"I do." He nodded and pulled his eyebrows together. "Have we met before?"

"No." Jillian scrambled for words. "I don't believe so."

"I thought you said the kid was a dude," David said, and gave Blake a questioning look.

"Maxine must have made a mistake."

David pulled the largest bag out and dropped it onto the asphalt. "You sure have a lot of stuff."

She watched him struggle with the next bag. "Oh, just bring in the two big ones for now. We can get the others later."

David grabbed one of the bags, Abby grabbed the other, and they both headed into the house. Jillian stood on the sidewalk watching Blake pull the rest of the luggage from the car before closing the hatch. She'd found him. He was no longer the tall, gangly teenager she remembered. He was definitely a man now. Could she trust him with Jamie's beautiful little girl? She heard Abby's voice echo in stinging complaint as she lugged her bag up the porch stairs. A little girl was how she'd remembered her, but she wasn't little anymore. She was an attitude-filled young woman.

When Blake looked up and his gaze met hers, she looked away quickly. *Don't blow it.* Spinning around, she walked toward the house, preparing to enter the so-called sanctuary she swore she would never set foot in again. Not able to do so immediately, she hesitated, trying to clear the knot developing in her stomach. She glanced back at Blake, and the knot immediately disappeared. Just watching him gather the rest of the bags in his arms before following her up the cobblestone walk was enough to make her forget the terrible horror that had happened within these walls.

The bags began to tumble back into his face, and he shouted, "I could use a hand with these."

"Oh, sorry." She hurried back to help him, swiped the small black cosmetic case from the top of the heap, and then bounced back up the steps and through the door.

"Thanks." He let out a chuckle. "That helps a lot."

Jillian stepped inside and took a deep breath. The house no longer smelled of her mother's famous meat loaf and home-baked chocolate-chip cookies. All that lingered now was the smell of fresh paint. "Where to now?"

"Up the stairs, to the right."

After climbing the U-shaped staircase, Jillian stood at the top, staring to the left toward her parents' bedroom. The room where it had all happened. Sweat formed on the back of her neck, and her stomach churned. She was going to have to visit them while she was in town.

"You have the two rooms with the Jack-and-Jill bathroom between them."

Forcing herself to move, Jillian headed the short distance down the hall, set her bag just inside the door, and looked around. She remembered the path well. She'd spent a lot of time in this room. The scent of fresh paint filled her nose. The color of baby blue now covered the pink walls she remembered. She walked through the bathroom to Jamie's room, and her stomach shot to her throat. Sadness overwhelmed her, and she grabbed hold of the door jamb. *Put it out of your mind, Jillian.* She took in a deep breath and forged ahead.

The furniture was sparse—a twin bed, nightstand, and lamp in each room. No dresser, mirror, or decorations. The rooms weren't nearly as comfortable as they were when she was a child, but more stuff wouldn't make it feel like home again.

"Kind of bare in here, isn't it?" she said, shrugging off the tingling chill climbing her spine.

"We haven't finished furnishing it yet. The department's a little behind with our funds. I think some of the original furniture is in the attic. I'll check on that this weekend."

"Thanks." It might be comforting to have some of her old stuff around her, but then again, it might not. The sun blinded her as she looked toward the window. "Are there any curtains?" They'd taken down the old frilly ones that had hung here when she was a child.

"Not sure if that's in the budget, but I'll check on it. If so, I'll get to it as soon as I can." He went to the window and glanced out at the setting sun. "You're on the west side. The sun shouldn't be too bright in the morning."

"Yeah, but I bet in another few hours it's going to be blazing hot in here." Thoughts of the blistering nights from her youth flashed through her mind. Endless tossing and turning, twisted in the sheets, unable to get comfortable. Then there were the hot sleepless nights she'd spent lying here with Amelia. Nights Amelia had sneaked out of her house and climbed up the trellis to be with her when the arguments in her house were so loud there seemed to be no escape. She shook herself out of the thought, flipped the latch on top of the wooden frame, and hoisted the window open. She stuck her head out of the opening. The old wooden trellises that led to the window in each room were gone, replaced by ones made of aged copper patina and now covered with beautiful roses. The wood had probably rotted away long ago, just like the family who had once lived there.

"None of these old houses have central air. It would cost a fortune to put it in now." Blake moved across the room and raised the other window. "If you open both windows, you can get a good cross-breeze going."

"It's too bad you don't have something newer."

"This is a good old house." Blake smiled and looked around the room. "I've spent some pretty good days here." His gaze drifted back to Jillian, and he seemed lost in thought. Maybe he did remember Jamie.

Jillian stepped across the room. "Is this the bathroom?"

"Yes, but..."

She closed the door before letting him finish. She had to. If she stayed out there one more minute, she would blow it. Her back against the wall, she slid down the door and squatted, holding her face in her hands. *Can I really pull this off?* The recurring doubts surfaced again. *This is the right thing to do. I can't possibly take care of Abby myself, can I?* She shook her head. *No, that can't happen.* She had no experience with children whatsoever. Besides that, she had a career to get back to, and Blake had experience. He had a child already, a teenager who couldn't be more than two years older than Abby. Two years older and she had no idea. *How could that happen?* It didn't make sense. The thought that Blake might have been sleeping with someone else when he was seeing her sister had Jillian's anger bubbling. What the hell was that about? Maybe that was why Jamie had never told him about Abby. Maybe Jamie had left him without a single word, no explanation, and no clue as to where she was going. Granted, there were extenuating circumstances, but she could have, and probably should have let him know, somehow. Her thoughts wandered to Amelia. Jillian should have done the same.

They had every right to go on with their lives or go back, as the case seemed to be for Blake. Would he love Abby in spite of Jamie's betrayal? Swiping her fingers across her tear-stained cheek, Jillian hoped when he found out the truth, Blake would love Abby no matter what Jamie had done. She smiled. Blake seemed like a good guy. He might hate Jamie, and possibly her for keeping it from him, but she was optimistic that he would accept Abby.

Seeing the toilet lid taped closed and the connections dangling from the back, she shot up to the basin and splashed a handful of cold water on her face. After she dried it with the only thing in sight, an old T-shirt that smelled of men's cologne, she grabbed the knob and sucked in a deep breath, hoping she hadn't been gone too long.

When she pulled the door open, Blake met her with his arms crossed and an if-you-had-listened-to-me look. "I'm not quite finished with the plumbing in there. I should have it done in a few days."

"I see that. Is there another bathroom I can use? It's been a long trip."

He led her into the hallway. "Down here to the right."

As she followed, Blake picked a T-shirt and a pair of dirty socks from the handcrafted, built-in bookcase she remembered. Her father had spent months building it. Giving her a prickly smile, he tossed the dirty clothes into the room across the hall, then reached in and pulled the door closed.

She pushed the door slowly, waiting for some sort of nasty critter to jump out at her. "In here?"

"Yeah. That's it."

Closing the door behind her, she walked gingerly, trying to avoid the magazines scattered across the floor. When she lifted the lid of the toilet, she was relieved to see that at least the bowl looked clean. At this point, running to the corner gas station wasn't an option. Messy, but clean. She could deal with that.

After she washed her hands, she reached down to straighten the magazines into a pile. As she looked at the covers, she could see they were probably all David's. *World Wrestling Federation, Hot Rod, MAD Magazine.* She smiled, thinking about her teen years. She used to read *MAD.* She remembered sneaking into her parents' bedroom to read her mother's copy of *Vogue.* The trendy fashions had dazzled her the first time she'd looked in mother's closet and the first time her mother had let her wear something out of it. It was a spectacular place, where Jillian could dream of being whoever she wanted, a place where she used to love to spend time.

The beginnings of a headache poked at the back of her head, and she took a deep breath before she flipped open the *MAD Magazine.* She wondered if it still had the same satirical punch. *When did they add so much text?* She flipped through a few more pages. *And pictures? Naked pictures!* She peeled the cover back. It wasn't *MAD Magazine.* Someone had glued the *MAD* cover onto an adult magazine. She picked up a few of the others and found the same had been done to those. *No, no, no. These will not stay.* Jillian gathered them all up quickly. Abby was much too young to be exposed to the realities of the male libido. *Okay, just settle down, Jillian. He's an adult, an adult male. If he wants to look at pictures of naked women, there's nothing wrong with that. He certainly doesn't have to explain it to you.* She'd met enough men *and* women with far worse habits than magazines.

Blake was standing by the top of the stairs when she came back out. Jillian shoved the magazines into his hands. "Please get rid of these."

"Sorry. The boys are kind of messy." He hedged his way down the hall and peered inside.

"You shouldn't leave stuff like that lying around." She eyed the magazines.

He looked puzzled. "*MAD, Hot Rod, WWF.* Nothing questionable here."

"Take a closer look."

She didn't know whether to be amused or irritated at his show of naiveté. This definitely wasn't the same man she knew from years ago. If the first hour was any indication, things might not go as planned. What was she saying? Her plan had to work. There was simply no other way. He flipped through the pages and his eyes widened.

"Changing the cover is a little extreme, don't you think?" She wasn't sure if it was from embarrassment or anger, but his face turned beet red. Maybe he didn't know.

"Sorry. I'll take care of them." He took the pile of magazines, and she followed him to the other end of the hall into her parents' old room. She peered into it as he entered. It looked different than it had before. The hardwood floor had been refinished and the furniture was new. It was nicely decorated in vibrant colors. He'd made it different. It wasn't her parents' room any longer. The bed was made, there were no stray clothes, and the dresser was neatly organized. A man who cleans up after himself. Every woman's dream. She heard him pull out a drawer and slap the magazines in before he reappeared and yanked the door closed behind him as he came out.

"Excuse me a minute, please." He headed straight down the stairs, his feet thumping in a quick rhythm as he descended into the living room where David and a couple of other boys were watching TV.

"I found your magazines." He waited with his hands on his hips for a response. Jillian stopped at the bottom of the stairs and watched as David's face paled. The boys seemed truly scared. What was Blake going to do? Punish him? Ground him for life? Blake moved closer, and David sank farther into the couch.

"Oh, no," she said, covering her mouth in a shuddered whisper. *He's a bully just like his father.* Remembering the repeated reprimands Blake had endured as a child, Jillian stepped into the room. David might deserve some sort of punishment, but she certainly wasn't going to let him hit the boy.

He looked at her, then back at David. "You get to cut the lawn this summer."

"The whole summer?" David asked with a tinge of protest clear in his voice.

"You wanna do the edging too?" His face was concrete, his eyes still and blazing.

"Okay," David said.

Blake rubbed his face as he turned away and then back to look at David again. "Don't bring anything like that into this house again. Any of you."

"Yes, sir." All the boys answered together.

Abby came bouncing down the stairs, dropping the book she was carrying onto the last step.

"Did you unpack?" Jillian asked.

"Why? I don't want to stay here. Can't we go to a hotel? There's no place to put my clothes."

Jillian crossed her arms. "We are staying, and you can hang them in the closet." Jillian had filled Abby in on the investigative report, only a half-truth, and Abby had begged Jillian to let her stay with one of her friends in New York. However, in order to carry out her sister's wishes, Jillian needed to see how Abby and Blake interacted.

"I'll do it later." Abby rolled her eyes. "Is there anything fun to do in this rinky-dink town?"

David's gaze followed her across the room. "You can hang out with us."

"Yeah." The rest of the boys hooted as they quickly made room for her on the couch.

Blake stepped in front of her. "Negative. She's only fifteen, boys."

David's head tilted, looking around him. "Doesn't look fifteen to me."

"Nevertheless, she is. I expect you to keep your distance."

Jillian saw Blake glance at Abby in a fatherly fashion. The man wasn't an idiot. He knew the girl had all of the right parts, and she was certainly putting them out there for everyone to see. "This is Shane."

He pointed to the boy who looked to be the oldest. "And this is his brother Logan." He pointed to the younger, skinnier one. "They're my foster sons and live here also."

Logan got up from the couch, walked over, and shook their hands. "Nice to meet you."

"Nice to meet you too, Logan," Jillian said before turning to Abby. "Maybe you should dress a little more conservatively while we're here."

"What's wrong with this? It's just a midriff, Auntie." Abby plucked the book off the steps where she'd left it.

"Look, dude. She's got a tattoo on her back." Shane bumped David's shoulder with his fist.

"It's not a tattoo. It's a birthmark," she shot back with a venomous look, swiping her hand across the jagged crescent-moon shape on her lower back, just to the left of her spine.

"Blue. That's an odd color," Blake said.

"Aunt JJ has one too." They all gave their attention to Jillian, and she nodded. Not that she wanted everyone to know.

"It's called a Mongolian blue spot." Jillian absently rubbed the similar one just below and to the right of her belly button. Hers had never faded. She was in the lucky five percent who were marked for life, just as her mother had been. They were considered sexy now, but it had never been revealed in any of her photographs, even when she'd done the story on modeling. In that world, body art, natural or artificial, was usually covered with makeup for all shoots.

"Mongolian blue spots are common among people of Asian, Native American, Hispanic, East Indian, and African descent." All eyes were on Logan as he spoke. "The color comes from a collection of melanocytes in the skin. The cells that make the pigment in the skin." He turned to Abby. "Are you Native American?"

"I don't know. Am I?" She looked at Jillian.

"You have a little Native American in your heritage."

"Oh," Abby said thoughtfully.

"Me too," Logan said.

"I'm gonna go outside and read for a while." Abby slapped the book cover with her hand.

"Is it okay if I come too?" Logan's voice had a waver. It wasn't nearly as steady as it had been when he was giving the anatomy lesson.

"Sure." Logan opened the screen door for her, and they went out on the porch. David and Shane sprang from the couch and went with them.

Jillian followed them to the door and said, "Don't wander off. Maybe later we can take a walk." Jillian looked back at Blake, and he smiled that charismatic smile she remembered.

CHAPTER THREE

This is unbelievable." Amelia jumped out of her car. "Jules, let me call you back." She headed up the front walk and into the house. "Whose car is that?"

"It's my Aunt JJ's," Abby said.

Amelia stopped, put her hand on her hip, and cocked her head. "And who are you?"

"This is Abby. She and her aunt are the new tenants," David said.

"Really. Well, that's just peachy." She blew out a breath and smiled. "Amelia Mathews. Nice to meet you, Abby." She held out her hand and Abby shook it. "So, where can I find your Aunt JJ?"

"I think she's upstairs."

"Thanks." Determination in her step, she strode into the house and up the stairs. "Blake, I hear you have a new tenant. Where is she?"

Jillian spun around at the top of the steps. "I'm, uh—"

"You're what? Sorry? You could've killed me this morning."

Jillian let it register. She was the road-raged woman in the car. "But I didn't." Her gaze raked up and down Amelia. "You look...fine to me."

Amelia narrowed her eyes, and Blake moved in front of her. "Amelia, I'm so glad you're here. This is JJ Davis. She and her niece are going to be living here for a while."

"I know. I met Abby downstairs. She said Aunt JJ, the crazy driver, was up here."

"I was just about to start painting. You want to help?" he said, a blatant attempt to deflect her attention.

"Do I look like I'm dressed for painting?" She motioned to her cream-colored Calvin Klein skirt and jacket. "Why don't you ask Aunt JJ to help you?"

"I feel a headache coming on. If you don't mind, I'm going to take a short nap," Jillian said.

"Take some Tylenol. We don't do a lot of napping around here," Amelia said, pulling her lips together into a tight smile.

"I understand. You've had a long trip, and the paint fumes probably aren't helping." Blake took Amelia by the elbow to guide her to the steps. "Come on, sis. Why don't you run home and change, and then you can help me paint."

"We need to go over the house rules," Amelia said over her shoulder.

Blake attempted to move her down the stairs. "What the hell are you doing?"

Amelia continued to glare at JJ, determined not to budge. "She needs to learn how to drive."

Blake changed directions and pulled her down the hall into his bedroom, closing the door behind them. "It's not like my day hasn't already been hard enough."

She shrugged out of Blake's grasp and straightened her suit jacket. "She practically ran me off the road, and she has the nerve to just stand there acting like she's done nothing wrong."

"You could be a little nicer, you know."

"And what's with the nap? Aunt JJ is in for a rude awakening if she thinks she's not going to have to pitch in around here." She snapped her lips together.

"Give her a break. She just got here."

"I hope she at least knows how to cook and clean. No slackers in this camp."

"What's the matter? You don't like my cooking all of a sudden?" Blake had to admit he needed some help with the domestic stuff while he worked on the house. Fae Cooper, their part-time cook, helped out a lot because her family was grown and had children of their own. But she was exactly that, part-time. "Come here." He took the magazines from the dresser drawer. "She found these in the bathroom."

She flipped through the magazines. "Shit. Are you serious?" She couldn't help the smile from spreading across her face.

He rubbed his face. "Here I was hoping David hadn't left his usual mess in there."

"Way to make an impression." She chuckled and dropped them onto the bed. "Did he steal them from you?"

"Funny." He clenched his jaw and scowled. "I don't know where he got them."

"Yeah, well, now that you have a young girl in the house, you're going to have to watch the boys more closely."

"Yeah. I know." He rubbed his eyes. "And now I need to figure out what to cook for dinner. Coop took the day off."

"Why'd you go and let her do that?" Mrs. Cooper had been part of the Mathews siblings' lives for close to two decades. She'd worked at the middle school and had taken them both under her wing after she'd caught Blake sneaking back into the school one evening after football practice because his dad was drunk and he didn't want to go home and be his target.

"She had something to do with her granddaughter."

"I guess we can give her a pass on that one." Amelia could see by Blake's bloodshot eyes that he'd been up all night getting the bedroom ready. Plus, the paint fumes were still thick in the hallway. Even though Amelia was beat from a long week at work herself, she felt the usual pang to help him. "I have some extra clothes in the car. Why don't you head down to the hardware store and get the stuff to fix the toilet? I'll stay here with the boys."

"Thanks, sis. If Maxine had given me a little more notice these two were coming, I would've made sure the bathroom was done. At least I had the toilet hooked up."

Amelia couldn't believe Maxine had placed the two of them with him. It wasn't as if he didn't have enough on his plate already with the three boys. The house wasn't even finished yet, and they were sending him this little princess and her niece. Weren't there any women out there with teenage boys who could help finish the renovation? Of course not. Amelia knew as soon as she saw them that they were both going to be a distraction. For everyone.

"I need to put the chicken in the oven before I go to the hardware store."

"No. You go get the stuff for the toilet. You have women living in the house now, and they can't be sharing a bathroom with the boys. I'll take care of dinner."

After they went down the back stairs, Blake headed out, and Amelia headed to the kitchen. She gathered up the dirty dishes the boys had left on the counter and slid them into the sink to soak before she poked her head out the swinging door into the living room to find

David and Shane on the couch playing video games. She peeked out the window to see Logan and Abby sitting on the steps, talking. It looked harmless enough, so she spun around to go back in the kitchen.

"You boys need to get your clothes off the furniture and put your shoes in your room. We have women in the house now." The house would never be totally clean. Since the boys hit puberty, the place always looked like a tornado just blew through.

Rattled, Jillian pushed the door closed and leaned against it. There she was in the flesh, Amelia Mathews, Blake's twin sister. Deep-blue eyes, long auburn hair, looking absolutely gorgeous. She was just as beautiful as she was the first time Jillian met her. So beautiful, she'd made Jillian's head spin. Still did. Amelia Mathews was the most attractive woman she'd ever seen. Jillian thought she would have been long gone out of this town by now.

She flopped down onto the bed. How could she begin to tell her the mistakes she'd made? Would she think she'd left town without giving her a second thought? Of course, she would. On the contrary, she hadn't been given a choice at the time. Over the years she'd given it a lot of thought and realized her grandparents had done what they thought was best for all of them. The deafening silence between then and now made it very clear how Amelia felt.

Jillian looked around the room. It was different now, but Amelia always said being here somehow made her forget the unbearable noise of her parents' arguments at her home. All the while she was filling Jillian's mind with stories and dreams of a life together, a life without hostility, expecting nothing in return except comfort.

Did she still think of those nights? No. Probably not. This Amelia Mathews was different—hard, in fact. She had house rules that weren't to be broken. Her first love had turned into a cold bitch. She was definitely not the same woman Jillian had fallen in love with so long ago.

Jillian thought about going back out the door and giving Amelia a few choice words that were floating around in her head, but her head was throbbing, and she was so tired right now, she was about to drop. Way too tired for quick banter.

❖

Amelia heard the door creak open and looked at her watch. A two-hour nap. Wouldn't she love to sack out in the middle of the day like that? No matter how tired she was, snoozing didn't fit into her schedule. During the time JJ had slept, Blake had already been to the hardware store and back, fixed the toilet, and helped Amelia paint the hall and part of the stairwell. They would've gotten more done if Blake hadn't let David off the hook to go hang with his friends. He should've grounded him for life for having those magazines, but he just couldn't do it. Amelia knew Blake couldn't stand to be like his father in any way, shape, or form.

"Hey. You want to take a walk into town?"

Amelia swung around and flipped the almost empty paint tray off the ladder. In what seemed like slow motion, droplets of powder-blue paint splattered across JJ's yellow camp shirt. Amelia climbed down the ladder quickly and was all set to apologize, but the disgusted look on JJ's face was so funny, she had to laugh. You would've thought she'd thrown rotten tomatoes on her.

"You think this is funny?" JJ wiped the paint from her face, smudging it across her cheek in the process. "I just bought this blouse."

"I'm sorry." Amelia tried to hold back the grin. "The look on your face was just so…"

"So what?"

"Um…cute."

"Cute?" JJ's anger vanished, and she seemed nervous all of a sudden. Amelia wasn't sure, but she thought she saw JJ's cheeks redden.

Amelia tipped her head sideways and assessed the giddy feeling that had just rushed through her. "Yeah, in an odd sort of way." She spread her lips into a wide smile.

JJ scrunched her cheeks into a forced smile. "Thanks. I guess this makes up for the almost-killing-you thing."

Amelia lifted an eyebrow. "This is water-based paint. You were never in any danger whatsoever." She swiped a droplet from JJ's collar with her finger. "Take it off. I'll put it in the wash. It should come right out."

"It had better. It's not like I have a huge wardrobe." JJ went back into her room.

Amelia shook her head and headed into the bathroom to wash the paint roller. How had this woman reversed the situation on her? She was usually pretty smooth with women, but even though she'd heard the doorknob turn and knew JJ was coming out of her room, her voice had startled her. Something about it rang deep within her, and it had definitely thrown her off. After rinsing the paint tray and roller in the bathtub, she folded the drop cloth and set the paint supplies at the end of the hallway with the ladder. They should be out of the way down there. She didn't need any more accidents with Aunt JJ.

She ran her hand across the stair railing as she waited for JJ. Something was familiar about her. Amelia couldn't place her, but she had the feeling she'd met her somewhere before. The door opened, and JJ came back out dressed in an old gray, form-fitting T-shirt. Amelia guessed she wasn't taking any more chances with Ms. Fumble-fingers.

"I'm sorry if I was nasty." JJ held up the shirt. "I don't have very many blouses, and this is one of my favorites."

"No problem." Amelia hesitated, trying to think of something witty to say, but for once in her life, she was speechless. Amelia didn't know what was the matter with her. She reached for the shirt. "Here. Let me take that. I'll just throw it in the wash." It was the least she could do. "You still want to take that walk?"

JJ nodded, giving her a more forgiving smile.

"Okay. Just give me a minute to take care of this." Amelia held up the shirt.

"I'll meet you on the porch." JJ slipped past her, bouncing down the steps.

Amelia heard the phone ring and shouted over the railing. "Can you get that, David?"

"I'll get it," JJ shouted back.

She'd been here only one day and was already taking over. Amelia went down the back steps to the kitchen and leaned through the doorway, trying to catch some of the conversation. She couldn't make out what JJ was saying, but her tone seemed pleasant.

"Who was that?"

"It was just Maxine, checking to see that we made it all right."

"Maxine, really? That's new. Maxine hardly ever calls the house." Amelia wondered when she'd become so attentive.

"Well, we kind of hit it off this morning. While we were talking, we found that we like a lot of the same things."

"Oh? Like what?"

"Clothes, reality TV—"

"Enough said. You lost me at reality TV." Maxine had a penchant for trendy clothes, but the reality-TV watching gave Amelia a completely different perspective on both Maxine *and* JJ. "Shirt's in the wash. It should be done by the time we get back." Amelia held the door open for her.

❖

Whew! That was close. Jillian hadn't expected Maxine to call so soon. She'd hoped she would let her get settled, but instead she'd called to tell Jillian about an open counseling position at the school that should work well with her undercover story. She also wanted to know if Jillian had time to have lunch next week. She'd even indicated she wanted to get to know her better, become friends. Jillian had lied and told her that there was too much going on at the house for her to have lunch. The plumbing had gone haywire, and the floor was going to take at least a week to dry out. The repairs would take another two weeks on top of that.

When Maxine had continued to probe her about the story, she'd lied again, telling her she needed to go, that David needed her help with his homework. Maxine continued to talk, telling her she was impressed about how quickly she'd eased herself into the household. She hadn't thought Maxine was the kind of woman to be starstruck, but after the phone call, she guessed she was wrong.

"You know all that reality-TV stuff is contrived, don't you?" Amelia trotted down the steps and scooted up next to her on the sidewalk.

"Possibly."

Amelia stopped, tilted her head, and raised an eyebrow. "No possibly about it. It is."

Jillian stopped abruptly. *Oh, my God. Stop looking at me in that incredibly sexy way.* She pulled her bottom lip between her teeth, focused on the bridge of Amelia's nose, and squelched her surprisingly powerful reaction. "A lot of it may be contrived, but some of the consequences are very real."

Amelia smiled. "Possibly." She turned back toward the pathway and walked slowly. "What do you plan to do tomorrow?" Amelia asked.

"I hadn't thought about it yet." The phone conversation from earlier with Maxine popped into her head. "Maybe look for a job."

"You should probably get Abby enrolled in school first."

"Where do I do that?" Jillian watched the leaves dance on the pavement in front of her as they walked.

"The administration building."

"On Walker Street?"

"No. They moved it a few years ago. It's on Flood now." Amelia's brows scrunched together, and Jillian knew she'd blown it. "How'd you know it was on Walker before?"

Her neck tingled and heat fled through her. "I kinda got lost on the way in and drove by it." *Shit, Jillian, just keep your mouth shut and listen.*

"Oh, yeah. They still have some of the signs on the building." Amelia tucked her hands in the pockets of her down vest and let her gaze move to the path in front of her. "So what did you do in New York?"

"I was a teacher."

"Really?" The surprise in Amelia's voice was unnerving.

"Uh-huh."

"While you're at the administration building, you should see if they have any openings. They're always looking for teachers at the high school."

She cringed at the thought of being around teenagers every day. "That's a good idea." *Damn it, you did it again. A minor in education does not make you a teacher.*

"I have a friend who works at the high school. I can call her, see if she can find out who to talk to."

"Thanks. That would be great." *Shut up, Jillian.* She could do this. The TV show had given Jillian plenty of experience in many areas. She was good at being anything she wanted to be. All it took was a lot of research.

"You'll probably fit right in over there." Amelia's lips pulled into a wide grin.

"What do you mean by that?"

"You just seem like the type of person they'd be looking for."

"And what type of person is that?" *Only known me for a day, and she already thinks she knows my type.*

Amelia stopped again and looked at her curiously. "I didn't mean anything by it. Really. I just thought…" She blew out a short breath. "Well, you have Abby, so you might be good with kids."

"Oh." Jillian could see the sincerity in Amelia's eyes, and instead of pressing the issue, she decided to take her at her word. Amelia was dead wrong. Jillian and kids didn't mix.

They rounded the corner and came upon the old park where the two of them used to meet when they were younger.

"You want to sit for a minute?" Amelia asked.

"Sure." Jillian plopped into a swing as Amelia leaned up against the beam of the metal A-frame anchoring it.

Closing her eyes, Jillian sucked in the all-too-familiar scent of the magnolia trees dotting the landscape and relaxed. She'd loved this place. Her mother had taken her here daily when she was a child.

"Are you okay?" Amelia's voice rang through her sanctuary of thoughts.

The swing slowed. "Yes, why?"

"You're crying."

"What?" She put her hand to her cheek, and the moisture heated her fingers. "Allergies," she said, choking out a cough. "It's just my allergies."

"Are you sure?" Amelia knelt in front of her and put a hand on her knee.

She looked deep into Amelia's eyes. They were the soft and warm eyes she remembered. Not the cold, dark ones she'd seen earlier in the day. She pulled her gaze away. "Yes, I'm sure. Can we go back now?"

"Of course." Amelia popped up and offered Jillian her hand.

Jillian took her hand and allowed Amelia to help her out of the swing, letting her hand linger in Amelia's for a moment. Her hand was soft and warm, her grip gentle. The tingle that shot through Jillian caught her off guard. She'd never forgotten the feeling. *Get a grip, Jillian.* All this reminiscing wasn't doing her any good. She needed to straighten up. Tomorrow would be the most challenging part of playing this role. She would have to find a normal job.

CHAPTER FOUR

A melia pushed through the front door of the law office she and her partner shared and shouted, "Dinner's here." She set the Chinese-food containers on the coffee table in her office and then went into the small storage area they called a break room and pulled a couple of bottles of beer from the refrigerator. "A new woman moved in at the house."

"Is she cute?"

"Infuriating is more like it." Amelia twisted the cap off one of the beers and handed it to Julie. Then she did the same for the other.

"Oh yeah? What'd she do?"

"She's the one who cut me off this morning."

"The one you were screaming about on the phone?" Julie chuckled. "Isn't that a coincidence? Or maybe just karma."

"I wasn't screaming." She took a sip of her beer and set it on the table.

"Yeah, you were." Julie nodded. "Did you scare the poor girl back to wherever she came from?" She opened all the containers and assessed the food. "Orange chicken?"

Amelia pushed one of the containers toward Julie and picked up another. "We rectified the situation when I splattered paint all over her shirt." She opened the container and plowed into it with a pair of chopsticks.

"You, my dear, should come with a disclaimer."

"It was accidental. We agreed to call it even and then took a walk to the park." Amelia slurped a lo mien noodle into her mouth.

"Oh, so you turned on the charm and got the newbie interested in you."

"Absolutely not. She's not interested, and I don't need that kind of trouble." Amelia recalled what had happened earlier. She didn't think she'd said anything to upset JJ, but something had definitely bothered her. The tears in her eyes hadn't stopped immediately, and Amelia knew they weren't caused by any allergy. The walk back had been long and silent. Any time she'd tried to draw JJ out again, she'd received very short answers. What could've made her so sad, so quickly?

"You wouldn't know interest if it was a runaway tire that hit you square in the face."

Amelia widened her eyes and shook her head. "That's not completely true."

"You never figured it out when I was after you."

"I think I must have. We got married, didn't we?"

"Not then. After the divorce."

Amelia stopped eating and put the container on the table. "After the divorce?"

She nodded. "I missed you, especially at night."

"For more than just sex? But you said you…"

"Needed more. I know. The divorce had to happen. That's why I forced myself not to call you and occupied myself with late-night movies."

"Jules…" Amelia's heart tugged, and she reached for her. She knew she'd been a terrible wife.

"Don't worry. That window closed a long time ago."

"I thought you stayed away because you were angry at me." Amelia swiped a napkin across her face. "Huh. How did I never know that?" She picked up her beer and took a sip.

"Because you don't pay attention, that's how." Julie took the lo mien container from Amelia's hand and replaced it with the orange chicken. "I'm not the only one you've lost because of that."

"Wow. Those are some strong words you're tossing around, Ms. Mathews. When was that?"

"Not long after the divorce. When you were dating Darcy."

Amelia tilted her head, trying to place the woman.

"That pretty little redhead at the high school." Julie put down the lo mien and picked up the fried rice. Having no luck with the chopsticks, she dropped them onto the table and grabbed a fork.

"Oh yeah, Darcy." She shook her head and smiled. "She was cute and really good in the sack, as I recall." She rolled her eyes. "But she was always around, bringing me food or coffee. It was very distracting."

"Because she was crazy about you." Julie poked her fork into the container Amelia was holding, snagged a piece orange chicken from it, and popped it into her mouth.

"That was during the Montgomery custody battle. I was pretty busy then."

"Exactly. Like I said, crazy about you and you didn't even notice because you're always working." Julie picked up her beer and flopped back against the couch. "You remember your girlfriends by the case you were working on at the time. Doesn't that tell you something?"

Amelia squinted and looked up at the ceiling. "Now that I think about it, you used to bring me food too."

"Yep. I got pretty good at cooking. Not that you noticed."

"I noticed." Amelia puffed out an irritated breath.

"Oh yeah? Name something I cooked for you."

"Umm." She scrunched her nose. "Spa...ghetti?"

"Lasagna, and it was a whole lot of work to make." Julie slapped her empty beer bottle onto the table. "After you let Darcy get away, I decided it wasn't about me. If someone as sweet as her couldn't get your attention, I never had a chance."

"But we still—"

Julie put up her hands. "That doesn't mean I don't enjoy sleeping with you on occasion. I just decided to remain unattached."

"I'm sorry, Jules. I had no idea."

"No worries, it's all good, but someday you're going to have to take those blinders off and find someone."

"That's just it, Jules." Amelia sucked in a deep breath and let it out. "I don't want to have to find someone. I've never thought of love as something you plan." She shifted to face her. "It just doesn't come to your door and announce itself. You meet someone by chance, and whether it's for a day, an hour, or a minute, it's an instant connection. It hits you like a lightning bolt, smoothing out all of your edges and filling all the gashes in your soul. All the chaos you've endured in your past dissolves, and you want to submerge yourself in it completely."

"Wow." Julie stared at her for a minute, seeming to absorb what she'd said. "Do you ever think about her?"

"Who? Darcy? No."

"That girl from high school?"

Amelia shuddered as the memory flew through her mind. "From time to time." *And every day in between.*

Julie picked up a magazine from the coffee table and thumbed through it. "I guess it would be difficult not to. She's been on plenty of magazine covers." She found a picture of Jillian and seemed to study it. "She is beautiful." She looked up at Amelia, seeming to gauge her reaction. "Ever thought about contacting her?"

"I'm sure she doesn't want to hear from me," Amelia said as she shifted uncomfortably, trying not to look at Jillian's picture.

"She's never gotten married, you know." Julie slapped the magazine closed and dropped it on the table. "Maybe she's just like you."

"Like me how? Busy? Not getting any work done because she has a chatty law partner?" She lifted a brow and cocked her head.

"Ha-ha." She squinted. "Waiting for the love of her life to come crashing back into her world."

"I'm not waiting for her."

"Could've fooled me." Julie popped up off the couch. "I'm going to leave you at that." She picked up her empty bottle and a few of the containers and threw them into the trash can on her way to the door. "I'll see you in the morning, love. Don't work too late."

Amelia thought about what Julie had said. She'd known from the very start that Julie had been in love with her, and Amelia hadn't been able to do anything to prevent it. She also couldn't control how she felt about someone who was long gone and so far out of her league now. Why couldn't she control whom she fell in love with? Everything would be so much easier.

Amelia remembered the day she fell in love with Jillian clearly. She'd never forgotten her smile, the sound of her voice, her laugh, the smell of her hair. It had all been magnified tenfold. Everything in her life became about Jillian at that point. Amelia wanted to do so many things with her, talking, laughing…kissing. She was older than Jillian by a couple of years and had pushed herself to stay away, not follow her like a lovesick puppy, but it was challenging. Amelia found it extremely difficult to accept what she felt and that she could be so vulnerable. Life was so unfair, sometimes.

If Blake hadn't taken a liking to Jamie, Amelia probably would never have met her younger sister, Jillian, and sometimes she wished she hadn't. Blake was the captain of the baseball team and had girls falling all over him. Why couldn't he have just chosen someone besides Jamie? She was younger than the rest of the girls, sweeter, a little naive even. Blake didn't even know her until Amelia became friends with her. Amelia knew their friendship would be short-lived because Blake would bask in the attention Jamie gave him for a couple of months and then toss her aside. Deep down, her brother wasn't a bad guy, but he'd liked the attention he got in high school.

After Blake and Jamie broke up, Amelia's friendship with Jamie waned as she kept her distance from Blake, but Jillian continued to come around. She waited for Amelia after practice, walked her home, and then invited Amelia to spend time at her house. They became best friends, and in Amelia's wildest dreams, she'd never seen what came next. One night during a sleepover, Jillian confided in Amelia that she'd had a huge crush on her from the first time they'd met. Amelia vividly remembered the emotions that rushed her. They'd spent the whole night holding, kissing, and touching each other. It was the most wildly intoxicating feeling she'd ever felt, and she hadn't experienced anything like it since.

Life was perfect for a little while after that. They kept their relationship to themselves, spending as much time as they could together, which was mostly after school and weekend sleepovers at Jillian's house. They made out a lot, held each other, and did some serious touching. But nothing nearly as serious as she dreamed of doing today. Amelia knew that was a dream that would never come true.

❖

Kelly slipped her newly cut key into the lock and flipped the deadbolt. "Jillian," she said quietly, entering the small one-bedroom apartment. With the bouquet of flowers she'd brought in her hand, she went through the quaint living area in search of her love. Not there. She went into the kitchen, plucked a crystal vase from the cupboard, and dropped the flowers into it before she headed into the bedroom. "Jillian. I brought you some flowers." Not there either, and the bed hadn't been slept in. She yanked open the closet door. Some of her work clothes were hanging in their usual side of the closet, but all of her casual clothes were missing from the others, as were some of her shoes. She went into the bathroom. All of her personal things were missing. She rubbed her forehead. Had Jillian gone on location and forgotten to tell her? The more she looked around the apartment, the more she saw the subtle differences. She didn't know where she was, but Jillian had left without leaving a hint as to where she'd gone.

"You bitch." She sent the crystal vase and flowers crashing to the floor. "You can't just leave me like this. You're mine."

"Where the hell are you?" She braced herself in the doorway, trying to focus. "You're with that bastard Christian." She looked at her watch. Ten a.m. She'd be at the studio. She raced through the apartment and out the door. Always at that fucking studio. She spent half her life there—with him, the man who never did anything wrong. She was at that fucking studio, fucking Mr. Perfect. She knew she couldn't trust her. All of her excuses and lies. Kelly knew what Jillian was doing.

❖

Jillian sat in the darkness, looking through the tiny cracks between the slats in the closet door as her mother whisked into the bedroom. She was smiling, but Jillian didn't dare let her know she was there. Her mother was meticulous about her clothes and wouldn't be happy Jillian was borrowing them without permission again. She heard her father's voice, which was loud, and he was calling her Judith. He was angry. He took her mother by the shoulders and shook her. He lowered his voice, and Jillian couldn't make out what she was saying, but her mother began to cry. Her dad rubbed his face, then went to his dresser, opened the top drawer, and took something out. Jillian couldn't see what it was. The dresser rocked back and forth as the drawer slammed shut.

She sprang up in bed, trying to focus. *Where am I?* The watercolor painting on the wall of her bedroom that usually kept her focused wasn't there. Sweat beaded on her forehead. She panicked and leaped out of bed before she remembered where she was. The nightmare had been one of the most vivid Jillian had ever experienced. She felt like a child again—alone, vulnerable, raw. This house was bringing her emotions out in full force. She searched through her purse at the side of the bed but couldn't find her pills. She slipped into the bathroom and closed the door connecting to Abby's room, then flipped on the light. She didn't want to wake her. She didn't want to have to explain.

The reflection she saw in the mirror worried her. Dark circles and sunken eyes. Who was this frightened child living inside her? She'd thought she'd left her behind long ago. It certainly wasn't the woman she'd been for the past ten years. She flipped off the bathroom light and closed the door, then crossed the room and turned on the bedside lamp. The clock read 12:23, and she was wide awake. Maybe some hot cocoa would help. She pulled on her robe and went downstairs.

As she moved across the living room, Jillian heard noise coming from the kitchen and could see light under the closed door. Who else was having a restless night? When she pushed through the door, she was surprised to see Logan and Abby at the table, huddled close together, studying.

"It's late. You two should be in bed."

"Logan says there's a geometry quiz tomorrow. He's helping me memorize the theorems," Abby said, glancing up from her book. "He's going to be a meteorologist."

"Geometry was always a b—I mean, really hard." Jillian took a pot from the cupboard. "You could definitely be a meteorologist if you set your mind to it."

"No. I could never do that much math."

Jillian poured milk into the pot and put it on the stove. "Do you two want some cocoa?"

"Ooh, that sounds good," Abby said and turned to Logan. "You want some?"

Logan nodded. "Are there any marshmallows?"

Jillian pulled open the cabinet and rummaged through the assorted boxes of cereal and crackers before she found a bag of mini marshmallows. "Yep." She took three mugs from the shelf and dumped a package of cocoa mix into each of them before filling them all with warm milk. After dropping a small handful of mini marshmallows into each cup, she set two mugs in front of the kids.

"What's this?" Jillian picked up the cartoon of the woman with an exaggerated butt and an even larger bosom, accentuated by a tight sweater, skirt, and three-inch heels. "It's a caricature of…me?"

"Isn't it funny? David drew it."

"Yeah, funny." She pressed her lips together into a thin-lipped smile. He'd made her look like a harlot.

"He drew one of me too." She pulled a drawing out of her notebook.

Jillian snatched it out of her hand. "Let me see that." If the one he'd drawn of Jillian was this outrageous, she could only imagine what Abby's looked like.

"Hey, give it back," Abby squealed.

Jillian's mouth dropped open. It wasn't a caricature at all but a tastefully done sketch. "It's very nice," she said and handed it back to Abby.

"I know. I told him I'd never talk to him at school if he drew one of those of me." She scrunched her face as she looked at the unflattering one of Jillian.

"I guess that's one way to go about it." Abby had certainly learned quickly how to manipulate David. She tossed the drawing of herself across the table. "Don't stay up too much longer. You're not going to remember anything if you don't get enough rest."

"Fifteen more minutes and I'll be up." Abby blew on her hot chocolate and then took a small sip. "I promise."

"Okay. If not, I'm coming back down to get you." Jillian stopped at the doorway, took a sip of her cocoa, and became lost in the past. She remembered the days when she and Amelia used to stay up late and do their homework at the table in the very same spot.

"Are you okay, Aunt JJ?" The concern in Abby's voice was jarring. Jillian gave her a soft smile. "I'm fine. Just thinking how nice it is that Logan is helping you." She turned and went back upstairs.

Since she couldn't sleep, Jillian booted up her computer and started checking email. First in line, an email from her assistant highlighting her fan mail for the week. When she'd become a celebrity, Jillian had made a practice of looking at all her fan mail. Now that the show had been on for several seasons, she had gobs of it. People asking for advice. People telling her stories of their life. Invasive people asking her for personal information that was strictly out of bounds. Many people who didn't know her and, for some reason, wanted to be her best friend. Now there was way too much email for her to keep up. She'd hired an assistant to handle the email as well as her social media. She didn't answer much correspondence personally, but usually a few emails each week garnered her special attention.

Next, she found one from her best friend and personal therapist, Marcus, indicating all was well on the East Coast, except that he'd gone on another failed first date and would require some serious talk time soon. When the nightmares had become too much to handle, Jillian had been referred to Marcus by a mutual friend. Somewhere along the line, their doctor-patient relationship had changed into a personal friendship, and over the past ten years, he'd become her best friend and confidant and vice versa. They clicked so well they probably would've been soul mates if either one of them had developed any romantic feelings for the other. It was clear from the start that neither of them was interested in each other romantically or, for that matter, anyone of the opposite sex. It just wasn't in the cards for them, so best friends they remained. She would make a point to call him soon and let him know who she'd run into here in town.

Jillian's stomach tightened at the next email, from Kelly, her ex-girlfriend. She'd discovered Jillian had left town without telling her. Jillian had hoped Kelly wouldn't come back after this last breakup. She'd done everything she could to be the woman Kelly didn't want, to make it Kelly's choice to end the relationship. Which she'd done a few weeks ago, very vocally in front of a number of Jillian's friends at a social event. Nevertheless, it seemed Kelly wasn't done with her yet.

Hey, love,
    I went by your apartment today to make up, but you weren't there. Looks like you went on assignment somewhere. Did I miss the communication? No harm done. Just let me know where you're at, and I'll come as soon as I can. I think we can forget about that silly argument we had at that dinner party and get our life back on course, don't you?
    Your one and only,
    Kelly

Her skin prickled, and she slapped the computer closed. Smiling back at Kelly had been one of the biggest mistakes of Jillian's life. She dumped the contents of her purse out on the bed, found her sleeping pills, and washed one down with a gulp of cocoa.

CHAPTER FIVE

Jillian yanked open the heavy metal door of the high school and let it clang shut behind her. The old-book smell filled her nose, and she suddenly felt inadequate. When she was a teenager, Jillian had cursed every day she'd walked these halls. She'd never dreamed she would end up working here someday, even undercover. However, taking college courses at night had been useful in her career. She'd always dreamed of being a reporter, but her parents had drilled into her head that she had to have something to fall back on if that didn't work out. A minor in education wasn't a big cushion, but it would help her now. God only knew she had dreams, but she'd never thought it would work out as well as it had.

She stopped for a moment, looking at her reflection in the glass trophy case. Dressed in a pair of black slacks and white blouse, she scrunched her newly dyed blond, shoulder-length hair with her fingers and blinked to re-wet her brown-colored contacts. She didn't like doing it, but she had to change the color of her hair and eyes to safeguard her anonymity. Her natural crystalline blue eyes, chestnut hair, and makeup were trademarks of Jillian McIntyre, super-journalist. For now, she needed to be plain old JJ Davis, super-aunt.

She shouldn't have any trouble fitting in here. This morning she'd made sure to wear low heels and a minimal amount of makeup. She didn't want to draw any extra attention to herself.

"Come on, Aunt JJ. I don't want to be too late."

"Coming." She rounded the corner and stood at the counter for a few minutes while the three women plucked at their computer keyboards, effectively ignoring both her and Abby.

"Hi. I'm JJ Davis," she said, trying to coax the closest older woman to look up. "My niece, Abby, is a new student."

She glanced up over the top of her reading glasses. "You have to register her at the administration building."

"We've already been there." She handed the enrollment sheet across the counter. She'd preregistered Abby before they arrived but had to drop off a few required documents.

The woman got up and rounded the counter. "You've already missed first hour, but you've got English second. Come with me." She motioned to Abby. "I'll show you where it is."

Jillian waited until the woman came back. "I'm also here about the counseling position."

"You have to apply for that at the administration building."

"As I said before, I've already been to the administration building this morning. They sent me over here."

"Have a seat," she said, sliding back into the chair behind her desk. After slipping her headset into her ear, the woman flipped the microphone around to her lips. "I'll see if Mrs. Patterson is available." She began to dial. "What was your name again?"

"JJ Davis." She reached into her purse and pulled out a half-sheet of paper. "The superintendent said to give you this."

A young woman came into the office and took the paper from her hand. "I got this, Carolyn." She stuck out her hand. "Hi. I'm Darcy Kennedy."

"JJ," she said, shaking Darcy's hand.

Darcy looked at the slip of paper. "Follow me," she said, leading her behind the counter to an office down the hall. The office was empty, but the nameplate on the desk read VICKIE PATTERSON, PRINCIPAL. The same as it had fifteen years ago. "Sorry about Carolyn. She's kind of cranky. I think she's been dealing with teenagers for too long." She motioned to the chair in front of the desk. "Go ahead and have a seat. It might be a few minutes. She's dealing with a disciplinary action right now." She turned to go and then glanced back. "Can I get you something to drink, JJ?" She flashed her a friendly smile.

"No thanks. I'm good," Jillian said, returning her smile and noting that she remembered her name.

Jillian waited for at least twenty minutes before she went out into the hallway to go back to the front desk. She stopped at the next office when she noticed it was no longer empty. Now a man, a woman she thought to be Vickie Patterson, and Blake's son, David, were in the office. They seemed to be having a one-sided discussion, and David was getting the brunt of it.

All she could catch was something about pictures he'd drawn before someone behind her coughed.

"Can I help you with something?"

She turned to find a balding man of average height standing behind her, wearing khaki pants and a polo shirt that seemed to be one size too small. She gathered he did that on purpose to advertise his physique. He was probably the gym teacher or one of the coaches.

"I'm here to see Mrs. Patterson, and I've been waiting quite a long time."

"She should be out soon. She's almost done in there." He smiled. "In the meantime, can I get you a cup of coffee?"

"Sure. I'd love one."

"Follow me." He led her into the teachers' lounge and poured her a cup.

"Cream? Sugar?"

Spotting the real sugar and powdered creamer, she opted out. "Black's fine." She might not be filming at the moment, but she still wanted to keep her diet on track.

"I'm Stan Burkess. I teach art." He pulled out a chair for her and she sat down.

"JJ Davis, new counselor."

"Oh, really." He smiled. "You should probably be sitting in on that student meeting with Vicki." He took a swig of coffee and winced. "I'm sure you'll be seeing that boy soon enough."

"I couldn't help but overhear. Is he in trouble for some artwork?"

"If you want to call it art."

She tilted her head in question.

"The boy draws caricatures."

"Cartoons?"

He nodded as he took another drink of coffee.

"What's wrong with that?"

"Not very flattering ones."

"Oh."

"His latest was of the principal herself."

She heard footsteps, and Stan looked over her shoulder.

"Vickie, this is JJ Davis. I was just keeping her entertained while you were finishing up."

"I'm sure you were, Stan." She gave him a look Jillian couldn't interpret. Mrs. Patterson's exaggerated expression changed into a warm smile when Jillian stood and extended her hand, and she shook it.

"I'm Vicki Patterson. Sorry to keep you waiting, I had a situation to deal with. Let's go back to my office." She turned and led her down the hallway.

"Stan was just telling me about it. The boy draws caricatures?" Jillian couldn't imagine what could be so bad about David's pictures that he needed to be called to the principal's office.

"You never know when you're going to find one of his drawings circulating throughout the student body." She floated a picture across her desk and sat down. "Fortunately, he usually directs the offensive ones only at the staff. If he starts on the students, we'll have a lot of unhappy parents."

JJ glanced at the drawing of the big-lipped, bubble-butted figure on the page and had to stifle a chuckle. Mrs. Patterson must have seen her, because she smiled.

"He's very good, I know." She turned it so Jillian could get a better look. "I'd probably pay at least twenty dollars for this at a theme park, but here at school, pinned to a bulletin board, it's considered disrespectful."

"I understand."

"I hear you're available to start right away."

"Yes. I can start today if you'd like."

"The social work on your résumé is impressive." Jillian had taken her sister's and fabricated a similar one for herself. "Any plans for continuing education? Something leaning more toward teaching, perhaps?"

"That's a possibility in the future, once I get settled in."

She frowned. "Normally I'd like someone with a little more experience in education."

Jillian let out a heavy sigh and started to get up.

"But I'm very shorthanded right now, and you look like someone who deserves a chance. So, welcome." She gave her résumé another quick glance. "I'll show you your office, and then Stan can give you a tour of the school."

"Thank you," Jillian said with a mixture of relief and disappointment. This would be a good way to remain inconspicuous and observe how Abby would get along here, but working at the school would probably interfere with her main goal of getting to know Blake better.

Mrs. Patterson waved a finger in the air. "Don't disappoint me."

"I won't. I promise." She felt like she was fifteen again, making promises she couldn't keep.

"Stan, are you out there?" Mrs. Patterson shouted from her desk. "Where is that man?" She grumbled. "He probably went back to the gym. Stan's the wrestling coach."

"I thought he said he was an art teacher."

"He does that too, but he spends most of his time on the mat." Now Jillian knew what Mrs. Patterson's facial expression earlier had been about. "We'll meet tomorrow, and I'll bring you up to speed on a few things. Okay?"

"Sounds like a plan." Jillian stood and reached across the desk to shake Mrs. Patterson's hand. "Thanks again for giving me a shot."

"Don't be thanking me too much until you've had a chance to meet some of the students." She rounded the desk and slipped her arm around Jillian's shoulder. "Your office is right down here." She took her into the office where she'd seen her meeting with David a few moments before. "Paint, pictures, decorations. You can change it however you like." She dipped her chin and narrowed her eyes. "Within reason, of course."

"Of course." Jillian said. The woman could be intimidating. She was about six feet tall, the same height as Jillian, but had a bit more meat on her. She definitely wouldn't want to be caught on a wrestling mat with her. Mrs. Patterson would take her down in a minute.

"You might want to take a look at this." Mrs. Patterson picked up the file on the desk. "David Mathews. He's usually in here a few times a week. He's not really a bad kid. He just does some stupid things. Maybe you can get through to him."

"I'll take a look at it. Thanks." Maybe this would give her some insight into the whole Mathews family. She opened the file and flipped through the numerous pages. It would take some time.

"We're going to meet with his parents tonight."

Jillian startled at the sound of Stan's voice behind her. She hadn't heard him this time. The man was so quiet it was spooky. "Parents?"

"Yeah. You want to sit in?" He spoke like an eager teenager, and Jillian was tempted. She wanted desperately to see what kind of woman Blake had married. However, she didn't think sitting in on a disciplinary meeting for his son would make a favorable impression. She didn't want to get off on the wrong foot with her new landlord or Abby's unwitting father.

"No, I don't think so. I'd like my first meeting with David to be under friendlier terms."

He nodded, tugging his lip into a half-smile. "I'll fill you in tomorrow." He took the file from her and dropped it onto the desk. "You ready for that tour?" He looked at his watch. "I've got about twenty minutes before my next class."

"Art or wrestling?"

"You found me out." He chuckled. "I was trying to show you what a sensitive guy I am. As soon as any woman hears coach, she assumes I'm an inconsiderate jock."

"Are you?"

"You've already spent a little time with me. What do you think?"

"Why don't we leave it at to-be-determined for now?" Jillian gave him a soft smile and wondered if he appreciated her honesty. "Which way first?"

"How about we hit the gym? That's where I spend most of my time." He led her through the cafeteria.

"How's the food here?"

"Salad bar's good and they have pizza twice a week, but the rest is marginal."

"Thanks. I guess I'll be brown-bagging it."

He opened the door for her, and she stepped into the gym. Her low heels clanked on the wood floor, and he looked down.

"You should take the heels off in here. It's not good for the floor." She obliged and dropped a few inches closer to his eye level.

She watched a group of pretty girls playing a miserable game of volleyball. She guessed swatting a ball back and forth across the net was just as boring for them as it had been for her.

"Do you play any sports? Softball, volleyball?"

"No. I'm not coordinated enough for that, but I do like to keep in shape. Does the community center in town have a fitness center?"

"It does, but you have to buy a membership. If you don't mind waiting until the evening, you're more than welcome to use the school facilities."

"Is that allowed?"

"Sure, a lot of the teachers swim laps in the pool, and a few even do some weight training. I'd be happy to spot you if you're interested." His lips tipped up into a sexy smile.

He was cute, friendly, and athletic. Might be a good cover. *Slow down, Jillian. Don't let yourself get sidetracked. You're here for one reason, and one reason only—Blake Mathews. Giving Stan the idea you're available would only complicate things.*

"Thanks. After I get settled in at home, I might just take you up on that."

He didn't break his stare. She knew what he was thinking, and it was making her nervous. She leaned against the cool, painted cinderblock wall, and he moved closer, placing his hand just above her shoulder. The man was way too far into her space. Jillian was just about to give him a push-back when the shrill of a whistle rang in her ears, and Stan swung around to see where it came from. She saw a short, plump, gray-haired woman herding the girls into the locker room. The woman gave Stan a wave and headed their way.

"Who's this?" the woman said as she approached.

"JJ Davis. She's the new student counselor."

Jillian held out her hand, and the woman crushed it with her grip.

"The name's Jan Smith, but everybody calls me Bubbles."

"Nice to meet you, Bubbles." Jillian pulled her hand loose and flexed it behind her back. She took note of Jan's tan, weathered face. The gray hair was deceiving. When she'd seen her coming toward them, she'd thought she was in her fifties. At closer look, the woman was probably in her early forties and was all muscle.

"Same here. Maybe we can have lunch sometime."

"Sure. That would be nice."

Bubbles nodded and gave her a wink before hurrying back across the gym to the locker room.

"Is she the tennis coach also?" That would explain the tan.

"She coaches all the girls' sports." Stan covered his mouth to prevent the gym-echo. "Sometimes she helps me out with wrestling."

Jillian laughed. "Where'd she get the nickname?"

"Don't know. She came with it."

"Bubbles. I would've never guessed that." Jillian smiled and shook her head as she headed back out the doorway. The bell rang, and kids sprang out into the hall from every door.

"You're starting full-time tomorrow?"

"Uh-huh. I'm meeting with Mrs. Patterson first thing."

"Don't rush. She won't be available until the second bell rings and all the kids are in class."

"Thanks."

"No problem. I'll bring lunch."

"Oh." That was unexpected. *Boy, he's a fast mover.* "I'm not sure what my day will be like. Maybe we should wait until later in the week."

"You have to eat, don't you?"

She nodded.

Stan smiled. "Meet you in your office at eleven thirty." He tossed her a quick wave and headed into the locker room.

She wandered through the halls, remembering teachers, classes, and friends. She'd left them all behind and never looked back, until now. Had she done the right thing? Should she have come back years ago when she'd found out the truth? That was a question she couldn't answer. She knew her life would be very different now if she had stayed. Maybe she'd have been working right alongside Amelia and Blake in their quest to save the scores of tortured children around here. Then again, maybe not. Maybe she would've ended up all alone with a broken heart.

As she entered the main office, she smiled at Darcy, the young lady who'd shown her to Mrs. Patterson's office earlier. She looked up from her computer screen for only a moment but managed an effortless smile. Jillian stopped by her office to pick up the file on David Mathews before she headed back out. On the way to the double doors leading to the parking lot, she slowed to look at the school history living behind the glass case in the hallway. Stan Burkess, quarterback and captain of the football team. She knew the name sounded familiar. She'd been trying to place him all morning. Now, as she looked at the aged picture, she knew exactly who he was. She remembered him hanging around a lot before Jamie started going out with Blake. Back then, he had a full head of blond hair and an ego to match. Jillian didn't want to have any part of that man. She rushed out to her car, rolled down the window, and fired it up. The air was so thick it was suffocating. She baked in the sunlight streaming through the windshield while the hot air blew in her face. Squeezing her eyes shut, she hoped to God the man hadn't recognized her. No, he couldn't have. Neither Amelia nor Blake had, and she'd been a lot closer to them than she ever had been with Stan. Her secret was safe for now.

CHAPTER SIX

Blake was painting the stairwell when Jillian came through the front door. She'd gotten the job. Now she needed to see about getting to know Blake.

"How'd it go today?" Blake asked.

"Great." She blew by him and headed up the steps.

"Did they have any job openings?"

"Yep."

"Well, did you get one?" He followed her upstairs.

"Yep."

"Hey, wait…" He dropped a fist against the closed bedroom door. "Don't use the toilet. I had to change one of the fittings," Jillian heard him say through the door.

She quickly changed her clothes, wrapped a bandanna around her head to pull her hair off her face, and headed back down the stairs.

"I'm ready," Jillian said, gliding down the last few steps.

"Ready for what?"

"To paint. You said you needed some help, right?"

"But I thought…"

"You thought what?"

"I thought you were gonna take a nap."

"You did?"

Blake smiled. "I'm glad to see I was wrong." He handed her a brush and a small container of paint. "Amelia's coming over later to help, but we may be able to knock this out ourselves."

"So what's with your sister?" She tried to say it casually. "Does she live here?"

"No. She does stay over on occasion, on the pullout in the den, but she has her own place across town."

"She certainly dresses nicely. What does she do?"

"She's a family attorney. Handles divorces, custody, and children's rights."

"I bet she makes a pretty good living at that."

"It all balances out. She does quite a bit of pro bono work for kids." He poured more paint into his container and moved to the molding around the door.

"She works for free?" Jillian couldn't hide the surprised lilt in her voice.

"Sometimes," he said, reaching for a high spot about the door.

"I would've never gotten that impression."

"You didn't get the best first impression. She actually has a really big heart." They painted in silence for a while before Blake moved across the floor and took the paint container from her hand. "I'll finish up here. I think Abby's on the porch. You wanna go see how her first day went?"

She looked out the storm door and saw Abby sitting on the steps. "I wonder why she didn't come in."

He pointed to the piece of paper taped haphazardly to the door. "Probably because of the Do Not Open sign."

She got up and was headed to the door when Blake stopped her and blotted her cheek with a paint rag. "You got a little on your face," he said with a smile.

"Thanks," she said and continued out the door. "How was your first day at school?" Jillian asked.

"It was all right."

"Did you meet any new friends?"

"Not anybody I'd really want to hang out with."

"Give it a few days. You'll make some."

"I don't want any. I want to go back to New York."

"We can't go back there."

"Why not?"

"Because I have a story to do here."

Abby dropped her head. "Why did they have to die?"

"I don't know, honey." Jillian slipped her arm around Abby's shoulder and sighed. "I've asked myself that a million times." She squeezed her tight. "Things will get better, I promise." Abby relaxed into her, and Jillian kissed the top of her head. She could hear her soft, muffled sniffles. Things had to get better. She wouldn't have Abby living through broken promises the way she had.

"So, what'd you do today?" Abby sat up and wiped her eyes.

"I got a job, and then I came home and helped paint the stairwell and the molding."

"Did you get any on the walls?"

"I didn't say I did it well. I just said I helped." She scraped a small glob of paint from her shirt and dabbed it on Abby's nose. She smiled, but Jillian didn't see the sparkle in her eyes she remembered. Abby was unhappy and she couldn't do a thing about it.

They heard a loud rumble, and an old red Trans-Am with gray-primer-spotted paint pulled up in front of the house. David was driving, and Jillian could tell by the way he was leaning on the armrest that he was trying to look cool. He rolled the electric window down, only to have it stop halfway. So much for looking cool. Smashing his palm across the top edge, he shoved it the rest of the way down into the door.

"You want to go for a ride?" He raised his brows mischievously, and Jillian knew he wasn't talking to her.

Abby let out a snort. "You've got to be kidding."

Turning quickly, Jillian drew her brows together. "Abby."

"What?" She raised her hands, palms up. "No self-respecting girl would ever ride in a heap like that."

David's grin faded quickly. "It's better than anything you've got." He threw the car into gear and pulled into the driveway and around the back of the house.

"That wasn't nice."

"Uh...did you see the car?" Abby hopped up and gave Jillian a stare. "If I set foot in that beast, my reputation at school would be gone before I even got one." She picked up her books and headed for the door.

Jillian held her arms tightly across her chest until she heard the screen door slap shut. When she thought Abby was out of earshot, she began to chuckle, and her whole body shook with laughter.

"That wasn't funny." Blake's deep voice resonated behind her. "He has feelings too."

"I know. I'm sorry." She covered her mouth to hold back another burst of laughter. "But he's even got a vanity mirror strapped to the side-view mirror."

"She's right about the car, Blake. It is a beast." Amelia stepped out on the porch. "Why don't you go make sure his ego hasn't been bruised too badly?"

"Yeah, sure." Blake jogged down the steps and around to the garage.

"Where'd you come from?" Jillian twisted around and followed the long, jean-clad legs up past the baseball T-shirt to the thick, dark ponytail before her gaze settled on Amelia's electric-blue eyes. *Wow.* The jolt shot through her without warning, and she knew Amelia had seen it.

"Back door," Amelia said, pulling one side of her mouth into what Jillian could only assume, after being caught looking, was a satisfied grin. "That was Blake's car when he was a teenager." She sat on the steps beside her.

"I rem—I mean, I'm sure he did well with the ladies." She snickered, leaning back on the heels of her palms.

"He did all right. How 'bout you? That little Honda of yours is… interesting."

"That old car?" She smiled as she fixed her gaze on the Honda. "It's just a perk." She'd picked up the ten-year-old Honda at the closest used-car dealership to the airport. The salesman didn't quite know what to do when she'd written the check without haggling.

"Because men love a good fixer-upper?" Amelia asked.

"Because women love them too." She saw the expression on Amelia's face change and her cheeks pink just a touch, which made her so much more attractive. "To be honest with you, I've never had much trouble interesting a man…or a woman." Jillian's body tingled. She shouldn't be putting herself out there like this, but she couldn't resist. After all, this was Amelia, her first love.

"You're pretty confident." Amelia raised an eyebrow, and another jolt hit Jillian.

"I try to keep it positive. You'd help poor little old me, wouldn't you?" she said with her best Oklahoma drawl.

"You would be hard to resist," Amelia said, her gaze glued to Jillian. "You *are* a beautiful girl."

The wind picked up, and Jillian watched the wispy straggles of hair that hadn't been captured in the ponytail dance around Amelia's eyes. She cleared her throat, broke the connection, and tried to suppress the prickle of heat rising on her neck.

"It's fun to have a little harmless banter once in a while, isn't it?" Jillian smiled, trying to play down the emotional hijacking she was experiencing.

"Is that all it is?" Amelia ran her thumb down Jillian's arm, and she shuddered.

Jillian's heart thumped rapidly when Amelia moved closer. Amelia's gaze fixed on hers again, and Jillian felt weak. She always could get lost in those deep-blue eyes. She let her gaze drift to Amelia's lips and wondered if they were as soft as she remembered, if her kiss could heat her through and through just as it had when they were young. She wanted—no, she needed to find out. She closed her eyes and leaned forward. She wasn't disappointed when she felt the warmth of Amelia's lips brush hers lightly. She let out an involuntary moan and Amelia pulled back, looked into her eyes, and then immediately came back for more.

Jillian didn't protest. She gave way when Amelia's tongue pushed through to dance with hers tentatively, slowly, as if one was gauging the other, pacing themselves for an elegant tango certain to happen. Every nerve ending fired, and Jillian thrummed with excitement she hadn't felt in a very long time. Amelia wasn't just Jillian's first love. She was the love of her life, the only love that had been able to penetrate the deep, dark depths of her soul.

David's engine roared in her ears and pulled Jillian back to reality. She broke away and stared into Amelia's eyes, emotions crashing through her. *Oh, my God. It's not over.* She hopped up and whirled around but wasn't quick enough to get away completely. Amelia grabbed her hand and tugged her back. She tried to resist but couldn't. *What am I doing?* Jillian didn't know, and she could see by Amelia's stunned expression that she was confused too.

"I...I need to get out of these filthy clothes," Jillian said, and pulled out of Amelia's loose grip.

❖

Amelia didn't follow. She couldn't. Her heart was still doing rapid flip-flops from this unexpected turn of events. *What the hell was that?* She took in a deep breath, trying to douse the heat still flooding her. *She's here because she needs help, and I just kissed her.* JJ could sue both Amelia and the department for sexual harassment. In one stupid move, Amelia could've put herself, Blake, and the boys out on the street for good. She twisted around and saw JJ looking out the living-room window at her. Amelia tingled all over again. *She wanted me to kiss her.* She pulled her bottom lip between her teeth and smiled. *If I'd had more time, I would have done it right.* She stared out into the street and waited a few minutes to cool down, then shook the thought of JJ Davis from her head and walked around back to the garage. Blake had the inside door panel off the car, and David was jiggling the window control.

"Whatcha doin'?"

"Trying to fix this beast," David said, disgust ringing clearly in his voice.

"Oh, come on. It's not that bad." Amelia patted him on the back.

"Abby's right. No self-respecting girl would be caught dead in this car." David kicked the door and dropped back against the driver's seat.

"That's not going to solve anything." Blake's tone was firm. "Maybe if we put our heads together, we can get it fixed up,"

"So, you'll help me?" David's voice rose with excitement.

"Sure. I still remember a little about this car." Blake swiped his hand across the spotted fender panel. "You're still in shop class at school, right?"

"Yeah."

"I bet I can scrape together enough money to buy some paint, and we can use the spray booth at school to cherry it out."

"Cherry it out?" David scrunched up his face.

Amelia chuckled. "That's old school for make it look brand-new."

"That would be awesome, but Mr. Wright would never go for it. Unless we're working on his car, we can't use that stuff."

"I'll give him a call and see what he says."

"Okay, but how do I get to school in the meantime?"

"It runs. You can still drive it."

"Not like this, I can't."

"Then take the bus like every other kid in town," Amelia said.

"No way."

"Then I guess you'll have to hoof it. Unless…" Blake stopped and gave David a thoughtful look.

"Unless what?"

"Maybe you can ride along with the little prima donna and her aunt."

"I'd rather walk." David tossed the screwdriver onto the passenger seat.

Amelia could see that Abby's comments had stung deep. David wasn't the coolest kid in town, but he did try.

"Do you have the key to the trunk?" Blake asked.

David got out of the car and pulled the key out of his pocket, slid it into the slot, and the trunk popped open. "What's in here?" Blake lifted a few things and pulled out a tattered old repair manual. "This is all we need, right here."

"You used to work on it?"

"All the time. Amelia and I both did. Right, sis?"

"Yep. As I recall, I put that stereo in." She took the repair manual from Blake and thumbed through it. "This thing is golden." She tossed it to David. "You'd better start reading."

Amelia peeked inside the car to check the condition of the leather and slid into the driver's seat. She looked over her shoulder into the backseat and remembered some of the wildly inappropriate things she'd done back there. Memories of tangled legs and sweet-hot skin flashed through her head. *Where did that come from?* She reached back and ran her hand across the smooth leather surface. Not the most comfortable place to get to know someone, but she had gotten to know someone very well there. She shook her head and smiled. She hadn't thought about that in years. The memory had all but faded from her mind.

Blake slammed the trunk shut, and Amelia was catapulted back to reality. She pushed out of the seat and looked up to see JJ watching them from the back porch, and the flip-flops started all over again.

She turned to Blake and said, "Hey. I forgot I have to be somewhere. I'll see you guys tomorrow." She didn't wait for a response as she got in her car and backed out of the driveway. She glanced back at the porch to catch a last look at JJ, and her body betrayed her again. *Jesus, Amelia. You need to get a handle on this immediately.*

CHAPTER SEVEN

The next morning, Amelia stood on the back porch, staring into the yard and listening to the buzz of lawn mowers in the neighborhood, while she waited for her clothes to dry. Her life had changed dramatically over the last ten years. If anyone had ever told her she'd be still be living in this college town working as a nonprofit lawyer, she would've bet everything she had against it. She *never* thought she'd be back in this old house. The memories it contained were bittersweet. She'd loved the family that lived here more than she'd loved her own. The girl whom she'd fallen in love with in this house had left a huge crater in her heart, which she'd spent the last fifteen years trying to fill, and now those memories were vivid, like they'd just happened. Amelia didn't know if it was the house, the car, or the woman living upstairs. Whatever it was, if she wasn't careful, that woman could very well destroy the shield she'd carefully constructed over the years. She hadn't meant to kiss JJ the other day, but the impulse had been so overwhelming she couldn't stop herself. There was something familiar about her that Amelia couldn't shake, and she couldn't stay away.

Pushing those thoughts from her mind, Amelia pulled open the screen door and went into the kitchen to refill her coffee cup. She'd just sat down and slipped on her glasses to read the paper when JJ stumbled down the back stairs and headed past her to the coffee pot. Amelia scoped her up and down. Pink sleep pants and a thin white cotton tee did wonders for JJ Davis. So much so, Amelia's libido was revving straight into high gear again.

"Good morning." Amelia smiled in amusement when Jillian jumped at the sound of her voice.

JJ spun around and slapped her hand to her chest. "Jeez, you scared me."

"How are you this morning? Did you sleep well? You look a little groggy."

"I'll be much more awake after I have some coffee." Jillian groaned and turned back to the pot. "I'm not a morning person."

What kind of a person are you, JJ Davis? The paper rattled as Amelia folded and dropped it on the table. "I was just thinking about what happened on the porch the other day."

"What about it?"

Amelia held back a smile as she got up to refill her still-full cup. "Since we're going to be seeing so much of each other here, I don't think we should let it happen again."

Jillian looked puzzled. "What do you mean, *we*? You kissed me."

Amelia reached up and adjusted her glasses. "As I recall, we were both involved. Maybe you should put something else on before you come downstairs." She moved her cup toward Jillian's chest before letting her eyes roam slowly down her long, slender body, then back up to her eyes.

"Me! Look at you." She motioned to her bare legs and the T-shirt hanging loosely from her shoulders. "Maybe *you* should put something on."

Amelia could do without the grumpy attitude, but God, she looked good. "You're lucky I put these on. This isn't the way I sleep."

"Wait. Did you sleep here last night?"

"No."

"Then what are you doing here so early?"

"My dryer's broken." Amelia strolled into the laundry room and pulled a pair of sweatpants on over her shorts. She had no idea what she was doing or why she was doing it. Amelia had managed to stay away all weekend, keeping herself busy with work, and had decided she wasn't going to pursue anything with JJ. Yet here she was on Monday morning, doing her laundry much earlier than necessary just to get a glimpse of her.

David rushed into the kitchen, pulled open the pantry door, and grabbed a package of Pop-Tarts off the shelf.

"Where's the fire, Dave?" Amelia asked, thankful for the interruption.

"I just wanted to get one of these before they were all gone." He held up the silver-foiled package.

"I was hoping to get one of those Pop-Tarts. Guess I'm out of luck now," JJ said, shooting David an ultra-cute pout that gave Amelia mixed feelings. Was that for her benefit or was she actually flirting with a teenage boy?

"You can have one." David ripped open the package, took one, and then handed JJ the other.

"How sweet." She smiled at Amelia, who promptly gave her an eye roll.

Blake came down the stairs next. "You're still here?" he said to David as he took a mug from the cabinet. "Are you going to take the bus with Shane and Logan?"

"I'll get there just as fast if I walk." David took off out the door.

"Don't forget, you might have to put in a little time after school," Blake shouted after him.

"Is he in trouble?" Amelia asked.

"No. I talked to Mr. Wright, his shop teacher." He poured himself a cup of coffee. "He said we could use the tools at school to get his car fixed up as long as it was after hours."

"The beast?" Jillian broke off a piece of Pop-Tart and popped it into her mouth.

Blake drew his brows together. "Not for long."

"If he's working on the car after school, why is he going in so early?" Amelia asked as she swiped the Pop-Tart from Jillian's hand and took a bite.

"Hey," Jillian said, her mouth dropping open.

Amelia raised an eyebrow at her before she returned her focus to Blake. "Is he working on the car before school too?"

"Not that I'm aware of. I don't know what's gotten into him. He's usually the last one out." Blake took a last swig of coffee and set his cup in the sink.

"New school year. Maybe learning has finally become interesting," Jillian said.

Amelia laughed. "It's more likely a girl."

"We can always hope, can't we?" Jillian smiled, glancing at the clock. "Oh, shoot. I'd better get moving or I'm going to be late." She snagged the last hunk of Pop-Tart from Amelia.

"Hey, that was my half."

"Half of my half is not your half." Jillian grinned and bounced up the back stairs.

Shaking her head, Amelia picked up the wrapper from the table where David had left it and tossed into to the overflowing trash can. She cursed as it bounced off onto the floor. Yanking the bag out of the can, she tied it and took it out the back door and around to the side of the house. Her eyes adjusting to the darkness, she could barely make out the shadowy figure perched on the fence.

"David? Is that you? What are you doing?" Without a word, David slid down off the fence to the pathway on the other side. *What the hell?* He'd left nearly fifteen minutes ago, so why was he sitting on the fence? Amelia let her eyes trace the path from where David was sitting to the house. She saw the light burning bright in the corner room on the second floor. She went over, climbed up on the fence, sat in the same spot, and stared up at the window. It certainly was a gorgeous view, she thought as she watched the curvaceous figure of JJ Davis undressing just on the other side of the glass.

"One more trip to the hardware store," she mumbled as she slid down.

She pushed through the back door, glanced at the clock, and picked up the phone. Maxine was an early riser. She should be in the office by now. She hoped to get a few more dollars out of her for the blinds. If not, they'd have to come directly out of Amelia's own pocket.

"Hello, Maxine. Amelia Mathews here."

"Good morning, Amelia. How's everything coming at the house?"

"We're working on it."

"And the new woman? JJ?"

"That's what I was calling about. We need blinds in the windows upstairs. Do we have money for that?"

"I'm afraid you'll have to wait another month until the others arrive."

"What others?"

"The woman and her boy." She said it as though Amelia should've already known.

"Maxine, we can't fit many more people into this house."

"Of course you can. It has three stories."

"The third floor is a storage room, not a bedroom. The whole space needs to be renovated."

"Then you and Blake better get to work on it. They'll be here in a month, maybe sooner."

"You can't expect us to renovate without any money."

"You should ask Ms. Davis if she can pay for the blinds." The line clicked and went dead.

"Ask Ms. Davis?" She slammed the receiver into its cradle. The thought was ludicrous. She wasn't going to ask JJ to pay for anything. She'd just gotten here and probably didn't have a dime to her name.

"Ask me what?" JJ said, fiddling with her bangs as she came down the back stairs.

Amelia's train of thought stopped. JJ was dressed in a green-and-white cap-sleeved, floral-print dress. *Beautiful.*

"Who was that on the phone?" JJ asked.

"Maxine," Amelia said, trying to get back to the phone conversation. "The woman must think we're miracle workers. We can't furnish a three-family household with the budget she gives me."

"Maxine called you?"

Amelia shook her head. "I called her." She pulled a fresh trash bag from under the sink and swung it in the air. Ignoring the loud pop as it expanded, she stuffed it into the can. "She's sending us two more people next month."

"Two more?"

"Yeah, the two we were expecting when you showed up. I'm not sure how she thinks we can manage on the minimal amount of funds we get from the foundation."

"Did she say something about me? I mean—" JJ swallowed hard. "Am I going to have to move out?" She looked honestly worried, as if they would actually put her and her niece out on the street.

"No. Of course not. We'll just have to make room." Amelia touched Jillian's arm and could see the look of relief whoosh across her face. "Don't worry. We'll work it all out. I'll have Blake go up in the attic today and see what kind of furniture is up there."

"Thanks." Jillian gave her a soft smile and held her gaze for a moment. "Well, I'd better get to work. How do I look? Is this okay for a school counselor?" She made a quick twirl, and her dress flew slightly up to her knees.

"It's perfect." The smile Amelia's comment brought to JJ's face was worth a thousand more of the same. She followed Jillian to the front door, watching her hips sway as she walked. Amelia refocused when they met Mrs. Cooper on her way in. A heavy-set Irish woman, who could be a little frightening at first, Coop was actually the most selfless person Amelia had ever known.

"Who's this?" Jillian asked, tilting her head.

"This is Mrs. Cooper, our savior. She helps with the cooking and laundry."

"You're the new one, aye?" Her voice was low and gruff.

"Yes, ma'am. JJ Davis. Nice to meet you." Jillian held out her hand.

"Welcome." Mrs. Cooper gave her a warm smile and swept Jillian into an embrace before letting her pass. "You can call me Coop."

Amelia held the door for Jillian before following her out. "I'll be right back, Coop."

"The foundation pays her salary?"

"I pay her salary."

Jillian gave her a puzzled look. "I thought the foundation funded the house."

"We're barely scraping by on the grant money from the foundation. Not that I'm not happy to have the house, but it's a huge expense in itself. It would just be nice to be able to give the kids some extras here and there."

"Oh." Jillian still seemed confused. "How did you find Mrs. Cooper?

"I've known her for a long time. She makes the place feel like home and keeps us all fed." Amelia shrugged. "Anyway, I could use some help finishing up a few things around here when you get home this afternoon."

"You're going to make me earn my keep, aren't you?" Jillian stuck her hand on her hip and rolled her eyes.

Amelia sucked in a deep breath at the sight. "That's the plan."

"Fine. I'll be home around four." Jillian smiled broadly, and Amelia knew she had her. Amelia couldn't help but watch her walk to the curb. JJ threw her a wave as she slid into her car and smiled as she pulled away.

"Looks like you got yourself a live one there," Mrs. Cooper said, startling her from behind.

"She's something, all right."

"You know what happens when you mix business with pleasure."

"I know." She couldn't keep the smile from her face and knew Coop could see right through her.

Coop shot her an I've-heard-that-before look. "Be careful, honey."

"I will."

Coop continued into the kitchen. "So, what are you up to today? Paint or wallpaper?"

"Neither. I'm putting up blinds. It gets a little hot in that upstairs front window." The sight of JJ's curvaceous body shot through her mind. She wasn't kidding about it being hot. All in all, she deemed the blinds a wise investment, if only to keep the hormones, including her own, from turning everyone in the house into oversexed teenagers.

"That where the new lady stays?"

"Her and her niece."

"Two more women in the household now." Coop's voice rose. "More trouble than you asked for, huh?"

"Blake's going to need help. At least the three he had were boys. Women in the house change the whole dynamic."

"At least we won't be outnumbered anymore. Plus, she's gorgeous."

Amelia nodded. "You have no idea."

JJ was a beautiful woman but got under Amelia's skin a little more than she liked to admit. Coop was right. Mixing would be bad, but it was already too late to stop that. Amelia would have to realign and make sure to keep the boundaries clear, if she could.

Jillian waited for the last bell to ring before she went to her office. She flopped down into the chair behind the desk and sat for a minute, deciding what she should do first. She'd read several books while prepping for the teacher role but was totally inexperienced at counseling high school kids. She picked up the phone and dialed Maxine's number. She was disappointed when it rang a couple of times and then went to voice mail. She wanted to be somewhere where she could dig into what was going on with the foundation funds, not sitting behind a desk at the high school. Maxine had insisted this was the only way she could get close to the goings on at Heartstrings House without drawing attention to herself.

"Hey, Maxine. I'm here at the school. Everything went as planned. I'll call you later and let you know how things are going." She started to drop the receiver into the cradle when she remembered her conversation with Amelia this morning about funding. "Oh, and Amelia said something about needing more money for something at the house. I'd like to discuss some of the funding issues with you. As part of the story, that is." Jillian couldn't fathom why there were any funding issues unless she needed to file additional paperwork. She'd funded the grant with plenty of money, enough so that the kids shouldn't want for anything.

She finally dropped the phone into the cradle before turning on her computer. Mrs. Patterson had left a few files with notes on her desk. She opened the one on top and thumbed through it. This particular girl had lost her mother to cancer last year, and her grades had gone down drastically since. She could relate. Jillian had enough personal experience with loss. She read the first few pages and reminded herself that she wasn't an expert on damaged children. Every child was different, and she certainly didn't want to do anything that would impact someone's life negatively. She'd need to call Marcus and get his advice before talking to this one. She set it aside and picked up the next file.

❖

It had been a long day of meeting kids, and Jillian seriously doubted she'd be able to keep up this charade. By the time she got home from school, Blake was installing the last blind in her room.

"Wow." She flipped them open. "I thought you said there wasn't any money for these."

"Amelia convinced Maxine to give us a little extra in the household fund this week."

That was a lie. She hadn't received a call back from Maxine today, and Jillian was sure she didn't move that fast. Amelia had probably paid for the blinds out of her own pocket. She'd have to remember to thank her and also pick up the tab for the next load of groceries. It bothered her that they had so little money. The grant was fully funded, so this was a sign something fishy was going on with the grant administration.

"I don't suppose you got enough money for an air conditioner as well," she said, hoping for a light reaction.

"'Fraid not. This was all she could spare. They weren't cheap, but installing them myself took a lot off the price." He climbed back down off the ladder and collected his tools.

"All finished?" Amelia said as she entered the room.

"Yep. It should be a little cooler in the afternoon up here now." He folded the ladder and hoisted it up on his shoulder.

"Thanks, Blake. These will help out a lot," Jillian said.

He dipped his chin and then headed out the door and down the stairs.

"Thank you, Amelia. I know you paid for these. Abby and I appreciate your thoughtfulness."

"You're welcome."

"How did you and Blake end up with this house?" Jillian knew full well how it happened but wanted to hear how Amelia felt about it.

"An old friend donated it."

"That was generous."

Amelia nodded. "It was *very* generous of her." She seemed to be lost in thought as she ran her finger along the windowsill.

"Does she live in Norman?"

"No. She lives in New York, but it sure feels like she's here." She turned to look deep into Jillian's eyes, and Jillian almost faltered. "But that's not possible. She's a hotshot TV journalist now. She wouldn't come back. There's nothing here for her."

"But you still consider her a friend." Amelia eyed her suspiciously, and Jillian knew she should back off. "I just thought if you were still in touch with her, you could let her know how grateful I am."

"I'm not in touch with her." Amelia walked to the window, peeked through the blinds, and looked outside. "You should probably keep these closed in the morning. There's an easement just on the other side of the fence. The kids use it as a shortcut to school." Amelia's gaze swept across Jillian intimately, and her cheeks warmed. "Young men kill for shows like that."

She yanked the blind up and looked down onto the easement. "Oh…oh! I had no idea." She widened her eyes. "Did you see me?"

"You were hard to miss." Amelia leaned against the window frame and smiled.

Jillian let the blind drop closed. "I guess you enjoyed the show too." Her voice rose as the full impact of what Amelia had meant hit her. "You could've told me."

"I just did." Amelia turned and went out the door. "Dinner's at six."

Jillian closed the door and fell onto the bed. "I just did," she said, taking a pillow into her lap and digging her fingers into it. The woman was infuriating, always wanting the upper hand. *Fuck.* She tossed the pillow away. That turned her on even more.

❖

Amelia heard the hum coming from Julie's office as she went down the hallway to see her. She stopped at the doorway and watched Julie move a clothes shaver across her chest.

"Why don't you just buy a new sweater?"

"Because I like this one, and they're expensive."

"Tell me about it. My bank account has seen better days." Amelia was still miffed about the money situation for Heartstrings House. "Do you have a lint roller?" Julie pulled one from the top drawer of her desk and tossed it to her.

"Do you need money? I can spot you." Julie dropped the shaver into her drawer and pulled out her checkbook. Most people in the working class would consider Julie rich. She'd come from old money, but Julie had also saved and invested well. She was always generous and willing to help if Amelia needed something, but after their divorce, Amelia didn't feel right asking her to fund projects unless she was also kicking something in herself.

"No. I'm fine." Amelia had saved and invested her money also, but the Heartstrings House expenses were adding up. First, it was paint, and then it was the furnace, and now the blinds. The new furnace had been a huge expense, and now having to buy essentials for a house she thought was fully funded was putting a strain on her bank account. "I had to buy blinds for the house yesterday." She ran the lint roller up and down the front of her jacket and then tossed it back to Julie. "The room where the new woman and her niece are living."

"Oh. What's she like? Is she nice?"

"She seems to be a little high class, spoiled, in fact. I'm kind of wondering why she's there."

"I'm sure she has a reason, or Maxine certainly wouldn't have sent her your way."

"That's true." Maxine was an excellent social worker, but she didn't have time for slackers. Even though they weren't able to get community housing assistance from the Emergency Solutions Grant program, the house would still be monitored by her as the program manager, and all requirements had to be met in order to have people placed at the house.

"Did she find her a job?"

"Yes. Something at the high school. A counseling position, I think."

"That will help out with the finances, won't it?"

"Maybe a little, but we can't accept more than forty percent of her monthly income. She has to keep enough to try to get on her feet alone, so it will probably be more like twenty percent to start. That probably won't be much, considering what the school system here pays."

"That makes sense, or people like her wouldn't need to be there in the first place." Julie slid both her checkbook and the lint roller back into the desk drawer. "Well, let me know if I can help."

"I will." Amelia turned and headed down the hall to her office.

Maxine had told her the funds for this month had been delayed, but more would be available soon. When she'd let her take over administering the grant, she'd thought it would be easier and she wouldn't have to deal with any of this. Amelia pulled the Heartstrings Foundation folder from her desk and looked through the pages. If the foundation wasn't going to fully fund the house, she had to find a way to bring in more money. Donations, fund-raising dinners, she'd even wash cars if she had to. At this point, anything would help.

CHAPTER EIGHT

Jillian and Darcy climbed up the bleachers and sat in the middle of the top row watching Shane and the rest of the team shoot baskets on the court as they warmed up for the game. Darcy gave her snippets of information about each faculty member as they found their seats in the bleachers below them. Darcy was like Jillian's own personal version of high school Google. She knew everything about everyone.

"Mrs. P is okay." She motioned to Mrs. Patterson sitting in the third row. "She's a little old-fashioned, so keep your personal life to yourself around her." She pointed to Mr. Wright, standing on the sideline watching the boys. "Steve's okay. If you ever need anything, he's your go-to guy. He's been at the school forever."

Jillian nodded. She'd thought she'd recognized him the other day in the office but hadn't been able to place him. She shifted her gaze and spotted Amelia coming up the steps. She looked up, caught Jillian's gaze for a moment, then turned and chose a row halfway up the bleachers below them.

"That one's difficult." Darcy dipped her head toward Amelia.

"You know her?" Jillian wasn't sure why she was surprised that Darcy knew Amelia. It made sense. In her line of work, she would have contact with the high school.

"Amelia Mathews."

"Why is she difficult?"

"She's super-hot and she's definitely a giver, if you know what I mean." Darcy wiggled her eyebrows. "But she stays totally detached, doesn't let anyone get close. Someone must have really fucked her over."

Jillian was a little startled by Darcy's profanity, yet thoroughly entertained by the way she switched her persona from sweet school secretary to faculty tabloid informer. "You know this how?"

"I went out with her for close to six months and never once went to her house. It was always my place…or her office." She winked. "We made good use of that desk of hers."

The visual made Jillian's stomach churn.

Stan came out of the locker room and clapped his hands, signaling the team off the court. "That man is a complete muscle, always working out. He has huge biceps and hair…" Darcy's eyes grew wide. "He has hair everywhere, except his head. He even shaves his chest."

Jillian had seen him with his shirt off when he was younger. She didn't remember him being extraordinarily hairy. She tried to shrug the thought off, but she couldn't stop the image of him from popping up in her head, chest covered with shaving cream, long ape-like arms hanging, and razor in hand. She chuckled at the vision. Those drawings of David's must be getting to her. Darcy definitely had her wondering if Stan groomed his whole body.

"So you've dated them both?"

"Stan and I didn't date." Jillian scrunched her brows together and waited for Darcy to spill more information, but she just winked.

"Oh, ohhh." Jillian surprised herself with the lilt in her voice.

"I don't date men, but sometimes I just need a little of something else." She wiggled her eyebrows. "If you know what I mean." She looked back down at Amelia. "I have to admit, I never needed that when I was with her." She let out a sigh. "Definitely a giver."

Jillian was officially on TMI overload. It was enough she had to hear about her escapades with Stan, but to hear the intimate details about her sex life with Amelia put her over the top.

"This is fun. Talking with you." Darcy smiled and put her hand on Jillian's leg. "We should go, uh, have a drink, sometime."

"Umm, sure." Jillian could already tell Darcy would be a good source of information. She seemed to know plenty about everyone, which could be very helpful to Jillian in the future. She had no intention of letting Darcy out of the friend zone, and it was clear she would need to make that known pretty quickly.

❖

The sun had already started to set and the sky to darken slightly when Jillian pulled up in front of the house. Things just weren't going her way today, but despite it all, the sight of Amelia sitting on the porch swing when she came home made her insides smile.

"You know you have a brake light out," Amelia said, using one foot to push the swing in a slow, steady rhythm as Jillian came up the walk. "And you missed dinner."

"I know. That's why I'm late. I got pulled over. Then I went by the Honda dealer to get it fixed, but they don't have an appointment open until Monday." She let out a sigh. "I'm pretty inept when it comes to cars."

"I can fix it for you." She put both her feet on the porch and stopped the swing.

"Really?" Jillian hadn't even thought to ask Amelia.

"Sure. Give me your keys. I'll be right back." Jillian handed them to her and watched Amelia walk to her car with determination in her step, her ponytail swinging from side to side. She stopped and yelled over the top before she got in the Honda. "I made you a plate and left it in the kitchen."

Jillian stood and watched her drive away. *She made me a plate. Who is that woman?* She shook her head and went inside, where she found Coop sitting at the table in the kitchen creating what looked like the shopping list for the next week's dinner menu.

Coop looked up briefly from the line she was writing. "You're late."

"I know. Long story." She found the plate of chicken and rice on the counter and put it in the microwave for a minute. "Looks good."

"It was. You're lucky you got any. The boys were hungry tonight."

"Thanks for saving me some." She sat at the table next to Coop.

"Not me. Amelia." She glanced up from her list again. "I'm not sure what you've done to her, but I like the result."

Done to her? "I haven't done anything. We haven't spent that much time together." Something Jillian was unsure she wanted to remedy.

"Maybe you should think about spending more." Coop got up from the table and took her bag from the hook inside the pantry door. "She likes you." Without another word, Coop was out the screen door, letting it slap closed behind her.

"She likes me?" *She likes me.* Jillian felt the familiar tingle in her belly and made an effort not to let her mind wander back to the kiss she and Amelia had shared. Instead, she put her mind to work on a new idea for an investigative report, maybe something about women and car repairs. How easy, how difficult, the cost. Energized, she grabbed the pad and pen Coop had been using and jotted down some notes. Her heart thundered in her ears at the thought of this new story. She was totally energized now. She had a new story, and it would be a good one.

She sat back in her chair and pondered her career. When she'd first started in investigative reporting, the adrenaline rush had come from the sheer terror of being discovered undercover. The edge-of-your-seat feeling she'd experienced for the better part of a year when she'd first embarked on the journey had been terrifying. Over the years, the rush had turned sweet and somehow rewarding. She savored the feeling now. It was incredible to have her image plastered all over TV and still be able to go unnoticed in the middle of hundreds of people, so much so that she couldn't wait for the next story to feel the thrill again.

Jillian finished her dinner and cleared her plate before she tucked her notes into her pocket and went outside to see if Amelia was back. She was there, at the curb, with the hatchback of Jillian's car up, her ponytail moving with the wind. She trotted down the stairs to see how Amelia was doing and made it just in time for her to pull the hatchback down and slam it closed. "No luck?"

"It's done." She held up the bad bulb.

"How much do I owe you?"

"It was under ten. I got it."

"Wow. I guess I should've come to you first."

"I'm always willing to help with a fixer-upper." She gave her a wink as she walked past her, and Jillian's cheeks warmed as she remembered their conversation about the car and their steaming-hot kiss.

"Are you going to the school dance tonight?" Jillian asked, prompting Amelia to stop, turn around, and pull her brows together. "I'm chaperoning."

Their eyes connected, and Amelia seemed caught in thought for a moment before she said, "Oh. That's not really my thing, but you have fun."

Jillian caught up with her at the screen door. Amelia opened it and let Jillian enter before her. "Well, I have to get ready, but thanks again," she said, turning back before she headed up the steps.

❖

Amelia walked into the kitchen trying to erase the vision of JJ standing in front of her outside in the evening dusk. The gusts of wind had moved her hair gently from her neck as she stood, so beautifully innocent, waiting for an answer. Such a beautiful neck. She flipped on the water, took the soap from the sink, and scrubbed her hands before dousing her face. Amelia was in trouble with this one. Sneaking looks whenever she could, making mindless conversation. She'd even left work early today because she wanted to see her. Amelia didn't know why she wanted to be close to JJ, but the desire was overwhelming. Time to flip the control switch back her way. She pushed through the back door, dropped down into a chair, and closed her eyes.

Blake's voice broke the silence. "What's wrong with you?"

"Nothing. Just tired."

"Oh. You going to the dance?"

"Not this one."

"Who's gonna help me check the punch?" he said lightly.

"JJ's going. Ask her." The words came out stronger than she expected, and Blake pulled his brows together. She knew he had more questions but wouldn't ask. The two of them had always kept clear borders about sharing.

"Okay then. I have to change. I'll see you when I get home?" He shot her a hopeful smile.

"Maybe." She pushed her head against the back of the chair and closed her eyes. It would be the first dance she'd missed since David had entered middle school. She felt a little sad at the thought of staying home, but she needed some space from JJ tonight. Accompanying her to a low-lit gym with music wasn't a good idea, even if it was a high school dance. It was probably time to let David go solo, anyway.

David straightened the collar of his polo shirt as he came down the stairs. "Can I borrow your car tonight, Aunt Amelia?"

Jillian heard Amelia's response from over her shoulder. "To the dance and back, Dave." Amelia crossed the room and straightened his already straightened collar before she took her keys out of her pocket. "Home before eleven, right?" she said as she dropped them into his hand.

"Right." He gave her a big grin. "Thanks," he said as he took off out the front door.

Jillian diverted her attention to the TV when Amelia passed on her way to the kitchen. No eye contact. It was safer that way. Abby had been in the bathroom for the last twenty minutes getting ready, so Jillian had opted to come downstairs and wait for her on the couch. Spring Fling, the last dance of the year before prom, and since Abby wasn't going to prom, Jillian knew she was looking forward to tonight. She'd helped Abby pick out the cute floral-pattern dress, which wasn't easy. They had very different ideas of what she should wear. In the end, they'd compromised and were both happy with the dress. It had good coverage up top and landed just above her knees. Abby had the body of a woman but the maturity of a girl. A dangerous mix at a high school dance. Jillian wasn't expecting the sight she saw when Abby came down the stairs. She'd put on mascara, eyeshadow, and lipstick, and it was like looking at her sister minus fifteen years.

"You're not going to let her go to the dance like that, are you?" Amelia's voice of disapproval resonated through the living room as she came out of the kitchen. "You need to go back upstairs and take off that makeup." Amelia waved her hand toward the stairs.

Jillian popped up off the couch. "Hold on a minute. Since when do you get to tell my niece what to do?"

"Since I know how boys react to fifteen-year-old girls who look like they're nineteen."

"She'll be fine. I'll be there to watch out for her."

"JJ, you have to be kidding." Amelia took a stance and propped her hands on her hips. "Do you have any idea what can happen in the time it takes you to walk across the gym looking for her?"

"I'm not an idiot," Jillian said, and Amelia raised an eyebrow.

Jillian could see Amelia was holding back an observation on her parenting technique. She took in a deep breath as her emotions battled within, the attraction and irritation competing in a razor-sharp duel. "You just let David walk out of here with the keys to your Camaro. Do you know what can happen in an hour in the backseat of a Camaro? How those actions can change a life forever?" Thoughts of her sister's experience flew through Jillian's mind.

Amelia eyed her strangely. "I'm aware. The new models don't have near enough room in the backseat for any of that."

"Where there's a will, there's a way." Jillian gave her a tight-lipped smile and kept her mouth shut, holding at bay the rest of the words she wanted to spew back. Amelia was not going to make her lose her composure in front of Abby. "Come on, Abby. Let's go." She opened the door, motioning Abby in front of her. "Don't wait up." She narrowed her eyes at Amelia and followed Abby out to the car. *What did I ever see in that woman?*

"Do you think I have too much makeup on, Aunt JJ?" Abby said as she got into the car.

"Maybe a tad too much eyeshadow." She reached over and squeezed Abby's hand. "We can fix that before we go in."

"My mom never let me wear any makeup."

"Then maybe we should just start with a little mascara," Jillian said, second-guessing her decision to let her wear makeup. She hadn't even thought about what Jamie would say. "You're a beautiful girl. You don't need much more than that."

"You think I'm beautiful?"

"Of course I do, but what I think doesn't matter." She rounded the last corner to the school. "What do you think?"

"I think a whole lot of girls at this school are prettier than me."

Jillian pulled into the faculty parking lot and put the car in park. "Maybe, but as long as you're happy with who you are, that shouldn't matter." She took off her seat belt and shifted to face Abby. "Now close your eyes and let's see about that eyeshadow." She pulled a tissue from her bag and stroked it lightly over Abby's eyelids, wiping away all but a tinge of the glittery eyeshadow Abby had applied. "Now the lips." She handed Abby a tissue, and she wiped off the lipstick. Jillian reached into her purse and took a tube of clear lip gloss. "I think you should stick with this for the time being, okay?"

"Okay." Abby swiped it across her lips and handed it back.

"You keep that." Jillian gave Abby a reassuring smile and reached for the door handle. "Ready?"

"Ready." Abby took in a deep breath and got out of the car.

When they walked into the gym, all heads turned, and Jillian could see they weren't looking at her. Abby was getting their attention, the boys with lovelorn eyes and the girls shooting daggers. Jillian's stomach tightened. She should have listened to Amelia. Abby was growing up way too quickly.

"Hey. I didn't know you were going to be here tonight. You two could've ridden with me and the boys." Blake motioned at Shane and Logan before he took a place beside her and looked at the growing crowd of teenagers.

"I had to wait for someone to get ready." She looked across the room at Abby, who was already surrounded by boys. "First dance at the new school and all."

"Looks like she's making some new friends."

Yeah, I know. All boys. She watched as Logan tried to squeeze between a couple of bigger boys to talk to her. Jillian was happy to see her give him her attention when he did. "Logan's a smart kid, huh."

"Very. He's in all AP classes." Blake glanced to the middle of the gym, where Logan and Abby had taken to the dance floor with a few other students. "They seem to get along well."

"They do, don't they." She smiled "And they look cute together." Jillian was thankful Logan and Abby seemed to have a lot in common. He was closer to her age and wasn't overly aggressive. She seemed to focus on him and didn't pay much attention to the other boys watching her. "What's with the eighties music?"

"I don't know, but I'm not sure they're going to get these kids dancing with the oldies they're playing," he said and looked across the gym. Jillian noticed the smile fall from Blake's lips and followed his gaze to an attractive woman with wavy blond hair who was talking to Stan. She was petite but wore heels tall enough to bring her to about Stan's height. "Do you know her?"

Blake nodded but didn't elaborate. She could see by the look in his eye that she was someone he still wanted to know. The DJ went way back, playing one of Jillian's favorites, Van Morrison's "Brown Eyed Girl." On impulse, she pulled Blake onto the dance floor, and they moved surprising well together. Blake threw her out and reeled her back in smoothly in a mix of swing and jitterbug moves. By the time the dance was finished, Jillian could tell Blake's mood had lightened and he seemed to be having as good a time as she was. The music changed to a slow ballad, and he placed his hand on her lower back and pulled her in close. Most of the single women in the room would love to be in her place at this moment, body to body with him, but being this close to Blake didn't stir any feelings in Jillian, physical or emotional. Her mind wandered to Amelia and how her body had reacted when she'd kissed her. Just the thought of the kiss made her body warm. No, not just warm, it was blazing with fire. That was the kind of feeling she wanted.

"That was fun," he whispered in her ear, and Jillian hoped he hadn't noticed the change in her body temperature.

"It was." She wasn't lying. Even though there was no chemistry between them, it was great to move in sync with someone. She scanned the crowd for Abby as they circled the room, caught sight of her near the food table with Logan. Then her gaze caught the petite blonde's, and Jillian found herself on the receiving end of a very unattractive scowl. Apparently, the woman Blake was pining after also had feelings for him. She wondered what the backstory was on the two of them but didn't dare ask. She didn't want to put Blake back into a sullen mood. The dance seemed to have brightened his spirits and, as a bonus, had sparked a bit of jealousy in Blake's love interest.

❖

Amelia had followed JJ and Abby to the dance. She'd also seen JJ's eyes widen as she'd become aware of how the other students were looking at her niece. Had the woman been raised in a box? Where had she gone to school? Hadn't she ever been exposed to boys when she was younger? Maybe not. Maybe she'd gone to an all-girls' school. Maybe she hadn't developed as early as Amelia had and hadn't been exposed to the attention of older boys or the cruelty of her peers. Surely, she'd have some inkling of how teenage cliques worked. Amelia wasn't even sure why she was so concerned. Looking after Abby wasn't her business. She caught sight of David off to the side, in a semi-darkened corner with his date, and JJ's words from earlier about the backseat shot through her mind.

David seemed just as surprised as Amelia was to find herself standing in front of him. "I don't want anything besides sitting to happen in the backseat of my car. Understand?" And she was even more surprised when the words flew out of her mouth.

"Uh, okay," David said, looking sideways to see if his date had caught the conversation. She hadn't, but Amelia knew she'd embarrassed him by just being there. She'd always trusted David to do the right thing. It seemed like only yesterday she was teaching him how to ride a skateboard, but he was a driving teenager now, and Amelia knew from experience that the backseat of a Camaro could be dangerous at that age.

"Have a good time, Dave." Amelia shook her head. She had no idea where this parenting urge had come from. As she spun around to leave, she caught the outline of JJ's dress from behind as she talked to Blake. It was a gorgeous sight, and Amelia knew exactly what she could do in the backseat of a Camaro, if given the opportunity. When

JJ turned around and glanced her way, Amelia ducked into the locker room and slipped out, hoping she hadn't spotted her.

It was almost eleven o'clock by the time Amelia heard footsteps on the front porch. She'd been on the couch, reading, since she'd returned to the house. No, that was a lie. She couldn't read, she couldn't think. She'd just been waiting for JJ to come back so she could apologize for her intrusive behavior. Laying her book on the table, she jumped up to open the door, and Abby scooted by her without a word, heading straight upstairs.

"I was beginning to worry."

"No need. I'm a big girl. I can take care of myself." JJ turned and seemed startled to find Amelia so close.

"I know you are." Her eyes met JJ's. *That's exactly what worries me.* "I'm sorry about earlier. I shouldn't have been so judgmental."

JJ's pink, heart-shaped lips looked so soft, so inviting. She closed her eyes, leaned closer, felt JJ's breath on her lips. Their lips had barely brushed when she heard Blake and the boys coming up the steps. *Thank God.* She turned away, touched her lips to cool the fire tingling in them. She went back into the living room, hoping no one had seen the heat in her cheeks.

"How was the dance?"

"Great. You should've come," Blake said. "This one really knows how to dance." He slipped his arm around JJ's shoulder.

"The two of you danced?"

"Most of the night," JJ said, smiling as she leaned into Blake.

"I haven't had that much fun in a long time." Blake turned to JJ. "Thanks."

"It was my pleasure." She smiled at Blake as he went up the stairs.

Amelia's stomach tightened. She didn't know what the hell was going on between JJ and her brother, but she didn't like it one bit. Her feelings were all over the place. One minute she was irritated as hell by this woman, and the next she was insanely jealous. She tamped her feelings down into the usual compartment she reserved for feelings of that kind and took in a deep breath. "Again, I'm sorry about the way I acted earlier."

"Me too." JJ put her hand on Amelia's shoulder and let it slide to her elbow before kissing Amelia on the cheek. "You should've stayed and danced with me."

Amelia's body buzzed as she watched JJ go up the stairs. She still didn't know why she wanted to be close to her, but she wanted to be even closer now. These crazy feelings she was having could turn out to be a huge mistake.

Jillian tried to slow the rapid thumping in her chest as she headed up the steps to her room. The evening had been full of surprises. Dancing with Blake had been fun, and making the blonde jealous had been an absolute blast. However, coming home to Amelia had been the highlight of the night. No matter how irritated Jillian was at her, she couldn't hold on to the anger. Whenever she looked into those big blue eyes, something inside her shifted, and all she wanted was to be wrapped up in her arms. The almost-kiss had been the topper. Thankfully, Blake and the boys weren't too far behind, or she might have found herself lost in Amelia...again.

Jillian changed her clothes, careful to hang up her dress before she went into the bathroom to wash her face. She gripped the counter and stared in the mirror at the reflection she'd created, wondering who this woman was whose stomach flip-flopped whenever Amelia was near. She'd dealt with all those feelings long ago. Hadn't she? She thought about Amelia and her pulse spiked again. *Apparently not.* She needed to get her shit together, focus on Abby and the foundation. She'd come here for specific reasons, and somehow those reasons had become blurred.

Jillian flipped off the light, and moonlight spilled into the room through the window, its silver beams reaching to the very corners of the space with its magic. The sheets felt cool to her skin as she slid between them. She put her mind to work on her new investigative-report idea about women and car repairs. She'd been surprised when it had taken Amelia only ten minutes to change the brake light in her car and the shop had quoted her an hour's worth of labor, plus the cost of parts. There she was again, Amelia. She closed her eyes, thought of Amelia's tanned skin and how she always seemed to smell like fresh flowers. She opened her eyes and shook the thoughts from her head. *Focus, Jillian. Cars, mechanics...Amelia. Fuck.* It was no use. Amelia was in her system, and she was going to have to work her out somehow. She pulled the covers up over her head, closed her eyes, and let fantasies of Amelia coming through the door, crawling into bed take over.

CHAPTER NINE

A melia rearranged her schedule and broke free from the office as soon as she could when she'd received Blake's text to come to the house ASAP. He didn't send those very often, so it must be important. When she got there, she found him in the kitchen helping Coop peel potatoes.

"What's going on?" Amelia sat at the table.

"David drew one of his caricatures in class today."

"What's wrong with that?"

"It was of Ms. Rand, his math teacher." Blake rinsed and dried his hands before sitting at the table next to her. "Here. Take a look." He slid a copy of it across the table, facedown.

"Lucy Rand?" Amelia recognized the name. "It can't be all that bad." She picked up the picture and let the edges of her mouth curl up as she looked at the head with scattered sprigs of hair shooting wildly about it, encompassing the huge open mouth and bulging eyes. "It looks pretty accurate to me."

"That's not the point." He snapped the picture away and stared at it, then exploded with a burst of laughter. "It is a pretty good likeness, isn't it?"

"Dead on, if you ask me. You should really get him into some sort of art program. He's a very talented young man, you know."

"Maybe, but I'm not going to that meeting."

"You haven't already met? Where did you get the picture?"

"JJ brought it to me at lunch. She said she'll go."

"Blake, you have to go stand up for him."

"Negative," he said, his voice firm.

"Don't you think your high school experience would've been a whole lot more tolerable if you'd had a father to support you?" Amelia's voice rose.

"I remember going to that high school once or twice to get your butt out of trouble," Coop said, as she continued preparing dinner. "David needs you to do the same for him. You gave up that college scholarship to be his dad. You can't stop because it's getting tougher."

"I'm not like you, Coop."

"No one is like me, Blake. But you're a strong man." She raised her arms and turned her palms up. "Look at all you've accomplished here. You changed your life, and you're making a difference with these kids. A weak man would have never chosen this path."

Amelia got up and took a soda from the refrigerator. "I can go with you, if you want."

"Strength in numbers?"

"Something like that." She opened the soda and the air fizzed out. "What time is the meeting?"

"Four. Right after school lets out."

"It's about that now."

"Go on. I'll finish up dinner." Coop shooed them to the door.

"Thanks, Coop." He grabbed his keys and they headed out the door. "We won't be long."

❖

Jillian sat speechless while the principal reprimanded David and Abby.

Mrs. Patterson looked at the picture. "Do you know how disrespectful this is?"

"I have never in my life had a student be so disrespectful to me," Ms. Rand said as she paced the office behind the principal's desk.

Jillian looked at her unique style of hair and clothing and decided that probably wasn't true. She'd probably just never caught them.

"What do you two have to say for yourselves?"

Abby spoke up. "It wasn't personal. We were just having fun. He draws them of everyone, including me."

"It's not any different than what you would buy at a theme park." Jillian shifted in her seat when Mrs. Patterson narrowed her eyes. It was like high school all over again. Fear skittered through her as though she were the one in trouble.

"High school is not a theme park, and these two had better pay attention unless they want to be working at one for the rest of their lives," Ms. Rand ground out.

Jillian shot out of her chair and went toe-to-toe with Ms. Rand. "They're both very bright students, so let's not pigeonhole them just yet." Jillian didn't know much about Lucy Rand, but she had a reputation for being a bully with the students as well as with the faculty. Jillian wasn't going to let her squash the spirit of either one of these kids. "Maybe if you'd treat your students with a little respect, they'd draw you in a better light. *And* they'd be in class rather than the office every day." The back of her neck began to tingle as her irritation grew. Jillian was just about to let loose on her again when she felt a hand on her shoulder and looked back to see Amelia standing behind her. "How long have you been there?"

"Long enough." Amelia gave her a soft smile. "I heard these two got caught with some questionable art in math class."

"If you can call it art," Ms. Rand said as she cautiously backed away from Jillian.

Jillian looked at Lucy and narrowed her eyes. Apparently, Lucy wasn't as tough as she seemed. She'd made her way to the opposite side of the room and was now using Mrs. Patterson as a shield. She held eye contact for a few seconds before turning back to Amelia.

"Is Blake with you?" She looked behind her into the hallway.

"He'll be here in a minute. He's trying to find a place to park around all the busses."

The door pushed open farther, and Blake stepped into the office. Mrs. Patterson hopped up and moved around her desk. "Well, if it isn't Blake Mathews, as I live and breathe."

"Good afternoon, Mrs. Patterson." He smiled, offering his hand. "I wasn't aware barracudas needed to breathe."

The kids chuckled, and Mrs. Patterson narrowed her eyes at them before returning her attention to Blake. "I can see you haven't lost your wit." She circled back around her desk. "I certainly haven't missed that."

"You're going to see a lot more of it, if you don't get off my son's back."

"Like father, like son," Lucy mumbled. Jillian shot her a look and moved toward her slightly. She was surprised to see Lucy flinch. Now she was sure there was a history behind her behavior.

"I may have been a challenging adolescent, Mrs. Patterson, but I had reasons for that. Reasons that don't exist in my son's life. I expect you to treat him individually and not pre-judge him because of your past experiences with me."

"All right, Mr. Mathews. I think I can do that." She sat down, eyes wide.

"Good. Now that we've got that straight, what's his punishment?"

"Three days' suspension." She slid the paper across the desk for him to sign. "I need your signature."

"And Abby?" Jillian asked.

"She didn't draw the picture. She'll just have detention the rest of the week."

"But—"

Jillian put her hand on Abby's shoulder. "That'll be fine."

Blake leaned over, scribbled his signature on the paper, and slapped the pen back onto the desk. "Let's go, David." He turned to Jillian as he opened the door. "We'll see you two at home," he said in a gentler tone.

She nodded and followed them out into the hallway and lightly touched Amelia's shoulder. "Would you mind taking Abby home with you? I have a few more things to take care of."

"Sure. Anything I can help with?"

"No. I've got this."

Jillian stood outside the door waiting for Lucy to vacate Vickie's office. She couldn't help but overhear Lucy ranting about the low punishment Vickie had given the kids. Lucy's face was stone cold as she exited the office, and her eyes drilled into Jillian's until Jillian raised a brow in challenge and walked toward her. She immediately scurried down the hall and out of the office. It appeared the woman was all show and no go.

Jillian ducked her head back through the doorway of Mrs. Patterson's office and said, "Can I speak to you in private for a moment?"

Mrs. Patterson looked up over her reading glasses. "Sure. Come on in."

"I'd like you to see something." She handed her the caricature David had drawn of her.

She glanced at it quickly, then threw herself back into her chair. "I don't need to see any more of these today." Pinching the bridge of her nose, she let out a short breath of irritation.

"I want you to look at it." Jillian's tone was unintentionally demanding, prompting a raised brow from Mrs. Patterson. "Please," she said, trying to temper the request.

Vicki leaned forward and looked at the picture. "Who's this?"

"That's me." She watched for her reaction as she looked at the cartoon of the Jillian with an exaggerated butt and even larger bosoms.

Her lip curled slowly, and she began to chuckle. "It's not very flattering."

"I know, but now look at this one." She slid the portrait of Abby across the desk to her.

Mrs. Patterson's amused look turned to one of astonishment. "This is Abby."

Jillian nodded. "It's very good, isn't it?"

"Yes. It's beautiful." Looking up at JJ briefly, she blinked. "David drew this one also?"

"He drew them both within an hour, sitting right in front of me."

"Amazing." She pulled the caricature of Lucy out of her desk. "I wonder why Stan hasn't mentioned this. I know of several art scholarships right now that David could benefit from, and I haven't seen anything at all about him come across my desk."

"That's what I was wondering." She sank into the chair in front of the desk. "From what David tells me, Stan's not a very engaging teacher. Apparently he gives assignments, then turns around and types on his laptop the rest of the hour."

"I didn't realize Stan had a laptop in his classroom."

"He built a roll-out shelf under his desk and hides it when any of the faculty come in."

"You've seen it?"

"The first week I started, I had to get something in his room, and I came across it."

"Why didn't you say something?"

"Like that would endear me to the rest of the faculty."

"I suppose you're right about that." She sat back in her chair looking at the three pictures. "Give me a few days to check into this."

"Thanks, I'd appreciate it, and I know Blake would also." She got up and headed to the door.

Vickie picked up her phone and began to dial. "Close the door on your way out, please."

❖

Amelia helped finish the dinner dishes as everyone else migrated to various places in the living room. Abby and Logan stayed at the dining-room table, doing homework. The other boys commandeered the couch and TV, and after JJ finished loading the dishwasher, she wandered out onto the front porch. After Amelia had dried and put away the last pan, she went out front and joined JJ on the porch swing.

"Are you okay?" Amelia asked. JJ had been noticeably quiet at dinner, and Amelia couldn't help but wonder why.

"This afternoon, in Mrs. Patterson's office, I felt like I was back in high school again. I was so nervous, I thought I was going to have a panic attack."

"You certainly didn't show it." Amelia had been totally impressed by the protective stance JJ had taken for the kids. Even more impressed that she'd done it for David as well as Abby.

"I don't know. When she started in that authoritative tone, I just couldn't speak." She rubbed her forehead.

Amelia fought the urge to put her arm around her shoulder. "Well, you sure put Lucy in her place." Amelia chuckled. "I've never seen her so ruffled."

A smile crept across JJ's face. "I guess I did, didn't I?"

Amelia let out a deep belly laugh. "I'm thinking that woman will be staying out of your way for a long time."

"In other words, I'll have the bathroom all to myself."

"Yes, you will, you big bully." Amelia poked her in the ribs, and her pulse spiked at the huge smile she received from JJ in return. She made eye contact, held it, and her stomach vaulted into somersaults again. The tension between them had somehow become thick, charged even. God, she was beautiful, even more so when she smiled.

JJ broke the connection and averted her gaze to her lap. "I showed Mrs. Patterson a couple of David's more serious drawings. She was impressed."

"Really?" Amelia turned sideways and put her arm on the top of the swing behind JJ. She resisted the temptation to reach over and drag her thumb lightly across JJ's shoulder.

"Uh-huh." JJ nodded. "A few deadlines have already passed, but I think she's going to see if she can find him a scholarship somewhere."

"Wow. That's awesome." Amelia was honestly taken aback. She'd seen David's sketches. Why hadn't she thought of that herself? "What made you talk to Mrs. Patterson about him?"

"He's just so good. I want him to have the best opportunities possible, and no one should stand in the way of that."

Click. Amelia felt the tumblers in the lock to her heart inch forward a tiny bit. All the warning bells were going off. This woman was doing crazy things to her, physically *and* emotionally, things she should ignore but couldn't.

❖

Jillian had said her good nights and gone upstairs after Blake had finished mowing the yard and joined them on the porch. She'd thoroughly enjoyed the time she'd spent with Amelia this evening. The mood between them had become lighthearted and playful. The temperature outside was delightful, and the sunset was beautiful, the perfect combination for combustion. It had been difficult to leave Amelia sitting there but imperative that she put some distance between them.

Jillian changed into her T-shirt and pajama pants before she plucked the book out of her nightstand drawer. It had been a long day, but she still had some reading to do in order to keep up with her false persona. She'd just opened the book when her phone buzzed on the nightstand. She looked at the name displayed across the screen and picked it up.

"Hey, handsome."

"Hey, love. It's good to hear your voice."

"Yeah? What are you up to?"

"Just delivering your voice mail."

Jillian tensed immediately. "Who called?"

"Your girlfriend, of course."

"Don't say that, Marcus." Jillian's body shivered at the thought of Kelly finding her. She'd gone to great lengths, including the purchase of a new cell phone and leaving her old phone with Marcus in New York, to hide her location to keep Kelly from following her. "What did she want?"

"She said she was getting ready to go out and meet some friends. Thought you might want to come along."

Fuck! "I wish she'd just leave me alone."

"You did make it clear you don't want to see her again, right?"

"You know I did." She kept her explanation short, not wanting to relive the whole agonizing experience.

"Should I call her back?"

"God, no. I hope she found someone else to occupy her time."

"Possibly, but you're hard to beat."

"Oh, Marcus, you such a sadistic charmer," she said evenly.

"When exactly are you coming home, anyway?"

"I don't know. There's been a complication." She paused. "Amelia is here."

"You knew that was a possibility."

"Yeah. I guess I did. I just didn't think she'd still be living here." She *had* known it was a possibility, and although there was probably no chance she and Amelia would ever be together again, a small part of her held out hope for a chance to reignite the fire that once burned between them. It was becoming clearer with each moment they spent together that the flame had waned but never gone completely out.

"She lives at the house?"

"No. She has her own place, but she spends a good amount of time here."

"And?"

"And it's still there, Marcus. The chemistry, the feelings, all of it." There, she'd said it out loud. Did that make it more true?

"Does she know who you are?"

"No. I don't think so, and I haven't told her."

"So what are you going to do?"

"I honestly don't know." Jillian heard someone coming up the stairs. "Hey, Marc. I gotta go. Let me call you back." She didn't wait for a response before she hit the red button.

She heard a soft knock as the door pushed open and Abby came in. "Who are you talking to?"

"No one. I was just practicing my speech for the assembly tomorrow."

"There's no assembly tomorrow. It's Saturday."

"Oh. I guess you're right. What are you doing home? I thought you were going to the movies."

"We are, but I forgot my jacket." She walked toward the adjoining bathroom.

"Here." Jillian went to her closet and took out her own cropped leather jacket. "Wear mine."

Abby's eyes lit up. "Are you kidding?"

"No. Go ahead." She held it up for Abby to slide her arms inside. "It'll look great on you."

"Wow." Abby ran her hand down the sleeve. "I'll be careful. I promise."

"I know you will. Have fun." She was surprised at the good feeling she got from the happiness she saw in Abby's face. All in all, it had turned out to be a good day.

CHAPTER TEN

Jillian sat at the dining-room table editing the information she'd gathered on community group homes. She was two weeks into her new identity, and everything was falling into place. She'd been making good headway in getting to know Blake and was finding he was a pretty good parent. She just didn't know when the time would be right to tell him about Abby. They seemed to get along well enough, but getting along and becoming an immediate parent were two different things. She was just biding her time at the school. She tried to avoid counseling kids as much as possible and spent most of her time working on the story about Heartstrings House. She'd originally made it up to get herself into the house, but after living here and observing the day-to-day challenges as well as the red tape involved in funding, she'd decided it would make a good feature story.

"Are the kids home from school yet?" Blake came out of the office and peeked through the blinds by the front door.

"Not yet. Abby has tennis practice this afternoon."

"Are you sure it's this afternoon?"

"Yeah. She has it every day."

"Must have been cut short today, and it looks like tennis isn't her only extracurricular activity."

Jillian pushed out of the dining room chair, darted over, and looked through the slit in the blinds as Blake held them down for her.

"What the hell is she doing?" She pushed the blinds farther apart.

Blake chuckled. "I think you can see what she's doing."

She yanked the front door open and raced out on the porch. "Abigail Davis, you get your butt inside this house, right now."

Abby rolled her eyes and turned back to the boy whose lips had just been glued to hers, which put her into even deeper hot water. Jillian rarely called her Abigail, and when she tacked the Davis on the end, it meant big trouble.

"See you tomorrow?" Abby said.

"No. You will not." Jillian's voice rose as he scurried down the front steps. "You will not see him here at this house, ever again."

"Lighten up, Auntie. You're embarrassing me." Abby went inside and headed upstairs.

Jillian followed her up. "I'm not kidding, young lady."

"I'm still going to see him at school, unless you plan to keep me out for the rest of the year." Abby's face flickered into a false smile as she rounded the banister and headed up the next flight of stairs, which made Jillian even more angry. "Or we could always go back to New York."

"And take that makeup off. I should've never let you wear it in the first place." Jillian flopped down onto the top step and mashed her face between her hands. She knew this would happen sooner or later, but later had been her preference. It wasn't something she was proud of, but fifteen had been the magic number in her life with a boy. It had been the loneliest, most horrible sexual experience of her life, and she hadn't done it again until she'd met Amelia. Now Abby was pushing those same boundaries, and Jillian knew Abby wasn't any more ready for it than she'd been at that age. Convincing Abby of that wasn't going to be easy.

"That went well." Blake smiled as he came up the steps and sat next to her.

"Did you see that?" She felt the heat rising in her cheeks. "The boy's tongue had to be all the way down her throat. And his hands." She shivered at the thought. "They were…everywhere!"

She hopped up, went down a few steps, and whirled around. "Why would she do that? Bring him here and let him fall all over her right in front of me."

"She needs some guidance."

"From me?"

"Yes, from you," he growled. "You're a beautiful woman, and she wants to be just like you." He shook his head. "Now with her mother gone, you're all she's got."

Jillian didn't know whether to take that as an insult or a compliment, but it sounded like a little of both. "She's got a funny way of showing it."

"You're right, but look at the bright side."

Bright side? What bright side could there be to a horny teenage boy feeling up her fifteen-year-old niece?

"She could be half-naked in the backseat of a car with him."

Her eyes flew wide again. Jillian had been half-naked in the backseat with Amelia more than once.

"But she's not. She brought him here...for you to see."

"Wouldn't it have been easier for her to just ask me?" Had being a teenager changed that much since she was one?

"She's feeling you out."

Jillian stared at Blake, still not quite understanding what he was saying.

"In essence, you're her mother now, probably a bit younger and cooler, and she needs some sort of a connection with you."

"How do you know all this stuff?"

"Raising David has been a learning experience."

"I didn't know it was going to be this difficult."

"No one said raising kids was easy," Blake said with a laugh.

"You're right about that." She threw her shoulders back and took in a deep breath before she headed up the steps.

After knocking lightly, Jillian turned the unlocked knob and pushed the door open. "Abby, we need to talk." Her eyes darted around the room, then to the closed bathroom door.

"I can't believe you embarrassed me like that." Abby's muffled voice came through the door.

You were embarrassed. What about me? Seeing her little niece in a lip-lock with a seventeen-year-old boy who had more facial hair than King Kong didn't give Jillian the most comfortable feeling. She dropped down onto Abby's bed and ran her hand across the fairy-tale pattern imprinted on the comforter. Abby was still so much a child that she couldn't fathom her with a boyfriend.

"Come on out and talk to me."

The door flew open, and out Abby came swaddled in her robe with a towel wrapped around her hair. "You just don't understand."

"Of course I do." She patted the space on the bed next to her. "Now come. Sit with me."

The bed bounced as Abby dropped down onto the end instead of next to Jillian.

"What was all that about?"

"I finally get a boy to notice me, and you have to go and blow it for me."

Jillian shifted around on the bed and tucked one leg up under her. "You shouldn't worry so much about men…in your case, boys. They'll always notice you."

"What do you mean?"

"Let me see. How can I explain this better?" She looked up toward the ceiling. "I was probably in my freshman, no, sophomore year in high school when I broke up with the quarterback of the junior-varsity football team."

Abby gave her a surprised look.

"It was the right thing to do, but he didn't take it very well. We had absolutely nothing in common. He told me, I'm sure out of anger, that I wasn't anything special and there were plenty of girls more beautiful than me out there." She laughed at the memory. "It seems funny now, but at the time I was devastated."

"What a jerk."

"Yes, he was, and that jerk went on to be the varsity quarterback, but that's another story." Jillian pulled her other leg up on the bed and sat with her legs crisscrossed. "After that, I always wondered if it was true, if there *wasn't* anything special about me." She smiled as confidence filled her. "Until I had been out of high school for a few years and something happened that changed the way I thought about myself." She touched her finger to her lips. "I can't remember where I was going, but I'd stopped in this coffee shop to get an espresso, and I noticed this absolutely gorgeous woman staring over her coffee cup at me."

"Why was she staring?"

"I didn't know. In fact, it made me very nervous at first." She did know, but that wasn't the point of this lesson. "Then I looked at her looking at me through the reflection in the mirror behind the counter, and that's when I knew just how beautiful I was."

"Huh?" Abby's nose wrinkled.

"She was looking at me the way I look at other beautiful women."

Her brows drew together. "You look at other women?"

Jillian laughed. "Yeah, I do. Sometimes I wish I could be as beautiful as they are."

"Oh, I get it. Like how Amelia looks at you."

"What?" Jillian played dumb. "Amelia was looking at me?"

"Yeah, she's beautiful, and she watches you all the time."

"Really. I hadn't noticed." That was a lie. Jillian had been unable to keep her eyes off Amelia since she got here, and now she guessed the impulse was mutual.

"I want to look like you. I mean like you used to." She reached under her pillow, pulled a magazine out, and slapped it into her lap.

"Where did you get this?" Jillian looked at the cover of the news magazine and smiled at the picture of her alter ego, Jillian McIntyre. She'd done the interview a few months before her sister had died.

"From Lucy. She got it in her current-events class. She noticed my eyes are the same color as yours and said I should wear the same color makeup."

Jillian stared for a moment, the unexpected emotion silencing her. "Sweetie, you're going to be much more beautiful than me." Jillian honestly believed she was already. She had the soft, sweet features of her sister, which made her so much more attractive than Jillian.

She perked up. "You think so?"

"I know so." She squeezed her up tight under her arm, unexpected maternal feelings exploding inside. Two months ago, this little girl was nothing to her, someone she was planning to dismiss from her life. Now Jillian wasn't certain she would be able to do it, even if Blake Mathews did turn out to be the perfect father.

❖

Jillian's stomach churned as she lay in bed, unable to get to sleep. She'd called Marcus, but he hadn't answered. Her talk with Abby earlier in the afternoon had replayed in her head at least a hundred times. Abby was a beautiful girl but lacked self-esteem, which could easily lead to a lack of self-respect and put her in a dangerous position with a boy. She got up and went to the bathroom, then slid open the door to Abby's room to look in on her. Not there. Jillian headed down the back steps. She was probably down in the kitchen doing homework with Logan. She'd make them all a cup of hot chocolate. Maybe that would help her sleep. When she reached the bottom of the stairs, she was surprised to find Amelia at the kitchen table.

"Hey," she said with a smile. It had been at least a week since Jillian had seen Amelia, and the buzz that shot through her made it clear she'd missed her. "I was going to make some hot chocolate. You want some?"

"Sure." Amelia got up to retrieve the packages from the cabinet.

Jillian headed for the door to the living room. "I'll see if the kids want any."

Amelia looked back over her shoulder. "David's the only one out there, and he's asleep."

"Are you sure? Abby's not in her room." She pushed open the door and searched the room with her eyes. No Abby.

Amelia followed her into the living room. "Maybe she went up the front while you were coming down the back."

Jillian rushed up the front stairs and checked her room again. No Abby. "Shit!" She ran into her room, pulled on some jeans and a hoodie, then rushed back down the stairs. "She's not here."

Amelia shook David's shoulder. "Where's Abby?"

David opened his eyes, groggily. "What?"

"Abby. Where is she?"

"Isn't she in bed?"

"No."

David sat up and rubbed his face. "We all watched a movie. Then she went up to her room."

"Then you fell asleep." Amelia closed her eyes and blew out a breath.

"I worked on my car all day. I was tired." David's voice rose in defense.

"Do you have any idea where she might have gone?" Jillian asked. She was starting to worry.

David let out a breath and stood. "She was talking about going out with Mike."

Amelia stood toe-to-toe with him. "Your seventeen-year-old buddy, Mike?"

"Yeah. I told her he's a jerk, but I guess she didn't listen."

"You should've told me." Amelia narrowed her eyes. "Where?"

"Muldoon's."

"She'd better be okay, David, or you're going to be in big trouble." She grabbed her jacket and took off out the door.

"What? I didn't do anything. She's the one who snuck out."

Jillian tripped down the steps after Amelia. "Are you talking about the old farm behind the high school?" She'd been to Muldoon's when she was younger. All she remembered was country roads, darkness, and beer.

"Yeah. Kids around here have been going there for years to make out." Amelia rounded her Camaro, got in, and fired the engine. "Get in if you're coming."

Jillian ran to catch up with Amelia and jumped into the car. "You've been there before?"

"Once or twice to retrieve a rebellious teen here and there," Amelia said.

"But you grew up here, didn't you?" Jillian said and thought she caught a glimmer of remembrance in Amelia's eyes. "Did you go there when you were younger?"

"Let's just say it's been a popular spot for a very long time."

After about fifteen minutes, Amelia pulled down the gravel road and turned off the headlights before circling the old barn and stopping the car.

"Why are you stopping?" Jillian asked.

"We go on foot from here."

"It's pitch-black outside." Jillian hated the dark, ever since she was a little girl.

"If they hear us coming, they'll just take off." Amelia got out of the car and slowly closed the door without making a bit of noise, but Jillian didn't move. Amelia poked her head back in the window and said, "Come on."

"I can't."

"Don't tell me you're afraid of the dark."

Jillian winced. "A little bit."

"Well, you can't stay here by yourself." Amelia leaned through the window, reached into the console, and took out a flashlight before she went around the car, pulled the door open, and offered Jillian her hand. Jillian took the hand and warmth flooded her. "Just stay close to me, and everything will be fine." Amelia clasped her hand firmly and pulled her toward the faint sound of voices.

After checking several cars first, they managed to locate Mike's car and pulled Abby out before she got herself into trouble.

"Do you know how embarrassing this is?" Abby whispered as Jillian pulled her along through the field.

"You're going to have a lot more embarrassing moments in life than getting caught in the backseat of a car with a boy."

Amelia chimed in. "Mike is too old for you. What were you thinking?"

"He's one of the most popular guys in school."

"This is not the way to become popular." Jillian opened the door of the car and flipped the seat forward. "Now get in."

"But I—"

"Not another word." Jillian looked over the top of the car at Amelia, who gave her a soft smile and nod of approval before she got in.

After they reached the house, Abby went straight to her room, and Jillian followed her. "What are you doing, young lady?"

"Nothing." Abby slid off the bed. "He wouldn't."

"Thank God."

Abby pushed her bottom lip out. "I'm fifteen. Everybody I know has done it."

"Losing your virginity at fifteen is not something to be proud of."

"Oh yeah? When did you lose yours?" Abby's eyes narrowed as she waited for Jillian to answer, and Jillian decided to let Abby in on her first meaningful experience.

"I was sixteen and in love." Jillian threw up a finger when she saw Abby's mouth open. "Even that was too young."

"Why would you say that if you were in love?"

"Sometimes our bodies and our minds just aren't in the same place. When your heart gets involved, it can be a disaster." Jillian raked her fingers through her hair. "I know it seems dreamy and romantic, but the first time can be very disappointing if it's not with the right person."

"So how do I know who the right person is?"

"Believe me, you'll know." She thought of her first time with Amelia and let a soft smile cross her lips. "You'll have feelings you've never experienced before, and he'll feel them too." She took in a breath. "Nevertheless, you have to be careful. Some guys only make you feel good to get you into bed."

"Did that happen to you, Aunt JJ?"

"It has." She nodded and pressed her lips together. "It's not a good feeling."

Abby looked as though she was processing what Jillian had said, but she could still see the curiosity in her eyes. She needed to end this conversation now before it went any deeper. "It's late. Get some sleep. I hope you brought a nice dress. We're going to church Sunday."

"I didn't."

Jillian's eyes swept Abby's body. Similar height and weight as herself, but with a slightly larger bust. "You can wear one of mine."

"Mom never made me go to confession."

"I'm not going to make you go to confession." She chuckled. "You don't have anything to confess anyway, right?" She dipped her chin and narrowed her eyes.

"Right." Abby gave her a huge grin.

Jillian kissed her on the forehead. "Sleep tight." Jillian closed the door and went through the bathroom into her bedroom.

"You did good." The voice startled her, and Jillian looked up to find Amelia sitting on her bed thumbing through a magazine.

"You're still here?" The sight of Amelia waiting on her bed made memories cloud Jillian's head. "You could've gone home. I mean, you didn't have to wait."

"I know. I just wanted to make sure you're okay." She set the magazine on the pillow and swung her feet to the side of the bed. "With Abby pushing the boundaries and all."

"I'm okay. The parent thing is new, but I'm getting used to it." That was a lie. Jillian was sure she'd never get used to nights like these.

Amelia pushed to her feet. "Are you really going to make her go to church? Sorry. I couldn't help but overhear."

"I'm not going to *make* her do anything, but attending church once in a while couldn't hurt."

"It's not going to make her stop thinking about sex." Amelia moved closer and held eye contact.

"Nothing makes a teenager stop thinking about sex." A tingle ran through Jillian's body. *Or me, apparently.*

Amelia's lips curved up into a sexy grin, and Jillian fought to contain the urge to kiss her. "Sixteen, huh?"

Jillian nodded, and another tingle shot through her. This was it. She'd been found out. Amelia finally knew who she was. The phone buzzed on the nightstand, and they both shifted their gaze.

"I'll get out of your way." Amelia crossed the short distance to the door, and Jillian's phone buzzed as the screen flashed on the nightstand. "You should get that. Marcus has been blowing up your phone for the past twenty minutes."

Shit! "He's a good friend." She'd forgotten that Marcus had put his name and number in her new phone.

"Must be. He sure does want to talk to you." Amelia stopped and looked back over her shoulder. "I was seventeen." She shot Jillian a sexy smile and continued out the door. "It was pretty amazing."

Amazing. Jillian shook her head. *It was fucking spectacular.* Jillian's body was telling her it would be again. Her heart thundered as she fell back onto the bed and let out a growl. She wanted Amelia, more than she was willing to admit. The phone buzzed again, and she grabbed it from the nightstand. Thank God, she had Marcus to talk things through with her.

Chapter Eleven

"Where do I put these?" Jillian asked, dropping the basket of dirty clothes on the floor of the laundry room.

"If you want them clean, I suggest you put them in the washer and turn it on." Amelia was using her serious tone again. "Nobody else is going to do it for you." Amelia must have seen her look at Mrs. Cooper, shuffling across the kitchen with a cast-iron frying pan. "Coop doesn't even do my laundry. She's certainly not going to do yours."

"Oh." Jillian looked at the clothes and then at the machine.

Amelia raised a brow. "You do know how to do laundry. Don't you?"

"Of course I do."

Amelia lifted the washer lid. "Then put them in, throw in some soap, and press the button." Jillian reached for the basket but looked up when Coop kicked another empty basket over next to it.

"Now come on, Amelia. You know better than to wash darks with lights." She laughed. "The first time she did laundry, she turned all Blake's undershirts pink."

Amelia pulled her lips into a wide smile, crossed her arms, and leaned against the door jam. "Thanks, Coop."

"Don't you have anything better to do? Like take the trash out?" As irritated as Jillian was, Amelia was a sight of which she never grew tired. She glanced at Coop, gave her a thankful smile, and began separating the clothes.

"I can do that." Amelia pushed off the wooden door frame with her shoulder and pulled the loaded trash bag from the can. "I'll be back in a minute."

"Take your time," Jillian mumbled.

"Now then." Coop picked up the basket and set it on top of the washer. "Darks are always separate. Lights and whites can go together. One scoop of detergent will do the trick." She pointed to the bottle on the shelf. "If your whites are very dirty, use one cup of bleach. Remember bleach is only for the whites, and wait until the tub is full to put it in."

"Thanks for not letting me look like an idiot. Is she always like that?"

"Only with the people she likes."

"She sure has an odd way of showing it." The mixed signals were getting old. Jillian stared out the window, watching Blake as he nailed up a loose plank in the fence. "He sure works hard around here."

"Yep. He makes sure everything is taken care of. I don't know what these kids would do without him."

"Even though the place seems to be falling down around him, he seems to love it here." Jillian watched Amelia head across the lawn and say something to Blake. "That one is hard to read. Just when I think I have her figured out, she changes."

"She's a feisty one, but don't let her fool you. She loves this place too. She's all about helping the kids."

She's way too good for me. Jillian had gone back to doing her laundry when she saw Amelia head up the steps.

"Did you get her all squared away?" Amelia said, letting the screen door slap closed behind her as she entered.

"She knew what she was doing. It's just a different machine than she's used to using." Coop gave Jillian a sly wink.

"You mean the kind that somebody else runs for her?" Amelia glanced at Jillian and lifted an eyebrow, and the constant battle of irritation and attraction flared inside Jillian again.

"Why don't you help me with this?" Coop shoved a square pan full of fried chicken into Amelia's arms. "Put it in the oven for me."

Blake came into the kitchen. "I can help with that."

Coop waved him off. "We got it." She followed Amelia to the oven and pulled the door open. "What are you doing, young lady?" Coop lowered her voice, but Jillian could still hear the conversation.

"I'm not doing anything." Amelia's voice was soft and seemed completely innocent, a sound Jillian hadn't heard before.

"The hell you're not. The heat in this room right now is enough to cook this chicken clear through." Coop let the oven door slam closed. "No mixing, remember?"

"Whatever you say, Coop." Amelia squeezed her lips together, and Jillian could tell she was holding back a smile.

She'd just crossed the kitchen to sit down when they heard Blake's name being chanted from the living room. Amelia and Coop looked at each other as if they smelled something bad as the voice got louder and closer. The chanting woman came through the swinging kitchen door, and Jillian could swear she saw a muscle twitch in Blake's jaw.

"There you are." The petite blonde from the dance waltzed into the kitchen smiling like the Joker, while Amelia and Coop eyed her suspiciously as though they were Batman and Robin. Jillian found herself skirting the edge of a huge pile of awkward. The woman raked her manicured nails across Blake's back and said in a slow, sexy voice, "I've got plans tonight. Do you think we can switch nights?" *Holy seductress, Batman.*

"Will you excuse me for a minute?" He took the woman by the hand and led her out the back door into the yard.

"Who is that?" Jillian darted through the door out onto the screened-in porch.

"Trouble, that's who," Coop said as she and Amelia joined her. They all watched through the mesh as the woman advanced and Blake retreated.

"Give," Jillian said without shifting her gaze.

"She's David's mother," Coop said.

"He was married…" Jillian turned abruptly and looked at Amelia for more information. When she received none, she glanced back outside to see that Blake had stopped retreating and was now brushing the woman's blond hair from her face. "To her?" The daggers the woman had thrown at her the night at the dance made sense now.

"Still is. He married her after his brother died." Coop supplied the rest of the information.

"Tyler's dead?" The news was such a shock, Jillian couldn't help the lilt in her voice. She knew he'd had drug problems but had no idea he was dead.

Amelia turned and looked at her curiously. "Did you know him?"

Jillian shook her head. "No. Blake mentioned you had a brother," she said, and Amelia didn't press. "What happened? I mean, was it an accident?"

"Car wreck," Amelia said, seemingly lost in thought. "I think I'll go run interference." She pushed through the screen door.

"It was a real shame too," Coop said with a slow shake of her head. "The boy was just getting his act together."

"David's not Blake's son." The words came out in a soft whisper. It all made sense now. She'd known he couldn't have a son David's age.

"Legally, he is. Blake adopted him. Genetically, David's his nephew." Coop turned and put her hand on her hip. "Kind of like you and Abby." Her eyebrows pulled together. "Isn't that a weird coincidence?"

"I guess it is. What's her name?" she asked, skirting that conversation.

"Suzie, with a *z*. He married her so there would be no questions about him being David's legal guardian. His biggest mistake was falling in love with her." Coop handed her a pile of laundry she'd pulled out of the dryer as they watched the backyard show. "She's tortured us ever since."

"He married her out of loyalty to his brother." The words bounced from side to side in her head until she needed more. "Isn't that kind of old-fashioned?"

"Don't get me wrong, I think he's enjoyed her, but she's a little too wild for him. She likes the bad boys."

Jillian looked out to see Amelia with her hands up, shaking her head as she walked away. She glanced up and caught Jillian's gaze, then took a hard left toward the garage.

"What in the world is he doing?" Coop's voice rose. "We'll never get rid of her now." Suzie was whispering something in Blake's ear, and he was grinning. "I can't watch this anymore." Coop shifted her attention from the show outside to Jillian. "I don't know what your story is, young lady." Coop took her hand and squeezed it. "I'm sure you'll let me know when you're ready."

Jillian looked at the heavy-set woman with her dark-red hair pulled up into a bun and didn't know what to say. Amelia was wrong about Coop. She wasn't frightening at all, and her hands were much too soft to be used for cleaning.

"Why don't you take that basket of clothes upstairs and fold them before Amelia comes back in here and gets herself into real trouble."

Jillian carried the basket of clothes up to her room and closed the door. Bleached-blond hair, oodles of makeup. *How could he marry someone like that?* She was so unlike Jamie, it was ridiculous.

❖

Kelly passed the house twice before coming up with a plan to park at the end of the street and walk by the house to the park. It was a perfectly normal route for anyone who lived in the neighborhood. She just wished she had a dog to make herself inconspicuous. Careful not to look suspicious, she pulled the stocking cap low on her forehead and headed down the sidewalk. She would've never figured out where Jillian had gone if it weren't for one of the researchers at the news network where Jillian worked. It had taken a few drinks and a fair amount of sweet talk, but she'd been able to find out everything she needed in one night.

As she got closer to the house, Kelly slowed her pace and dropped down to the concrete to tie her shoe. She glanced up carefully and saw there wasn't anyone on the porch, so she walked past the driveway and then by the house, noting the position of the door and windows. The headlights of a car shined on the shrubs that bordered the yard, and she looked over her shoulder. A car had pulled up at the curb. She passed the shrubs that bordered the yard and turned back to watch as a woman she didn't recognize got out of the passenger seat and went to the door. Kelly looked to her left and smiled. *Jackpot.* She'd spotted a pathway next to the house that would make it much easier for her to get a full view.

Jillian watched from the slight opening in the kitchen doorway as Suzie handed Blake David's baseball uniform. "His game tomorrow is at eleven. He already has his hat."

"You want to come in and have some dinner with us?" Blake asked.

Suzie looked over her shoulder toward the car at the curb. "Thanks, but I already have plans. I'll pick him up tomorrow afternoon."

Blake stood in the front entry watching as she went down the walk to the car and got in. Jillian crossed the living room and stood in the doorway next to him.

"Who is she?" Jillian already knew Amelia and Coop's opinion of Suzie, but she wanted Blake's as well. She had a huge decision to make about Abby, and Suzie was becoming an integral factor.

"She's David's mother." He hesitated.

"The two of you must have had David when you were very young."

"It's complicated." He continued to stare straight ahead, watching Suzie. "David is my brother's son."

"Oh." She feigned surprise. "So you're not married?"

"We're married."

"Was she married to your brother before you?"

"No. Tyler was pretty messed up. He never took responsibility for David."

"Then why did you marry her?" she said in a whisper.

"Every child needs a father." He shifted his gaze to Jillian. "I wasn't a very good husband. We were young and it was difficult."

"Do you love her?"

"It didn't start out that way."

"But you do now." Jillian could see it clearly in his actions. She'd watched him earlier. The excitement in his eyes when she'd arrived, the clenching of his jaw as he'd watched her rush to the car waiting at the curb.

"It doesn't matter." He shook his head. "I'll never be the kind of guy she likes." He motioned to the shaggy dude in the leather jacket waiting for her in the car.

Jillian could see the disappointment in his face as the car drove away. "Well, how about I help you out with that."

His brows drew together. "How?"

"Why don't we start with this?" She reached up and mussed his hair, then rubbed her fingers across his cheek and gave him a light pat on the face. "You need to invest in an electric shaver, so you can leave a little stubble on that baby face of yours." She smiled and cocked her head. "If you don't have anything else going, I'm up for a little shopping."

Kelly stood just on the other side of the fence and looked through a knothole in the wood. The back of the house was lined with a screened-in porch, and on the other side was a detached garage where the driveway led. She waited for the sun to go down before she pulled herself up and peeked over the fence. Through the kitchen windows, she could see a man and a woman who seemed to be cooking together. It was difficult to make out through the screened-in porch, but the woman looked to be about the same size as Jillian, yet her hair and clothes were all wrong. She scanned the second floor, noticing a trellis to each window on the side, no lights on upstairs. Either they were the only two home or everyone was downstairs. She saw headlights across the yard, and a car pulled into the garage. She could tell by the leaded exhaust fumes that it was an old one. She ducked down while the person came across the yard and went inside. Another man.

She strolled back to her car, watching through the windows as she walked. She saw boys in the living room, and she stopped when the girl caught her eye. *Abby.* She crossed the yard to the side of the porch and peeked through the window. *Jillian must be here somewhere.* All she saw were kids. She sprinted back to her car and looked at the documents she'd printed before she left New York. The house, previously owned by Jillian's parents, had been donated to social services. It had been up and running for close to a year now. *Why would Jillian come back here to do a story she could just as easily do in New York?* She fired the engine, threw the car into gear, and sped off to the motel she would make her home until she figured all this out.

CHAPTER TWELVE

Faded jeans. Check. Plain gray T-shirt. Check. Black work boots. Check. Leather jacket. Check. The transition was amazing. Blake had changed from the all-American boy to a laid-back, cool dude overnight. Now he would just have to get Suzie to notice. It was her weekend to have David, so Jillian knew she'd be here soon to pick him up.

"Okay, give me the jacket." He took it off, and she hung it on the old oak hall tree by the door. "Sit on the couch and relax." He sat in the middle, sitting straight up with his hands on his legs. "No, over here." She pointed to the corner. "Lean back, put your arm on the back, and spread your legs."

Jillian heard the engine as the car drove up and looked out the window. "Okay, now I'm going upstairs. I'll be back down in a few minutes."

"Okay. What do I do?"

"Just sit there. Don't get up when she comes through the door, and when I come back, go with whatever I say." Blake pulled his brows together, skepticism in his eyes. "Okay?"

He nodded, and Jillian climbed the stairs and sat on the step just past the landing. She heard the door open and then Suzie's voice in the foyer. She waited, listening to their conversation.

"What's with the hair?" Suzie asked.

"Thought I'd try something new."

Jillian peeked around the steps and watched as Suzie let her gaze rake over Blake. Mission one accomplished.

"Looks good. You should keep it that way."

"Thanks."

"What are you doing tonight? You want to get something to eat with David and me? We're going to the new Mexican place downtown."

That was her cue. Jillian popped up and headed down the stairs. "Hey, baby. I'm ready." She went to the couch and gave Blake a soft kiss on the mouth. "Sorry I took so long. Did you make the reservation?"

"I uh…yeah." He pushed up off the couch.

She went to the hall tree, pulled their leather jackets from the hook, and handed them to Blake. Blake helped her on with hers and then slid into his own.

There they were, right on cue. Daggers coming straight out of Suzie's eyes at Jillian. Mission two on schedule. Jillian pushed further. "Thanks for letting David stay with you tonight. We haven't had a night alone in weeks." She locked her arm with his, looked up, and gave Blake one of her sexiest smiles.

"Yeah, thanks," Blake said and opened the door for Jillian. "We'll see you tomorrow."

"Yes, you will. Bright and early. David, let's go," Suzie shouted up the stairs.

Jillian leaned into him and giggled, trying to hold her laughter in until they got in the car.

"Wow, did you see the look in her eyes?" Blake said.

"I did. She hates me. Now we know she's not over you."

"You certainly know how to stir it up, don't you?"

"It's a gift." She pulled her lips into a smile. "Where's this new Mexican place you're taking me for dinner?"

"I guess I owe you, don't I?"

"Yep, and to cement this in her head, she needs to see us together."

The host seated them at a table for four, and Jillian opted to sit next to Blake rather than across from him. The waiter brought the menus and took their drink order. They had been there for only a few minutes when Suzie walked into the restaurant with David. As soon as Jillian spotted them, she snuggled up close to Blake and whispered in his ear. "Don't look now, but they're here. Just pay attention to me like we're actually dating."

They continued to chitchat and look at each other until they heard David's voice. "Hey, Dad. I didn't know you were coming here tonight."

"We weren't," Jillian said. "Blake said your mom mentioned it." She looked over at Blake and smiled. "It sounded good. Right, honey?" She looked back up to see Suzie's eyes widen. *Bam!* Mission number three accomplished. "Do you two want to join us?"

"Sure." David pulled out a chair and sat before Suzie could get a word out.

Blake started to get up, and Jillian planted a hand firmly on his thigh, reminding him he was here with her. "What do you think I should order?" Jillian leaned over and looked at Blake's menu.

"Why don't we get the fajitas for two?"

Good boy. "That sounds great." She gazed into his eyes. "You know just what I like."

"Blake and I usually split those," Suzie grumbled from across the table.

"Oh." Jillian pulled her brows together. "Maybe you can split an order with David."

"Uh-uh. I'm having the mucho burrito with double beans," David said.

"Oh well. I think they have single orders." Jillian reached across the table and pointed to them on Suzie's menu.

Suzie narrowed her eyes. "Yes. I see that."

The waiter came with their drinks. He put a strawberry margarita in front of Jillian and a bottle of beer in front of Blake.

Suzie pointed at the drinks and crisscrossed her hands. "You've got those orders wrong. He doesn't drink beer."

"No, that's right," Jillian said, picking up the margarita and taking a sip from the straw.

"Yep. JJ convinced me to try one of these the last time we were here, and I have to admit, it's pretty good." Blake squeezed the wedge of lime into the beer bottle and took a long pull.

Suzie's mouth dropped open as she watched Blake drink the beer, and Jillian fought to hold back a grin.

They made it through dinner, Blake filling Jillian's corn tortillas with chicken for her and feeding them to her once in a while. It would've been a very romantic date for anyone who had the slightest interest in Blake. On the flip side, it was clearly torture for Suzie, who couldn't get through her meal quickly enough and had left Blake with the check.

"I don't have to drink any more of this beer now, do I?" Blake said as he picked it up and looked at the small amount left in the bottle.

"No." Jillian lifted a brow. "But you need to learn to like it if you want to hook that woman. She's got some deep-seated stereotypical ideas about men."

❖

Amelia sat on her couch flipping the TV from channel to channel. When she'd stopped on her way home to pick up her take-out chicken-enchilada dinner, she was shocked to see Blake and JJ together at the restaurant, his arm across the back of her chair, her leaning into him. She had no idea her brother was dating JJ. Amelia would've never kissed her if she'd known. She replayed the kiss in her head, just as she had over and over for the past few weeks. *She kissed me back.* She hit the power button and slapped the remote onto the coffee table. *Now she's all cozied up with my brother, having dinner.* She knew it was too good to be true. She'd finally found someone who made her feel something, and now she was messing with him. *What the hell kind of game is JJ playing?* She picked up her cell phone and hit the favorite button for Julie.

Julie answered on the second ring. "Hey, what's up?"

"You want to get a drink?"

"I would, but I'm kind of already settled in here. I've got a bottle of chardonnay. You want to come over?"

"I've got cold chicken enchiladas."

"Sour-cream sauce?"

"Always."

"Sounds great. Come on."

The door was unlocked when Amelia arrived, and Julie met her at the entrance to the kitchen. "The wine is on the counter." She took the enchiladas into the kitchen and slid them into the oven. Amelia followed her in, poured herself a glass, and drank it down.

Julie eyed her. "Are we going to require two bottles tonight?"

"Why is it when I finally find someone I click with, she's taken?" Amelia pushed herself up and slid onto the counter.

"My luck is rubbing off on you." Julie picked up her glass and clinked it against Amelia's.

"Luck." She pulled her lip up slightly. "Is that what you call it?"

"You know me. I don't like attachments. I didn't think you did either." Julie moved closer and put her hands on Amelia's thighs. "Isn't that why we're so good together now?" She leaned in and kissed Amelia softly.

Amelia felt nothing—no spark, no tingle, nothing. Not at all like the kiss she'd shared with JJ. "I've been rethinking that lately. I don't know if I want to be alone forever."

"Oh." Julie backed up, took a sip of wine, and set it back on the counter. "Because of this someone you click with, whom you can't have?"

"Something like that."

"So, does that mean no more friends-with-benefits for us?" She traced her finger along the neckline of Amelia's shirt.

"I didn't say that." She slid off the counter, captured Julie's mouth with hers, and kissed her hard. Maybe a good round of sex with Julie would get JJ out of her mind.

Later, Amelia sat up and tucked the sheet under her arms as she and Julie shared the pan of chicken enchiladas. "These are a little dryer than usual."

"That's probably because they spent an extra two hours in the oven." Julie shoveled a spoonful of rice into her mouth.

Amelia frowned. "Sorry. It takes me a while."

"I know. This isn't my first rodeo, cowgirl. You know I never give up a challenge." Julie winked. "Seeing as how this may be our last time, I gave it my all."

"That you did." She gave her a soft smile. "I'm sorry, Jules."

"Stop. We both know what this is. Just promise me you've never faked it."

"Never." She threw up three fingers. "Scout's honor."

"So what are you going to do about click-girl?"

"I honestly don't know." Amelia slipped her T-shirt over her head and slid out of bed. She took the empty pan of food into the kitchen, then came back and put on her jeans.

"You don't have to go, you know."

"Yeah, I do." She leaned over and gave Julie a kiss on the forehead. "I'll see you tomorrow." Amelia knew the encounters she and Julie had had still meant more than just sex to Julie, and the only way to squash those feelings was to stop having them.

CHAPTER THIRTEEN

Jillian drove past the brick pillars and down the long gravel road to where her parents resided. She parked the car and sat for a few minutes staring out the windshield, steeling herself for the visit. It had been almost fifteen years since she'd been here. Jillian got out of the car, made the short walk across the perfectly groomed lawn, and stood quietly gazing at the granite stones in front of her. The last time she'd been here, there were only two mounds of dirt. She took a few steps closer and dropped to her knees. She couldn't stop the burning ache within, and her body heaved as she sobbed. She missed them so much.

She looked at the marble headstone. A flash of nausea swept through her as she read the name below her mother's. EMILY MCINTYRE. The date below was the same day her mother died. "You were pregnant?" she whispered, swiping at her cheeks. How could her grandmother keep that from her all these years? She traced the name with her fingers before noticing the single red rose that had been placed at the base of the headstone. She looked around to see if any others had red roses at the base for Mother's Day but saw none. She picked up the flower, held it to her nose, and took in its sweet scent. It was a welcome change from the cold, metallic stench that filled her memory. She didn't know blood had a scent until the day she'd found her parents dead on their bedroom floor. That was all she could remember from that day, and it haunted her.

She set the rose back in place and got up to leave. She glimpsed someone walking toward her from the road and took off toward her car. She wasn't in any shape to see anyone, and she didn't want to be caught in this particular spot. She'd just pulled on the door handle when she heard the voice. "Good morning, Miss Davis."

Jillian shivered as she turned to see Steve Wright standing behind her. "Good morning, Mr. Wright. What are you doing here?"

"I'm one of the caretakers. Teaching doesn't pay all that much, so this helps supplement my income a little." He smiled. "I'm sure you can relate to that."

"Yes. I know what you mean." She smiled.

"You have relatives out here?"

"No." She shook her head and looked away, hoping her bloodshot eyes and mussed makeup wouldn't give her away. "I just have a weird curiosity about cemeteries."

"I'd be happy to give you a little history on the place if you'd like."

"Oh, that would be nice. It looks like some of these stones have been here for decades." She really wanted to get the hell out of there as soon as possible.

"They have been. In fact, some are dated as far back as 1910." He walked a little distance past where she'd been sitting earlier and pointed out a grave with a single rectangular stone featuring odd-shaped edges. "This one's been here since 1915. It's got the whole family listed. Two daughters and three sons. A few of them died pretty young."

"Thank God for modern medicine," Jillian said.

He weaved in and out of the plots to another old stone. "This one's been here since 1932. A farmer and his wife who owned a mess of property around these parts. Their kids sold most of it over the years, and now it's all shopping centers and housing." He walked back to one they'd passed, a bronze marker that was flat with the surface of the ground. "Military colonel, war hero, 1953." He shrugged. "No one was left to buy him a stone other than the one the military provided."

Jillian walked back to her parents' headstone. "Do you know anything about this one?" Her voice wavered, and she fought to keep it steady.

Steve followed her, kept quiet for a few minutes, and then he spoke, his voice soft and low. "Can't tell you much about this one, but jealousy can do terrible things to a relationship." He sucked in a deep breath. "It was a tragedy. I mean, with her being pregnant and all."

Jealousy? Jillian's head started to throb, and she kneaded the back of her neck with her finger.

"Well, I'd better get back to work. You have a nice day, Miss Davis." Without another word, he turned and walked back in the direction from which he'd come.

❖

The weekend had flown by quickly. Blake and David had spent most of it working on David's car, and Amelia had been noticeably absent from the house. Jillian had settled in at work, and Abby seemed to have taken Jillian's advice. She was spending more time with Logan and other kids her age rather than the older boys. She'd also started riding the bus, which gave Jillian more time after school to do research on the group home. Today she'd had enough and had come home to help Coop start dinner.

Jillian heard the bus arrive from the kitchen and pushed through the door. Abby dropped her books onto the coffee table in front of the couch where Shane and Logan were playing video games. "I'm never gonna get it all done tonight. Logan, can you help me?"

"He can't right now. We're in the middle of a game," Shane said.

Logan looked up briefly and then went back to the game. "I will when I'm done."

Abby plucked her books from the coffee table, crossed to the dining room, and let the pile drop with a thud on the table. "I can't believe how much homework that witch gave us."

"What class?"

"Geometry. I'm never going to be a meteorologist."

"Is Ms. Rand giving you trouble because of the drawing incident?"

"No, but I thought she was going to be so cool at first. She's even got a huge tattoo of a tree on her back." Abby's face scrunched. "She gives us freakin' homework almost every day."

"Well, why don't you start on it now?"

"I'm starving."

"I'll fix you a snack. Peanut butter and celery?"

"Chips and salsa."

"So nutritious." Jillian wished she could eat like a teenager again.

Jillian had just set the snacks on the table when she heard the roar of an engine. "Are you expecting someone?"

"No. Who is it?" Abby popped up off the couch and looked out the window. "Wow. Nice car. Whose is it?"

"I think it belongs to the guy you've been so nasty to for the past couple of weeks."

Abby pulled her brows together. "I haven't been nasty to any guys."

"You sure about that?"

Abby went out the front door and onto the porch to take a closer look. "That's David's old heap?"

Her expression made Jillian burst out laughing.

David slipped out of the car and shouted to Abby. "You wanna go to Sonic and get something to eat?"

"Sure." Abby was already down the steps and halfway to the car.

"Hey, what about your homework?"

She gave her a backhanded wave. "I'll do it later."

"They shouldn't be gone too long. I'm sure David has homework too." Blake flipped through David's textbook, pulled out a loose piece of paper, and unfolded it. "Damn."

"What's the matter?"

"David's having a little trouble in school." He handed her an English paper with a bold, red D written across the top.

"Oh, wow. I'd say that's more than a little trouble."

Blake dropped the book onto the couch. "Do you think you could help him out? Maybe tutor him a few days a week?"

"Yeah, sure. I guess." She could tutor a faltering teen. How hard could it be? "What subject is he having trouble in?"

"History, math, English. I'll pay you, of course."

"No need to pay me. You could let up on the household chores a little instead."

He smiled. "I'll think about it."

"David's a smart boy. I don't know what's going on." She glanced out the window where the car had been parked. "Look at what he did with that car." She spun back around. "I know what his problem is. He doesn't pay attention."

"Hence the D." He plucked the sheet from her fingers.

She chuckled. "No. I mean, he's bored and his mind wanders." She picked up the chips and salsa and headed toward the kitchen.

"What do we do about that?"

"Maybe he's not in the right classes." She dipped a chip in the salsa and then popped it into her mouth

"What kind of classes should he be in?"

Jillian wiped her hands on a napkin and then planted them on her hips. "I don't know. Let me see what I can figure out. In the meantime, I'll set up a study group with Logan and Abby. Then he can get into the habit of doing his homework at a certain time." She'd sit in, of course. It would make a good spin in her story.

"Better make it quick, 'cause he's tanking fast." Blake lifted the top from the pot on the stove. "What's for dinner, Coop? It smells great."

"Beef stroganoff, but I need some sour cream." She pulled open the refrigerator. "There's not much left in here. Did you go to the store this weekend?"

"Nope. I was busy with David's car. I'll go now." He took the list stuck on the front of the refrigerator and wrote on it. "Big or little sour cream?"

"I'll go with you," Coop answered. "We need to pick up a few other things for later in the week."

"Could you get some of those little yogurt cups? Please?" Jillian said in a sugary-sweet tone as she smiled at him. "Abby and Logan like them too."

He pulled one side of his lip up in return. "All right. We'll be back in a few." He held the door to the living room open for Coop, and they were gone.

Jillian turned to the stove, took the lid off the stewing meat, forked a cube, and ate it. It was wonderful. She would never be able to cook like this.

"Are you dating my brother?" Amelia's voice came from nowhere.

The lid clanged and dropped back onto the pot as Jillian jumped and spun around at the sound. "*Jesus*, you walk like a cat. Someone should put a bell on you." Amelia had slipped in without her noticing again, and she must have heard the exchange from the living room.

"Clearly." She propped herself against the door molding. "Are you?"

"Am I what?" Jillian was playing dumb and could see by Amelia's raised eyebrow that she was annoyed. *God, she's cute when she's like that.*

"Dating Blake? Because I got the feeling the other day you're more interested in women." She moved closer into Jillian's space.

"Does a girl have to make a choice? Can't it just be about the person?"

"No, I guess not." Before Jillian knew it, Amelia had her backed up against the table with her lips pressed to hers. *Sweet Jesus.* She was tossed back in time to those steamy days of her teens, only this kiss didn't feel tentative at all. It was powerful, aggressive, yet soft and tender. It sent her mind swirling like an F5 tornado, and Jillian had no choice but to surrender to it.

Her knees buckled, and she melted into Amelia as she skillfully maneuvered her tongue through the opening Jillian had given her. Their tongues met in an intense dance that could only be described as euphoric. Then, before she knew it, the whole experience was over.

Amelia pushed herself away and created some distance between them. "That's done. There will be no more kissing between us."

Jillian swallowed hard, staring into beautiful cobalt-blue eyes, still reacting in ways she didn't want to. Didn't know she could. "I get no say in this?" She moved forward, and Amelia put up a hand.

"No, you don't. Blake is my brother. If you're interested in him, you can't have me." Amelia turned and stalked into the living room.

"But I..." Jillian, still wobbly from the mind-blowing kiss, followed her. When Amelia glanced back, Jillian saw the uncertainty in her eyes.

"You can't have it both ways." Amelia sucked in a deep breath and headed out the front door.

CHAPTER FOURTEEN

The kiss was a bad idea. Amelia was still reeling from the multiple reactions it had provoked within her. JJ had proved to be more than an expert kisser, and Amelia hadn't been able to resist. If she was going to bow out of this triangle, she'd had to kiss her one last time. She slid into her car and drove the short distance to her office.

"I need to see the papers on the McIntyre place. Now," she rattled off as she flew by Julie and flopped into the chair behind her desk.

"What's got you so fired up?"

"We have a couple of new tenants, and I think Blake is expecting more by the end of the quarter. I need to see what the capacity limit is. I was planning to move in over there, but I may have to rethink that."

"You know there's enough room in that house for twelve people, if necessary. What's really going on in that head of yours?" Julie had always been able to read Amelia, even before they'd become partners.

"I'm not sure about the new woman. She's dating Blake."

"So. Blake's a big boy. He can take care of himself."

"Yeah, I know he can, but she kissed me." Amelia stared at Julie, waiting for her reaction.

"Oh, shit." Julie sank into the chair across from the desk. "When did this happen?"

"The other day." She picked up a file and flipped through it. "Then again, just now."

"This is off-limits girl?" The rhythm of Julie's voice told Amelia it wasn't a question.

Amelia blew out a heavy breath and answered anyway. "Yep."

"I take it the kiss was good, or you wouldn't be this upset."

"It wasn't just good. It was phenomenal." She tossed the file onto her desk. "Do you know how long it's been since I've had a kiss that made my toes curl like that?" She hopped up from her desk chair. Julie followed her into the small break room as she grabbed a couple of bottles of water from the refrigerator and handed one to Julie.

"I do, and now you're going to give it up because…"

"I'm not going to compete with my brother for a woman." She took a long drink of the water.

"Who says you have to compete? If she's kissed you…*twice*, she's clearly interested in you."

"It doesn't matter. It's not going to happen again. Not at Blake's expense." She had some emotional places she didn't want to go, and a jealous rivalry with her brother was one of them. Her life had been in a good place, with no complications and no emotional strings. That's the way she liked it. She needed to find a way to get back there.

"You ought to stop keeping that door to your heart locked down so tight, or no one's ever going to try to get in." Julie moved closer and lightly tapped her on the chest. "I never could find that key."

"I'm sorry. I know you tried really hard." She took in a deep breath.

"I'm only telling you this because I care."

She went back into her office. "I'm fine with my life just the way it is." *Loving someone hurts too much.*

Julie followed right behind. "That may be what's coming out of your mouth, but that's not what your body is saying."

"Don't you have work to do?"

"If you're not going for it, you want to introduce her to me?"

"Hell, no."

"Just as I thought." Julie shook her head and pulled one side of her lip up. "No matter what you say, you're not finished with her." She turned and left the office.

Nope. Not even close. Amelia closed the door behind her and flopped back into her chair. *What am I going to do about this?*

❖

Jillian heard the screen door slap closed and hoped Amelia had come back. She needed to tell her some things, like how she had no interest in Blake whatsoever. She was caught off guard when she saw Maxine standing just inside the doorway. Since when did social workers let themselves in?

"Dad, Maxine's here," Shane shouted from the couch, where he was busy playing video games with Logan.

"Blake's not here. He's gone to the grocery store," Jillian said as Maxine, smartly dressed in a navy Calvin Klein suit, carrying a Fendi bag, burst into the living room. Social work was certainly paying better nowadays.

"I came to see how your story is going."

Jillian looked behind her to make sure the boys hadn't caught what Maxine had said. They still seemed to be engrossed in their video game. "I need to check on dinner. Why don't we talk in the kitchen?" Jillian turned, and Maxine followed her.

Maxine was barely through the door when Jillian blasted her. "I thought you were going to keep that quiet."

"I thought you were going to include me in the story."

"I am. We just aren't at that part of it yet." Jillian kept an eye on the door over Maxine's shoulder. "I do have a question, though. Why is there no money to fix anything? Is there a bottleneck somewhere? I checked with the grantor, and there doesn't seem to be a lack of funds."

Maxine's hand went to her hip, and her demeanor changed immediately. "I don't know."

Jillian watched closely as Maxine averted her eyes and touched her chin. *She's lying.* "A lot of things in this house need attention. Not to mention that they need window air conditioners in the bedrooms before summer hits."

"Yes." She nodded. "Those will be necessary."

Blake and Coop came through the back door with the groceries. "Hey, Maxine. We weren't expecting you today. Is everything all right?"

"Yes. Everything's fine."

"She just came by to tell us she's received more funding," Jillian said, and she thought she saw Maxine's eyes narrow a tiny bit.

"Awesome," Blake said as he put the groceries away. "We could certainly use it."

"I'll have the funds transferred by the end of the week. If it's all right with you, I'll just take a look around and be on my way."

Jillian followed her up the back stairs and down the hall. She pushed open Blake's bedroom door, then hers and Abby's. When she reached the first of the boys' rooms, Jillian grabbed the knob and pulled it shut. God only knew what they'd find in there.

"We're not quite finished painting in there yet."

"Can I take a look?" Maxine reached for the knob.

"I'd hate for you to get white paint on that nice suit of yours." She gave her the once-over.

Maxine hesitated for a moment and flattened her collar. "I'll take your word for it." She turned and headed back down the steps.

"That's a very nice purse, also." Jillian followed her down the front staircase into the living room to find that David had taken Logan's place on the couch, and Logan was sitting with Abby at the dining room table, studying.

"Thank you. It was a gift." Maxine let her fingers move down the strap to rest on the bag. "Looks like things are shaping up nicely around here. I'll see you all next time."

"The funds?" Jillian raised her eyebrows.

"I'll check on that first thing tomorrow, and we can talk about the story."

"Sure. It was so good seeing you again." Jillian rushed Maxine out the door to the front porch. "I'll call you tomorrow, and we'll set up some time to outline your part of it. Okay?"

Maxine's lips spread into a huge smile. "Okay. I've got plenty of ideas."

I'm sure you do. Jillian walked Maxine to her car, and then Blake joined her on the porch. She was going to have to be more careful from now on.

"The house looks great," Maxine shouted and threw them a wave as she pulled away from the curb.

"Did she say great?"

"I think she did."

"The woman's never been that nice before."

Jillian widened her eyes. "Maybe she likes you."

Blake raised his eyebrows. "That would be surprising. Amelia's the one she was after."

"She dated Amelia?" *Did everyone date Amelia?*

"I wouldn't say they dated. They spent a good amount of time together working on the grant paperwork, and I think Maxine got the wrong idea. Getting money out of her has been an uphill battle ever since."

Now things were starting to make sense. Jillian hadn't realized the situation when she'd let Maxine take over the administration. She was going to make sure the difficulties stopped, one way or another.

CHAPTER FIFTEEN

Amelia had successfully stayed away from the house this week. She had plenty to do at work. Keeping her mind occupied made it easier to avoid stopping by, but she'd still found herself thinking about JJ more than she should. It was Thursday night, and she craved a home-cooked meal. She hadn't eaten anything but fast food all week.

"What are you cooking there, Coop? It smells wonderful," Amelia said as she came through the back door.

"Roast chicken."

"With mashed potatoes and gravy?" She glanced through the door into the living room, hoping to see the woman she'd been avoiding all week.

"They come together." Coop dipped out a spoonful of gravy and stuck it into Amelia's mouth.

"Oh, that's wonderful. Do you mind if I stay?"

"You'll have to fight for your share, as always."

"She can have mine. I'm going out," JJ said as she came down the back stairs.

"Out? With who?" Amelia turned, leaned back against the counter, and swallowed hard as she took in the gorgeous sight in front of her. JJ was dressed in black leggings and a printed T-shirt covered with a faded gray vest. Damn, she looked good.

"Darcy," JJ answered.

"Darcy? Seriously?" Amelia's voice rose.

"She asked me if I wanted to have a drink, so I said yes." JJ tilted her head. "Is there some reason I shouldn't go?"

"I just didn't picture you with someone like her."

"Oh?" JJ lifted her eyebrows. "Just who do you picture me with? You?"

Amelia crossed her arms and rolled her eyes. "No. Definitely not me."

"Good, because that's not going to happen."

Amelia narrowed her eyes. "Well, now that we've got that settled." She turned around and pulled the plates from the cabinet. "Anyone else hungry?"

"There's no school tomorrow, and Abby's spending the night with a friend tonight, so I might be late," JJ said as she pushed through the door into the living room.

With that news, Amelia fumbled with the plates, almost dropping them.

"What was that?" Blake said, taking the plates.

Amelia stared at the kitchen door, calming the urge to follow JJ through it. "Nothing. She's just irritating."

Coop let out a chuckle. "You keep telling yourself that, honey."

Amelia couldn't get through dinner fast enough. As soon as she reached her car she called Julie, told her she needed help, and to meet her at her place. She'd gone home and changed into jeans, boots, and her sexiest form-fitting black sweater. Darcy wasn't going to get her hooks into this one.

"Hey, I'm here." Julie had let herself in. "What's up?" She stopped, scrunching her eyebrows together. "Are you going out?"

"Yes, and I need *you* to go with me."

"You could've given me a heads-up." She motioned to her jeans and T-shirt.

"You always look fabulous."

"Can I at least borrow a blouse?"

"Sure." Amelia opened her closet. "Knock yourself out."

Julie chose a form-fitting gray tee and an oversized button-down blue plaid camp shirt that fit more like a tunic than a blouse. She decided to stick with her ballet flats instead of letting her size-eight foot swim in Amelia's size-ten boots.

"Who are we going to see?"

"No one. We just haven't been out in a while, and I thought it would be nice."

"Don't bullshit me, Amelia. You never want to go out. I always have to drag you."

Amelia chewed on her bottom lip, debating what she should tell Julie. She still straddled a fine line in their friendship when it came to dating other women. "Darcy's going to be there with someone I know."

"Someone you want to go out with." Julie crossed her arms and cocked her head. "Click-girl?"

"Possibly." Amelia steeled herself for a big fat no and started thinking about how she could go to the bar alone without being too obvious.

"Okay, then. Let's let Darcy know she's got competition."

"Thanks, Jules. You're the best." She gave Julie a quick hug and followed her out the door.

It wasn't a large house—two, maybe three bedrooms, she guessed, surrounded by a chain-link fence on a corner lot. With standard locks and deadbolts, it wouldn't be difficult to breach. Getting information was easy. All it took was a friendly disposition, a little twang in her dialect, and the right questions. Within minutes, Kelly knew everything she needed to about Amelia Mathews. She'd sat next door, on Mrs. Jones's back porch, enjoying a delicious piece of apple pie while the sweet elderly woman spilled information about the entire neighborhood. Fortunately, a house down the street was for sale, and it was easy for Kelly to pretend she was a prospective buyer. No one had answered the first two doors she'd knocked on. Finding Mrs. Jones in her front yard trimming her roses had been just plain dumb luck.

People in this town knew nothing about privacy, let alone security. The houses sat on good-sized lots, but having neighbors who knew everything about you, plus could look right into your backyard, was much too invasive for Kelly. She'd had a bird's-eye view into the back of Amelia's place from Mrs. Jones's rear porch all afternoon and had been able to get a pretty good idea how the house was laid out and that Amelia still wasn't home. The blinds in the living room had been left open, so Kelly had slipped into her backyard to take a look. She could never live in a town like this and was surprised no one had been smart enough to figure out Jillian McIntyre was masquerading as a teacher at the high school.

Jojo's wasn't the fanciest bar in town, but it was some distance from the university and wasn't filled with young college students drinking themselves into oblivion. It was Thirsty Thursday, as deemed by the students, and the bars on Campus Corner would be spilling out with stressed undergrads trying to forget about their courses for the night. Jillian followed Darcy past the tall tables to the far end of the bar and grabbed a stool facing the mirrored wall, while Darcy took the one adjacent to her on the corner. Jillian could see that it gave her a good view of the whole place, and Darcy was using it to her advantage, already surveying the crowd. Jillian's stomach rumbled. When Darcy had suggested dinner and drinks, Jillian had thought dinner would consist of more than a couple of tacos at the place down the street. If she'd known, Jillian would've opted to stay for the delicious-smelling roast chicken at home.

Darcy leaned in close to Jillian and whispered, "This isn't a gay bar per se, but it gets a pretty mixed crowd."

Jillian could see that right away by the number of looks they got as they came in. The cute bartender came over and took their drink order, a Bombay martini for Jillian and an IPA beer for Darcy. She mixed the martini first, slid it in front of Jillian, then popped the top off a bottle for Darcy and offered to pour the glass. Darcy waved her off, opting to drink straight from the bottle.

"Don't look now, hazardous hotness alert," Darcy said before taking a pull on her beer.

"Where?"

Darcy dipped her head toward the far end of the bar.

Jillian leaned forward, looked around the various people enjoying their drinks, and her stomach tightened. There, sitting at the end of the bar, was Amelia with a knockout blonde. Smiling and laughing, she was propped way too closely, touching her face intimately. Jillian downed her drink. She wasn't supposed to give up so easily. She should still be pining away for her, just as Jillian had for all those years. She must have been an idiot to come back to this town. It wasn't as if they could pick up where they'd left off. It was stupid to think Amelia didn't have needs. Jillian had plenty of them. Only one problem—Amelia had never left her thoughts, not for one blasted minute over the past fifteen years. She'd plagued every relationship Jillian had ever had or, to be more accurate, tried to have. How could she expect anyone to live up to the memory of her first love?

Jillian glanced down the bar to get another look at Amelia, but the seats where they'd been sitting were now occupied by two men. She almost jumped out of her seat when she heard the familiar voice behind her.

"I didn't think I'd see you here," Amelia said.

"Ditto." Jillian let her eyes sweep Amelia's body, and her mouth went dry. She was wearing a V-neck sweater that accentuated all the right parts, bootleg jeans, and plain black boots that had made her two inches taller. She was looking way better than any woman had a right to look.

"You two know each other?" Darcy said, raising her eyebrows.

"JJ lives at Heartstrings House." The woman next to Jillian got up, and Amelia slid onto the stool in her place.

"You live with Blake Mathews?"

"My niece and I occupy a room in the house, as do a few others."

"Oh." Darcy seemed disappointed that she wasn't going to have any gossip to spread tomorrow. Well, she did have some, but it wasn't juicy.

Jillian motioned to the bartender, who mixed her a martini, grabbed another IPA for Darcy, and scooted them across the bar. Jillian's throat burned as she downed her drink.

"What's that you're drinking?" Amelia asked.

"Martini." Jillian slid the glass back across the bar.

"I tried to get her to try a Leg Spreader, but she wouldn't go for it." Darcy smiled.

"Smart girl." Amelia didn't take her gaze from Jillian.

"You want something?" Darcy asked Julie.

"Crown and water." Julie looked at Amelia, then nudged her on the shoulder when she didn't look up. "Club soda for you?"

Amelia nodded, and Darcy waved down the bartender. She ordered their drinks and Jillian pointed to her glass.

"You sure you need another one of those?" Amelia asked.

"Aren't you here with someone else?" *Someone other than me?*

Amelia took in a deep breath and nodded. "I am, but she seems pretty tied up right now with the woman *you're* here with." The bartender slid her club soda across the bar, and she raised her glass. "Let's make the best of it, shall we?"

Jillian picked up her martini. "Cheers," she said, tapping it lightly to Amelia's before downing the drink. The burn wasn't as intense this time, but she was beginning to feel the effects of the gin. She glanced around the room, her face numb and her view beginning to skew. She probably should've nursed that one for a while.

❖

Amelia poured JJ into bed and sat on the edge, making sure she was settled for the night. She couldn't help but smile about the multiple times she'd told Amelia how beautiful she was, as well as the times she muttered nasty things and pointed at Julie. It was clear the woman was jealous, and Amelia had to admit, the same feeling had hit her hard when she'd spotted JJ with Darcy.

She hadn't planned to bring her home with her, but no way in hell was she was going to leave her intoxicated like this in Darcy's hands. Darcy would definitely take advantage of her condition. It wasn't that Amelia hadn't enjoyed drunken sex before, but tonight wasn't the night it was going to happen. Not with this woman. Thankfully, Julie was a team player. She'd seen JJ's condition and had offered to keep Darcy busy while Amelia got JJ out of the bar.

Amelia looked at the woman passed out in her bed and took a deep breath. She was gorgeous and looked kind of sweet in her sleep. It was tempting to crawl in next to her just to hold her through the night. *Bad idea, Amelia.* She shook the thought from her head and got up. After taking a blanket from the closet, she headed out into the living room and settled in on the couch, thinking about the evening. It had passed quickly and was kind of a blur at this point, except for the parts that included JJ. The bar had been pretty busy when they got there. She hadn't spotted JJ right away, but Jojo's was Darcy's hangout, and they were bound to be there somewhere. She and Julie had snagged a couple of seats at the end of the bar, and that's when she'd seen Darcy directly opposite her at the other end of it. JJ had to be close by.

They'd just ordered their drinks when she caught Darcy watching her. She saw her turn to someone adjacent to her, and that's when JJ's head popped into view. Amelia had turned quickly to Julie and told her she had something on her face. Julie leaned in right on cue and let Amelia brush her cheek with her fingers. When Amelia looked back down the bar, Darcy was glaring at her and JJ was downing her drink. It couldn't have played out more perfectly. She just hadn't expected JJ to drink two more martinis after that.

When they'd talked, the observations JJ had made about Julie were spot-on to a certain degree, until the jealousy factor kicked in. The night had grown pretty amusing after that. JJ's thoughts seemed to be scattered at times. She'd said some things that made good sense and then some that didn't make sense at all. She had Amelia confused about what was happening between the two of them. When JJ had pushed Amelia against the car, hooked her hand behind Amelia's neck, and kissed her, JJ's intent was crystal clear, and Amelia gave in to it.

JJ had immediately changed the radio station from NPR news to a mixed music station when she got in the car, and the bass blaring through the speakers vibrated the windows. Other than that, the drive home had been uneventful until Amelia looked over and caught JJ gazing at her. When JJ reached out and took the clip from Amelia's hair, she couldn't mistake the thrill that shot through her. Amelia had thought she was going to have to pull the car over right then and there. They had shared plenty of wet, hot, arousal-piquing kisses on the way into the house, but the puking after that had been a reality check. Amelia was absolutely not going to sleep with JJ when she was drunk.

Jillian opened her eyes and gazed around the room. *Where the hell am I?* She heard the water running in the shower. *Darcy. Shit. I must be at her place.* The room was decorated nicely, but subdued with muted greens and dark furniture. She glanced around and took in the rest of the room. Funny. She never would've pictured Darcy's bedroom like this. She'd expected it to be more bright and vibrant.

"Hey, you're awake," Amelia said as she came out of the bathroom dressed in a terry robe, rubbing her long, dark hair with a towel.

Jillian couldn't help but pause a minute to take in the picture of deliciousness. *Holy hotness. Am I dreaming?* A flash from the night before shot through her mind. She'd kissed someone at the car, the front door…lots of kissing. "Did we?" She lifted the sheet, looked at her clothes or, more accurately, lack thereof. No leggings and someone else's T-shirt. She widened her eyes and bolted up. "Oh, my God, we did." She sank back into the pillow and let out a slow breath. *How could I not remember?*

Amelia let out an unrestrained laugh, and Jillian let the amazing sound wash over her. The incredible rush made her tingle all over. "No, we did not. You were a little drunk. I thought it best not to take you back to the house." She touched Jillian's chin with her finger. "Believe me, if we had, you'd remember it."

Jillian pulled the sheet up and tucked it under her arms. "I don't hold my liquor very well."

"Apparently, but not many women do after three martinis." Amelia raised an eyebrow and pulled her lip up to one side into an irresistible smile. "Just be thankful I didn't let Darcy take you home. You'd be waking up in a whole different situation."

"Yeah. Thanks for that." She glanced over at the clock, nine thirty. "Damn!" Jillian jumped up quickly, taking the sheet with her as she grabbed her clothes and ran into the bathroom.

"What's the matter?"

"I'm supposed to pick Abby up at ten."

She came out of the bathroom searching for her shoes as she pulled on her vest. "Where's my car?" she said, looking out the window.

"Still at the bar. I can only drive one car at a time."

"Shit." She sank down onto the bed. "I hate to ask, but could you take me to get it?"

"How about you call her and let her know you're running late? Then you can shower, and I'll take you over to pick her up. After that, we can get a bite to eat." Amelia sat next to her. "We'll get your car later."

"You don't have to do that. You can just take me to my car."

"I want to." Amelia patted her thigh. "Now, go shower and I'll get you some clean clothes."

❖

"How about some fresh air?" Amelia pushed the button and the top retracted, then stowed itself away in the back of the Camaro. "It's a beautiful day." She looked over at JJ and could see how bloodshot her eyes still were. "For most of us. Want me to put the top back up?"

"No. I'll be fine once I get a little air movement." Amelia watched as JJ leaned back and let the sun hit her face. *Amazing. Beautiful even after a night of serious puking. Where did this woman come from? More importantly, how did she end up in the middle of my life?*

Amelia flipped the air-conditioning on and pointed the vents toward JJ. "Better?"

"Hmm…thanks," JJ said, giving her a soft smile.

As they pulled up to the stoplight, Amelia pointed to the license plate on the small Hyundai next to them. The license plate read TURBO. "That's just not right. A car like that has absolutely no power compared to this one." She put the car in neutral, revved the V-8 455 horsepower engine, and it roared. The guy in the car next to them looked over, revved his engine, and it hummed. "See what I mean?" Amelia laughed and threw him a wave. "Good try, buddy."

"Are you always so competitive?"

"I wouldn't call myself competitive."

"Then what was that back there?"

"Just a little fun. Making the boys jealous." She looked over and smiled at JJ. "Showing them what I have versus what they have." Her gaze returned to the road as her voice became softer. "Nice car, beautiful girl...you know." *Shut up, Amelia!*

"Beautiful girl?"

"Well, you're a little off this morning, but beautiful just the same." That comment garnered her a slap to the shoulder, which Amelia gladly accepted. It had lightened the mood, and JJ seemed to enjoy the ride after that. She reached over and pushed the button for the radio, and the mixed station from the night before blared through the speakers, the bass rocking the car. People gave them looks at each stoplight, which would've usually made Amelia uncomfortable, but she didn't care today. She was doing one of her favorite things, driving her car with someone special in the passenger seat.

CHAPTER SIXTEEN

Jillian had managed to dodge Darcy all morning but was taking a chance going into the faculty lounge to get a diet soda. She'd just slid her dollar into the machine and pushed the button when Darcy came in and headed straight for her.

"What happened the other night? One minute you were at the bar, and the next you were going out the door with Amelia."

Jillian reached down and pulled the can from the machine. "I'm sorry about that. I was tired, and you seemed to be having a good time with Julie. I didn't want to spoil your night and Amelia was leaving, so we walked out together."

"No worries. It was nice getting to know Julie a little better."

"How'd that go?" She popped open the can and took a sip.

"We're going out next weekend."

"Wow. That's great." She gave her a hug.

"Actually, it is. We have a lot in common and *I* got a good-night kiss."

"Now that deserves an ice-cold Diet Coke." Jillian fed another dollar into the soda machine, hit the button again, took the soda from the machine, and handed it to Darcy. "Here's to new beginnings." Jillian clanked her can with Darcy's. "I hope it works out for you."

"How about you? Did you get one too?"

"No. No good-night kiss for me." Jillian clamped her lips together to suppress the smile that began to creep across her lips. She wasn't about to tell the biggest faculty gossip that she and Amelia had exchanged more than one heated kiss that night.

Darcy's voice rose. "That's surprising. Amelia is notorious for quick starts."

"You said you went out with her. Is that how it started?"

Darcy raised her hand. "Guilty."

"I guess I'm just not her type."

"Go figure." Darcy sank into her chair. "You guys were so intensely focused on each other all night. When you left together, I thought for sure she was taking you home."

"Discussing politics always gets me focused, and as for leaving together, we were just ready to go at the same time. That's all." It seemed apparent Darcy had been keeping an eye on them all night. Fortunately, she hadn't seen Jillian's car when she left. Either that or she was very good at playing dumb. Maybe she'd been too busy with Julie to notice.

Amelia slid into her car and fired the engine. When music blared through the speakers, she automatically reached for the knob and changed the station to the news. She listened for a minute to all of the terrible things going on in the world and flipped back to the music station. From today forward, she planned to focus on the good things in life. She was still humming the last song played when she wandered into the office.

"You're in a good mood this morning," Fran said as she got up from the reception desk and followed Amelia down the hallway.

Julie joined the parade and immediately assaulted her with a string of questions as she entered her office. "So, what happened with you and JJ the other night? Did you take her to your house? Did you kiss her again? Did you sleep with her?"

Amelia dropped her briefcase and purse on her desk before turning around. "You know me better than that. I'm not going to take advantage of a woman when she's drunk."

"Oh, wow, what'd I miss?" Fran said.

"We went to Jojo's the other night, and Amelia hit it off with someone."

Amelia looked at Fran, scrunched her eyebrows together, and shook her head. "Not really."

"She was definitely into you."

"I wouldn't say that."

"Amelia." Julie smiled widely. "I saw her kiss you in the parking lot." She turned to Fran and widened her eyes. "I got hot just watching."

"Seriously?" Fran slapped her hand to her mouth.

"Jeez, Jules. You watched?" The words came out in an unexpected squeal.

"Calm down. I was just making sure you got to the car all right."

"If there was kissing, there must have been interest," Fran said.

"I got the feeling she's interested, but she was drunk." Remembering JJ's attempt at modesty the next morning, Amelia opted to keep JJ's alternate personality to herself for the time being. "Really drunk."

"You know they say people are at their most honest when they've had a few drinks," Julie said.

"If that's the case, then she really doesn't care for you at all." Amelia shot her a grin.

"What did I do?"

Amelia winked. "You showed up with me." She pulled her lips into a satisfied smile.

"Not a girl who likes to share, I take it," Fran said.

"No, not at all. In the car, she kept saying, 'I can't believe I'm here, with you.' Like I've got some kind of amazing reputation."

Julie's forehead creased. "What do you think that's about?"

"I have no idea."

"Well, she's in for a surprise. You're not all that special."

Amelia lifted an eyebrow and shot Julie an evil look. "Gee, thanks."

"Just kidding." Julie bumped her with her shoulder. "You're very special. Right, Fran?" She winked. "In your own kind of way."

"I'm not even going to ask what you mean by that."

"Are you going to see her again?"

"I don't know. We picked up her niece from her sleepover and had breakfast. After we took Abby home, I dropped JJ off at her car, and that was that."

"I can't believe you didn't set something up to see her again. That's so unlike you," Fran said with a tilt of her head.

"I think her head was still throbbing a bit. I was surprised she could eat breakfast. She had at least three martinis while we were at the bar, and who knows how many she had before we got there."

"I don't think she had any before that."

"How do you know?"

"Darcy."

"What did Darcy say?"

"She said she got the feeling the two of you had something going on. They'd gone out before, and she hadn't seen her drink like that."

"They went out before? Are they dating?" Amelia's adrenaline spiked, and a nervous tingle ran through her. It was becoming apparent that JJ was pretty friendly with a number of people.

"I don't think so. It was just for a drink after work. She said she'd hoped to go out with her again, but now that the amazing Amelia Mathews was interested, she didn't think that was going to happen."

"Since when am I amazing?" She spun around to face her. "And who says I'm interested?"

"Uh…everyone who saw you in that bar with her the other night."

"Was it that obvious?" Fran asked.

"Oh, yeah. Sparks were flyin'."

"Okay, that's enough of my life for today." She shooed them with her hands, moving them toward the door. "Time to get to work." Amelia couldn't argue with Julie on the sparks. When she'd spotted JJ at the bar, she'd ignited like a red-hot flare. She'd felt the warning signs but couldn't steer away from the danger she knew JJ encompassed. The night had been filled with hazard zones, and Amelia had barely managed to avoid the big one. Searing kisses flashed through her mind, and she smiled. JJ Davis was definitely becoming a necessary detour around a huge roadblock.

❖

Jillian wasn't a very good cook, and she never had the time at home, but making dinner with Coop had been fun, and it actually smelled wonderful. She'd left work early today, hoping to get in a little writing time on her story, but she'd been shanghaied in the kitchen and had only made it upstairs to change her clothes.

"Is there a church close by?" Jillian asked Coop as she stirred the spaghetti sauce.

"A few. It's Oklahoma," Coop responded. "Why? You have to confess?" Coop looked over her reading glasses at her.

"I thought maybe it might be good for Blake and the kids to go once in a while."

"Blake doesn't go to church anymore." Coop's answer wasn't surprising. Jillian hadn't spent time in church other than a wedding or two since her parents were killed. "He doesn't make the boys go to church, and he doesn't make them pray."

"Does he teach them anything at all about God?"

"Nope." Her attitude became rigid.

"They need to be taught something, don't you think? Then they can make up their own minds about it."

"Probably, but they won't learn it from Blake or Amelia." Coop filled a pot with water and set it on the stove before wiping her hands and leaning back on the counter. "These kids could spend every waking hour praying to God, and it won't bring their parents back. Or make their mother put down the bottle. Or guarantee their father will just be in a good mood tonight, so he doesn't slap them across the room. Most of these children are throwaways. Praying doesn't help. Shit still happens every single day of their lives."

Jillian touched her arm softly. "Until God brings them here." *Did I actually say that?* Coop's gaze rose slowly to Jillian. "They need some sort of faith, something to believe in. Don't you think?"

Coop turned back to the stove. "What I think doesn't matter. I'm not in charge here."

Amelia came through the kitchen door. "What doesn't matter?" She took a spoon from the drawer and dipped it into the spaghetti sauce.

Coop turned back around and looked at Jillian. "You're on."

Jillian contemplated her words as Amelia blew on her spoon. "Is it all right if I say grace before dinner?" Jillian asked Amelia.

Amelia stopped, spoon midstream into her mouth. "Do whatever you want. I don't care. Just don't expect us to chime in." She ate the bite of sauce, then dropped the spoon into the sink. "The sauce is great, Coop. What can I do?"

"The bread needs to be heated." Coop gave Jillian a slight smile as Amelia turned on the oven, took the foiled loafs of bread from the counter, and put them in the oven.

Everyone had been through the kitchen and filled their plates when Amelia took the last seat at the dinner table. It was nice to have a family meal where everyone was present. She glanced around the table, realizing what she'd just thought. This was her family now. It was comforting to see the kids happy and smiling, and it was good to see Blake that way as well. Her gaze fell on Jillian, and she took a deep breath. *Is she family? Could she be?* Hope was not something Amelia experienced often. She steeled herself and halted her thoughts. She couldn't let them go any further.

The Parmesan cheese and bread were making their way around the table when Jillian spoke up and said, "I thought if everyone's willing, it might be nice if we said grace before eating tonight and then went around the table and said what we're thankful for today."

Blake picked up his fork, spun a wad of pasta on it, and shoved it into his mouth. All eyes were on him.

"What?"

"You don't have to join in, Blake, but do you think you could possibly wait until I'm finished?" Jillian made sure her voice was soft and nonconfrontational.

Blake's gaze darted from Jillian to the kids as they all stared at him. He swallowed the mouthful of spaghetti and dropped his fork onto his plate. "By all means." He sank back into his chair and crossed his arms.

Amelia knew it probably wasn't the response Jillian had hoped for, but it was what it was. Jillian turned her attention back to the kids and said grace before she added, "I'm thankful to have a roof over my head and for being here with all of you tonight." She turned and looked at Abby, who was seated next to her.

"I'm thankful to have brothers." Abby looked at the boys and smiled.

"I'm thankful to have somebody who actually listens to me." David grinned and everyone laughed.

They went through each one of the kids, and Amelia realized they all had something to say. Maybe this was a good thing. She sat back in her chair and thought for a moment about what she might say. So much in her life had changed in the past few weeks. Did she dare to be thankful? Silence filled the room. She hadn't realized it was now her turn to speak. She shifted in her seat and looked across the table at JJ. "I'm thankful to have hope in my life again." Amelia's gaze didn't falter, and JJ's sparkling amber eyes became glassy, almost luminous. JJ cleared her throat, and Amelia knew she had gotten her message.

Blake's voice rang through and the moment was broken. "I'm thankful we have Coop to cook us this wonderful food."

JJ broke eye contact with Amelia, and a subtle smile overtook her face. "It is wonderful, isn't it?" She looked to Blake and then back to Amelia. "It seems we have much to be thankful for."

From then on, all Amelia heard were the clicks of forks on plates. None of the conversation registered. Only the deep-brown eyes of the beautiful woman sitting across from her caught her attention as she mindlessly forked spaghetti into her mouth. Her world was changing rapidly, and she didn't know quite what to do about it.

Making dinner with Coop had been fun, and it actually tasted good. Now Coop was gone, and Jillian and Amelia were alone in the kitchen. They'd finished up the dishes, and nothing was keeping them otherwise occupied. The small talk was getting noticeably ridiculous. She heard the doorbell ring and was thankful for the distraction. Jillian looked through the kitchen door to see who had arrived. "What the hell is she doing here?"

"Who?" Amelia squeezed in next to her and looked through the opening. Jillian's senses fired when Amelia's body brushed against hers. She closed her eyes and took in the sensation. This was *so* not the way she wanted her night to go after the glances she and Amelia had exchanged during dinner. The tension was growing between the two of them, and Jillian was finding it hard not to want her, to kiss her, to touch every part of her just as she had in the past.

Jillian pushed the thoughts from her mind and tried to focus on Blake and Suzie. She had DVDs in her hand, and it looked like Blake had invited her to stay and watch. All the kids had gone to Shane's basketball game tonight, so all who left to watch were Blake, Amelia, and Jillian. *What fun.*

"I'm gonna go." Amelia's voice was soft and low as she backed up.

"You don't want to stay and watch movies?" It was a stretch, a lame attempt to keep Amelia from leaving, but that's all Jillian had right now.

"No. I don't want to be a third wheel…or a fourth." Jillian could see the ambivalence in Amelia's eyes.

"You wouldn't be."

"I'm afraid I would." She took her keys out of her pocket and crossed the kitchen to the back door. She turned back momentarily, as though she'd had a second thought. "We could go for ice cream." Amelia's expression was sweet, hopeful even.

Yes, yes! I would love to go for ice cream with you! Jillian's heart screamed, but she'd promised to help Blake with Suzie. "Can I meet you later?"

"Never mind." Amelia rolled her lips together and shot Jillian a thin smile, then went out the door.

Fuck. Why does everything you do have to be so complicated, Jillian? Jillian pushed the door open again slightly and watched as Suzie came out of the bathroom and flopped down onto the couch next to Blake. He kept his arm at his side. Jillian knew it was difficult for him to ignore the reflexive urge to move it up and around her shoulder. If he did that, Suzie would surely curl in under it, and all his work would be lost. Jillian hadn't decided when to enter the picture, but she could see Suzie was giving Blake all the right signals, and he wanted to move forward, no matter what Jillian had told him to do.

"What do we have to watch tonight? Something girlie, I suppose." Jillian could hear the playfulness in his voice.

"Actually, I picked up one of those action flicks you like."

"Really?" Blake jumped up and looked at the title. "This is awesome. I didn't even know this was out."

His excitement seemed to make Suzie smile, and she genuinely seemed to be enjoying his company. Only she wasn't really *with* him. They were still separated. Maybe it was time for Jillian to remove herself from this unfinished story.

Blake slid the video into the player and then, in an effort to keep his distance, slid into the chair next to the couch.

Suzie frowned, seeming to notice his deliberate change of seating. "You won't be able to see from there."

"I'll be fine."

She moved to the middle of the couch. "Come sit over here where you always sit."

Jillian took her cue and walked quickly into the living room. "Is there room in that chair for two?"

Blake looked up at her and smiled, then patted his thigh. "For you. Always."

Suzie's eyes darted from Blake to Jillian, then back again before she hopped up and flopped down in the opposite corner of the couch. Just then, the power went out, and everything was dark while Jillian's eyes adjusted. The room slowly became lit by the glow of the moonlight.

"Not again," Blake grumbled, and Jillian stood so he could go check the fuse box. Before Jillian heard the screen door slap shut, Suzie was on her feet and in Jillian's face.

"Blake is *my* husband."

"Not for long, right? From what Blake tells me, you've moved on."

"Blake told you that?" The look on Suzie's face was a mixture of anger and surprise. Either she didn't want anyone else to have Blake, or she was still in love with him. "That's none of your business."

"Could be," Jillian said evenly, not moving an inch. "Looks like you haven't moved on. I suggest you stop being such a prima donna and let him know. Sooner or later he's going to find someone else." Jillian heard the back door close and sidestepped Suzie to meet Blake halfway as he came back into the living room.

"I'm going to have to get a padlock for that lever. Someone pulled it again," Blake said as he entered.

"Again. Has it happened before?" Jillian hadn't remembered that.

"Last week. I think you were out with Darcy." He shook his head. "It's just kids messin' around."

"That's weird. The kids aren't even home." A slight shiver ran up Jillian's back.

"Apparently someone doesn't know that."

JJ shook the feeling off and went back to the task at hand. She took Blake by the shoulders, lowered her voice, and whispered in his ear. "I'm going to bed. Here's your shot. Sit on the couch, but play it cool." She squeezed his arms before looking over her shoulder at Suzie and giving her a nod. She pushed through the kitchen door, rushed up the back stairs, then back down the front to the first landing. Jillian moved slowly as she peeked around the corner to make sure everything between the two of them moved in the right direction. She just hoped Blake didn't fuck it up.

Blake took a seat in his usual spot at the end of the couch just as Jillian had told him, and it wasn't long before Suzie was sitting next to him. "Ready for some action?"

Jillian had to pull back and put her hand over her mouth to stifle her laughter. He had no idea how loaded that question was. When she peeked back at them, Suzie had pulled her leg up underneath her and moved to face Blake.

"Can we talk for a minute first?"

"Sure, about David?" Blake said, and Jillian shook her head. The man was oblivious.

"About us." Suzie looked down and was silent for a moment. Jillian suspected she was gathering her thoughts. "I'd like us to try again."

Stay calm, Blake. Jillian thought the same words over and over in her head, hoping he remembered what she'd told him. His forehead creased. "Only if you're sure you want this. It's been pretty hard on David. I don't want to give him any false hope."

"I do…really want this." Suzie took Blake's hand and held it between hers.

Jillian's job was done. She quietly went back upstairs. She only wished it were that easy to get her own love life in order. She thought about Amelia and how she would've loved to be with her the rest of the evening. Instead, she would spend another night in her room researching the foundation, which she loved. Her work had always been her passion, but remembering how Amelia had looked at her earlier and knowing she was just across town meant the pull to see her would be a major distraction tonight. She took her laptop out of the closet and got comfortable on the bed. *Focus, Jillian, focus.*

CHAPTER SEVENTEEN

Kelly waited in her car until she saw Amelia Mathews come out of the building, get into her car, and drive off. She admired the woman's taste in cars, she thought as she crossed the street and climbed the short flight of stairs that led to the family-practice law firm of Mathews and Mathews. Kelly pulled her brows together and remembered the information she'd read about Amelia and Julie Mathews. It had been a short marriage, just a little over a year, yet they still worked together. Odd relationship, she thought. Kelly couldn't do it. She pulled the wood-framed glass door open and walked into the small office. The walls were unfinished brick, some would call the style rustic, quaint even, but Kelly wasn't impressed.

No one was at the receptionist's desk, but Kelly heard a faint mechanical hum coming from one of the offices. She looked inside to find an attractive woman with long blond hair, who appeared to be in her mid-thirties. She was running what Kelly thought to be a clothes shaver across her ass. She slipped past the door and headed to the next office, knowing it had to be Amelia's. Surprisingly, the door was unlocked, so she slipped in and quietly closed it behind her. Kelly could tell by the furnishings that Jillian's suitor was doing well in her profession. She pulled at the filing-cabinet drawer. Locked. She slipped around the desk and did the same with the drawers there, also locked. At least they had some sense of security. She picked up the computer keyboard and took a picture of the back before crawling under the desk and hiding her surveillance device.

It didn't take her long, and she could still hear the humming of the clothes shaver as she exited Amelia's office. She peeked around into the doorway to see the woman using the shaver across the front of her sweater now. She stepped into the room and cleared her throat, and the woman looked up.

"Sorry. I didn't hear you come in." Her eyes widened in clear surprise.

"Probably because of that gadget you have there."

"Oh, yeah." Julie flipped the switch and dropped it into her drawer before rounding the desk and holding out her hand. "Hi. I'm Julie Mathews," she said with a broad smile.

"Sandy Mason," Kelly said, shaking her hand.

She looked at her watch. "I was just about to head out the door for court, but I have a few minutes. What can I do for you, Miss Mason?" Julie motioned for her to sit down.

"Please call me Sandy." Kelly took a seat.

"I'll be happy to as long as you call me Julie," she said, giving her a warm smile.

Kelly thought she might throw up. The woman was just like the rest of the people in this state—too polite and too happy. She had no idea why Jillian wanted to spend a day here, let alone a couple of months. Oklahoma wasn't on the top of Kelly's vacation list, but if she had to come here to get her woman and take her home, she would.

"Through an unfortunate accident, my girlfriend's sister was killed, and now she has custody of her niece. We'd like to see what we need to do to adopt her."

"Oh, I'm so sorry to hear about your girlfriend's sister." Julie sat behind her desk, took out a notepad, and began taking notes. "Was her husband killed also?"

Kelly nodded.

"Have you and your girlfriend been together for very long?"

"Eight years."

"The child is how old?"

"Ashley just turned fifteen."

Julie sat back in her chair. "First off, it sounds like your girlfriend already has custody, so I don't think she'll have any trouble legally. Are you worried about something specific regarding the child?"

"If something happens to my girlfriend, will I have custody of Ashley?"

"There probably wouldn't be any question unless another family member contests it. If you're worried, you should get married before starting the adoption process."

"I'd already planned to ask her, but I've been saving for the wedding. I want to do it right."

"You can always get married at the courthouse and have a larger wedding later. Just make sure you check with the courthouse you plan on going to. Some are friendlier than others." Julie reached into her desk drawer, took out a piece of paper, and slid it across the desk. "Here's a list that may help."

"Thanks. I guess I'll just have to speed my plans up a little." Kelly stood. "What do I owe you?"

Julie smiled. "There's no charge for the first consultation." She handed Kelly one of her cards. "Let me know if you need further assistance." Julie looked at her watch again and stood up. "I'll walk you out."

"I will." She headed for the door and then turned back. "Thanks again for the advice." The woman was oblivious to the fact she'd planted wireless recording devices in both the reception area and Amelia's office. Julie had also provided her with some well-needed advice about completing her little family with Jillian and Abby.

❖

Jillian took the thirty-minute drive to Oklahoma City on her lunch break. She didn't have any counseling sessions scheduled this afternoon, so it was a good time to retrieve any important mail her agent had managed to forward. She opened her post-office box and pulled out the Priority Mail envelope that contained a few bills and one hand-addressed letter from Marcus. When she opened it and found the additional unopened envelope inside, the hair on the back of her neck stood up. It was from Kelly. She slid her thumb under the flap and tore it open.

Jillian,

I'm sending a letter, since you've chosen not to respond through your email. I've come to terms with your decision to split. I'm sorry for getting angry about it the way I did. I know it wasn't an easy decision, and me saying all those nasty things made it even worse. I've regretted it ever since. I'd like to erase all those ugly words and replace them with something happier. I don't know where you are right now or what you're doing, but once upon a time, we were in love.

Deeply, passionately in love. Do you remember that? I do, and it hurts to think we'll never be back there again. All I ask is for you to think about that and reconsider your decision.
  Your one and only,
  Kelly

"I was never in love. Definitely not passionately. Not anywhere close to deeply." Jillian shivered at the thought and had to stop herself from ripping up the letter and tossing it in the trash. She laid it on the counter, snapped a picture of it with her phone, and emailed it to Marcus before she jammed it into her purse and rushed out of the post office to her car. She fired the engine, flipped the air to high, and took a deep breath. *Why can't you just leave me alone?* Her stomach threatened to lose its contents as the torturous control Kelly had on her flashed before her. Jillian closed her eyes, breathed deeply again, and cleared the thoughts of their miserable relationship from her mind before she took out her phone and called Marcus.

"I got the letter you forwarded from Kelly today. I emailed a photo of it to you."

"Hang on a minute. Let me pull it up," he said, and she could hear him typing.

"Has she been texting me?"

"Of course."

"How often?"

"At first it was all day, nonstop, but it's slowed down to once or twice a day now."

"Are they still crazy possessive?"

"You're not softening, are you?" From the elevated tone of his voice, she could almost see Marcus's expression, raised eyebrow and all.

"God, no. I could never go back to that insanity. Forget I asked."

"Good. You were lucky to get out of that one when you did. Who knows the extremes she might have gone to in order to keep you." His voice settled back into his normal tone.

"She hasn't given up yet." Jillian fished the letter out of her bag. Marcus had advised Jillian to keep everything Kelly sent just in case she didn't leave her alone. "I should never have slept with her again."

"You mean after I told you not to?"

"Yes, after you told me not to, smart-ass."

"Sleeping with her again only gave her reason to hope."

She heard a few clicks, and he was silent for a few minutes. She slid the letter out of the envelope, unfolded it, and squirmed as she read it again.

"Hmm," he said, and she could imagine his brows pulling together, then rising as he read. "Doesn't seem like your one and only has come to terms with your decision to split." He let out a heavy breath. "You need to be careful of her."

"Hopefully, by the time I get back, she'll have moved on to someone else, and I'll no longer be the object of her obsession." She slipped the letter back into her bag and pulled into traffic.

"What are you going to do if she's still deeply, passionately in love?" he asked with a slight upward lilt in his voice.

"I guess I'll have to move in with you and tell her I've sworn off women."

"Hmph," Marcus said lightly. "Deal. As long as you do the cooking."

"I hope you're okay with grilled cheese and tomato soup."

"As long as it's gruyere, I'm happy."

Jillian had only driven a few blocks from the downtown Oklahoma City post office when she spotted someone, Amelia, dressed in a sleek navy suit coat and pencil skirt. "What the hell is she doing here?"

"Who?" Marcus's voice sounded urgent. "Is Kelly there?"

"No. It's Amelia." She watched her walk toward the courthouse. The suit seemed a little high-end for Amelia, but it certainly fit her figure well. The horn of the car behind her blared, and Amelia turned her head to look. Dark sunglasses covered Amelia's eyes as the wind blew her long, dark hair across her face. Jillian ducked down behind the steering wheel. Shit! "Marcus, I have to go. I'll call you back."

Jillian snagged a parking spot farther down the street and hustled through the lunch-hour crowd. She sprinted inside the courthouse and ran directly into a man crossing the hallway in front of her.

"Oh, I'm so sorry," he said, placing his hands on her shoulders to prevent her from falling. "You seem rushed. Can I help you find where you're going?"

"Is there a ladies' room close by?" She smoothed her shirt and glanced around the hallway, but she'd lost sight of Amelia.

"Yes, it's straight over there and to the left." He pointed down and across the hallway.

"Thank you so much," she said softly and moved quickly into it.

She took out her cell phone, looked up the number for Amelia's law firm, and hit the call button.

"May I speak with Amelia Mathews, please?"

"Ms. Mathews is in court today. May I take a message?" the perky voice on the other end informed her.

"No, that's okay. I'll try and catch her at the courthouse. Cleveland County?"

"No, she's in Oklahoma County today, room 409."

"Perfect, thanks." Jillian hit the red button on her phone and slipped it back into her purse. By the time Jillian got to room 409, court was back in session. She slipped through the doors and took a seat in the back of the courtroom. She spotted Amelia right away up front, sitting at a table talking to a woman who Jillian assumed was her client. Her hair was now neatly twisted up into a bun at the base of her skull where it met her long slender neck. Amelia stood to address the judge, and Jillian followed the length of her, from Amelia's navy pumps all the way to her shoulders as she paced in front of the judge, speaking. Amelia's expression was intense, her voice clear and powerful. The focus and passion she exhibited were insanely attractive. Mesmerized by her confidence, Jillian felt her stomach flutter when Amelia turned to the gallery and zoomed her focus in on her. Captured by Amelia's gaze, Jillian couldn't move. She'd been caught but couldn't take her eyes off the passionate, confident woman owning the courtroom.

Amelia tilted her head slightly, reached up, shifted her glasses, and then looked away as she continued her eloquent statement delivery. She was beyond sexy. Amelia didn't falter, even after seeing Jillian watching her. She simply finished her statement, strolled back to the table, and took her seat behind it between her client and another woman, who Jillian now identified as Julie. After Amelia sat, she leaned slightly into Julie, who then turned to Jillian and narrowed her eyes. Time to leave. Jillian slipped out quietly and didn't stop to think until she slid into her car, fired the engine, and flipped the air to high. She fanned herself with the mail she'd picked up only an hour before, but no amount of air-conditioning would cool the fire burning inside her. The absolute passion she saw in Amelia ignited something within Jillian more powerful than she'd ever felt, and it unnerved her.

CHAPTER EIGHTEEN

Jillian climbed the steps, pushed through the door of Amelia's law office, and checked in with the receptionist. Jillian still wasn't sure how she was going to explain why she'd been in the courtroom the other day, but after the third phone call to the house asking her to come to her office, Jillian knew she couldn't avoid it any longer. The receptionist led her to the back of the space past one office into another farther down the hall. She opened the door slowly, looked inside, and then motioned for Jillian to go in.

Amelia was in a heated conversation on the phone when Jillian entered. She looked at Jillian and held up a finger, signaling her to wait. Amelia's phone conversation seeped into the back of her mind as she took in the floor-to-ceiling bookcases filled with law books, the brown leather couch placed perfectly under the large double windows that looked out onto the street below. Several awards hung on the wall next to the bookcase. Jillian zoomed in on the United Nations Association Public Service Award and the article framed next to it with the headline LOCAL ATTORNEY RECOGNIZED FOR HER EFFORTS TO DEFEND THE RIGHTS OF CHILDREN. The next one read LOCAL PARK SAVED BY CHILD ADVOCACY ATTORNEY. She'd saved the park beside the house from being demolished.

Jillian was pulled from her thoughts as Amelia's voice rose. "Prior authorization? Up to five days. Are you kidding me?" Amelia threw herself back in her chair. "By the time we get that, he'll be using again." She shook her head. "That's ridiculous. The man is asking for help, and all we do is tie him up in red tape. Can't we make this happen any faster?" Amelia tapped her pen rapidly on the antique mahogany desk as she spoke on the phone, and the image of Amelia and Darcy pushed up against the massive wood platform flew through Jillian's mind. She shook it from her thoughts and spun around to head back out the door, but ran smack-dab into Julie.

"Oh, sorry. I didn't see you there," Jillian said, steadying herself against the door frame.

"No problem." Julie stuck out her hand. "I'm Julie Mathews. I was at Jojo's with Amelia a couple of weeks ago. I don't think we were actually introduced."

"No. I don't think we were." She held out her hand. "JJ Davis."

"Why don't you come have a seat in my office while Amelia's on the phone?" She led her back down the hallway, stopping at the small break room to grab a couple of bottles of water on the way.

"Okay." Jillian glanced over her shoulder her to see Amelia craning her neck, watching as she entered Julie's office. "You and Amelia have the same last name. Are you related?" Jillian didn't remember any cousins living here when they were growing up.

"Not anymore." She smiled and handed her a bottle of water. "She's my ex-wife."

Jillian's mouth dropped open, but nothing came out. The information floored her. She had no words.

Julie seemed to notice Jillian's confusion and tilted her head to one side. "After the other night, I assumed you knew she was gay."

"I just didn't know she'd been married." Jillian adjusted the flow of conversation she thought was about to happen in her head, contemplating the direction of her next question. "You still work together?"

Julie looked at her and pulled her brows together, seeming to wonder why Jillian was so curious. Possibly gauging what she should tell her. "We found we're better off as friends."

"But you kept her last name." For so many personal reasons, Jillian needed to know if that was about status or possession.

Julie continued to study her as though she were assessing her next move. "It was just easier this way. We'd have to change the logo, letterhead, business cards, etcetera. How about you? Are you married? Divorced? In...volved?" Julie let the last word roll out of her mouth slowly.

"None of the above."

Julie hit her again with the contemplative look. "Amelia tells me you live at Heartstrings House."

"I do. My niece and I have been there for a few weeks now. It's a wonderful place." She sat in one of the chairs facing the desk. "Maybe you could tell me a little about the grant. I'd like to thank whoever funds it."

"I don't have the information on the Heartstrings Foundation. That's Amelia's passion."

"Passion?"

"She and her brother worked long and hard to get that place up and running." She sat back and crossed her legs. "She's had a lot of obstacles to overcome, and Maxine hasn't made it any easier."

"Maxine?" She played dumb, wondering when Julie would get tired of being led.

"Maxine Freeman. She's the grant administrator."

"Maxine controls all the money?"

"Yep, and from what Amelia says, there's not a lot of it."

"That's ridiculous." Jillian knew for a fact that there was plenty of money. Something fishy was going on. "I mean, it's too bad there isn't more. The place could use some fixing up."

"Don't worry about that. Amelia won't let the place fall down. She's already put a good amount of money from her own pocket into it."

"She has?" Jillian knew that wasn't necessary.

Julie nodded. "She would never let her brother's dream fail. Speaking of Blake, are you two dating?" Julie didn't pull any punches.

Damn! What have I gotten myself into here? "I wouldn't call it that."

"What would you call it?"

"We've just enjoyed each other's company a couple of times."

Julie's eyes narrowed. "Sounds like dating to me."

Jillian started to give in, but since Julie wasn't going to let up, neither was she. "That's really none of your business." She heard Amelia's heels clicking down the wood hallway, and then she felt her presence right behind her.

"What are you two chatting about?"

"You," Jillian said, not swerving her stare from Julie.

"Me?" Amelia's voice rose, uncharacteristically innocent.

"Among other things." Julie stared back at Jillian and pursed her lips.

"Seems your partner is also your guard dog." Jillian stood, set the unopened bottle on the desk, and moved toward the door.

"Jules?" Amelia's brows pulled together.

"It's okay." Jillian took Amelia's hand, led her back into her office, and closed the door. "You didn't tell me the two of you had been married."

"That's not something that usually comes up with an acquaintance in casual conversation."

"Is that what I am?" Jillian moved closer and could feel Amelia's breath on her lips. "An acquaintance?" Her body buzzed at the proximity. She couldn't focus when they were this close, so she continued across the room and leaned against Amelia's desk.

Amelia surveyed her from head to toe, made an obvious gesture of taking in every inch of her, and Jillian felt the familiar bounce in her stomach. Amelia cleared her throat. "We got married because we could. To prove a point. Then we found out I wasn't good at it." Jillian shot her brows up, which prompted Amelia to explain further. "Now we use our experience to show our clients that couples can get along after divorce."

"Okay. Then I'll give her a pass on the interrogation this time." Jillian pushed herself up on the desk and crossed her legs, fully utilizing her sexuality. "Do you think there's any money in the budget for an air conditioner upstairs? It's already been pretty warm this spring. It's going to be unbearable during the summer." Jillian glanced at the thermostat on the wall. It was a currently a cool sixty-eight degrees in Amelia's office, but Jillian could feel the heat all the way down to her toes.

"I'm not sure, but I'll see what I can do." Amelia strolled to the bookshelf. She seemed to be keeping herself distracted as she reached up and pulled one of the law books from the shelf.

"Do you have to ask Maxine?"

Amelia nodded, then plucked her glasses from the top of her head where they'd been resting, slid them on, and thumbed through the book. "She holds the purse strings."

"Do you want me to talk to her?"

Amelia gave her legs another glance. "No. That would be a bad idea. She needs to be worked in a certain way."

"Worked?"

"Complimented, stroked. She's more agreeable when she's feeling good about herself."

"Okay." Jillian rubbed her hand across the mahogany desk and then pulled her lip up into a smile. "This is a beautiful desk."

"It's an antique. I bought it at an estate sale and refinished it."

"You did this?"

"I did." Amelia smiled with obvious pride.

"What an amazing job. The lines and the color are just perfect." Jillian knew how to stroke as well.

"Thank you."

"Have you ever had sex on it?"

Amelia's eyes went wide. "What? No." She walked to the side of the desk, careful to keep space between herself and Jillian.

Amelia's shocked expression was thoroughly amusing. It was difficult for Jillian to hold in her laughter. "Word on the street is you have." She pulled her lip up to one side.

"I can assure you, I have never had sex on this desk." Amelia took in a deep breath as though she were contemplating her next words. "Not that it's any of your business." She reached up, adjusted her glasses, then pulled them off and dropped them on the desk. "I think you should go." She walked to the door, grabbed the knob, and opened it.

"Let's get something straight." Jillian followed her and pushed the door closed with her hand. "If there's going to be no more kissing, you're going to have to stop all that stuff you do." She moved her finger in a figure eight at Amelia.

"What stuff?" Amelia cocked her head and raised an eyebrow.

"That right there. The cocking of the head, eyebrow thing you do when you know exactly what I'm talking about. The rubbing of your temple when you're deep in thought. The shifting of your glasses when you're nervous. Not to mention the twisting of your hair when you're daydreaming."

"And if I don't?" Amelia did it again, cocked her head and lifted an eyebrow. That was a dare, if Jillian ever saw one. She closed the distance between them, and Amelia's back thudded against the wall from the motion. Air whooshed out of her lungs, and Amelia's lips parted in surprise. Jillian ran her thumb across them, amazed at how soft and full they were. When she looked up into Amelia's eyes, they were no longer filled with surprise. They were dark, heavy with arousal. Jillian plunged forward, reaching up, hooking her hand behind Amelia's neck, pulling her into a kiss. Her mind went a bit hazy at that point, and then she felt Amelia's hands on her waist, pulling her closer, leaving no space between them. Jillian's lips parted, and to her surprise, Amelia deepened the kiss, plunging her tongue inside, touching, baiting, dueling with Jillian's. It was the most wonderfully arousing kiss Jillian had ever experienced, even better than the ones before. She could honestly kiss Amelia forever, and she wanted more…so much more. Jillian let her free hand travel inside Amelia's perfectly tailored suit coat, up Amelia's side to find a surprisingly full breast. She cupped it in her hand, flicked the nipple with her thumb, and felt it harden beneath the silk camisole. Amelia let out a moan that sent Jillian's arousal soaring, prompting her need to feel the warmth of the skin beneath the shirt. She tugged at it, trying to free it from her slacks, but she felt Amelia grip her wrist with one hand, then the other pressed against her chest, pushing her back.

"Stop," Amelia said breathlessly. "I can't do this. You're dating my brother." Her head fell against Jillian's.

They stood for a moment, forehead to forehead, chests heaving, still close enough to feel each other's breath on their lips. Jillian backed up slowly, shook her head, and quirked her lip up into a half-grin. "I have absolutely no interest in doing that to your brother."

"I certainly hope not." Amelia rubbed the back of her neck. "Jesus."

"Yeah. I know." Jillian pressed her lips urgently to Amelia's and let out a growl. "We will definitely have sex on that desk." She blew out a breath, then spun around, pulled the door open, and left.

Amelia followed her to the front door of the office and then walked to the waiting-room window. JJ glanced up and smiled before she got in her car and drove away. Amelia was so hot, she was sure she was going to burst into flames at any moment. This was wrong in so many ways. She raked her teeth across her bottom lip, looked down the hall at her desk, and smiled. She'd always had a strict no-sex policy at the office, but she'd seriously consider making an exception for JJ.

Julie's voice pulled her from her thought. "Look at you. Lips all swollen, cheeks all pink." Julie gave her a wink. "Another phenomenal kiss?"

Amelia shook her head. "Understatement."

Julie let out a chuckle. "I guess that meeting didn't go as planned?"

"Shut up." She went back into her office and flopped into the chair behind her desk. "There's something about her I can't resist."

"Clearly. I've never seen you like this." Julie sat on the edge of the desk. "You want me to run a background check on her?"

"That's not the way I like to start a relationship."

"Oh, my, she is special. I haven't heard you say the *R* word in a long time."

"I don't know any other way to describe it. I honestly have no idea what it is, but I want more than just a hookup."

"Tell you what. I'll run the check, and if nothing shows up, no harm done."

"No, don't. If she's got a past, I don't want to know about it right now." Amelia just wanted to enjoy the amazing feelings she was experiencing for as long as she could.

"Whatever you say." Julie got up to leave. "Did you find out why she showed up in your courtroom the other day?"

"No. Sorry. I got distracted."

"It seems she has a way of doing that." Julie headed for the door. "I'll be in my office if you need me."

Julie was spot-on. Amelia couldn't focus when Jillian came into the picture. Just her presence could jumble every cognizant thought and every bit of reasoning Amelia contained. When she'd seen Jillian seated in the back of the courtroom earlier in the week, her train of thought had gone right out the window. She'd had to force her arms to remain at her sides as the nervous tingle washed through her and settled on the back of her neck. *What the hell was she doing there? In my courtroom, messing with my mojo?* She'd taken a deep breath, settled her nerves, and thankfully, she'd gotten her bearings back. It wouldn't have done her client any benefit for her to get flustered in the middle of her summation. Judge Johnson was a stickler for protocol, and asking for a recess midstream because the woman in the back row had sent her mind into a tizzy would have totally pissed him off.

❖

Traffic had been light this morning. It was after ten when Julie arrived at the Oklahoma State Bureau of Investigation office in Oklahoma City. Not wanting to explain where she was going, she'd slipped out of the office after Amelia had gone to court and Fran was fully engrossed in her newest *People* magazine. She wouldn't even notice she was gone for at least another hour.

Inside the OSBI office, a couple of people were sitting in the chairs that lined two of the walls in the small waiting area, but the usually busy office was somewhat deserted today. Julie pulled the Criminal History Record Information Request form out of her purse. She'd filled it out earlier this morning with whatever information about JJ Davis she could gather without making Amelia suspicious. She wanted to abide by Amelia's wishes, but at the same time, Julie wanted to make sure JJ Davis wasn't going to hurt her best friend. JJ had asked her some interesting questions yesterday, questions she wouldn't expect from a woman who merely needed assistance. She was awfully curious about Amelia and the Heartstrings House foundation funding. Too curious.

"Good morning," Martha, the OSBI officer, said over the rattle of the sliding-glass window as it opened.

"Hey, Martha. How are you? I bet those kids of yours are keeping you busy." Julie had become friendly with Martha years ago, when she'd worked with her on a foster-kids charity event. Martha and her husband had adopted three foster children last year, who'd been living with them previously. They'd had a couple of kids of their own before that, so now they had a full house.

Martha's smile widened. "They keep me so busy I have to come to work to relax. Seems you're busy too. I haven't seen you in a while."

"Yeah. I know. Haven't needed many background checks lately." She handed Martha the form along with the cash payment. She knew her name would be on the form as the requester but didn't want any record of the payment going through the law firm's accounts.

"You want the works run on this one?"

Julie nodded. She'd requested record checks on name, sex offender, and violent offender as well as a name and fingerprint check. After JJ's visit yesterday, Julie had taken the bottle of water she had left in her office and put it into her desk drawer. She'd waited until after Amelia had left for the day to pull the prints and transfer them to the fingerprint card. They weren't the best, but she'd gotten a good thumbprint, which should be enough to pull at least a DMV record.

"Just give me a minute," Martha said.

Julie paced the small waiting room, truly hoping this woman came back legit. She didn't know what she'd do if some kind of criminal activity showed up. She heard the glass window rattle open and stepped back to the counter.

"Good news and bad news." She slid a small stack of papers across the counter. "Your lady doesn't have a criminal record, but she's lying about who she is."

Julie pulled her brows together as she read the name on the report. "Jillian McIntyre." *Holy shit.*

"Looks like she's using Davis as an alias, and she's from New York, not Missouri."

"This is very helpful." Julie folded the report in half and slid it into her purse. She'd have to wait until she got in the car to read the rest of the multiple-page report.

"Sure thing. Let me know if you need anything else on her, and I'll see what I can dig up."

"I think this will be sufficient, but thanks, Martha." She smiled and headed out to her car. How was she going to handle this newfound information? Clearly, Jillian McIntyre didn't need monetary assistance. She got into her car and started the engine. The cool air flowed through the vents and slowly brought her body temperature down. *Fuck! What the hell is she doing here?*

Julie thumbed through the pages. The report was thicker than the one page she'd expected. She took a few minutes on each page to scan for important information. One page in particular caught her eye, where she found that at least one piece of information Jillian had given Amelia was true: Abby was her niece. Her heart clenched as she read the circumstances in which she'd gained custody of Abby and honestly hurt for both of them. Julie hadn't experienced any similar losses but knew the impact they would have on her life if she had. She continued flipping through the pages and came across more than one incident report where Jillian had been the victim of domestic abuse. The last one was dated just a month ago. *She's hiding from someone.* She read further and realized not even fame and money can protect you from a crazy ex-lover. She tossed the papers onto the passenger seat.

"Kelly Hammond." She pulled a blank form from her briefcase and filled it out. "Let's see what we can find out about you." She grabbed some cash from her wallet and went back inside.

Chapter Nineteen

The office had been slow this morning, and Amelia's thoughts had wandered too many times to JJ Davis. She'd wanted to talk to Julie several times, but each time she'd wandered into her office, she wasn't there. Fran hadn't seen her leave and had no idea where she was. Amelia had thought she'd possibly gone for coffee, but when she didn't materialize back in the office within twenty minutes, Amelia ruled that out. Instead of waiting for her sounding board to come back, she'd decided to take a drive and get some fresh air. She ran by the flower shop, picked up her usual order, and headed to the cemetery.

Amelia sat on the small worn patch of grass in front of the marble stone and laid the single red rose on the small ledge at the base. "Your flowers look nice. Mr. Wright's been taking good care of your spot. I know he keeps telling me to call him Steve, but I still remember him as the shop teacher and just can't seem to do it." She reached over and rearranged the fake spring mix in the vase on each side of the headstone. "I have something to tell you, and I hope you'll be happy for me." She looked at the ground, pulled a blade of grass from the turf, and rubbed it between her fingers. "I've been kind of seeing someone new. She's not like the other girls. She's smart and sassy, not afraid to challenge me. There's something different about her, and I can't seem to keep her from my thoughts."

She sat quietly for a few minutes. "I've always asked you to bring your daughter back to me someday, but instead you've brought me someone else." She blew out a breath. "I have to believe you have. I've never felt like this about anyone besides your Jillian. It's absolutely wonderful and positively terrifying to let myself feel like this again." She brushed a few blades of fresh-cut grass from the base of one of the vases. "Please don't let her break my heart." She closed her eyes, faced the sky, and let the sun warm her cheeks. All she could do was hope JJ felt the same way.

"I'm not sure how soon I'll be back. If I'm going to give my new someone a chance, I need to let your daughter go. You'll always have a special place in my heart. You were my parents when my parents weren't. I'll always love you for that." And she would. If it weren't for Joe and Judy McIntyre, Amelia might never have made it past her senior year, and she definitely wouldn't have gone to college. When Amelia had received the news from the probate lawyer that she'd been named as an heir in the McIntyres' will, she was stunned. They'd provisioned enough money to pay for both her and Blake's educations to the colleges of their choice. After that, she knew what her path in life would be, with or without Jillian. Up to that point, she hadn't known such generosity, and until the McIntyres' house had been donated last year, she hadn't since. With tears streaming down her face, Amelia pushed herself from the ground and left the cemetery.

Julie gripped the steering wheel as she drove to the house. She'd called the school, and they'd told her JJ had taken the day off. Hopefully, everyone would already be gone to their respective activities and she'd be able to talk with JJ alone. Julie wasn't expecting JJ's abuser to be a cop. Hell, she wasn't expecting JJ to be *Jillian*. That put a whole new light on the problem. Julie had been a little rattled yesterday when she'd discovered JJ Davis was actually Jillian McIntyre, a ghost from Amelia's past. A very prominent ghost at that. The feelings Amelia held for Jillian were strong and had been a demon to contend with throughout their marriage. It was one of the very reasons it had ended. You can't expect someone to give themselves fully to you when they've left a piece behind, and Amelia had left a big chunk with Jillian. It was her own fault. Julie had known about Amelia's first love when she went into the relationship. Ridiculously, she'd thought she could fill the hole Jillian had created. She'd underestimated the size of the colossal crater the implosion had left. The jagged edges had only grown sharper as time passed.

After reading the full report, Julie wasn't wondering why Jillian had come all the way to Oklahoma to escape her psycho ex. She was worried Jillian had left breadcrumbs Kelly could use to find her and how it might impact Amelia. From what Julie had read, the woman was not only crazy, but she was also dangerous. She had to figure out how she was going to approach Jillian McIntyre, aka JJ Davis, with this newfound information and how she was going to tell Amelia.

She pulled up behind Jillian's car in front of the house and collected her thoughts. No matter what she did at this point, it would probably go badly. She just didn't know how badly. Julie had just stepped on the porch when the door swung open.

Jillian stopped mid-step out the doorway. "No one's home. I'm the last one out."

"Just the person I need to see."

"Like I said, I'm on my way out. I have an appointment, and I don't want to be late."

"Oh yeah? Where?"

Jillian looked at the small piece of paper she was holding in her hand. "Edmond."

"Edmond can be pretty confusing. How about I give you a lift?"

"That's not necessary. I can find it. But thanks." Jillian slipped by her and down the steps.

"What kind of an appointment could Jillian McIntyre possibly have in Edmond, Oklahoma?"

Jillian stopped and turned to face her. "What did you say?"

"I want to know what kind of business you need to take care of in Edmond, Jillian." Julie stepped down to the walkway. "Yes, I know who you are." She moved closer. "Why are you here, Jillian? More importantly, why are you pretending to be someone else?"

Jillian slung her bag onto her shoulder. "Okay, if we're going to do this, let's go, or I'm going to be late." She turned and headed toward Julie's car, holding the slip of paper up in the air. "I need to be at the television station by ten. Can you get me there?"

Julie snatched the paper out of her hand and looked at the address. "Yep."

Jillian hadn't expected her cover to be blown so soon, especially by Julie, of all people. The woman was sharp, suspicious, and well versed in all things Amelia. How could she pacify her without giving her all the details?

"Talk," Julie said as she pulled away from the curb.

"I'm here because of Heartstrings Foundation. I think what Amelia and Blake are doing is wonderful, and I want to help out."

"I don't buy it. You could've made a donation from New York."

"I wanted to see what it was like in person. We have history."

"I know. So why the fake name and the makeover?" She could see now that Jillian was wearing colored contacts.

"I wasn't sure how I'd be received. Davis is the name I always use when I'm not being me."

"What about all the questions you asked me the other day?" Julie wasn't letting up. Jillian was going to have to give her some valid information.

"Okay. I'll be straight with you if you promise not to tell Amelia who I am."

Julie shook her head. "I'm not making any promises."

"I'm here doing a story on the Heartstrings House Foundation."

"There are plenty of other foundations. Why Heartstrings House?"

"Because it's my foundation."

Julie's head snapped around. "What?" The car veered into the next lane, and Julie quickly jerked it back.

"I donated the house, and I fund Heartstrings House anonymously."

Julie glanced back at the road. "Are you investigating Amelia?" Then it dawned on her that they could all be suspect. "Are you investigating *me*?"

"No, but I don't understand why there's no money."

"I told you the other day. Maxine handles the funding."

"Okay. Then tell me about Maxine."

"Maxine. That'll take more than the few minutes we have left in this ride."

Jillian could see the TV station sign in the distance. "Just the highlights, then."

"Single. Beautiful. Extremely sexy. Dangerously high maintenance."

"Sounds like you've had firsthand experience with her."

"She almost broke me, and she never has gotten along with Amelia. She blames her for our breakup."

"Is she seeing someone now?"

"Currently dating a petroleum engineer." Julie pulled into the studio parking lot and rolled into a parking spot close to the door.

"Plenty of money there, huh?"

"You would think." She killed the engine and looked at Jillian. "Somehow I get the feeling I've given more information than I've gotten."

"I'm an investigative reporter." Jillian pulled her lips into a smile before she got out of the car. "I'm good at what I do."

Julie watched from the control booth as Jillian recorded the lines. Her voice slow and even, she didn't miss a beat. She *was* very good at what she did. Julie had called the office and told Fran she wasn't feeling well and wouldn't be in today. She hadn't planned to take the day off to help Jillian, but it was a good opportunity to gain more information. Julie had tried to hit Jillian hard and heavy on the way there. She'd wanted to see her reaction, but she'd found the tables turned on her.

The control-booth door opened, and a fiftyish-looking man with salt-and-pepper hair came through the door and stood next her. "Hi." He stuck his hand out. "James Cochrane. I'm the station manager here." Julie shook his hand and returned her attention to Jillian in the studio.

"She's doing very well," James said.

"Seems to be." Julie glanced over, wondering why he was here.

"Not even one mistake," he said as he watched Jillian.

"Is that unusual?" Julie asked.

He nodded. "I've never seen anyone speak so smoothly. I wish I had someone like her here."

"Do you have an open position here at this network?" Was it possible Jillian would move back to Oklahoma to be with Amelia?

"Not currently, but for her, I'd create one." He seemed very impressed.

"Do you think she'd consider it?" Julie suddenly had hope for a good outcome to this situation.

"I doubt it. No one comes to a market like this from New York. She has a job most people only dream about." His smile flattened.

"I guess you're probably right." Her hopes dashed, Julie shook her head. Jillian would be crazy to leave her job in New York.

"When I heard she was here at the studio, I thought I'd at least come down and meet her. Maybe take her to lunch."

Julie smiled. She'd thought lunch would probably be a good idea after this, but not with the station manager. She wanted an opportunity to get to know Jillian better without someone else in the mix.

Jillian finished the last lines of the voice-over. The session had gone smoothly and, hopefully, would be air-ready from here, with no other editing necessary. She couldn't help but laugh at Julie, all bundled up in a blanket as she sat against wall waiting for her. It might have been seventy-five degrees outside, but it was only a little above sixty in the studio. Even though the situation between her and Julie was contentious at best, she was thankful Julie had been her chauffeur this morning. She'd managed to garner some useful information from their conversation and hopefully had gained a little of Julie's trust as well. Plus, she would've never found the studio with the directions her assistant had sent to her cell phone. The only hiccup today had been the receptionist, who didn't recognize her right away with her blond hair. With a phone call to the station manager and Julie's reinforcement, she seemed to accept Jillian's explanation of trying to remain incognito while she was here on assignment and eventually let them inside.

When she stepped out of the booth, a tall, well-dressed man with a huge smile approached her. "Hi. I'm James Cochrane, the general manager here at the station." He reached out and took her hand.

"Oh, yes. My producer said he spoke with you about using the studio. Thank you so much for accommodating us." Jillian winced as he shook her hand with an iron grip.

"You're very welcome." He stared at Jillian for a moment, then said, "May I get a picture?"

"Of course," Jillian said. It was the least she could do.

He took out his phone and handed it to Julie. She snapped a couple of pictures, and they chatted a little about local opportunities and markets before James looked from her to Julie and then back again. "It would be my pleasure if the two of you would accompany me to lunch."

"I'm afraid we have to get back to Norman." She tilted her head and glanced at Jillian. "We have a previous appointment. Right, Jillian?"

"Right." She offered the station manager her hand. "Perhaps another time."

He took her hand and squeezed it gently before handing her his business card. "Just let me know when, and I'll come to you."

"That's very sweet. Let me check my schedule, and I'll get back with you."

As they left the studio, Julie whispered in Jillian's ear. "Do people fall all over you like that all the time?"

"Not always, but it happens."

"Ugh, that's ridiculous."

"That he's falling all over me or that he thinks I'd consider moving to a small market like this?"

Julie stopped mid-step and turned to Jillian. "Would you?"

"That would depend on a few key factors." What a total lie. At this stage in Jillian's career, it would be career suicide to consider moving anywhere outside of New York.

"What factors?"

"Salary and creative freedom, among other things."

"By other things, you mean Amelia?"

"Yes. Amelia." Amelia *had* become a big factor in Jillian's life, whether she liked it or not. If it came down to it, she hoped Amelia would come to New York with her.

"You still own a piece of her heart, you know."

Jillian stopped, let the information wash through her. "She told you that?"

"Didn't have to. You were there every day of our marriage." She pulled open the car door and slid into the driver's seat.

"I don't know what to say."

"Say you're not going to fucking tear her heart out again."

"Hurting Amelia isn't something I would ever set out to do." *Falling in love with her again wasn't either.* Jillian leaned her head against the headrest and closed her eyes. "If she's told you anything about us, you know the choice to leave wasn't mine."

Julie was conflicted. Amelia had mentioned her first love but never divulged any details of the relationship. Finding out she was a famous television journalist had been a complete surprise at the time Amelia had told her, and Julie wanted to know more of their history. "I've heard her story. Why don't you tell me yours?"

"Falling in love with Amelia blindsided me. When I was younger, I followed my sister around most of the time. She'd dated Blake in high school, and that's how I first met Amelia. My sister was always annoyed at my presence, pushed me off on Amelia every chance she could. Amelia was so sweet to me. At first, I thought she was just being polite. Then we started hanging out together without Jamie and Blake." She shook her head and let out a heavy breath. "I was so young. I had no idea what love was or how it felt. All I knew was, when we were apart, I wanted to be with her, and when we were together, I wanted to be closer."

Julie watched Jillian intently as she glanced up and stared out the windshield. From the smile on her face, Julie knew she must have been thinking back to the time she and Amelia spent together, and a sudden spark of jealousy shot through her. Julie had never heard any of this from Amelia, and it made her gut twist. She almost reached over and took Jillian's hand but stopped herself.

"Our first kiss rocked my world. I was excited and terrified all at once. I had no idea it was normal to have such feelings about another girl." She reached forward and turned the air-conditioning up a notch. "When my parents were killed…" She stilled herself, and Julie could see the tears gather in her eyes. "I was lost. I couldn't live at home. Living with Amelia was out. Her parents would've never let that happen."

"So you just left?" Julie's voice was more accusatory than she'd meant it to be.

"It wasn't like I had a choice. I was only sixteen. My grandparents took me and my sister to live with them in New York."

"You could've stayed in contact. Why didn't you?"

"I tried to call a few times, but her dad was such an ass." She closed her eyes and shook her head. "I guess he found out we were more than friends somehow and wouldn't let me talk to her. After that, I sent letters. I suspected he intercepted those as well, but my grandmother had a hand in keeping us apart too. I never heard from Amelia again." She put her hands to her face and wiped the tears from her cheeks.

Julie squeezed Jillian's hand. "I'm sorry you had to go through all that." She didn't want to feel sorry for her, but she'd have to be made of stone not to feel something.

Jillian straightened her shoulders. "I'm okay. I went on with my life." She moved her hand from beneath Julie's. "I'm sure you've heard all of this from Amelia."

Julie nodded. "Yeah," she said. But she *hadn't* heard any of it from Amelia, and it made many things so much clearer.

Jillian turned and stared at her with huge, red-rimmed eyes. "I need you to keep this to yourself for the time being. Will you do that?"

Julie studied her for a moment, debating her next move. "What are you hungry for?"

"I'm actually not very hungry at this moment."

"I'll keep your secret for the time being." Jillian's story had gotten to her, and Julie wasn't happy she'd let it happen. She put the car into gear, looked over her shoulder, and backed out of the parking space. She glanced at Jillian as she turned back to the windshield, and Julie could see the gratitude in her eyes. "There's a new Mexican place downtown. We'll stop there."

CHAPTER TWENTY

Jillian stared out the window of her office. Her conversation with Julie had raked up all the past emotions that had settled at the bottom of her heart. Now they were swirling about, trying to find a new place to settle. The door to the gym flew open, and one by one, the pom-pom girls filed out. Her stomach tingled as she remembered the times Amelia would push through the very same door and spot Jillian waiting for her. She was gorgeous, sweet, and so unassuming. Her beautiful smile would broaden as she came closer, always with that hint of surprise in her voice when she'd asked Jillian what she was doing there. The chemistry was undeniable from the beginning. She didn't doubt Amelia had loved her. Jillian had felt the same, and it was increasingly evident that she still did. She'd been attracted to Amelia since the moment she saw her again. Her feelings might have been easier to ignore, or maybe even faded altogether, if she hadn't had to see her so much over the past few weeks.

She thought about her life in New York and tingled all over. She had fame, fortune, success, and a job she loved. The one thing she'd never been able to capture was the contented state of love she'd had with Amelia. She'd never found anyone who touched her as deeply as Amelia had done so many years ago, and she didn't know if she ever would again.

Jillian rubbed her eyes. She'd had appointment after appointment of college-bound kids today. The school year was almost over, and they all needed guidance about where to go and how to get there. She was writing a few notes on her last student for the day when Darcy's voice startled her out of her thoughts. "Where were you yesterday?"

"I had a doctor appointment in the city."

"Is everything okay?"

"Yeah. It was just for my allergies."

"You want to go grab a drink?"

"Sure. Let me check on Abby first." She picked up her cell phone and typed in a text. She took the folders strewn in front of her and filed them in her desk drawer. "Can we go somewhere besides Jojo's? I don't want to deal with other women tonight."

Darcy nodded. "I'm with ya there."

Jillian's interest was piqued. "That's new. I was expecting resistance."

Darcy scrunched up her nose. "I'm kind of seeing someone."

"Oh yeah, who?" Jillian dropped the last file into the drawer and gave Darcy her full attention.

Darcy's gaze hit everything in the room besides Jillian. "I'd like to keep it to myself for now. It's very fresh, and I don't want to jinx it."

"Oh, okay." Darcy seemed nervous about the whole thing, so Jillian decided to leave it alone. Her phone chimed and she read the text from Abby. "Abby's going to a friend's to study for a little while, so I have some time." She pulled her purse from her desk and stood.

"Wow. Is that new?" Darcy motioned to Jillian's sundress.

"Since I was already off yesterday, I did some shopping. Like it?" Jillian did a little twirl.

"I love it, but it looks expensive." Darcy reached over and stroked the fabric. "Was it on sale?"

"Of course. I never buy anything unless it's on the sale rack." After returning from her outing with Julie, she'd had a lapse in willpower and had gone to the mall and indulged in some over-the-top shopping in the Tommy Bahama section of Dillard's. She'd picked up a couple of camp shirts, a long skirt, and the sundress she was wearing. She had no idea Darcy was so fashion conscious.

"You and I need to set up a shopping date. I could use a little help getting my wardrobe updated."

"She must be special," Jillian said, and the color in Darcy's cheeks reddened.

"She is."

Jillian wrapped her arm around Darcy's shoulder as they walked out. "Just say when. I'm at your service."

They took the short drive to one of the restaurants on Campus Corner and settled into a table in the corner of the restaurant.

"Anything eventful happen at work yesterday?" Jillian asked.

"Not much. Maxine came by to check on you."

"To check on me?"

"Yeah. She said she needed to visit with you about something. I asked her if I could help, but she wouldn't tell me."

"And?"

"Then she wanted to see Mrs. P."

"Did she talk to her?" Jillian was getting concerned that Maxine had opened her big mouth.

"I hate that pretentious bitch, so I told her Vicki was in a meeting at the administration building. She seemed to buy it."

The waiter came to the table. "What can I get you two ladies to drink?"

"Mic Ultra for me," Darcy said, then looked at Jillian.

"For me, also."

"You're a little early for happy hour, but they're putting the food out now." He pointed to the table across the room covered with silver food warmers and trays with vegetables and dips.

"Awesome. I'm starving," Darcy said as she got up. "Come on. Let's get some before the place fills up."

Jillian made it back to the table with only half of what Darcy had on her plate. "Is this your dinner?"

Darcy gave her an isn't-that-obvious look and said, "It's free."

Jillian laughed and took a bite of a mini-eggroll. "So you're not going to tell me anything about this new woman in your life."

Darcy took in a deep breath. "You may not like her."

"Of course I'll like her. Why wouldn't I?"

"You kind of already know her." Darcy picked up a nacho and added a jalapeño pepper to the top.

Jillian widened her eyes. "Please don't tell me it's Maxine."

Darcy choked on her food. "God, no. Didn't I just tell you I don't like her?"

"You never know." Jillian popped the rest of the eggroll into her mouth.

Darcy finished chewing and wiped her mouth. "It's Julie."

Jillian snapped her gaze back to Darcy. "Amelia's Julie?"

"She doesn't belong to Amelia. They're divorced."

"I know. I'm sorry. I just…" *That was a blindside.*

"You just what?"

"I don't know. I just hadn't thought about you two…together."

Darcy tilted her head and shrugged. "Me neither, but I really like her." She speared a meatball with a toothpick and popped it into her mouth.

"How did this happen?"

"That night at Jojo's when you decided to OD on martinis, we stayed and talked for a while after you and Amelia left."

"Well, that's great." She gave her a light punch on the shoulder. "I can't believe you waited this long to tell me." She smiled but cringed on the inside. Another complication she would have to deal with sooner or later.

The way things were going, maybe Jillian didn't need to worry about Julie. She thought about their excursion yesterday. While she'd been explaining the history between her and Amelia, she suspected from the expression on Julie's face that she understood. She'd agreed to keep Jillian's secret for the time being, which she was thankful for. Julie had given her an unreadable stare before looking back and pulling out of the parking space. She'd seemed sincere about keeping her secret. Jillian just didn't know how long the "time being" would last.

"Have you seen the way Stan has been following Lucy around lately?"

"The hard-assed math teacher that gave David so much trouble? No. I hadn't noticed."

"They probably have something going on. They're kind of made for each other, don't you think?"

"I don't know. I've never paid much attention to either one of them."

Jillian's mind drifted from Darcy's idle gossip about the school faculty. Speculating about other people's lives just didn't interest her. The day before, being at the television station had exhilarated her. She absolutely loved what she did. There was no getting around it. The general manager had made a special trip in from his vacation just to meet her. They'd had a nice chat before Julie nudged her and pointed to her watch. During their short visit, he had made it very clear he would love to have a talent like hers on board. Always keeping her options open, Jillian had been very polite in her response.

Moving to a market like Oklahoma City would be a step down for Jillian, and she wouldn't consider it. Would she? Could she give up what she had in New York for Amelia? She shook the thought from her mind. Her passion for her job had hit her square in the face when she'd been in the television studio yesterday. The rush she'd felt when they'd listened to the final product was immense and, when she'd known she'd nailed it, was downright overwhelming. She picked up her beer and drained it. Her life was in total disarray, and she didn't like it one bit. She had many decisions to make in the near future, and thinking about them right now was not an option. She motioned to the waiter and ordered another round of beers.

Amelia headed into her office and flipped on the radio to get the latest weather report. She'd been in Oklahoma City court and hadn't gotten on the road soon enough to miss the mass exodus as everyone hit the road home to avoid the incoming weather. The meteorologists on every TV channel had been scarecasting since the morning before, making everyone aware there was a better than good chance for a tornado or two to touch down in the state.

She swiped the screen on her cell phone and then hit the favorite button for Julie, who picked up on the first ring. "You all right over there?" Amelia slid down on the couch next to the window.

"Yep, you comin'? I've got the cellar stocked."

"I think I should go to the house and check on things." She stared out the window at the clouds scudding across the sky.

"I thought the boys all went camping?"

"They did, but I'm not sure JJ is familiar with Oklahoma weather."

"A phone call can easily remedy that."

"I just want to make sure she and Abby aren't freaked out by the meteorologists on TV. They get a little excited."

"Okay." Julie laughed. "Can I come? I want to watch you play with that fire."

"That's a big no."

"I expect to hear all the details tomorrow."

"We'll see." Amelia hit the red button on her phone and slipped it into her pocket. She hadn't seen JJ in almost a week, since she'd come to her office to explain why she was in the courtroom a few days before, which she hadn't done. Somehow, they'd ended up kissing instead. Amelia had needed some distance after the impact she'd felt from the kiss. The distance hadn't helped. JJ still invaded her thoughts frequently. She was going way out of her comfort zone tonight, but she'd decided to just let go and see what happened.

❖

The front door flew open, and Amelia rushed in. "Have you heard from Blake? I hope he and the boys are in for the night 'cause it's fixin' to blow." Amelia hung her jacket on the hall tree and swept into the living room. "Where's Abby?"

"The boys are staying in a cabin away from the storm, and Abby is spending the night with one of her friends," Jillian said.

"They have a shelter, I hope." Amelia raised her eyebrows, waiting for an answer.

"They do. I talked to her a little while ago." Jillian knew that one of the prerequisites of letting your kids sleep over in Oklahoma during the spring was knowing the house they were staying at had a storm shelter.

"Is she okay?"

"Actually, she's doing great. I don't think she knows enough about the weather here to be freaked out." Jillian was fully aware and had been jittery all day.

"Great." Amelia grabbed Jillian's hand and pulled her off the couch. "Let's go sit on the porch and watch the storm."

"I really don't like thunderstorms." Jillian stopped, held her ground.

"Come on." Amelia tilted her head and nodded toward the porch. "The lightning is beautiful."

Amelia smiled, and Jillian couldn't resist. She took in a breath, swiped a throw from the couch, and followed her out. They sat thigh to thigh on the porch swing, legs covered with soft chenille, and prepared to take in the spectacular light show. A red glow blanketed the sky in the distance. Lightning, brilliant and white-hot, flashed through the blackening sky. Its jagged fingers sparked randomly across the horizon. The rolling sound of thunder followed, filling the air with the crackle of its might. Intervals of time between the bursts of lightning and thunder kept growing shorter.

The air was stifling. The afternoon sky had darkened considerably, murky clouds billowing across it. The storm was well on its way to showing its power. If it became much stronger, there would be severe wounds and permanent scars left on the structures surrounding them.

Trees began to creak and moan, swaying as the wind picked up.

Jillian shivered and Amelia snaked her arm around her shoulder, urging her closer. "Isn't it beautiful?"

Jillian stared at Amelia, studying her face. The small, delicate nose, creamy light skin, lovely full lips. She remembered every facet of it except the tiny creases at the corners of her eyes. "Yes, beautiful."

Amelia seemed to feel Jillian's gaze on her and turned to stare into her eyes. The air between them was thick. Amelia held Jillian's gaze for a moment, then skittered to her lips and slowly back again. She moved closer and brushed Jillian's lips gently with her own, then pulled back, searching Jillian's eyes, as though asking for permission. The bolt of electricity that flew through Jillian at that moment was more powerful than any thunderstorm she'd ever known. She reached up, slid her hand behind Amelia's head, and pulled her in. The kiss that came next wasn't urgent like those before. It was soft, tender, seeking, a kiss Jillian could get permanently lost in. The wind kicked up, whipping harder through the trees. The urgency of the storm seemed to make the kiss more intoxicating, more powerful. Jillian was no longer cold. The fire spreading throughout her body astonished her. She let her tongue roam Amelia's mouth, seeking more of the warmth she encompassed.

Rain trickled across them lazily, and soon the blanket covering them was soaked. Only when hail began pelting them did they break apart, lips swollen, chests heaving, staring in wonder at each other.

The hail became thick, dime-size. A piece hit Jillian's ear, and Amelia touched it with her fingers. "Are you okay?" Then Amelia took a hit to the cheek. "Ow." She chuckled and pulled the blanket up, covering their heads. "We'd better go inside and check the weather."

Unable to form any kind of response, Jillian nodded and huddled with her under the blanket as they made their way back into the house.

Jillian flipped on the TV and watched the meteorologist point at the red blotches on the map. The excited voice rang through the speaker, saying something about F0 gustnados and to stay away from windows. It was going to be a long night. More storms were moving this way. Hail pelted the windows and wind howled in the eaves. This thunderstorm was coming in strong. Jillian hated storms, had never gotten used to them as a kid. They'd always kept her on edge all night. At least this old house had a basement, and Amelia was here to keep her safe. She looked up. Amelia was standing at the end of the couch watching the TV as though she were keeping her distance. Jillian was grateful for the space, even though every nerve ending in her body was telling her differently.

Amelia glanced over at Jillian, smiled, and headed into the kitchen with the wet blanket. "You want some popcorn?"

"Sure. If you're making it," Jillian shouted after her.

"I am," Amelia shouted back. "Coke or Dr Pepper?"

"Is there any diet?"

"Nope. Only the strong stuff." After a few minutes, Amelia came back out with a big bowl of popcorn in one hand and a couple of sodas in the other.

"Okay. Give me a Dr Pepper."

"I was hoping you'd say that." Amelia winked and sat next to her on the couch. "What's the meteorologist got to say?"

"Heavy thunderstorms right now, but there's a possibility of funnels developing to the west. So, no *Amazing Race* tonight."

"I can fix that." Amelia handed Jillian the bowl of popcorn, then got up and crossed the room to the office. She came back out with Blake's laptop and set it on the coffee table in front of them. "We can watch it online as long as the power and internet hold up."

"Wow, if I'd have known you were so resourceful, I would've called you during *Wheel of Fortune*."

Amelia raised a brow. "You should have. It's a sad day when you have to miss out on watching Vanna White sashay across the stage and flip letters."

"Tragic." Jillian let out a chuckle as Amelia flopped back against the couch next to her. The show intro came on, and all the racers flashed across the screen. "Can you zoom the screen in a little bit?"

"I can." Amelia handed the popcorn to Jillian again, took the laptop from the coffee table, and plopped it in her lap.

"Wow. That's what I call technology."

"It's a new feature. Not many people know about it yet." Amelia grinned.

Jillian couldn't help but smile. She'd forgotten how funny Amelia was and how good it felt to be near her. No matter what the circumstance, she was always upbeat. They placed their bets on who was going to get kicked off that week and then settled in to watch the show.

Jillian focused on the laptop, trying to ignore the fact that her leg was pressed up against Amelia's. She didn't even take her eyes off the screen when the jolt shot through her as their fingers brushed in the popcorn bowl. She somehow managed to get through the show without tossing the popcorn bowl to the floor and kissing Amelia senseless.

"I knew they would come in last. They fight way too much," Amelia said confidently.

"They'll bounce back. They didn't get eliminated." Jillian hated that she'd been wrong but was totally turned on by Amelia's confidence.

"Only because it was a non-elimination round. They still came in last because they don't work well together."

"So you think if they collaborate more, they have a shot at winning?"

"Not a chance. They're definitely going to lose, and I'll be glad when they do. They annoy the hell out of me."

"Oh, I see. It's all about you, not the race." Jillian bumped her shoulder.

"Always." Amelia winked as Jillian got up to carry the empty popcorn bowl into the kitchen.

"You want another soda?"

"No. I should probably head home." Amelia got up and stretched. Jillian couldn't help noticing the bare skin of her stomach as her shirt pulled up.

"But it's still storming." The words whooshed out of Jillian's mouth softly as she walked to the window and peered out. The rain was still coming down in a steady rhythm.

"I think all the severe stuff has passed." Amelia turned, looked at Jillian, and seemed to notice her agitation. "I can stay a little while longer." She sat back down on the couch and fiddled with the laptop. "Do you want to watch something else? A movie maybe? There's a new superhero film on Netflix."

Jillian curled her lip up at that. "How about a drama?"

Amelia rolled her eyes. "How about you stab me with a fork?"

Jillian laughed loudly. "Why don't we meet in the middle with a comedy?"

"I can do that." Amelia flipped through the selections until they found one they both agreed on and settled back on the couch with the computer on Amelia's lap and her feet on the coffee table. Jillian pulled the chenille throw off the chair and settled back next to her, tossing it across their legs.

When Amelia opened her eyes, the power was out, and the only light in the room was the glow from the laptop teetering on her thigh.

She didn't know how it had happened, but she'd somehow slid to her left, and JJ was snuggled up close next to her. She was sleeping soundly, with her head tucked up under Amelia's chin, and Amelia's arm was wrapped around her as though it were the most natural thing in the world. She used her free hand to move the laptop to the couch and then took in a deep breath. The scent of cucumber and melon filled her nose.

Amelia knew she should go, but freeing herself out from under JJ would undoubtedly wake her, and Amelia was honestly enjoying her current position. Lying here on the couch, warm and toasty, under the blanket with a soft, beautiful woman pressed up against her was nice—really nice. Amelia hadn't felt this comfortable around anyone in a long time. Besides, the power was out, and the rain was still coming down steadily outside. It was probably a bad idea, but she twisted a blond lock of JJ's hair around her finger and decided to stay put.

❖

The next time Amelia woke, it was light outside. She was cold and alone on the couch, which hit her hard. It would've been nice if JJ had woken her. Her heart hammered. Maybe JJ hadn't liked waking up in her arms. She squeezed her eyes closed, let the sun warm her face, and took in a deep breath to calm herself. The scent of coffee wafted into her nose, and she cracked open her eyes to see JJ sitting on the coffee table in front of her holding two steaming cups.

"I thought this would get you moving." JJ handed her one and then raised the other to her lips. "You're a heavy sleeper."

Not usually. She sat up and raked her hand through her hair. "What time is it?"

"A little after nine. The boys will be back soon."

She studied JJ's face. *How can a woman look so beautiful all the time?* She felt a familiar tingle in her belly, and it unnerved her. "I should go." She set the cup on the table, then stood and looked around for the laptop.

"I put it away." JJ dipped her head toward the office. "At least have some coffee." She picked up the cup and held it out to her. "Black, right?"

Sensing the plea in JJ's voice, Amelia nodded as she sank back in to the couch and took the cup from her. She sipped the coffee slowly, enjoying the deep, rich flavor. She made the mistake of making eye contact, and they sat quietly, peering over their cups at one another for a few minutes. Amelia didn't fight the tingle this time. She let it wash over her, warming every inch of her body. It was spectacular.

"Do you want some breakfast?" JJ asked.

"No, but thanks." Amelia shook off the wondrous feeling and took one last gulp of coffee before she got up and headed toward the door. "I should get home. I have some work to finish up before Monday." That was a lie, but she needed to get out of there. These new feelings were a lot to manage.

JJ touched Amelia's hand, and she spun back around. "Thank you for staying with me last night. I really hate storms."

"It was my pleasure." Amelia gave her a soft smile. She wasn't lying. She hadn't enjoyed the company of another woman like that in a very long time. "Maybe we can do it again sometime." She pulled her lips into a soft smile. "Without the storm." The words were out of her mouth before she knew it, but there it was. She'd put it out there.

"I'd like that." JJ held Amelia's hand for a bit longer, then let it drop and followed her to the door. "Amelia?" JJ's voice was almost a whisper. Amelia turned around and found herself on the receiving end of a wonderfully soft kiss. She stumbled backward out the door, wishing she didn't have to go. But she *had* to go.

Little streams of the night's rain raced through the empty streets to their edges. Tree limbs littered the yard. This town would have to do a lot of cleanup today. Mother Nature had been angry last night, very angry. Was it due to the fact she was making out with her brother's new love interest? Maybe. She took in a deep breath and let the sun warm her face. She could finally see the light, the promise of a new day. The lock to her heart was slowly opening.

Amelia glanced back at the house to see JJ watching her from the doorway, and her body heated. She slid into her car, fired the engine, and turned the air-conditioning on high. *I'm for sure going to hell now.* She flipped down the visor, assessed herself in the mirror, and swiped her finger over the black smudges left below her eyes from her eyeliner and mascara. "Well, aren't you a sight this morning?" She flipped the visor back into its place. "That's enough to scare any woman away." A smile crept across her face as she drove away. *It didn't scare JJ.* She finally had a reason to look forward to tomorrow.

CHAPTER TWENTY-ONE

Jillian pressed her head to the door after she closed it. *What the hell am I doing?* She peeked out the window beside the door and watched Amelia walk to her car. She smiled as the morning flashed through her mind. She had felt so warm and cozy when she'd stirred. The slow and steady heartbeat under her ear had soothed her, and she hadn't wanted to open her eyes. She'd been alarmed to find her hand splayed across Amelia's belly under her shirt, her fingers tucked just inside the waistband of Amelia's jeans. Her leg had been draped randomly across Amelia's, holding it with the possessiveness of a familiar lover.

She hadn't wanted to budge, and removing herself from the position had been tricky. Thankfully, Amelia was a deep sleeper. She sipped her coffee and smiled. She couldn't remember the last time she'd slept so soundly, without a nightmare. She crossed the room into the kitchen and plucked a dust cloth from the laundry room before heading back to the living room to flip on the stereo.

She felt the phone buzz in her pocket, pulled it out, and saw it was Marcus. She hit the green button at the bottom of the screen and pressed it to her ear. "Hi there, handsome."

"You know just the right way to answer the phone, don't you?"

"What? I'm just stating the truth."

"Alas, if I were only single," he said with a sigh.

"Too late again." She returned the sigh. "Plus, I don't have a penis."

"That's definitely a problem." He chuckled. "How are things going out there?"

"So far, so good, but I miss you terribly." She hit a button on the stereo, and music blared even louder through the speakers.

"It doesn't sound like it. Are you having a party?"

"No. Just getting ready to do a little cleaning."

"Well, that's totally out of character. Where's Jillian? Put her on the phone, please."

Jillian laughed. "I'm trying to blend in, remember?" She fiddled with the knobs, trying to figure out how to turn it down.

"Have you told Blake who you are yet?"

"No, not yet. We had some weather last night."

"I saw that. The news kept calling it a gustnado."

"It's not as bad as it sounds. Just a lot of wind and rattling windows." She paused. "There's been a complication."

"What kind of complication?"

"Amelia was here with me last night during the storm, and she stayed over."

"Did you two—"

"No, but I kissed her."

"That is a complication." She heard him blow out a long breath. "How was it?"

"Spectacular." She pulled her bottom lip between her teeth, remembering how wonderful it felt.

"Sounds like it was more than a gustnado that shook your shingles last night."

"It wasn't the first time."

"Then I'm guessing it was good for her, also."

"I think so." She smiled at Amelia's nervousness this morning. It was so fresh and innocent, something she hadn't seen in Amelia before.

"Do you plan to pursue anything with her?"

"I don't know. I've been pretending to date Blake to make his wife jealous, which complicates the situation even further."

"His wife?"

"It's a long story."

"Oh. Well…could you use a little on-site support? Maybe I should come that way."

"Oh, my God, Marcus." Her voice rose with excitement. "Would you? That would be so awesome."

"Just let me cancel my appointments, and I'll be on the next flight out."

"Marcus, you're the best."

"I know. I'll call you with the details in a little while."

She dropped the phone to the table and danced around the room. Marcus would be able to help her sort out this whole thing.

Kelly sat in her rental car across the street. She was still soaked to the bone from last night's rain. She seethed as the sight of Jillian and Amelia lying on the couch together, sleeping. Amelia had been touching Jillian in ways only Kelly was allowed, and Jillian had let her. Amelia had to go, and Jillian would be punished for that error in judgment. She'd waited patiently for Amelia to leave the house, and her anger had spiked when she'd seen Jillian kiss Amelia again.

She got out of the car, ran across the street, and slipped in between the holly bushes, just as she had the night before, to look through the living-room window. Jillian was dancing around the living room and it looked like she was dusting, which was so unlike her. She reached in her pocket and pulled out her cell phone. It must have been someone she knew because she was smiling as she talked. Kelly couldn't make out what she was saying, and she hated that.

Jillian went to the stereo and fiddled with the knobs. Music blared through the speakers, and Jillian jumped before she found the off button. After a few minutes, she dropped her phone to the table, turned the music back on, and danced into the kitchen. She was gone for a few minutes, and then she danced in from another room with a spray can of some kind in her hand. Kelly enjoyed watching her move around the living room, dusting as she danced. She got caught up in memories of their nights together. Jillian shouldn't be this happy, not without her. She should be missing her as much as Kelly missed her.

❖

Amelia found herself standing just outside Julie's door, the usual place she went when she needed help figuring things out in her life. She let herself in, put on a pot of coffee, and poured herself a cup before going out back to sit on the deck. It was still pretty early, but Amelia knew the scent of the freshly brewed coffee would bring Julie out of her sleep soon. Within fifteen minutes, Julie was pushing through the back door and settling into the wicker chair next to her.

They sat quietly together, enjoying the sounds of the morning. Various birds were singing their morning songs, tweeting, chirping, and, in particular, the regular pair of doves cooing to each other.

"You're here early. What's up, sunshine?" Julie asked, breaking the serenity. She assessed her appearance. "Weren't you wearing those clothes yesterday?"

Amelia nodded. "I stayed at the house last night."

"I wondered if you would. Did you all have fun watching the lightning?"

"Sort of. It was just me and JJ." She shifted her gaze sideways to catch Julie's reaction.

"Fuck me." Julie bolted forward in her chair. "You slept with her."

"No. I didn't." She shook her head. "But I did wake up with her sprawled out across me during the night."

"Oh, my God." Julie chuckled. "Now I need details."

Julie listened intently while Amelia told her how the night had gone. How comfortable she'd felt with JJ and how cold she'd felt when she'd woken up alone this morning.

"You asked her out?"

Amelia nodded. "I was trying to get out of there, and the words just came out."

Julie let out a huge belly laugh. "Why don't you just tell her you're in love with her?"

"I'm not in love with her."

"Well, you're definitely in *something* with her."

"Love is a big word. You know how hard that is for me to say. I've been in relationships where we said 'I love you' all the time, and it didn't mean anything."

"Yes, I know, but that doesn't mean you should take it out of your vocabulary."

"I can't get that close, Jules."

"Seems to me you already have."

Amelia's gaze snapped back to Julie's. "I've only known her a few months."

"Are you sure?" Julie seemed to stumble over her words. "I mean, is there a time frame on love? Have you created a new rule?"

She shook her head and gave her a soft smile. "There should at least be a green light signaling it's okay to proceed so I don't get broadsided."

"If you need that, I'll give it to you." Julie waved her hands in front of her. "Green light flashing, right here. Green means go, and if it's already changed to yellow, that means go faster."

"Shut up." Amelia popped up out of her chair. "I need more coffee."

"I bet JJ makes spectacular coffee." Julie shouted after her.

Amelia turned around and peeked back out the door. "As a matter of fact, she does." *She does a lot of things spectacularly.*

CHAPTER TWENTY-TWO

A melia waited in front of the restaurant for JJ to arrive. Before she'd set up the date with JJ, she'd decided it would be safer to meet at the restaurant rather than to pick her up and be faced with the choice of where to take her at the end of the evening. What she saw when JJ came around the corner was nothing short of breathtaking. The sleek black slip dress, the slightly curled hair, the confident strut. JJ was sexy as hell. *Fuck! Why didn't I tell her it was casual?* Not that Amelia was dressed casually herself. It had taken her close to three hours at the department store the night before to pick out the tropical-patterned maxidress she was wearing, and she hated going to the mall.

"You look beautiful," JJ said and kissed her on the cheek.

"As do you," Amelia said with more difficulty than she expected. "Shall we?" She pulled open the door for JJ.

The hostess led them to a table in the middle of the restaurant, and JJ turned to her. "Can we have something a little more private?"

"Sure." The hostess glanced at Amelia for approval. Amelia nodded, and she led them to a quaint little table toward the back of the restaurant.

"This is a nice place. The hostess seems to know you. Do you come here often?"

"I wouldn't say often, but it is one of my favorite places in town."

Amelia glanced up from the menu to catch JJ watching her. She gazed back at the menu and shifted in her seat. *Where the hell are you, Blake?* After she thought about the situation between JJ and her brother, she'd had serious reservations about having dinner alone with JJ and had invited Blake to come along. The bell chimed as the door opened, and she was relieved to see the hostess leading Blake to their table.

"Oh, look, Blake's here." Amelia threw up a hand and waved him over. "Do you mind if he joins us?

"Uh, I guess not." JJ seemed a little annoyed but scooted her chair around the small round table closer to Amelia.

"Hey," Blake said as he slipped into the chair across from her.

"Fancy meeting you here," JJ said.

"It's my favorite place. When Amelia suggested it, how could I resist?"

JJ cocked her head and smiled slightly at Amelia. "No. I'm sure you couldn't."

Awkward. Tiny jolts of electricity coursed through Amelia. Now JJ was fully aware she had invited him. No easy way to backpedal out of this one. She picked up her menu, only glancing up from it long enough to give JJ a soft smile before she diverted her gaze to Blake. "Do you want to pick out a bottle of wine?"

"Sure. How about a nice pinot noir? It always goes well with Italian."

"That sounds good. I love a good pinot." JJ looked back at the menu. "So, what's good at your favorite place, Blake?"

"I'm partial to the chicken-and-spinach manicotti."

"Lots of cheese in that. I think I'll stick with the vegetable pasta marinara." JJ looked over at Amelia and caught her watching her. "Something catching your attention tonight, Amelia?" She lifted her eyebrows.

She cleared her throat. "I think I'll have the Mediterranean pasta with shrimp."

"That sounds delightful. Maybe you'll let me have a taste later?" JJ said with a suggestive lilt.

"Of course. I'd love a taste of yours as well." Amelia could throw around innuendo with the best of them.

The hum of conversation filled the restaurant. Blake ordered a bottle of wine and a few appetizers. By the time the entrees arrived, Amelia was having a nicer time than she'd imagined. So far, the food had been good and so had the company. Apparently, she'd been unnecessarily nervous about the whole thing. After the last kiss she and JJ had shared earlier in the week, Amelia's hormones had kicked into full gear, and all she needed to complicate her life right now was being swept away by an irresistibly beautiful woman who had a habit of pushing her buttons.

Blake picked up the bottle of wine to refill his glass. "I thought you said you loved pinot noir?" he said. JJ's glass was still almost full.

"I do, but this is not pinot noir." JJ pushed the glass away.

He picked up the bottle and looked at the label. "That's what it says."

"I don't know what it is, but it's certainly not a pinot. This is some kind of red swill." JJ waved the waiter down. "Could you bring us a bottle of 2011 Carpe Diem pinot noir?" She smiled at the waiter and then, as if on second thought, picked up the other bottle and swung it his way. "Please take this away."

"Would you like it recorked and bagged to take home?"

"God, no," JJ quipped. "I'd *like* it poured down the sink."

Amelia choked, spitting wine across the table as she laughed uncontrollably. "I'm sorry." She wiped her mouth and then blotted the tablecloth with her napkin. "She's right. This is terrible."

"I order it all the time," Blake said.

"Maybe that's why your social life has been so dull lately." Amelia quirked an eyebrow up.

The waiter brought the new bottle of wine, uncorked it, and gave JJ a taste. She nodded her approval, and he poured three new glasses.

Blake picked up his glass, swirled it around, and studied the wine. "Now I suppose you're going to enlighten us with what's good about this wine?"

JJ raised her glass to her lips and took a sip. "Umm, it's just good." She raised her brows.

Amelia, captivated by JJ's nonchalance, followed her lead and took a sip. The wine was exceptional.

"It's good? That's it?" Blake stared at JJ.

"That's it," JJ said easily as she set her glass down.

Trying to head off the debate she knew was coming, Amelia glanced over at Blake and cocked her head. "Other than loving the way it tastes, why else would you drink a certain bottle of wine?"

"Possibly because of the aged oak and citrus undertones."

JJ lifted a brow. "Well, this wine has limited oak undertones. That's what gives it the soft texture." She took another sip. "I drink it because it has an incredible taste that doesn't bite the back of my tongue."

Amelia looked over her wineglass at JJ and watched her amber eyes sparkle in amusement. She let her gaze trip down to her lips, taking in their sensual fullness as she spoke. She was caught off guard by the flutter in her stomach when she looked up to find JJ staring back at her. Would she ever get used to that? When JJ tugged her lip up to one side and winked, Amelia gulped down the remaining wine in her glass. *Get control of yourself, Amelia.*

"Are you okay?" Blake asked.

"I'm fine. I just need to use the ladies' room."

JJ tossed her napkin on the table. "I'll join you." She rounded the table and slipped her arm into Amelia's as though they were old friends. "Are you afraid to be alone with me?"

"No. I just thought Blake might enjoy a night out." A total lie. She *was* afraid. Yet, walking arm in arm with JJ right now felt like the most natural thing in the world.

JJ stopped in the darkened hallway, pulled Amelia around to face her, and stared into her eyes. "What are you afraid of, Amelia?"

"I can't"—Amelia turned her head—"look at you."

"Why not?"

"When I see your lips move, I want to make them stop."

"Oh." JJ leaned closer, and Amelia felt her warm breath on her ear. "What are you going to do to make them stop?"

Amelia closed her eyes and tried to resist but couldn't. She turned her head slowly, reached up, and cupped JJ's face in her hands. "This." She nipped at her bottom lip, captured it between her own, and pulled it into her mouth. Then she let her tongue slip inside JJ's mouth and reveled in the warm abyss awaiting her. Her body thrummed with excitement. Amelia was fully engaged instantly, buzzing as tiny electrodes zapped through each one of her senses. Kissing JJ was one of the most tantalizingly sensual things she'd felt in…forever. JJ stirred feelings in her she'd purposely kept dormant for quite some time. It felt so good to feel again. They were both silent for a moment, enjoying the crackle of heat passing between them.

"Wow." JJ blew out in a whisper.

"Yeah…Wow." Amelia blinked and tried to focus.

"You are absolutely breathtaking," JJ whispered against her lips, then turned and went into the ladies' room, leaving Amelia standing in the hallway still wondering how this woman could ignite every one of her senses so easily. Amelia marveled at the mixture of contentment and arousal that continued to circle through her. She didn't know where these feelings were coming from or what she was going to do about them. Amelia liked being in control, but she'd just been thoroughly and completely kissed by the most gorgeous creature she'd met in a long time. It was the most wonderfully exciting experience in the world. She definitely wanted more.

Amelia took a few deep breaths to calm herself before she walked the short distance back to the table and squeezed her brother's shoulder. "I have to go," she said, and floated out of the restaurant.

❖

Julie answered the door in her pajama pants and T-shirt. Amelia had called her from the parking lot after she'd left the restaurant, and, as always, Julie had told her to come on over. Amelia's mind was still whirling. She couldn't go home. She needed to sort this out and needed Julie to help her do it.

Julie's eyes widened as she surveyed Amelia's dress. "Wow, you look nice."

"I was out to dinner with Blake."

"You put on that knockout dress for your brother?" She scrunched up her face. "That's a little creepy."

Amelia let out a chuckle. "Yeah, it is. JJ was there too."

"Ah, the forbidden fruit." Julie slid down onto the couch and patted the spot next to her. "So why do you think you can't seem to stay away from her?"

"I don't know. There's just something about her. She's beautiful, smart…and outrageously sexy." The view of Jillian walking away from her tonight in slow, confident steps had made Amelia acutely aware that Jillian seemed to have some sort of clandestine power over her. She had gone from nothing to ninety in under three seconds flat.

"I'm with you there." Julie nodded and pulled her lip up to one side. "What about the kissing?"

"Off the charts."

"Well then, I suggest you remove the restriction and get whatever this attraction is you have for her out of your system."

"I don't know if I'm ready for that."

"Why not? As you said, she's beautiful, smart, and sexy. She's bound to be an exciting adventure."

"She'd be more than an adventure, and I think that would be very dangerous for me."

"Oh." The word came slowly from Julie's lips. She pulled her bottom lip between her teeth, then sprang up off the couch and moved toward the kitchen. "You want a glass of wine?"

"Sure. Do you have any pinot noir?" Amelia smiled, thinking about the wine interaction between JJ and Blake earlier in the evening.

"I have chardonnay and chardonnay."

"Then I guess I'll have the chardonnay."

Julie poured them each a glass and handed one to Amelia as she sat back down on the couch.

"I need you to help me get her out of my head, Jules." Amelia took a drink of her wine before setting her glass on the coffee table.

"Okay, how can I help? More work? Play? What?"

"Definitely play." She scooted closer to Julie and leaned in to kiss her.

"Whoa." Julie put a hand on Amelia's chest. "Not this time. The only way you're going to get this woman out of your system is to let whatever this is run its course *with her*."

"I don't know if I can do that, Jules."

"I've never known you not to go after what you want, Amelia, and she's definitely something you want." Julie pulled her knee up under herself, creating space between them. "I can't help you with this one. Not that way. In fact, I can't do that with you anymore at all." Julie shook her head and looked at her lap. "Do you have any idea how hard this is for me? Watching you fall in love with someone else." Julie's voice was barely a whisper.

As Julie looked away, Amelia caught a glimpse of something in her eyes she'd thought was gone long ago. She reached over and lifted Julie's chin to regain eye contact. "What do you want from me, Jules?"

"Honestly?"

"Always."

"I want what any girl wants. That all-consuming love that pulls you into a blissful fog of infatuation, lust, and need. I want someone who forgets there's work to be done at the office. Someone who calls me first when something happens in her life, whether it's good or bad. I want more than anything for someone to burn for me like you do for JJ."

"Wow." Amelia took a gulp of wine. "I…"

"I know that was a lot of information. Don't freak out on me. I don't want any of that from you now." Julie rubbed Amelia's shoulder. "There was a time when I did. When we were married, I wanted all of it from you, but we both found out you couldn't give it to me." Julie took the glass from her, set it on the table, and held her hands. "I do still want that...and I want it for you too."

"Is this your not-so-subtle way of telling me you're seeing someone?"

Julie tilted her head. "Since you brought it up."

"What? Who?"

Julie took in a deep breath. "Would it bother you if I dated Darcy?"

"You want to ask Darcy out?"

"Actually, she asked me out, and we've already gone out a few times."

Wow. Amelia dropped back into the sofa cushion. "I didn't even realize you two knew each other that well."

"We've been seeing a lot more of each other since I've been mentoring at the high school, and then there was that night at the bar a couple of weeks ago. I'll stop if it bothers you."

Amelia could see by the spark in in Julie's eyes that she didn't want to stop. "No." She shook her head. "You should go out with her. She's a sweet girl." Amelia rubbed the back of her hands with her thumbs. "You deserve someone who pays attention to you like she does. I'm just not good with relationships, Jules."

"Maybe it just takes the right one. You don't want to admit it, but you know that weird little flip-flop feeling you get in your belly every time you see JJ? That's love." Amelia stared at her and didn't flinch. "Don't act like you don't know what I'm talking about. I never thought I'd see you like this."

"Like what?"

"Off center, unstructured. Completely, hopelessly in love." Julie swiped at the tears forming in her eyes. "You need to give this one a shot."

"I haven't felt like this in a long time, Jules. I can't think straight. My head is spinning all the time."

"Oh, honey." Julie touched her cheek. "Love does that. It makes you dizzy, throws your mind into a contented haze. It opens you up to everything life has to offer. Passion, excitement, adventure. It changes your life."

"It's scary as fuck." The last time Amelia felt like this, she'd lost everything in what seemed like a second. She didn't know if she could risk it all again.

"It *is* incredibly scary." Julie chuckled. "But scary can lead to wonderful. Love is so much more than a happily-ever-after, and you'll never regret it. I promise."

"What if it doesn't work out?"

"Amelia." Julie blew out a breath and tilted her head. "Don't worry about the ending. Just enjoy what's happening *while* it's happening." She held her glass up. "To new beginnings."

"For both of us." Amelia clinked her glass against Julie's. "Wherever they may lead."

CHAPTER TWENTY-THREE

Julie stared out her office window at the sparse traffic traveling Main Street. Not many people were up early on Sundays in town unless they were going to church or had forgotten to buy eggs for breakfast. Her conversation with Amelia the night before had concreted the fact that Julie had to help Jillian and make sure her story was on the up-and-up. Julie had given Amelia permission to move forward with Jillian, not that she needed it. Yet Julie could see she was still hesitant, even though she was clearly falling in love with her. Julie's stomach churned. Her whole existence was about to change. Amelia wasn't in love with her anymore, but she'd always been there. Would that change?

Of course it would. Her best friend and ex-wife could possibly leave her and move halfway across the country with another woman. She felt a tear stream down her face and wiped it from her cheek. *Stop. You don't know that will happen, and you'll be happy for her if it does.* She saw the familiar Honda pull up in front of the building and plucked a tissue from the box on her desk. She wiped her nose before heading to the bathroom. She couldn't let Jillian see her in any kind of vulnerable state. This was her best friend's life she was messing with, and she needed to be sure Jillian wasn't going to tear her heart out.

Jillian was waiting in her doorway when Julie returned from the bathroom. "You shouldn't leave the door unlocked when you're here alone."

"It's fine. We're in Oklahoma, not New York." She glanced at the door to see that Jillian had flipped the deadbolt after she'd come in. She left it that way just in case Amelia decided to make an unannounced appearance, although she had no idea what excuse she'd come up with for her being at the office alone with Jillian on a Sunday. "Have you seen Amelia this morning?"

"No. I imagine she's still in bed sleeping. It's the crack of dawn on Sunday. Besides, how would I know?"

Julie raised her brows and gave her an unrelenting stare. "You'd better be careful with her."

"Whether you believe it or not, she means a great deal to me."

Julie stilled and took in a deep breath, trying to keep her emotions in check. "I'll come after you if you hurt her."

"I'm sorry."

"For what? Showing up? Or scarring her for life?"

Jillian shook her head. "For being the reason she couldn't love you."

Julie straightened her shoulders as the words reverberated loudly in her ears and hit deep in her gut. "She loved me."

"Not like she should have." Jillian offered a tentative smile. "I know because I can't do it either." Jillian moved toward her, and the room suddenly got smaller.

"Don't." Julie squeezed her eyes closed to stop the tears and went behind her desk. She'd promised herself she was going to move on, and she was damn well going to make it happen. Even if it meant helping Jillian. "Let's get to work. Were you able to get the papers?"

"Yes. I had them emailed to me, but I haven't had an opportunity to print them."

Julie clicked a few keys on her keyboard, got up, and motioned to her chair. "Pull them up and we'll print them."

Jillian typed in her credentials and waited for her mailbox to open. She looked over the screen at Julie. "Is your computer always this slow? There seems to be a lag when I'm typing."

"No. It started acting up a week or two ago after I updated it. I think it might have been the patches I installed that slowed it down."

"Have you defragged it lately?"

"Have I what?"

"Run a defrag on it. It takes all the tiny bits of memory and throws them into one place. Your drive is fragmented above ten percent, so it will probably help your response time." She clicked a few more buttons, and the printer whirred. "I can run it for you after we're done here."

She rounded the desk to see what Jillian was talking about. "Uh, okay." She looked at the box on the screen indicating her C drive was nineteen percent fragmented. "How do you know all this?"

"I did a story on computer repair shops."

"Oh." Julie wasn't sure if she should let her do it or not, but it seemed plausible. "Okay, thanks."

Jillian clicked a few more buttons and got up. "It should be done in about fifteen minutes or so." She picked up the papers from the printer. "Where do you want to do this?"

Julie pointed to the small, rectangular wooden table in the corner of her office. "We'll have more room to spread out over there." Julie pulled the file from her desk, followed Jillian, and sat adjacent to her.

They went through the line-item expenses one by one, noting only a few discrepancies that could be corrected easily. Nothing that would account for a lack of thousands of dollars. The expenses matched exactly, but from Jillian's paperwork, they could see that all the money wasn't making it into the foundation account.

Julie pinched the bridge of her nose. "From this, it looks like Amelia might be siphoning funds off the top."

"She wouldn't do that. Would she?" Jillian's voice went up, her disbelief evident.

She answered Jillian immediately. "No. Amelia would not take from the kids. She would beg, borrow, and steal *for* them, but she would never take *from* them."

Jillian looked at the bank statements. "These numbers are different." She pointed to the account number on the statement and then the one on the paperwork.

"They shouldn't be." Julie thought for a minute. "So the money goes into one account, and Maxine moves it to another. That's why Amelia has to run everything by her before any funds are disbursed."

Jillian's brows pulled together. "Why would she do that?"

Julie dropped the statements on top of the pile of paperwork in front of her. "Because she's a vindictive bitch. That's why."

"I'll take care of it." Jillian snatched the statements from the desk. "Can you handle the administration for the time being?"

"Sure, but Maxine will know who you are."

"She already knows. I had to tell her in order to get a spot in the house."

Julie blew out a breath. This secret had just become more complicated. "She's a mean little witch, and if she gets wind of who you are to Amelia, she'll expose you."

Jillian nodded. "We'll just have to keep that between us, then. Right?"

Jillian seemed sincere about her intentions, but Julie wasn't sure how much longer she could keep the information from Amelia. "I told you I would, and I meant that." Julie gathered the rest of the papers into the folder and slapped it shut. "You just get Maxine under control."

❖

Jillian hopped out of her car and waved her arms wildly when she spotted Marcus coming out the door to the passenger pick-up area at the airport. He pulled his carry-on down the sidewalk and left it teetering on the curb as she rushed into his arms.

"I'm so glad you're here." Jillian wrapped her arms around him and squeezed.

"Whoa. Let me breathe, will you?" He chuckled.

"You have no idea how much I've missed you."

"You look so plain, I almost didn't recognize you." He gave her the once-over. "You can't disguise those legs."

"They *are* a curse." She looked at her khaki-capri-clad legs and winked.

"A curse any man…" He paused, lifted a brow. "Or woman would gladly endure to have them wrapped around their body."

"Shut up and get in the car." She shook her head and slid into the driver's seat. She knew he was going to give her a hard time about Amelia. "I made you a reservation at the Skirvin downtown."

As they took the thirty-minute drive to the hotel, they talked about anything and everything that didn't have to do with Amelia. Marcus had told her how he'd broken it off for good with his on-and-off-again guy back in New York and wasn't waiting it out this time. He was on the hunt for a new man. Jillian pulled up in front and let the valet take her car. She watched Marcus scan the lobby with its massive wood columns as they moved through the rotating doors.

"Wow. This is fancy."

"I want to keep you happy while you're here."

"So I'll stay longer?"

"Yes. That's my goal." She motioned toward the piano bar. "Why don't you go order us a drink while I get you checked in?"

"After that flight, I'm ready for one."

After she took care of the details, Jillian met Marcus in the bar. He'd ordered her the usual gin martini and a scotch old-fashioned for himself.

"The Presidential Suite was taken, so you'll have to suffer with the Rotunda Suite." She slipped onto the padded leather bench seat next to him. "Apparently, they don't know you're the most important person in town this weekend."

Marcus let out a short gasp. "Who could be more important than me?"

"Some country-western star playing at the Chesapeake Arena this weekend."

"I bet that goes over well here."

"Yep. We hometown folks love us some country music," Jillian said, using her best Oklahoma drawl.

"You do like it here." His voice was certain.

"Oddly, I do. But I miss work so much it's ridiculous."

"Well, then get this finished and come home."

"It's not that simple, Marcus. I can't just drop Abby off on Blake's doorstep." She'd become rather attached to her niece and wasn't sure she wanted to leave her. "Plus, there was a problem with the distribution of funds for Heartstrings House. The money wasn't getting delivered in a timely fashion, so I had to change administrators this morning." Maxine had denied holding the funds at first, but when Jillian had threatened to go public with the information, she backed down. "It turned out to be a bitter woman whom Amelia refused to date. What is it with some women and their pride? Can't they just take no for an answer and move on?"

"Don't ask me. Some men are the same way. Speaking of men, have you told Blake anything about Abby?"

"No. Not yet."

"What can I do?

"Just having you here helps."

"I have to say happy looks good on you." He motioned up and down with his finger. "So, are you in love with Amelia?"

Jillian didn't answer, just sucked down the rest of her martini.

"Hmm." Marcus studied her for a moment. "Well, you certainly have a glow about you."

Marcus left the Amelia subject alone and moved on to Blake. Jillian explained the situation with Blake and his wife. Marcus wasn't keen on the idea of her being a decoy to make Suzie jealous, saying that was an emotion he didn't feel people should mess with. She did point out that the ruse had brought some of Amelia's feelings to light.

"Come on. Let's get you settled in upstairs." She led him to the elevator. "I think you'll like the Rotunda Suite." She pressed the button for the fourteenth floor. "After that, we can go back down to the restaurant and have dinner, if you want."

"How about we call room service and talk in the suite?"

"We can do that." Jillian knew Marcus wanted to get into her head and find out what was going on, and she was okay with that. She needed to let it all out and get his opinion.

While Marcus cleaned up, Jillian ordered a pot of coffee and an assortment of sweets that were delivered within fifteen minutes. She'd already helped herself to a bite of chocolate cheesecake when he came out of the bedroom and sat opposite her on the couch.

"Dessert first. One of the things I miss about you," he said, forking a chunk of cheesecake from the same plate.

"It's wonderful." She set her fork down and pushed it toward him. "Now eat it so I don't. I've gained five pounds since I've been here."

"Happy weight." Marcus smiled and shoveled another forkful into his mouth.

"Coop doesn't cook anything light." She let her lips tip up slightly. "It's all comfort food and always family style."

"Coop?"

"The cook at Heartstrings House."

"They have a cook? I thought you said there was no money for anything."

"Blake pays her out of his own pocket. She doesn't do any housework, but she does do most of the cooking."

"Speaking of the house, how are you getting along there with your drab persona and all?"

Jillian took a sip of her coffee and sat quietly for a moment looking out the window, gathering her thoughts before focusing back on Marcus. "Did you ever lose something and think you were never going to get it back?"

"All the time. This brain isn't getting any younger."

"I'm serious, Marcus." She took in a deep breath. "I never thought I'd see Amelia again, let alone still have these feelings for her."

"And?" Marcus was great at leading questions.

"And I don't know what to do. I have a life in New York, and she has a life here."

"But?" He sipped his coffee.

"But everything I felt is still there, even stronger. I want to be with her."

"So?"

"Stop it, Marcus. I need your advice on this one."

Marcus set his cup on the table, scooted back into the corner of the couch, and turned to face her. "Are you happy with your life in New York, Jillian?"

"I love my job," she said immediately, adrenaline pulsing through her at the thought.

"That's not what I asked. I know you're doing what you love, but are you happy with your life?"

"I don't know. I've never thought past my career."

"You've never thought about what you're going to do when you're finished with broadcasting? About whether you want to be alone or share the rest of your life with someone?" Marcus said it so simply, as if everyone planned it out years in advance.

"Not really." She drew her brows together. "Every time I've tried to share my life with someone, it's been a huge fucking disaster."

"Because?"

"Because I can never go all in." She blew out a breath. "I've never been able to imagine my life with anyone beyond next week."

"Can you see it now? With Amelia?"

She nodded and stared out the window. "I can."

"Because you're in love with her."

I'm in love with Amelia. She'd been ignoring the increasingly persistent thought pounding in her head over the past few weeks. She flopped back against the couch and closed her eyes. "What am I gonna do, Marcus?"

"I think you already know what you *need* to do. You just have to act on it."

"She doesn't even know who I am."

"Shouldn't she? I mean, she *is* the love of your life."

"What if she freaks out?"

"Then she freaks out. At least you'll know how she feels. What could be worse than what you're going through right now? Talk to her, Jillian." He leaned forward and patted her on the thigh before he got up. "More coffee?"

She shook her head. She was already on edge. More coffee would just throw her over. "I have to get back." She gathered up her purse and moved toward the door. "Order whatever you want from room service, and if you need anything else, call me. Otherwise, I'll talk to you in the morning."

On the drive home, Jillian contemplated what Marcus had said. He knew her better than anyone did. Maybe he was right. Maybe she shouldn't try so hard to deny her feelings for Amelia. Playing these games with her was only making it harder, but she didn't know if she was ready to expose herself fully. Especially to Amelia, the one person who could shatter her very existence if she didn't feel the same way. Leaving herself raw and unprotected terrified her.

CHAPTER TWENTY-FOUR

A melia blew through the front door of Heartstrings House, expecting to see everyone in the living room watching TV as usual, but Blake was sitting all alone on the couch. She was happy not to find JJ cozied up next to him, but another week had gone by, and she couldn't fight the pull to see her.

"Where is everyone?" She meant JJ but didn't want Blake to call her on it.

"There's no school tomorrow. The kids are at the movies, and I think JJ went to bed."

"What's with that?" She plopped down on the couch next to him. "It's only nine o'clock."

"She missed dinner. I guess she had a busy day."

Amelia sat quietly for a minute, then turned to face him and pulled her leg up under her on the couch. "What's going on between you and her?"

"Who?"

Amelia tilted her head toward the stairs.

"JJ?" Blake's eyebrows rose.

"Yes, JJ." Amelia motioned to his hair and face with her finger. "What's with all this new stuff? Are you trying to impress her?"

Blake gave Amelia a wide smile and chuckled.

"What's so funny?"

"We've even got you fooled."

Fooled? Amelia cocked her head. "Okay, give."

"JJ's just been helping me out. She fixed my hair and gave some style tips to make Suzie jealous."

"But I saw you two at the Mexican restaurant." Amelia was

confused. She'd seen how close they were that night, and it sure looked like they were dating.

"Yeah. That was for Suzie's benefit." He sat back and smiled.

The permanent knot in Amelia's stomach loosened. "So you and JJ have no interest in each other?"

"Nope. None whatsoever."

"You *did* fool me. I had no idea." This was game-changing information. Now no obstacles were standing between them, which excited and terrified her all at once.

"I know. Isn't it great? It's driving Suzie crazy. She's calling me all the time now." He looked over at his phone as it buzzed on the coffee table. "See?"

"Why aren't you picking up?"

"JJ said I should wait until she calls at least three times before I do."

Amelia shook her head. "The girl certainly knows how to work it, doesn't she?"

"Yeah, and it's working." He looked at the phone as it buzzed again.

"Okay, Romeo. That's call number three. Pick up." She swiped the remote and muted the TV.

He grabbed the phone and hit the red button. "Hey, what's up?" Blake grinned, pushed up from the couch, and went into the office.

Amelia leaned back on the couch, put her feet up on the coffee table, and flipped through the channels. Then she heard a sound she didn't quite recognize coming from upstairs. She got up and went to the foot of the stairs, stopped for a minute, but didn't hear it again. As she started back to the couch, she heard a blood-curdling scream. She took the stairs two at a time as she raced up to the second floor. The sound was coming from JJ's room. Amelia rushed through the door to find JJ in a fitful sleep, legs thrashing and her face in a tortured grimace.

"JJ." Amelia shook her, but she didn't wake. "JJ," she said louder, and JJ's eyes flew open.

"Ames?" Her eyes began to focus as she gripped Amelia's arms.

Amelia zoned in on the crystalline blue eyes looking up at her, and her heart raced, pounding loudly in her ears. "It can't be." Adrenaline pushed her pulse to the limit as she pulled back the sheet and lifted the bottom of Jillian's shirt. She saw the crescent-moon-shaped birthmark on her stomach. "It *is* you."

"Oh, my God, Ames." JJ grabbed at her hands as she came out of the dream.

Jillian. Amelia pulled out of her grasp and stared at her for a moment before she stumbled across the room to the window. So many things were crowding her head at that moment, so many unanswered questions. Why had she come back after all these years? Why was she hiding who she really was? Why had she never heard from her before now? It wasn't long before she felt Jillian come up behind her and put her arms on her shoulders.

"You're…" She couldn't speak.

"Jillian McIntyre, cold, heartless journalist."

"Why didn't you tell me?" Amelia's voice wavered as she choked back her emotions.

"I'm sorry. I couldn't."

"Why not?" Amelia swiped a tear from her face.

"It's complicated."

Amelia spun around. "Uncomplicate it for me." The air was stifling. All she could smell was the cucumber and melon scent that seemed to always accompany JJ…Jillian. "Why are you here?"

"My last relationship ended badly." Jillian's gaze flickered to the window and back. "It's been difficult. She wasn't ready to let go."

"You came back here pretending to be an abused woman on the run?"

"I'm not pretending, and I didn't know where else to go. I didn't plan to stay this long, and I didn't know you would still be here."

Jillian's eyes were pleading, and Amelia wanted to gather her into her arms, hold her, and tell her everything would be all right. But she couldn't, not until she knew more. "Unlike you, I never left."

"Amelia, please. You don't know how many times I've thought of you over the years."

"You broke my heart." Soon enough it would be split in half again.

"When my parents were killed…" Jillian's voice cracked.

Amelia stared into her eyes. They weren't cold and emotionless, as she'd imagined over the years. With the soft amber gone now, they were blue. A pale blue so stunning it could hypnotize any woman and had done so to her many years ago. "Now what are you planning to do?"

"I don't know." Jillian shook her head. "I have all these things pulling at me. Memories of my parents, Abby, *you.*"

"Me?" Moonlight danced around the room, and the space between them became dangerously intimate.

"Yes, you." Jillian looked into her eyes, and the air crackled between them. Then she closed the space between them and captured Amelia's mouth with hers. Amelia tumbled into the kiss, her head spinning, her body hot, ready to burst into flames any minute. She felt it as though it were their first kiss, only so incredibly better. It was wonderfully warm, intoxicating even. It awoke all kinds of yearnings Amelia had buried long ago.

Amelia's heart pounded as she pulled back and held Jillian's gaze, gauging her response. She forged forward, hooking a hand behind Jillian's neck, pulling her in for another searing kiss. Their tongues mingled as the kiss deepened. Warmth ran throughout her and settled low in her belly. She pushed Jillian to the wall, and the full length of their bodies pressed together, kick-starting a whole new array of sensations. Her mind went hazy. Jillian could do things to her no one else ever could.

"I'm sorry. I've waited a long time to do that," Amelia whispered.

Jillian traced Amelia's lip with her thumb. "I never thought it would happen again. Then when I got here and saw you, I knew what we had is still there."

Amelia pulled away, stared into Jillian's eyes. The moment of excitement was laced with anguish, hurt, and anger. "I haven't seen or heard from you in fifteen years, and you think what we had is still the same?" She was thoroughly excited and totally pissed off in the same moment.

"Ames, after my parents were killed, I—"

"They were my parents too. The only real mom and dad I ever had." Jillian reached for her, and Amelia batted her hand away. "You *left* without even a good-bye."

"You think I wanted to leave? I was sixteen years old." Her voice rose as she drew the words out slowly. "I had no choice, Ames. My grandparents took me."

They heard the front door swing open downstairs. Then the kids' muffled voices.

"I have to go." Amelia spun around and ran down the stairs. She had to get out of there. Now. She hated this woman yet loved her at the same time.

"Amelia, wait," Jillian shouted. Her stomach was in her throat.

She'd just had the kiss of her lifetime, what she'd been wanting for weeks, and now Amelia was gone. Jillian stood at the top of the stairs, gripping the banister, her fingers pressed to her lips, wondering exactly what had just happened and what she should do about it. She had to talk to Amelia, and she had to do it tonight.

She ran back into her bedroom, threw on a hoodie, slipped on some flip-flops, and sped down the stairs after her. She slammed directly into Logan when she leaped off the last step. "Oh, my God!" she screamed, and they both went tumbling to the floor. "I'm so sorry. Are you okay?"

"I'm good," he said. "Are you?"

She got up, straightened her hoodie. "What are you two doing home so early?"

"There was some creepy guy at the movies. He kept following me around, wouldn't leave me alone."

"What?" Jillian's stomach clenched. "Have you seen him before? Do you know who he is?"

"Yeah. He's one of the jocks at school. David told him to back off."

"Oh." Relief washed over Jillian. "So what are you two going to do now?"

"We're going to hang out here, watch some TV." Logan flopped down onto the couch. "Everyone else is coming over after the movie."

"Oh, okay." She looked over at Blake, who was coming out of the office. "Are you going to be here for a while?"

"Yep. Suzie's coming over." He grinned.

"Great." At least that was working out. "Do you mind if I go out for a little bit?"

"Nope. Go ahead. What happened to Amelia?"

"That's where I'm going." Jillian raced out the door.

Jillian had never driven so fast in her life. By the time she pulled up at Amelia's, she'd broken a half dozen traffic laws. She killed the engine and rushed up the pathway. The door swung open before she reached the porch, and Amelia squelched anything she was going to say with her mouth. She was met with an earth-shattering kiss—deep, primal, and thorough. She felt it all the way down to her toes. Amelia pulled her close, and Jillian's body hummed.

"I want you now." Amelia hauled her inside, slipped her hands under Jillian's hoodie, and tugged it over her head. She didn't wait for an invitation, not that Jillian wouldn't have given it to her. She pushed up Jillian's shirt, exposing her unpadded bra. She slid a thumb over one of her nipples, and it materialized through the silk fabric. She reached around, undid the clasp, and pushed it up for better access. She took one nipple into her mouth and sucked it hard while she pinched the other between her fingers.

"Oh, my God." A bolt of erotic electricity coursed through Jillian as she fell back against the wall and let Amelia devour her. She slipped her hands into Amelia's silky auburn hair, so wrapped up in the blanket of sensations shooting through her she didn't notice Amelia had reached into her pajama pants until she felt the light touch of her fingers graze across the top of her center. She let out a moan that turned to a soft whimper and pulled Amelia's face up to hers.

"Should I stop?"

She shook her head. "Bedroom." She pressed her mouth to Amelia's and let out a low growl. "Now."

Amelia quickly obliged, pulling Jillian down the hallway to her bedroom. The room was filled with a massive king-sized bed, which she immediately pushed Jillian back on.

Jillian tugged at Amelia's shirt. "This needs to come off." She slid down to the button of her jeans. "All of it."

Amelia stood, removed her shirt, started on her jeans. Jillian sat up, stopped her, moved her hand, and placed a soft kiss on Amelia's belly before she looked up into Amelia's wondrous blue eyes. She unfastened the jeans, pushed them from Amelia's hips, slowly, but with purpose, while softly teasing her thighs as she removed them, then her panties. Jillian didn't want to rush, but when she slid her hand across Amelia's thighs, then into the space between them and felt the wetness, she couldn't stop. She dropped to her knees, pulled a leg over her shoulder, and pressed her mouth to Amelia's center.

She felt Amelia's knee buckle as she let out a moan. "I can't do this standing up."

Jillian twisted around and let Amelia fall onto the bed, half on, half off. She lifted her legs onto her shoulders and settled in between them. She took a quick swipe with her tongue up the wonderful crevice before her and felt Amelia quiver. She did it again before circling her tongue around the plump, fleshy cherub of her center. Amelia let out a whimper, and Jillian sucked her hard into her mouth. Jillian's tongue moved in and out in quick rhythm. Going slow was not an option.

Amelia's hands were on her head, pulling her in deeper as her body quivered. Amelia's whimper became stronger and louder until it ended with a low, guttural moan that seemed to last forever. Just the sound of it almost put Jillian over the edge. She crawled up on top of Amelia and silenced the moan with an urgent kiss that morphed into a deep, slow mingling of tongues. She pulled back, looked into Amelia's eyes, and soon found their positions reversed, with her under Amelia, feeling the rapid beat of Amelia's heart against her chest.

There were no words, just the sound of soft kisses and caresses as Amelia explored her. She felt the warmth of Amelia's mouth on her breast and sucked in a deep breath as Amelia's tongue circled the nipple and flicked it back and forth. She squeezed her breasts together, dividing her time between them. Jillian wiggled beneath her. She couldn't take much more. Amelia seemed to read her and moved slowly down her body, the warm wetness of her tongue igniting each and every sense as she moved. *God, this has never felt so good.*

She quivered when she felt Amelia's tongue move to her center, flicking at it, making it swell with anticipation. The heat rose within her, and she couldn't stand it anymore. "Amelia…please." The words came out in a pleading whisper.

She felt her hot breath against her and bucked as she felt Amelia's fingers enter, curling inside her. Her mind fragmented into blinding shards of color as the staggering orgasm overtook her, and she let out a cry as she grabbed a fistful of sheet to ride it out.

Amelia rested her head against Jillian's thigh as she stroked a finger slowly through her folds. "Jesus, that was…"

"Mind-blowing, to say the least." Jillian put her hand to her forehead as an occasional jolt still hit her. "Why didn't we do this years ago?"

"Too young. Naive. Scared." Amelia crawled up next to her, kissed her tenderly on the lips.

"I've overcome two out of the three." Jillian felt her insecurities creep in.

"Me too."

"You've learned a few things over the years."

"As have you." Amelia quirked up an eyebrow in that sexy way Jillian adored. "And where did these come from?" She cupped one of Jillian's breasts in her hand.

"A plastic surgeon in Beverly Hills."

"Remind me to send a thank-you card." She traced a finger around the nipple.

"I never forgot you, Ames," Jillian said, and Amelia turned to face her. "I missed you so much." She shook her head slowly, tears welling in her eyes. "*So, so* much. I cried myself to sleep for months after we left. I wrote you hundreds of letters, and you never wrote back."

"I never got any letters." Her brows pulled together, and she propped herself up on one elbow.

"I know. It never occurred to me my grandmother wasn't sending them. She thought it would be easier if I believed you didn't care. When she finally told me, I looked you up. You were doing well, working for some nonprofit company. I figured you'd moved on, found someone else, and were living your life." She swiped at a tear on her cheek that had escaped and chuckled. "It's probably a good thing you didn't get them. By the time I sent the last few, I was pretty angry you hadn't responded, and I'm sure I said some things I'd regret."

"I did live my life, Jillian. But I never found anyone else like you." Amelia searched her eyes. "Did you?"

Jillian held her gaze. "No. No one like you." She touched Amelia's lips softly with her own.

"So why are you here after all these years? Looking like this?" Amelia brushed a few blond strands from her face. "You look different."

"I was in a car accident this past year and...I had some reconstruction done." Jillian touched her nose. "You don't like it?"

"You'll always be beautiful, Jillian."

"I had to get out of New York, to become someone else for a while. My last relationship *did* end badly." It was only half the truth, but that was all Jillian was prepared to give at this point. "It's been difficult. She wasn't ready to let go. Still isn't."

"Did you file an order of protection?"

Jillian nodded. She *had* done that. Not that it made a difference to Kelly. "That didn't stop her. She's a cop. I met her when I was doing a story on self-defense. She was the instructor. Then my sister and her husband were killed in the car accident." She squeezed her eyes closed, trying to hold back the tears.

"The same accident that caused your reconstruction?" Amelia asked softly.

Jillian nodded. "Now I have more than myself to worry about. The life I've lived wasn't meant to include a child." She swiped at the tears. "I'm sorry. I thought I was done with this."

"Oh, baby." Amelia pulled her into her arms and kissed the top of her head. "It's okay. I'm here now."

Jillian stayed there, warm in Amelia's arms, feeling safe and loved. Sleep claimed her quickly.

CHAPTER TWENTY-FIVE

K elly sat in her rental car across the street watching for activity in Amelia's house. Jillian had left Heartstrings House quickly after Amelia, but Kelly had been able to follow and soon knew exactly where she was going. Her gut had twisted when she'd seen Amelia kiss her at the door. She'd almost gone in after her right then, but she had a plan and needed to stick with it. She had to be smart about this or she'd be caught, and that just wouldn't do. She'd made her way around back and found a dark, grassy spot in the corner of the yard by the shed to sit. The blinds had been left partially open in Amelia's bedroom, and Kelly's heart thundered in her ears as she watched them kiss, watched Amelia take Jillian to her bed, seduce her.

Kelly hadn't planned to hurt anyone this time, but this woman clearly had to go. Kelly was not going to be second choice. The last woman Jillian had become friendly with in class had been easy to divert. Kelly had made her feel as though she had a gift for martial arts, and referred her to a higher-level class held on a different night in a different place. It was amazing what you could accomplish with a woman, or man, by stroking their ego.

The sound of a barking dog woke her. She'd dozed during the night, something Kelly would punish herself for later. There was no room for slacking in her world. She'd hopped the fence and had barely made it back to her car before sunup. An hour later, she watched a truck pull up in front of Mrs. Jones's house next door. Three men piled out. One rolled a push mower off the trailer, another took a trimmer from the hooks of the wire mesh, and the last drove the zero-turn mower from the trailer onto the street. The two with the push mower and trimmer went around back, while the one on the rider started on the front yard.

Kelly was parked around to the side, where she had a good view of the backyard. She narrowed her eyes and seethed at the sight of Amelia standing on the back porch with her hands on the railing as she looked out at the yard. Jillian came out the door in only a tank top and panties. Kelly's anger bubbled. Jillian's body was only hers to love. Who did Amelia think she was, seducing her girlfriend?

Amelia gripped the railing of her back porch and let the sun warm her face. The night with Jillian had been more than wonderful. Amelia had lain in bed watching Jillian sleep. She'd memorized every line, every crease of her face. She was every bit as beautiful as she remembered. She thought about how their lives had played out. Jillian hadn't left willingly. She'd been taken away. She couldn't very well blame her for not coming back. After all, Amelia hadn't gone looking for her either. Pride was a stupid emotion, and she refused to let it prevent her from being happy. She didn't want to spend any more nights on useless dates with women who couldn't measure up. She was in love with Jillian. She'd always been in love with her.

"Doesn't anybody ever sleep in around here?"

Jillian's voice washed through Amelia, and she glanced back. Her eyes swept Jillian's body, and she shivered at the beautiful sight of her clad in just a tad more clothing than she'd left her with in bed. "They mow every Friday."

"Do they have to do it at the crack of dawn?" As Jillian's eyes fixed on her and darkened, Amelia immediately felt vulnerable. Jillian had an effect on her like no other, and it scared the hell out of her.

"It'll be eighty degrees out here by nine." Amelia took her denim shirt off the porch railing and wrapped it around Jillian's shoulders, then took her face in her hands and kissed her. The familiar jolt shot through her midsection. "Good morning."

"Good morning." Jillian slipped her arms around Amelia's waist. "I somehow forgot about the sweltering heat and humidity Oklahoma can produce."

Amelia kissed her again, thoroughly, deeply. She broke away, took a ragged breath, and looked around the yard. "Unless we want the yard crew to start talking, we'd better finish this inside."

"Excellent idea." Jillian took her hand and pulled her through the doorway. She looked around the spacious living room as they entered. A leather couch and tweed club chair and ottoman circled a square glass coffee table in the middle of the room. She looked up, and her gaze caught a framed charcoal sketch on the wall. She moved in to take a closer look. It was her sitting on a blanket at the park, a day she remembered vividly from her past. She turned to Amelia. "Is this me?"

Amelia nodded.

"I don't remember you doing it."

"I sketched it when I got home that night." Amelia moved closer, ran her thumb across Jillian's cheek. "How could I have not known it was you? I remember every line, every crease in your face."

"I have a few more now." Jillian took Amelia's hand, pressed it to her lips.

"Just a little character, that's all." Amelia smiled. "How about some music?" She pulled Jillian across the room to the stereo and turned it on. Static crackled through the speakers, distorting the sound. "I don't know what's wrong with this thing. It's been doing that for the past couple of weeks." With Jillian glued to her backside, lips on her neck, Amelia turned the dial, trying to adjust the station.

"Let me try." Jillian set her chin on Amelia's shoulder, reached around, and flipped the frequency to AM. No change. She flipped it back to FM and moved the dial to one of the major stations, but the interference was still there. "Guess we'll just have to suffer with it," Jillian said, holding Amelia close before she whispered in her ear, "Somebody may have you bugged." She put her finger to her lips, then turned and ran her fingers under all the shelves in the entertainment center. Probably not the best place to put a listening device. She went to the breakfast bar, nothing. She went to the end table closest to the front door, felt underneath around the wooden braces, and found it. She plucked it from its perch, took it into the kitchen, and dropped it into a glass of water. The radio still had interference, so there had to be another one.

"What the—"

Jillian crushed Amelia's words with her mouth and then whispered, "There's another one." She took her hand and led her into the bedroom, then ran her hand behind the dresser and the nightstands. She came up with another one behind the one closest to the door. After she removed it, she took it into the kitchen to meet the same fate as the previous one. The interference in the radio was gone. "Has anyone been here who might want inside information on one of your cases?"

"No. No one."

"Someone had to have let themselves in to do this." Jillian looked at the alarm pad next to the door. "Do you use that?"

"Only when I'm out of town."

"You need to start using it all the time, even when you're home… and you need to get a sweep device so you can make sure it doesn't happen again."

"That's ridiculous. No one is going to break in here when I'm home."

"Amelia." Jillian widened her eyes. "Someone has been in your house, and you didn't know it." She pulled her close, put her arms around her, and stared into her eyes, hoping to see a flicker of understanding as to the urgency of the situation. "That scares the hell out of me."

"Okay," Amelia said. "I'll use it."

"Now get dressed. We need to go check your office." Jillian took her hand and pulled her toward the bedroom.

"I have no idea who would've done it." Amelia's voice wavered.

Jillian pulled her back into her arms, brushed the hair from Amelia's face, and kissed her lightly. "Don't worry, baby. We'll figure it out, but first we eliminate the devices, okay?" Amelia nodded, and Jillian waited for her to let the situation settle in before heading to the back of the house to get dressed. "Is there an electronics store close by?"

"On Main Street."

"Good. We'll need to stop and get an RF signal detector."

"How do you know all this?"

"I'm an investigative reporter, remember? I did a story on surveillance last fall. I've learned a lot of things along the way."

"Right." Amelia smiled. "Should we call the police?"

"Probably, but they can't do anything until we have something to go on. Let's do some investigating on our own first."

Amelia pulled her lip up to one side and stared at Jillian.

"What?" Jillian said.

"Seeing you in action like this is incredibly sexy."

"Yeah?" Jillian cocked her head.

"Oh, yeah." Amelia crossed the room and kissed her. "It's kind of fun to watch you."

Jillian gave Amelia a wide smile to keep the moment light. *It might be fun, if I wasn't so fucking scared.*

When they reached Amelia's office, Julie was already there

working at her computer in her office. Amelia pushed through the door first and Jillian followed, sweeping the room with the RF detector. "What's going on?" She stopped typing and stood.

Amelia held her fingers to her lips and reached for a pen and a legal pad. "I had to come by and pick up something before we head over to the house to see Blake." She wrote Julie a note explaining the situation, and Julie's eyes widened.

Jillian closed the door. "Nothing in here. I'll check the rest of the office." She opened the door and went into the reception area.

"What the fuck? Off-limits girl is some kind of a private detective?"

"She's an investigative reporter. That's Jillian McIntyre." Amelia pulled her brows together at Julie's non-reaction to the news. "You already knew that, though. Didn't you?"

Julie nodded.

"How long?" Amelia wasn't angry, but she was hurt that her best friend hadn't told her the most important person in her life had come back to town.

"A couple of weeks."

"Why didn't you tell me?"

"She wasn't here to hurt you, and it looked like you both needed to resolve this one way or another." Julie seemed to assess her. "Which it looks like you may have done."

"Stop psychoanalyzing me, Jules."

"Someone's got to look after you."

"How did you know it was her?" *How did she know?* Amelia had kissed her more than once, and she hadn't even figured it out.

"I didn't at first, but I know you, and you don't trust many people. So I ran the background check."

"I told you—"

Jillian came through the door and set a glass of water on the desk with two listening devices sitting at the bottom. She also dropped a phone charger onto the desk. "Okay. You're all clear."

"Is that my phone charger?" Amelia picked it up and sank into one of the chairs in front of Julie's desk.

Jillian sat in the chair next to her. "It's not a phone charger. It's a wireless key sweeper disguised as one."

Julie took it from Amelia, studied it for a minute. "What's a key sweeper?"

"It captures everything you type on your computer and transmits it over the Internet to a web interface." Jillian scooted her chair up close to the desk. "Do you have a small screwdriver?"

Julie opened her desk drawer and searched inside before setting a couple of different screwdrivers on the desk alongside the key sweeper.

"Do you have anything smaller?"

Julie reached back in and took out a short, skinny one. "Only this one that I use for my glasses."

"That'll work." Jillian took the small Phillips-head driver from Julie's hand and went to work opening the small device. "It has a microcontroller, a radio frequency chip, and a SIM card inside." She separated each element from the others as she named them. "It also has a battery, so it continues to run when it's unplugged." She picked up the small, thin rectangular battery, studied it for a moment, and then set it back on the desk. "All they had to do was get the FCC identifier from the back of your keyboard to find the frequency information they needed to set it up."

"Why only me? Jules does the same kind of work." Amelia swallowed hard. This wasn't so much fun anymore.

Jillian touched the wire that ran from the keyboard to the computer. "Julie doesn't have a wireless keyboard. Someone would need access to her computer to load this kind of software on it."

"There wasn't a listening device in here either."

"Are you working on any cases that might warrant someone needing inside information?"

A shiver ran through Amelia as she tried to think of who might have done something like this. "That's always a possibility, but I don't think any of them would go to this extreme."

Jillian reached into her back pocket, pulled her phone out, and looked at the screen. "I'll be right back."

Amelia watched as Jillian lowered her voice and moved down the hallway. After a few minutes, she followed her, catching a word here and there. All she heard clearly was the tail end of the conversation. "I told you soon. Don't worry. You know I want that too." When Jillian turned around and spotted Amelia behind her, she smiled, pulled the phone from her ear, and touched the red button with her finger.

"Is everything okay?"

"Yeah. Everything's fine." She shoved the phone into her back pocket before she took Amelia's hand and pulled her back to Julie's office. "You need to think long and hard about who might want information, because someone has you under surveillance big-time." She glanced back at Amelia, who was still focused on the phone conversation she'd just overheard.

Jillian slipped her arm around Amelia's waist, kissed her on the cheek, and said, "Come on. We need to check the house."

Amelia snapped out of her thoughts. "You think someone may have gotten in there too?"

"Not necessarily, but we need to be sure. Someone seems to be watching you."

CHAPTER TWENTY-SIX

Jillian watched the numbers change above the elevator door as she rode to the tenth floor. She'd been disappointed her Saturday morning with Amelia had been cut short, but they'd made up for it on Sunday, Monday, and this morning. They'd started the Fourth of July holiday off with multiple fireworks. Jillian hoped they would have many more mornings to spend together now that Amelia knew who she was.

Saturday they'd combed the house for bugs and had come up with only two: one in the kitchen and the other in the living room. The placement was interesting, and to Jillian, it meant someone was gathering information from Amelia, probably about a case. But who? Neither Amelia nor Julie could think of any case where someone would go to such measures.

She slid her key card in and out of the slot quickly and waited for the light to turn green before she opened the door. "I brought bagels. Did you order coffee?" Jillian said as she dropped her purse on the chair in Marcus's suite. She'd sent him a text as soon as she'd left Amelia's this morning and invited him to come to the holiday cookout at the house. He'd replied that he had other plans already and for her to bring New York food. The closest thing she could find were bagels. Even though they weren't quite the same, they were close.

"It's on the desk. Did you bring cream cheese?"

"Plain, hazelnut, and blueberry." She set the food out on the table and poured herself a cup of coffee. "What do you have planned this afternoon?"

"I'm going to the fireworks display downtown. I hear it's accompanied by the symphony."

"You met someone in the bar." He must have. Marcus wasn't the kind of guy to go to an event alone.

"As a matter of fact, I've met a few people since I've been here." He gave her a wink. "Enough about me. What's going on at the house?"

"I found listening devices at Heartstrings House, Amelia's office, and her house." She spread plain cream cheese on half a bagel and took a bite.

"You were at Amelia's house?" Marcus dipped out a portion of all three kinds of cream cheese and spread them together on his bagel.

"Yes. I found two bugs there." She scrunched up her nose and motioned to his bagel. "That looks awful."

"Mind your own business. You have yours the way you like it, and I'll have mine my way." He took a bite and washed it down with a drink of coffee. "Is that why you went there?"

She dropped down onto the couch. "I had another nightmare Friday night, and when I woke up she was sitting on the bed beside me. I didn't have my contacts in."

"She recognized you?"

She nodded. "She told me how she felt about me leaving, among other things, and then she took off."

"So you followed her."

"I couldn't leave it that way." She took a bite of bagel and gazed across the room past him. "When I got there, she was waiting for me and it was…" She closed her eyes, and her body heated as she remembered the raw sensations that had run through her. "It was undeniable."

"Wow, you certainly did an about-face on that one."

"I didn't mean for it to happen. I've wanted her so badly for such a long time, Marcus. I just couldn't stop."

Marcus eyed her in that certain way he always did when he understood. "So, we're calling it a force of nature."

"Yes." Jillian smiled shyly and nodded. "That sounds right."

"Where does that leave your future?"

"I have no idea. I don't even know what she sees in me. I mean, she helps kids, Marcus. Abused kids. How can I measure up to that?" Jillian had never had anything to do with kids until she'd been forced to care for Abby.

"Uh…you do investigative reporting. You expose bad people who take advantage of weak people."

"I'm paid a *lot* of money to do that."

"What do you do with that money? You fund Heartstrings Houses all over the country."

"It's not the same, Marcus. It's easy to give money." Jillian picked up her cup and set it back down without taking a drink. "She gives her time and fights for them in court."

"Don't sell yourself short, Jillian. Funding is a big deal. Amelia wouldn't be able to accomplish everything she does without it. Plus, many people who make more money than you don't give anything back to the community." He finished off his bagel and poured himself another cup of coffee. "How was it?"

Jillian didn't have to ask what he meant. She and Marcus always knew what the other was thinking. "Spectacular. Just as I imagined it would be."

"That's going to make things more difficult for you when it's time to leave." He rubbed his chin. "Did you tell her about Abby?"

"No. I couldn't. I don't want her to think that's the only reason I'm here."

"It is the reason you came."

"Yes, but I didn't know Amelia was going to be here, and that changed everything."

"Hmm."

"Stop analyzing me, Marcus."

"Can't. It's what I do, remember?"

"Then help me figure this out. Tell me what to do."

"Okay. You asked for it." He sat across from her. "What exactly do you have in New York besides a job?"

Jillian felt the familiar adrenaline rush. "It's not just a job. It's my life, Marcus." Jillian's voice faded. "It's all I have."

"Is it?" Marcus tilted his head slightly. "Look at what you've got here, in Oklahoma. A home, a child, a woman who loves you. Whether you like it or not, Jillian, you matter to these people. You need to give this thing you have with Amelia a chance, whether you're here, she's there, or you have to do it long-distance. I don't think you'll ever be happy if you don't."

The thought of leaving Amelia made her stomach churn, but the thought of not returning to New York did the same. "Do you think I'll ever be happy, Marcus?"

"I hope so, but that's all up to you, sweetheart."

Jillian's phone buzzed on the table, and she didn't recognize the number. She picked it up, thinking it was probably her assistant calling from her cell. "Hello."

"Hey, baby." The sound of Kelly's voice made Jillian physically ill, and she couldn't speak. "Surprised? I thought you would be," Kelly said.

"I wasn't expecting you to call." She looked up and saw the concern on Marcus's face. "I'm on assignment. How did you get this number?"

"I'm a cop. I can get anything I want." Kelly's voice was firm, almost authoritarian. "I was surprised you left without telling me where you are."

Jillian pushed off the couch, went to the door, and looked through the security hole. Her stomach settled slightly when she didn't see anyone in the hall. "Like I said, I'm on assignment, and this one's pretty hush-hush."

Marcus motioned for her to put the call on speaker phone, and she did. Jillian could hear Kelly take in a deep breath. "When are you coming home? I miss you."

He took the pad of paper from the desk and wrote, "Gentle, but firm."

Jillian nodded. "Kelly, we've been through this. It's not going to work between us. You and I see life very differently."

"I'm willing to change."

"I don't want you to change. You need to be who you are, but with someone else." There was silence on the other end of the line. "Kelly, are you there?"

"I'm here. We'll talk about this when you get home," Kelly said, and the line went dead.

"Fuck!" Jillian turned the phone completely off and threw it across the room.

"You had location services turned off, right?" Marcus said as she fell into his arms. Jillian nodded and sucked in a big sob against his shoulder. "I'll call her supervisor again and see if he can do anything."

Jillian had had no idea the kind of hell she was going to experience when she'd first met Kelly. Her life had turned into the most miserable hell since. The emotional and physical abuse was devastating, but the worst of it all was the control. Jillian hadn't even known the manipulation was happening until well into the relationship. It was all clear to her now, and she couldn't escape Kelly's forceful determination to own her.

❖

Amelia had worked a half day and then gone to the market to pick up the hamburgers and hot dogs for the cookout. The last few days had been nothing less than spectacular, and now that she and Jillian had talked, she wanted to spend every moment with her. She carried the bag of groceries in the back door and set them on the kitchen table. She'd called Coop, filled her in on the new status between her and Jillian, and let her know she would pick up the food for the cookout. Amelia was in the mood to celebrate.

"The flowers you sent are beautiful," Coop said as she took the food out of the bag.

"I didn't send any flowers."

"Well, someone did, and they're beautiful." She pushed open the kitchen door and motioned to the huge bouquet of lilies on the dining-room table.

Amelia plucked the envelope from the holder, slid the card out, and read it.

Hey, baby,
    It was great to hear your voice last night. Can't wait until you get back to your real life. Our bed is pretty empty without you.
        All my love, Kelly

Amelia's stomach dropped, and she covered her mouth to hold back its contents. "She's involved with someone in New York." She shook her head, thinking back to the phone conversation she'd overheard when they were at her office. "I should've known better." She jammed the card back into the envelope and left it on the table.

"What?" Coop picked up the card and read it. "Huh. You never would've known."

"I didn't, or I wouldn't have…" Tears streamed down her face.

"Oh, honey. Come here." Coop pulled her into her arms. "Maybe there's some explanation for this."

"It looks pretty clear to me."

"You never know. Don't you think you should let her explain?"

"I have to go."

"What about dinner?"

"I'm sorry, Coop. I can't see her right now."

❖

Jillian parked in front of the house and got out of her car, then glanced around the neighborhood to see that everything looked normal. She'd been a nervous wreck after Kelly's call. She couldn't keep from looking over her shoulder everywhere she went and was terrified she'd turn a corner and run into Kelly. She was probably being paranoid, but the woman knew how and where to get information. It wasn't the first time she'd gone into hiding from Kelly. It was just the first time she'd done it so far away. She was surprised not to see Amelia's car. She'd called her earlier and said she was on her way to the store. Maybe she got hung up at work.

"Wow, these are beautiful. Who are they for?" Jillian leaned in and took in the scent of the gorgeous lilies on the dining room table.

"You." Coop plucked the card from the holder and handed it to Jillian.

"From Amelia?" She smiled and slid the card out of the envelope. Fear tore through her when she saw the note. *She found me.* Jillian ran to the window and looked outside. "Have you seen anyone new in the neighborhood this week?"

"No, but just an FYI, Amelia was here earlier."

"Oh, my God. She saw these?"

"And read the card from your girlfriend."

"She's not my girlfriend, Coop. I haven't seen her in months." It dawned on her. The surveillance devices and the odd things happening at the house. No one was following Amelia. Kelly was following *her.* Fear flooded her. "Where did she go?"

"I don't know. She tore out of here like a bat out of hell. My guess would be home."

Jillian raced to Amelia's house, but she wasn't there. Next, she went to her office, but again, not there. *Where else could she be?* She pushed the favorite button for Blake and held the phone to her ear. "Hey, Blake. I'm looking for Amelia. Have you seen her?"

"Not today. Did you check her house?"

"Yeah. I've checked her house and office. Do you know where else she might be?"

"Could be at Julie's. Even though they're divorced, they've had a pretty steady friends-with-benefits thing going since they split."

You could've provided that tidbit of background information a little sooner. "Address?" She hit the speaker button. Blake rattled off the address, and she typed it into the maps app on her phone. "Thanks."

Jillian was relieved to see Amelia's car parked in front of Julie's house when she pulled up. She would explain to Amelia about Kelly and get this whole mess straightened out. She knocked but had no answer. She knocked again, and after a few minutes, she heard the deadbolt flip. Julie answered the door dressed in a mid-length silk robe.

"Is Amelia here?" She looked around Julie into the living room. Amelia was nowhere in sight. She had to be there. Her car was out front.

"She doesn't want to see you." Julie blocked her from going any farther.

"I need to talk to her."

"What do you want, Jillian?"

"Okay, we're going to play this game, are we? Amelia, please come out here and talk to me." Jillian pushed by Julie and went down the hallway, opening each door as she traveled until she finally found Amelia in the master bedroom pulling on a T-shirt. She scanned the room, saw the remnants of clothing scattered about. "Seriously? Is that all it took? One minute of doubt?" Jillian narrowed her eyes. "You didn't even give me a chance to explain." She bit her bottom lip. "I—"

"You have someone in New York waiting for you."

"Are you okay, Ames?" Julie's voice rang in Jillian's ears, and she sucked in a deep breath, trying to keep the tears at bay. She shook her head and cleared her throat. "And apparently, you still have someone right here." She spun around, rushed by Julie, and ran full force into Darcy.

"Hey. I didn't know you were gonna be here." Without a word, Jillian pushed by her and out the door. "What the hell?" Darcy said as she fought to keep her balance and stumbled out of Jillian's way.

Julie saw the smile on Darcy's face fade when she took in Amelia's lack of clothing as she appeared in the hallway. She seemed to come to the same conclusion Jillian had. Amelia and Julie weren't finished with each other.

"Oh, my God." Darcy looked from Julie to Amelia and then back again. "I thought we had something going here."

"We do." Julie's stomach clenched. She knew how it looked.

"Not if you're still sleeping with her." Darcy turned toward the door.

"Darcy, wait. Please let me explain." She tried to get ahead of her, but Darcy was already out the door.

"You should've told me you were still seeing her," Darcy shouted without looking back.

"I'm not." Julie started out the door after her, but Amelia grabbed her by the arm. "Let her go, Jules."

Julie whipped around. "What the fuck are you doing?" She pulled her arm free. "Enough of these games, Amelia. You need to get your shit together. You may not want a relationship, but I do. I'm not going to let you destroy it." Julie looked out the front door to see Darcy speeding away in her car and then back at Amelia to catch the shocked look on her face. "Jesus, Amelia. You're like a fucking steamroller. You destroy everything in your path." Julie pushed by her into the bedroom, threw off her robe, and pulled on a pair of jeans and a T-shirt. "I can't do this with you anymore."

"Don't you even want to know why I did it?"

"God, you're selfish, Amelia. This is exactly the reason we're not married anymore. It's always about you." She shook her head. "No. I don't want to know why you did it." She threw her hands out to her sides and raised her shoulders. "I don't care. Did you ever think I might want a little happiness in my life?" Amelia stood silent, wide-eyed, watching her. "I have to go find Darcy now and hope she believes me when I tell her what she saw wasn't really what she saw and that you're a fucking lunatic."

"I'm sorry, Jules. I'll come with you and explain."

"No." Julie held up a hand. "You won't. You've done enough damage for one night. Now get dressed and go home. I don't want you here when I get back." Julie saw an unexpected look of hurt on Amelia's face, and a pang of guilt hit her. "If you want to be any part of my life, you have to stop acting like what I want doesn't matter. I can't handle this kind of destruction."

"Jules, I'm sorry. I'll tell Darcy it was all me." Julie actually thought she heard a touch of vulnerability in Amelia's voice, and it made her stop for a minute.

"You're damn right you will." Julie headed out the door, leaving Amelia standing in the hallway. She didn't have time to deal with her drama tonight. She had to see if she could salvage what she'd started with Darcy.

CHAPTER TWENTY-SEVEN

The thought of Amelia with another woman sent a jealous shiver up Jillian's spine. Especially Julie. "It makes me crazy, Marcus. She said all those things to me, and then, with one minute of doubt, she goes and sleeps with Julie."

"Did you tell her you wanted to be exclusive?"

"No. I have no claim on her." She covered her face with her hands. "I just thought…"

"You just thought she loved you without question?"

"I don't know what I thought." She kneaded her forehead with her fingers. "It won't work. I knew that from the beginning. I have a life that exists fifteen hundred miles away."

"Have you thought about how it could work?"

"No. I haven't even considered it. Every time I think about leaving, I feel like I'm going to throw up."

"No one says long-distance relationships can't work. You can afford to fly back and forth, can't you?"

She nodded. "I don't want her for just a couple of weekends a month, Marcus. I want her all the time."

"Maybe you should be telling her that instead of me."

Jillian touched the button on Marcus's phone after she left a message for Abby and held it between her hands. It immediately rang back. Jillian knew the number would be strange to her, and Abby wouldn't answer until she'd listened to the message.

"Hey, sweetie. What are you doing?" She cleared her throat.

"Kristin and I are in her room watching a scary movie. Her mom won't let us watch it on the big TV in the living room because of her little brother." Her tone went up and down as she spoke, letting Jillian know she wasn't happy with the situation.

"You wouldn't want him to have nightmares, would you?"

"I guess not. Whose phone are you on?"

"Marcus is in town. It's his. I forgot mine in the car. What time is the movie over?"

"We just started it. I've been trying to call you. Can I stay over here tonight? Kristin's mom said it's okay."

Jillian looked at her watch. It was after ten. She hadn't realized how late it was. "Sure. Tell Kristin's mom I'll come get you two in the morning and take you to breakfast."

"Can we sit at the bar and watch them flip the pancakes?" Jillian could hear the excitement in Abby's voice.

"Sure." Jillian smiled. She'd never known anyone who got so excited about watching someone cook. "I'll come after ten so you two can sleep in."

"Thanks, Aunt...I mean Mom."

"You're welcome, honey. I love you." The emotional tingle that spread through her had been so powerful when Abby had called her mom. The three words that followed came out so quickly she couldn't stop them.

"Mom." Abby's voice was low, almost a whisper. "I love you too."

The line went dead. Tears welled in her eyes as Jillian dropped the phone to the table.

"What's wrong?" Marcus said as she came out of the bedroom.

"She called me Mom." She looked up at him, tears streaming down her face. "She called me Mom and said she loves me."

"Oh, honey." Marcus moved the short distance across the room, sat beside her, and took her in his arms. "That's wonderful."

"What am I going to do now?"

"So, it would've been easier to leave before she called you Mom and told you she loves you?"

"Now I'm something to her." *And she's something to me.* "Before, I was just mean Aunt JJ." She rubbed her arms, trying to defeat the chill of the air-conditioning. "When did I become that girl, Marcus? The one who hurts everyone?"

"I'm going to order some food." He went to the desk and picked up the phone receiver. "You've had one hell of an emotional roller-coaster ride today, and you need to eat."

"I'm not hungry."

"Well, then, I need to eat." He pushed the button for room service.

"Do you mind if I stay here with you tonight?" Jillian picked up her bag.

"That extra room over there is reserved just for you. They have an excellent filet here. Eric had it the other night in the restaurant."

"Who's Eric?"

"He's here on business from New York. I met him in the bar."

"That's quite a coincidence. What are the chances you'd run into someone here from New York?"

"I know. I'm taking it as a sign." His voice rose. "We're going for a boat ride on the canal after lunch tomorrow."

"I probably threw a monkey wrench into your plans tonight, didn't I?" She headed into the bedroom.

"No worries. It's all good. I'm going to order you some food, and you're going to eat," he shouted after her.

She unzipped her bag and pulled out a pair of yoga pants and a sweatshirt. She'd stopped back by the house and picked up a few things before heading into the city. She knew there was a good possibility that Abby would sleep over at one of her friends'. She wouldn't get much sleep tonight, but at least she'd have a good mattress and air-conditioning.

❖

Jillian awoke to the smell of bacon and the sound of Marcus in her doorway chanting, "Breakfast is here, Princess." She rolled out of bed, still in her yoga pants and sweatshirt. Her stomach rumbled. At Marcus's insistence, she'd eaten a few bites of the food he'd ordered last night. It was after three when sleep had finally captured her. She made her way into the main room of the suite to find Marcus had already fixed her a plate of eggs, bacon, and fruit.

"What have you decided to do?"

"I'm going to talk to her." Jillian picked up a slice of bacon and bit into it.

"Good. Let her know how you feel."

"I'm not going to do that, Marcus. I'm going to break it off. There's no future for us. I can't change that."

"Yes, you can, and you know it. What I'm hearing is you won't change it."

"I have a contract and an obligation to fill it. Do you know how hard it was for me to even get this sabbatical to come here?" She poured herself a cup of coffee. Caffeine would be her only savior today.

"No, but I know contracts can be amended and even broken. It may cost you some money, but isn't she worth it?"

"She sleeps with other women, Marcus."

"Minor detail." He shook his head and took a drink of his coffee. "Once you tell her you want to be exclusive, that will change."

"You don't know that."

"Of course I do. You're Jillian McIntyre. Who wouldn't want to be exclusive with you?"

She twisted her lips into a frown. "There's nothing special about Jillian McIntyre. Plus, I've been lying to her since I got here."

"You haven't lied. You just kept a few things to yourself."

"Like she kept the fact she's sleeping with her ex-wife to herself." She lifted an eyebrow and curled her lip up to one side. "Lied."

"So you're just going to let it all go? What about the reason you came here?"

"I'm not going to tell Blake about Abby. I have to go back to New York, and I'm not leaving without her." Her stomach tightened, the bitterness of the coffee rolling inside. She knew Blake would be a wonderful father, and it tore at her knowing Abby would never know. "Abby will be fine with me." She took one last bite of fruit and reached for her coffee. "I'm her mom now. I'll take care of her."

Marcus's expression was solid—no smile, no frown. "Just a few months ago, you were having trouble taking care of yourself. That's quite a change."

"I guess I've grown up. Abby makes me realize I have more important things in life to worry about other than whether my shoes match my dress." Jillian knew Amelia and her work had a lot to do with her change in outlook. Coming back home had been good for her.

A wide grin spread across his face. "That's a big step. I'm proud of you. And the nightmares?"

"I've only had a few." That was a lie, but she didn't want Marcus talking her out of what had been the hardest decision she'd ever had to make.

"And Kelly?"

"I can't worry about her right now. I need to settle things here and get back to New York."

"I'm worried about you, Jillian."

"I'll be fine." *It may take a while, but I will be fine.* Another lie.

The emptiness was unbearable. It was as if someone had reached into her chest and squeezed the life from her heart. She wiped her mouth and dropped her napkin onto the table. "I need to go pick up the girls. I promised to take them to breakfast."

"Would you like reinforcements?"

"No. You go have fun with your new friend. I have to do this on my own."

"Okay. Let me know how it goes." Marcus didn't seem at all disappointed Jillian had opted to handle the day on her own.

Jillian and the girls had bypassed the line of people waiting for tables and snagged three seats at the end of the counter, Kristin against the wall, Abby next to her, and Jillian flanking her on the other side. Though the girls each ordered eggs and pancakes, Jillian opted for coffee and a small bowl of fruit. She'd eaten plenty earlier but felt she needed to order something since she was taking up space in the packed restaurant.

"What do you think about heading back to New York soon?"

Abby set the forkful of pancake back down on her plate. "You want to go back?"

"I thought *you* wanted to go back."

Abby slid a glance at Kristin, who was still eating. "I like it here. Don't you?"

"I do, but I have a job to get back to."

"Can't you get a job here? What about the place you went to record for your show?"

"I can't do that all the time, honey."

"But I've made friends." Jillian could see the angst in Abby's eyes.

"Don't worry about it, honey. I'll figure something out."

The beautiful smile returned to Abby's face, and she dug back into her pancakes.

Jillian hadn't considered that in the short time they'd be here, Abby had grown attached. She wanted to stay, and it was apparent that leaving would hurt more people than just her.

CHAPTER TWENTY-EIGHT

Get up, sleepyhead. It's almost noon." Julie pushed through the door of the bedroom and plopped down on the bed next to Amelia.

"I don't want to. I just want to go back to sleep and dream about how my life was five days ago."

"No do-overs. We only move forward. We have a fund-raiser to finish planning, remember?" Julie shook her shoulder. "I brought muffins from that little place on Main Street and nice strong coffee." The last word rang out of Julie's lips in song.

Amelia rolled over and put her head in Julie's lap. "I swore I was never going to do this again. It hurts so much, Jules."

"I know, honey." Julie swept the hair out of Amelia's face.

"For so long, I wondered if something was wrong with me because I never felt a connection like this."

"Honestly, I did too. Now we know there's not."

"And I hurt you." She looked up at Julie, and a tear ran across her cheek. "I hurt so many women."

"Don't go all crazy and start calling them." Julie widened her eyes and shook her head. "I'm sure they're fine now."

"No. I won't do that." She chuckled lightly, and then her smile faded. "Thanks for still loving me. I don't think I could lose both you and Jillian at the same time."

"Don't thank me. Thank Darcy. I wouldn't be so forgiving if she hadn't believed me." Julie stroked her back. "Are you going to tell me what the big charade was about?"

"I was stupid to think Jillian was in love with me." Amelia sat up, leaned against the headboard, and pulled her knees up to her chest. "I won't be that girl, Jules. The one who has to ask her to choose me.

I need her to want me. Only me." She took a drink of the coffee Julie handed her and winced. "Is there cream in this?"

Julie took the cup from her and switched it with the one in the carrier. "That's mine."

"You take cream in your coffee now?"

"Always have."

Amelia shook her head. "I am a shit."

"Yes, you are. Now back to the subject at hand. You thought you'd beat her to the punch? Let her know you have other options? Which you really don't." Julie's brows drew together as she broke off a piece of chocolate muffin and stuffed it into her mouth.

"Something like that." Amelia refused the piece of muffin Julie tried to give her. "Did you bring blueberry?"

"Of course." She opened the box and put it in front of Amelia. "You know how much I love you, Amelia, but I can't be part of this game you're playing with her."

"No more games, Jules. It's done." Amelia broke the blueberry muffin in half and took a bite.

"Did you see her face when she came into the room? You really hurt her."

"She'll get over it." She dropped what was left of the muffin back into the box and then swiped her hand across her face, wiping away the tears she couldn't hold back any longer. "She'll go back to her girlfriend in New York, and everything will be fine. I should have realized a woman like Jillian was bound to have someone waiting for her somewhere."

Julie choked on the sip of coffee she'd just taken. "What? Who?" She wiped the droplets of coffee from her mouth.

"Kelly. Her name's Kelly. I overheard a phone conversation between them. Jillian told her not to worry and that she'd be back soon. I didn't put it all together until she sent flowers to the house. From the looks of the card, she's very much still involved."

"Oh, Christ. She found her." Julie moved the muffin box to the bedside table and pulled her leg up on the bed in front of her. "Amelia, Kelly is her crazy ex-girlfriend."

"How do you know that?" Fear raced through Amelia.

"I ran a background check on her. Jillian has filed numerous assault complaints against Kelly. That's why she's here in Norman. She's hiding from her."

"Jesus, Jules." Amelia jumped up and pulled on her jeans. "Don't you think you should've told me this before now?"

"She asked me not to."

Amelia's eyes widened. "The two of you discussed this, and neither of you thought it might be important to tell me?" Her stomach clenched as the feeling of betrayal washed through her.

"Don't hate me. I thought you deserved another shot with the woman you've been comparing everyone to since the beginning of time. I didn't want the ghost of an ex-girlfriend to get in the way." Julie sat on the edge of the bed clenching the mattress. "I'm sorry. I should've told you, but you were so happy."

"Damn right you should have." She put her hands to her head and let out a slow breath. "How am I going to fix this?"

"Just tell her."

"She's never going to believe we weren't sleeping together. Why would she? Look at what she walked in on."

"It did kind of fall into place in an odd sort of way."

"It fell into place spectacularly. *Jesus*." Amelia shook her head as she remembered how Julie had been in the middle of changing when Amelia came through her door. She'd thrown on her robe and sat with her on the couch to console her. When Jillian showed up, Amelia had rushed into the bedroom to wait while Julie sent her away. That's when Amelia had decided she was the one who was going to come out on top of this breakup. So, she'd taken some of her clothes off and made a path with them from the bedroom door. It had all made sense at the time, considering the frame of mind she'd been in.

"You want me to go with you? Tell her what happened?"

She swung around. "You can come, but I need to tell her myself." Amelia had to fix this fuck-up herself. She'd gone off half-cocked with minimal information.

Julie took Amelia's hand, laced their fingers together, and squeezed. "Okay. I'll keep my mouth shut unless you need me."

"You're not off the hook yet." She kissed Julie on the cheek. "I'm still mad at you." She headed to the bathroom.

"We're probably even now, don't you think? I'll leave your half-eaten muffin in the kitchen, but I'm taking the rest of these."

❖

Amelia growled and slapped the phone to the table as Jillian's phone went straight to voice mail for the tenth time. She'd been at the house for hours, and Jillian hadn't come home or called. "You'd think she'd have the courtesy to call and let you know she's all right."

Blake set his phone on the table. "Abby said she's with some friend named Marcus."

"Marcus? Who the hell is Marcus?" She narrowed her eyes at Julie.

"I don't know." Julie shrugged. "She never mentioned him."

"Are you sure it's not one of those things you're keeping from me for my own good?"

"Okay." Julie pushed away from the table and stood. "I'm going home now." She took her empty cup into the kitchen. "That's where I'll be if you want to be civil to me again."

"You're being kind of hard on her, don't you think?" Blake said. "Boys, turn that game down. I can't hear myself think."

"Negative," she said, using his words. "This never would've happened if she'd told me about Kelly." She picked up the card from the flowers and looked at the note again.

"She was just trying to look out for you."

"Well, she's doing a shitty job of it."

"What are you going to do now? Call every hotel in the city?"

She got up from the table. "If I have to, I will."

"Amelia." Blake popped up and grabbed her arm. Amelia turned around, narrowed her eyes, and glanced from Blake's hand to his eyes, and he let go. "I'll see you in the morning."

CHAPTER TWENTY-NINE

Jillian followed the tall blonde into the restaurant. She'd met Wendy the week before at the TV station when she'd gone back to do some more voice-overs. She was one of the evening news anchors and had asked Jillian to dinner. Jillian had accepted, hoping it would take her mind off Amelia since nothing else had. Now she was regretting that decision. She'd been avoiding Amelia all week by staying at the hotel with Marcus, which was inconvenient and also made her miss seeing Abby outside of school.

The ride up the elevator was longer than Jillian anticipated. She hadn't realized it was on the top floor. She realized her date was a regular as the hostess, without hesitation, picked up the menus and guided them to a table by the window. Looking out at least fifteen stories higher than any other building in the city, the view was spectacular.

Jillian heard the waiter's voice from behind as she watched the lights of the city twinkle. "Your usual bottle of wine, Ms. Williams?"

She felt a hand cover hers and turned to Wendy. "Red or white? Or would you prefer a cocktail?"

"Red would be perfect." Jillian studied her date as she paged through the wine list. Short blond hair parted on the side and tucked neatly behind her ears. Long narrow nose and perfectly plucked eyebrows. She was gorgeous. Exactly what any TV station needed to bring in viewers.

"We'll have a bottle of the 2008 Spottswoode cabernet sauvignon," Wendy said, looking across the table at Jillian as she handed the wine list to the waiter.

Jillian smiled. "That's a very nice bottle of wine."

Wendy tilted her head. "You know something about the subject."

"I've tasted a few different varieties here and there." The Spottswoode was a nice red, not too cheap and not too expensive for someone who could afford it. Good for impressing a first date, and she imagined Wendy was pretty good at impressing.

"Have you been to Oklahoma City before?" Wendy asked.

"Once or twice."

"For business or pleasure?"

"Mostly business."

"Maybe pleasure in the future?"

"Possibly." Jillian smiled but cringed inside. She hated dating and hated the future speculations that came from it even more. At this moment in time, she had no idea if she would ever see the woman sitting across from her again or whether she even wanted to. Wendy was in television. She had to know what it was like to have women contact her. Women who wanted so much more than she was willing to give.

"That's good to know." Wendy smiled widely before picking up her menu. "The blackened salmon is fabulous, as is the lamb. We can start with the seared shrimp if that sounds good to you."

"Sounds wonderful."

When the waiter came back, Wendy ordered the shrimp, two mixed green with goat cheese salads, the salmon for Jillian, and the filet mignon for herself. They'd settled into comfortable conversation when Jillian spotted two familiar faces across the room watching her. She'd told Darcy where she was going but hadn't expected her and Julie to show up in the same place.

Julie shifted slightly to peek over Darcy's shoulder. "Is that Jillian over there?"

Darcy turned slightly. "Looks like it."

"Who's she with?"

"Wendy Williams, the channel five news anchor."

"Do you know her? Did you set them up?"

"No and no. But I did tell her the best way to get over someone is to get under someone."

"Why would you tell her something like that when you know Amelia is trying to get her back?"

"Because I don't like Amelia."

Julie frowned. "She's my law partner."

"She's also your ex-wife, and she takes advantage of you."

"What the hell, Darcy. You can't just get in the middle of Amelia's business."

Darcy's brows pulled together. "You can't expect Jillian to keep getting mind-fucked by Amelia."

"So you think she should jump into the sack with the next woman that comes along?"

"The next beautiful one, yes. Sex doesn't have to involve the mind. It just needs to be good."

"You know Amelia's in love with her."

"That may be the case, but Jillian wants to move on. So, being the team player I am, I've encouraged her to explore other women."

Jillian made eye contact with Julie and then looked at Darcy, discreetly motioning her to the front of the restaurant.

"That doesn't seem quite fair." Julie watched Jillian get up from the table and move across the dining room, and Darcy pushed back in her chair to get up. "No, you don't." She placed a hand on Darcy's shoulder, keeping her in her seat. "I think the other team deserves a little assistance, don't you?" She followed Jillian out the restaurant door to the elevator area.

When Jillian turned around, she seemed surprised to see Julie. "What are you doing here?"

"I'm guessing it's because Darcy knew you were going to be here, also."

"Oh." Jillian tightened her jaw. "Not much of a confidante, is she?"

"Nope."

"If you're going to try to convince me to talk to Amelia, you can save your breath."

"I'm not going to try to convince you of anything. I just want to deliver a little nugget of information I think you should have."

❖

When Jillian sat back down at the table, she was still stunned by the story Julie had told her about the evening she'd found Amelia in Julie's bed. She looked across the table and smiled at the beautiful face staring back at her, but all she could think about was Amelia.

"Do you like the view?" Wendy asked.

Jillian nodded. "It's amazing that they built something this tall in Oklahoma. How high is it, exactly?"

"Close to eight hundred and fifty feet. Almost as tall as the first observation deck in the Empire State Building."

"Yes, I would say so, but the view is very different." Her heart began to pump wildly, and everything around her was silent as she stared out the window at the city. She watched the twinkling lights disappear into the darkness as she lifted her eyes to the distance where the city of Norman would be. Julie had explained, sworn nothing happened, said Amelia had thrown her clothes off when she'd heard Jillian at the door just to make the break easier for herself. *How could Amelia think I would sleep with her while I was in a relationship with someone else? Does she think so little of me? Does she think so little of herself?*

It seemed Amelia was no better at dealing with conflict than Jillian was. She'd moved into the hotel with Marcus and vowed to stay away, knowing it would be easier to make the break clean. But it wasn't clean. It was savagely messy. Her heart had been ripped from her chest, left bloodied and beaten. The huge crater that remained had refused to heal, the jagged edges not willing to fuse together again. No matter what had happened and what Jillian told herself, she was still hopelessly in love with Amelia.

Wendy touched her hand, and Jillian realized she wasn't listening to a thing she'd said. "You seem far away. Are you okay?"

"I'm sorry. I'm not feeling well. Something didn't agree with me." She wasn't lying. The news Julie had delivered had her stomach rumbling.

"Oh. Let me get the check, and we'll get you home." The look of concern on Wendy's face only made it worse. She was nice girl, but Jillian's heart already had too many strings attached to it.

Jillian saw Amelia's car parked in the driveway when she pulled up in front of the house. She debated whether to go in. She didn't know if she wanted to see Amelia tonight, didn't know if she could. Amelia had left a number of messages that she'd ignored, all of them filled with explanations and apologies for jumping to the wrong conclusion. The piercing pain shot through her as she remembered the moment she'd found Amelia at Julie's. The little fantasy world she'd been living in had been shattered. The reality of it all had hit her head-on. At that moment, her life had been totaled and she hadn't seen any coming back from it.

She'd resigned herself to stay in Oklahoma long enough to let Abby finish out the summer camp she'd signed up for before she went back to New York, immersed herself in her work, and moved on as best she could. She loved Amelia more than she had when they were younger, more than she thought she could ever love another woman. The vulnerability she'd discovered in herself was terrifying. When she'd seen Amelia at Julie's, it seemed the choice to leave had been made for her, but now she knew differently, and the decision was right back in her court. It would be agonizingly difficult to leave now because it would be her choice. Her stomach lurched at the thought. She closed her eyes for a few minutes and cleared her head before heading inside.

When she entered the kitchen, she was surprised to find Coop still there, looking out the back door onto the screened-in porch.

Coop turned as she came up behind her. "Well, look what the cat dragged in." She gave her the once-over. "Where've you been all snazzied up like that?"

"I was out…on a date." Jillian sighed. As soon as she'd talked to Julie, she'd wanted to bolt from the restaurant. She didn't know why she'd gone in the first place.

"How was it?"

"You know, Coop? I meet these gorgeous women and we click in certain ways, but others not so much."

"And this one?" Coop dipped her head toward Amelia.

"This one." She took in a deep breath. "The perfect click." Jillian peeked over Coop's shoulder to catch a glimpse of Amelia standing, tiptoe, on an old wooden step stool with her arms stretched above her head. "What's she doing out there?"

"Changing the lightbulb she asked Blake to change three days ago," Coop said.

"Oh, geez." Jillian peered out at her. "She's going to fall and break her neck." She pushed past Coop and through the screen door. "Do you need some help?"

"No. I've got it." Amelia was stretched to the limit but looked like she was going to get it done.

"Here. Let me help you." Jillian slipped her hands on Amelia's hips to steady her. Amelia glanced down and froze. Then the stool went one way, and Amelia went the other, falling right into Jillian.

With her arms wrapped firmly around Amelia's soft body and her head pressed against her belly, Jillian was fully encompassed in Amelia's aura. Jillian tingled as all her senses fired, and her heart thudded. She let Amelia slide farther down into her arms and felt the warmth of Amelia's breath on her cheek. She didn't dare turn to face her. "You okay?"

"I'm fine." Amelia looked at the ceiling. "Lightbulb made it."

Jillian looked up. "Yeah. I guess it did."

Their eyes met, and Jillian let it happen. She covered Amelia's mouth with hers. The warm, wet sensation sent her mind spinning. Her body temperature soared as her senses spiraled to a scorching high.

She heard a muffled pop and then a loud chuckle from Coop. "Well, it's about time."

When they broke away, Jillian felt the heat rising in her cheeks and saw it mirrored in Amelia's. Neither one of them took their eyes off each other to look at the lightbulb shattered across the floor. There it was, all out in the open. Jillian still had feelings for Amelia. Now she just had to figure out how she was going to make it work.

"I'll get the broom," Jillian said, releasing Amelia.

"I'll get the ladder."

"Well, I'm going to leave you two to do whatever you need to do." Coop turned and headed for the front door. "Don't forget to lock up."

Amelia climbed the ladder and twisted a new lightbulb into the socket as Jillian swept the glass from the broken bulb into the dustpan and emptied it into the trash.

"Are you're okay? You didn't get any glass on you, did you?" Amelia pulled her brows together and searched Jillian's head and shoulders.

"I'm good." Hell, that was an understatement. Amelia had kissed her. She was fantastic, awesome…fantastically awesome. She watched Amelia's gaze sweep across her, seeming to notice how she was dressed.

"You look incredible."

"I went out to dinner." Jillian pulled her bottom lip between her teeth, hoping Amelia would leave it at that.

"With someone? Like a date?"

Jillian nodded, not wanting to explain any further. It didn't matter now with whom she'd been.

"Oh." Amelia's smile faded as she folded the ladder and held it in place next to her. "Did you have a nice time?"

Jillian shook her head. "No. Not at all."

"No?"

Jillian thought she saw a slight smile cross Amelia's lips, and she took a step closer. "All I did was compare her to you all night."

Amelia cocked her head, raised an eyebrow, actions that made Jillian's belly tingle. "I'm guessing I came out ahead, or you wouldn't be here."

Jillian pulled her lips up into a soft smile. "Miles ahead." She took another step, gave up all attempts to slow the thundering in her chest. "No one can compare to the love of my life."

"Are you saying?"

She nodded. "I love you, Amelia. I want to try to make this work."

Amelia dropped the ladder against the wall and closed the distance between them. "You still love me?"

Jillian nodded. "I've tried not to, but I do with all my heart," she whispered, lowering her mouth to touch Amelia's lips, kissing her tenderly. Amelia returned the kiss, gently at first, and then with the same hunger she had the last time they'd been this close. Visions of their night together roared back, and Jillian had to physically calm herself. Dragging her lips away, she brushed a strand of hair from Amelia's face. "I need to touch you." She looked into the kitchen. "Where is everyone?"

"Blake took the boys camping again." Amelia kissed Jillian's neck.

"Abby's at a sleepover. She won't be back until morning." Jillian took Amelia's face in her hands, captured her mouth, and plunged her tongue deep inside.

"Jesus," Amelia said, breaking free. Her eyes were dark, hooded with desire. That was all Jillian needed. She took Amelia's hand, pulled her up the stairs to the bedroom, and pushed open the door. "Shit." They both stared at the twin-sized bed for a moment before Amelia pulled her back down the hallway into Blake's bedroom.

Amelia couldn't contain herself, couldn't believe Jillian was here, wanting her, loving her. She'd thought this would never happen again. Only when she struggled to unzip her dress did Amelia realize Jillian was nervous.

"Wait," Amelia said, taking Jillian's hands in hers. "I've got you." She pressed her lips to Jillian's neck and felt her shudder beneath them. Liquid rushed to her panties. Amelia reached around, unzipped the dress, and backed up slightly, letting the dress fall to the floor. Next, she took her time unfastening the bra clasp, pushing the silky straps from Jillian's shoulders before taking a nipple into her mouth. First one, then the other, while she slipped her fingers under the band of the matching panties and pushed them to the floor. She dropped to her knees, kissing Jillian's belly, taking in every bit of her she could.

"Come back up here." Jillian pulled her to her feet again, reached under the hem of her shirt, and slipped it over her head. "Turn around."

Amelia did as she was told. Jillian unfastened her bra, reached around, and cupped each breast in her hands. Amelia's knees went weak. She leaned back into her and uttered an involuntary moan as Jillian let her palms float lightly across each nipple before she took her breasts into her hands possessively. Amelia tried to turn, but Jillian held her tightly and whispered, "Not yet."

Jillian slid her hands down Amelia's belly and unfastened her jeans, kissed down her back as she pushed the jeans and panties to the ground. Once Amelia was free of them, Jillian moved closer behind her, pushed her gently to the bed. The skin-on-skin contact set Amelia aflame. She grabbed at the comforter, unsure, a little scared even, of letting Jillian have control. She felt soft, tender kisses in the crease of her knees, and an erotic tingle zipped through her. She didn't know how so little could do so much. Jillian's mouth moved up her thigh, circled the bottom of her ass, and teased the inside her thighs. Then she kissed the tenderest parts at the small of Amelia's back. Her body quaked.

"I'll have to remember that spot," Jillian said. Amelia felt her lips smile against her back as she slid her hands up her sides to her breasts. Jillian kissed each shoulder, slowly, softly, then shifted Amelia's hair to the side and brushed her neck with her lips. It was the most erotically sensual experience Amelia had ever had, and Jillian hadn't even come close to the throbbing ache mushrooming between her legs.

Amelia let Jillian's name escape her lips in an urgent moan.

"Are you ready for me now?" Jillian whispered against her neck.

"God, yes."

Jillian flipped her over and kissed her deeply. When she pulled away, Jillian's eyes darkened, and a jolt of electricity flashed through her at the sight. "Jillian, please."

Jillian reached a hand between Amelia's legs, slipped a finger through her wet folds, and Amelia's body jolted as the full impact of Jillian's touch tore through her. "Okay, baby." Jillian moved her tongue in a hot, wet trail down Amelia's body and settled in between her legs. She swiped her tongue across Amelia's center, and the pleasure was unreal. She felt Jillian's fingers slip inside. Stroking her rhythmically, she pushed her fast and hard. Amelia tightened her fingers in Jillian's hair as the wave of orgasm ripped through her, traveling to the very ends of her limbs, awakening every nerve. Amelia's body reached a level of sensitivity she couldn't explain, let alone understand. Jillian continued until Amelia spiraled down slowly from the ecstasy she had just encountered, spasming here and there, not wanting to let go of the wondrous feeling, not comprehending how it was even possible.

Jillian moved back up Amelia's body and smiled. "You are so beautiful."

"You are incredible." Amelia pulled her down and kissed her, tasted herself on Jillian's lips. She reached down and slid a finger between Jillian's silky folds and felt the wetness. "I want you inside me." She slipped her finger into Jillian, then into herself.

Jillian let out a primal growl that had Amelia wet all over again. Amelia flipped her onto her back, spread Jillian's legs, lowered her body, settled her hips in between them, and felt the amazing sensation of skin to skin. She kissed her as she rocked back and forth, creating a delicious friction between them. She stroked her breast, around the top, underneath, then a light touch across her nipple. That produced a tiny whimper from Jillian's lips, so she pushed her tongue into her mouth and did it again, rewarded with a soft moan. She let her mouth roam down her neck, to her ear, back across her jaw, and plunged her tongue deep into her mouth again. The feeling was intoxicating. She could seriously do this with Jillian forever. She couldn't get enough of the way she tasted, smelled, felt beneath her. The woman was like a drug, and Amelia was deeply addicted, so much so, it was affecting her ability to remain in control.

Jillian wiggled beneath her, wrapped her legs around Amelia's as she continued to rock against her. Amelia slipped a hand down between them, slid her fingers across the hot moisture of Jillian's center, and buried her fingers deep inside. Jillian threw her head back into the pillow, raised her hips against her, and let out a soft cry. Amelia snaked her fingers up through Jillian's wet folds, then back inside in a continuous pattern. Jillian's body tensed, and her fingers dug into Amelia's back as she increased the rhythm. Amelia slid her thumb between the folds and focused on a particular spot that produced moans of pleasure between ragged breaths. Jillian's eyes flew open, connecting with Amelia's as she flew into a staggering orgasm. Her body continued to pulse until she reached down, took Amelia's hand, and forced her to stop.

Amelia placed a soft kiss on her lips, put her head on Jillian's chest, and snuggled in close. Mind racing, body totally sated, neither one of them spoke. No words could describe the experience. It was real, raw, totally unfiltered. So much better than any sex she'd ever had. Amelia's body connected with Jillian's in ways it never could with anyone else. Amelia was feeling things that were totally new to her, and it wasn't just about the mind-blowing sex.

When Jillian woke a few hours later, the warmth she'd been holding all night was gone. It was still dark. She looked at the clock. "Ames?" No answer. "Ames?" she said louder.

"I'm here." Amelia rushed through the door, turned on the lamp on the bedside table. "Hungry?" She slid back under the covers with a huge bowl of macaroni and cheese.

"Starving."

She slid a spoonful of macaroni into Jillian's mouth. "And you thought I couldn't cook."

"My favorite, right out of the box."

"Mine too." Amelia grinned.

Amelia's phone chimed, and she ignored it as they ate their way to the bottom of the bowl.

Amelia spooned the last bit of macaroni into Jillian's mouth and then kissed her. "I'm sorry. I was such an ass."

"You were an ass, but I would've reacted the same way." Jillian took the empty bowl from her and set it on the table. "It was kind of nice to know you cared."

"I've always cared, Jill." She brushed a strand of hair from her face, tucked it behind her ear. "I never stopped loving you."

"Me neither." Jillian kissed her softly, slowly, and her body began the automatic process Amelia prompted within her. The phone chimed again. "Who the fuck is that?"

"It's probably Jules," she whispered between kisses. "She's been following up on some details for the fund-raiser we're having for the house."

Another chime.

"Would you please answer her before I toss that thing across the room?" Jillian felt Amelia smile against her neck.

"If you insist." Amelia reached over, read the string of texts, typed a message back, and turned off the phone. "Now where were we?" She went back to kissing her neck.

"I could help you out with that."

"With this?" She continued down her neck. "Am I not doing it right?"

"The fund-raiser, silly. I've done my share of charity work."

"Would you?" Amelia sat up gazed at her with big blue eyes, heavy with arousal.

Jesus, keep looking at me like that, and I'll do anything for you.
"There's nothing I would rather do more."

Amelia raised an eyebrow. "Nothing?"

"Well, almost nothing." She pushed Amelia onto her back, nipped at the tender skin at the base of her neck. "I would much rather do this." She continued across her collarbone with a trail of light kisses on down to the top of her breast. Let her tongue trail farther down, circle Amelia's pebbled nipple. "And this." She sucked the nipple into her mouth, teased it with her teeth. Amelia let out a moan, and Jillian was wet instantly. She made her way across the smooth skin of her belly, felt it quiver beneath her lips, stopped just below her belly button. "This is what I would rather do most of all." She pushed Amelia's legs apart, took in the beautiful sight, and then kissed the inside of each thigh.

"Jillian, please." She grabbed at the sheets.

"Please what?" She smiled and let her lips hover just above Amelia's center, feeling the silkiness of the small patch of dark hair tickle her lips.

"Touch me."

"Your wish is my command." One light stroke of her tongue produced a moan from Amelia that almost sent Jillian over the edge. "God, you're gorgeous." She slid a finger inside, took another stroke with her tongue, and reveled in the tangy taste of her. Amelia let out a growling whimper, and Jillian watched as she continued to push her closer to climax. Her belly rippled with each spasm, her breasts rising with each breath. It was the most breathtakingly beautiful sight Jillian had ever seen. She buried her face in Amelia's center and held on tight as she herself launched into orgasm. The incredible wave of glorious ecstasy ripped through Jillian, left her astounded and breathless. Never in her life had that happened.

"Did you just?" Amelia asked breathlessly.

Jillian chuckled, nodded, and let out a contented sigh.

"That's not fair." Amelia reached for her. "Come up here."

"It's your fault. Coming all beautiful like that." She crawled up Amelia's body, kissed her, and was surprised when Amelia flipped her, quickly reversing their positions.

"It doesn't count unless I make it happen."

"Has anyone ever told you you're kind of a control freak?"

"All the time." She covered Jillian's lips with hers, explored the inside of her mouth with her tongue as she settled a thigh between her legs, pressing against Jillian's center.

Jillian was on fire, responding to Amelia in ways she never had to anyone else. She moved her hips against Amelia's thigh, begging for release. Amelia broke free from her mouth, dipped her head down, took a nipple into her mouth, swirled her tongue around it. With that, Jillian let out a cry and nearly came undone. That seemed to spur Amelia on, and she moved down, bathing Jillian's skin with her tongue as she traveled. She spread her legs, slipped underneath, wrapped her arms tightly around them, and then plunged her tongue into her center, sending a rush of orgasm through Jillian. Her mind splintered into bursts of color as Amelia drove the climax higher with each stroke of her tongue. It was carnal, sensual, and surreal, so much more than Jillian ever thought it could be, even with Amelia.

Jillian lowered her hips and Amelia slowed her pace, Jillian still spasming with each stroke. Just when Jillian thought she was finished, Amelia plunged her fingers deep inside, and Jillian launched into orgasm again, sensations tearing through her. The depths of pleasure that rocked her were immeasurable.

Amelia rested her cheek against Jillian's thigh. "Wow."

"Absolutely wow. Overachiever."

Amelia laughed loudly. "I get called that too." She moved up, gathered Jillian into her arms, and let out a contented sigh.

No words could describe how she was feeling now. Jillian listened to the soft, slow rhythm of Amelia's heartbeat. It wasn't long before she began to drift off to sleep. She felt Amelia kiss the top of her head and then heard her whisper into the darkness under the moon, "If you'll let me, I promise to make you happy for the rest of your life." Jillian squeezed her eyes shut, trying to hold back the tears. *I wish there was a way I could let you do that.*

CHAPTER THIRTY

Kelly fumed, watching through the window as Amelia groped and kissed Jillian all the way across the living room. When they reached the bottom of the stairs, Amelia even pushed her up against the wall and forced Jillian to kiss her before she pulled her up the stairs. When they were out of view, Kelly went to the front door. She could see the alarm pad through the side window. That was new, but the light was green. Not armed. Kelly turned the knob. The door was locked. She made her way around the side of the house to the back door. Unlocked. She slipped quietly in through the kitchen and silently climbed the stairs, stopping just short of the top landing.

The bedroom door was open, and she could hear Amelia seducing Jillian. Her blood boiled at the thought of that bitch touching her girlfriend. She clenched the railing and sucked in a deep breath to calm herself. When the time was right, she would make her pay for that. She took soft, slow steps to the door and peered through the crack below the hinge, watching as the two naked women touched each other. When Jillian dropped to her knees in front of Amelia, it took all of Kelly's strength to stop herself from bursting into the room. She closed her eyes, trying to clear the vision from her mind before she walked quietly down the hall to Jillian's room. She couldn't watch her woman have sex with someone else.

It's okay, Kelly. It's only sex. She doesn't love her. She paced quietly within the small space of the bedroom. *Everyone needs sex. Remember when you had sex with that woman from the bar last week? It didn't change how you feel about Jillian.* She took in a deep breath. *It's just sex. She'll always come back to you. She loves you.*

She pulled open the top drawer of the dresser and reached inside, took out a pair of Jillian's panties, and held them to her nose. She crumpled them up and tossed them back into the drawer. She went into the bathroom, found the hamper, and picked up a T-shirt lying across the top. She immersed her face in it, took in Jillian's intoxicating scent, and felt dizzy. She stumbled back out into the bedroom and fell onto the bed. *Why is this happening? We were so happy.* Crushing the T-shirt in her hands, she glanced around the sparsely furnished room. Jillian had nothing here. If she came back home, Kelly would give her everything she could ever want or need. She had to figure out how she was going to capture her attention away from that bitch.

She heard the familiar sound of Jillian's orgasm from the room down the hall and shot up on the bed. She ran to the bathroom and vomited. She couldn't stay here any longer. She slid the T-shirt into her jacket pocket and slipped back down the stairs. She could forgive Jillian for her transgression because she loved her, but she would never forgive the bitch.

Small rays of sunshine were just starting to peek through the windows when Amelia woke. Jillian was snuggled in close, her head on Amelia's chest and legs intertwined together with hers. Amelia buried her face in Jillian's hair and took in a deep breath. She no longer smelled like cucumber. She smelled feminine, sweet, musky, all woman. She smelled like Jillian, the scent that filled Amelia's memories from years ago.

She heard voices downstairs and shook Jillian awake. "Blake's back."

"You're wearing me out." Jillian looked up at her with a lazy smile. Then her eyes went wide when Amelia's words seemed to register. "Shit." She hopped out of bed and searched for her clothes, bumping into Amelia, who was doing the same. They gathered various pieces of clothing and pulled them on before they peeked out the bedroom door. The coast was clear, so they sprinted down the hallway to Jillian's room. Jillian slammed the door behind them and fell back against it.

Amelia couldn't resist the half-naked, gorgeous sight. She moved near and captured Jillian's mouth with hers. "God, how do you do that to me?"

Jillian nipped at her bottom lip. "The same way you do it to me."

They heard footsteps on the stairs. Jillian pulled the dresser drawer open and tossed a T-shirt and a pair of yoga pants to Amelia. She took the same out for herself and pulled them on. "I'll go first."

"He has to find out sooner or later. This is going to happen now." Amelia pulled open the door just as Blake was reaching the top of the stairs.

"Hey. I didn't know you were here." He stopped, seemed to assess them. "Did you spend the night?"

Amelia reached up, scrunched the back of her hair. "Yep."

"Oh, okay." He shrugged, and then headed for his bedroom. "I'm going to hit the sack. I didn't get much sleep last night."

Amelia jogged ahead of him and blocked the doorway. "I need to change the sheets first."

He stood quietly for a minute and then turned, keeping them in his view as he pointed at them. "The two of you?"

Amelia nodded. He looked at Jillian, and she nodded.

"It's about time."

Jillian made her way to Amelia, took her hand. "Did everyone know?"

"Pretty much." He yawned. "I'm happy you two finally figured it out, but I'd be much happier if we could get the sheets changed so I can get some sleep."

"Just give us a minute." Amelia started stripping the bed, and Jillian went for a clean set.

After they finished making the bed, Jillian and Amelia went into Jillian's room and closed the door. For the next few hours, they held each other and discussed everything between frequent kisses. Jillian wanted to donate a substantial amount to the fund-raiser, but Amelia wouldn't take it. She finally agreed to have a dance and dinner date with Jillian put into the blind auction. Jillian hadn't been able to take part in the planning since she and Amelia weren't speaking at the time, but she wanted to contribute in some way.

Jillian filled Marcus in on her night with Amelia and the words she'd spoken when she'd thought Jillian was asleep. Words that Jillian hadn't been able to get out of her head since Amelia had said them. *If you'll let me, I promise to make you happy for the rest of your life.*

"She really said that? You weren't dreaming?"

"No. I heard it loud and clear." She paced the room. "I don't know what to do, Marcus."

"Do you love her?"

"I do. Even more so now." She spun around. "She's everything she was and more. Mature, smart, and put together."

"Then why are you holding back?"

"I'm afraid she'll hate me when she finds out why I'm here."

"You didn't make the choice not to involve Blake in Abby's life. That was Jamie's decision."

"I didn't tell her the truth, Marcus. I'm scared. These are big fucking stakes I'm dealing with here. I have this beautiful girl to take care of, and I don't even know how to begin to be her mother. Or if I can be at all. Jamie was the perfect mom, the nurturer my grandmother never was. She knew everything. If I ever had a question about anything—sex, girls, hormones—she always had the answer. She constantly encouraged me to be who I am, no matter what, and not to let anyone question it. Ever. Jamie made me feel worthy, like I could be something in the world. I don't know if I can do that for Abby, and I certainly can't do it alone. Amelia may not want anything to do with me when she finds out Abby is Blake's daughter and I kept it from her all these years. If that isn't enough, I still have obligations back in New York. I don't know if I can just walk away from those."

"Are you finished?"

Jillian nodded.

"You're going to have to start living your life, Jillian. No one's going to live it for you. Why don't you ask her to come with you?"

"I can't ask her to leave Oklahoma. She makes a difference here."

"I think you may underestimate her."

"I don't know, Marcus. I'm not sure how I'd react if the situation were reversed."

"Don't you think it's time you were able to lean on someone else?"

"I've been doing it myself for so long, I'm not sure I know how."

"It's easy, honey. Look at her and look at yourself. You've already started."

Marcus was right. She'd started depending on Amelia since the first moment she saw her again. She'd needed her smile, her optimism, and even her smart-ass banter to keep her sane, or she would've never stayed this long.

"So I have to tell her about Abby?"

"Yes. You do."

Jillian picked up her purse and strode to the door, only looking back to get a reassuring nod from Marcus. Her next line of business was to tell Amelia about Abby and hope she didn't toss her out on her ear.

CHAPTER THIRTY-ONE

A bby is Blake's daughter."

"What?" Amelia's eyes widened. "You're serious, aren't you? Jillian nodded, and Amelia felt like her head might explode. It was enough to find out Jillian had come back, but to discover Abby was Blake's daughter was just too much. She must be having some crazy nightmare.

Seeming to contemplate her next words, Jillian blew out a breath and rolled her lips in. "It wasn't something she was particularly proud of. It was only one time, and by the time she knew she was pregnant, we were already living in New York." She stared into Amelia's eyes. "I haven't lied to you, Amelia."

"No." She shook her head. "But that's a big detail to leave out, Jillian." She paced across the room, her mind racing. Had she been that blind?

"She didn't even know she was pregnant until after my parents were dead. Blake was set to go to college. No way would he have been able to raise a child."

Amelia didn't offer any words of solace. She wanted to hear Jillian's reasoning for keeping such a huge detail a secret.

"The only other choice was your parents, and no way in hell was she going to let that happen." Jillian raked her fingers through her hair. "She couldn't see herself aborting and couldn't see herself as a young mother either. My grandparents helped her while she was in college, and then she met Ken. Once they were married, everything in her life was perfect. I never expected any of this." She looked up at Amelia, but Amelia didn't flinch. She just stared out the window. "I always thought Jamie would be here to take care of Abby."

"You never expected to see me again, did you?"

"No." Jillian cleared her throat. "But I was in love with you." She took Amelia's hand in hers. "I still am."

Amelia turned slightly, glanced at Jillian. "Abby's really my niece?"

She nodded. "I did what I thought was best at the time."

"It's been fifteen years, Jillian. How could you not have told him? How could you not have told *me*?"

Blake's voice came from the doorway. "Abby's your niece?" He stared at Amelia. "How's that possible?"

Jillian removed her brown contact lenses. "I'm Jillian McIntyre."

His brows rose. "The investigative reporter?"

She looked at Amelia. "He doesn't even remember."

Amelia prodded him. "Remember my best friend?" Still no spark of recognition. "The girl who used to live here?"

"Oh yeah. The cute little brunette." He glanced over at Jillian. "I didn't recognize you. You look different."

"Do you remember my sister, Jamie?"

"Yeah. I remember her. Didn't we go out once or twice?"

"Jesus, Blake. You slept with her. You should remember." Amelia narrowed her eyes. "Abby is *your* daughter."

"What?" Blake looked from Amelia to Jillian. "Why didn't she tell me back then?"

"Would you have believed her? You were going to be a big baseball star. Jamie wasn't in your plans, and I'm sure a baby certainly wasn't."

Blake raked his fingers through his hair. "Jesus. I've got another kid?" He glanced over at Amelia, and she nodded. "Does she know? I think I'd like to be part of her life." He hesitated. "Yours too, if that's what you need."

"Sounds like you got what you came for." Amelia stared into her eyes and pressed her lips together, holding back everything else she wanted to spew at Jillian.

"You can be part of Abby's life, Blake, but I don't want anything else from you." She stared back at Amelia. "I'm in love with your sister."

"This is the way you love someone? Secrets and lies? Wow. I can't believe I let you get close to me again." Amelia started for the front door.

"Amelia, wait. Please let me explain." Jillian grabbed her arm and swung her back around.

"You ruined my life once. I'm not going to let you do it again." She shrugged free of Jillian's grip and took off, letting the door slam against the wall as she sped down the front steps.

Jillian raced ahead of her and blocked the door to her car. "I ruined your life? Do you know I haven't been able to stay involved with anyone for more than six months at a time?"

Amelia stopped and put her hands on her hips. "We could've avoided all this if you'd just had your attorney send Blake a registered letter." At least then, she wouldn't have had to deal with the huge gaping hole Jillian had left in her heart. Twice. "A mistake made one night in the past is easily resolved in court."

Jillian's steel-blue eyes fluttered angrily. "That mistake made so long ago, with my sister's egg and your brother's sperm, turned into a beautiful little girl." Jillian was so close, Amelia could feel her heated breath on her face. "So, why don't we just leave it at that and go from here?"

"Because my niece is practically a stranger to me, as is she to her father, and I have you to thank for that."

"It wasn't my choice to make, Ames. Please tell me you understand that."

"I can't." Amelia shook her head. "Because I don't understand. This thing between us has all been a crazy fantasy. You have too many secrets, Jillian. Too many hidden agendas. Does it ever stop? Life isn't something you can make up to fit your needs. I can't be molded to react the way you want me to. This is…" Amelia shook her head and blinked. "Too much." She moved past Jillian and tried to pull the car door open.

"Amelia, please." Jillian took her by the shoulders. "I never meant to hurt you." Tears were streaming down her face.

Amelia pulled free. "I'm sure there are a lot of things you never meant to do."

Amelia's head was spinning with the newly discovered information about Abby, not to mention that was the only reason Jillian was here. Did Abby even know Blake was her father? Was Kelly really her ex-girlfriend? Was she really stalking her, or was she indeed waiting for her back in New York? Was anything she'd ever told her true? Who exactly was this woman Amelia had fallen in love with? She certainly wasn't the innocent young girl she remembered. Jillian's newest confession had hit her hard. Amelia dropped into the driver's seat, fired the engine, and took off. A rolling wave of despair flooded her as she looked in her rearview mirror and saw Jillian crumple to the curb.

Amelia fell into Julie's arms when she opened the door. "She—" A huge sob interrupted her words. Her tears came out in full force, choking any voice she thought she had. The ball of anger inside had turned to grief. Her very being had been torn from her, thrown to the ground and squashed at her feet. Her world had been ripped to shreds... again.

"Whoa, whoa, whoa. What the hell happened?"

"She lied to me again." She let out another sob. "Blake is Abby's father." The back of her neck heated as she pushed back from Julie. "Did you know that?"

"No. God, no." Julie pulled her back into her arms. "I had no idea."

"Is everything okay?" Darcy's voice rang through Amelia's desolate, foggy mind.

"No. Nothing is okay," Amelia said, glancing up at Darcy and not hiding her pain. She didn't care if the biggest gossip in town knew her heart had been broken.

"I'll call you later." Darcy rubbed Amelia's back as she went by them out the door, pulling it closed behind her.

"I'm sorry. I should go."

"No. Don't." Julie took Amelia into the living room and sat her down on the couch. "Wine or coffee?"

"Whiskey."

"Whiskey it is." Julie went into the kitchen, came back out with a bottle of Jack Daniel's, and poured a finger's worth into a highball glass.

"Tell me how this all happened."

Amelia drank down the whiskey and poured herself another before she began to recount the story of Abby's conception and the subsequent concealment of her parentage.

Julie sat looking stunned for a moment before responding. "It all makes sense now. I couldn't figure out why she chose *here* to get away from her ex."

"She came to fuck with my life."

"Don't you think you're being a little hard on her? I mean, that's quite a predicament she was put in, wouldn't you say?"

"She lied to me, Jules. Again."

"I can't say that I don't understand why." Julie shifted to face

Amelia and pulled her leg up under her on the couch. "Her sister *died* and left her with the challenging, *at the least*, task of letting her dead sister's high school boyfriend know he'd become a daddy fifteen years ago."

Amelia rolled that around in her brain for a moment. It sounded different when Julie said it that way. "She could've easily done that through her attorney."

"Yes. She could have. Maybe she just wanted to make sure Blake was fit to be involved in Abby's life."

"Of course he is."

"Jillian didn't know that. Then she gets here and finds you. The long-lost love of her life."

Amelia's gaze snapped back to Julie. "She told you that?"

"She didn't have to, honey."

Amelia wiped her face with the palms of her hands and shook her head. "I've been living in this fairy-tale world like nothing else matters, ignoring the fact that she lives halfway across the country."

"Is she going back?"

"I'm sure she is. I would."

"Wow. No concessions there."

"What do you mean?"

"Have you thought about going with her?"

"You know I can't leave the kids."

"How can you expect her to consider giving up her career and moving here, if you won't consider doing the same?"

"Truthfully, I have thought about it. More than once." The possibility of leaving everything she knew and depending on someone threw her whole world into a panic, but she felt empty and alone when she wasn't with Jillian. "Jesus, Jules. What am I gonna do?"

"You have plenty of reasons to walk away from her, but if you can think of one reason to stay…" Julie glanced at the ceiling and then back at Amelia. "What does your heart want to do?"

"I love her, Jules, and against all of my better judgment, I want to be with her."

"Forever?" Julie asked with a soft smile.

Amelia took in a deep breath and let it out slowly. "Forever." *Damn. What has this woman done to me?* She reached for the bottle, and Julie grabbed it away from her.

"No more. Big day tomorrow. You've got a lot to think about. You can sleep on it." Julie pulled her up from the couch, and she headed for the door. "No, you don't." She pulled her toward the bedroom. "Come on. You can bunk with me tonight and figure out what you're gonna do about Jillian tomorrow."

❖

Jillian couldn't eat, couldn't sleep. She felt more than empty inside, and it was her own doing. She'd been stunned by the hurt in Amelia's eyes and wasn't sure why she hadn't expected it. She'd fought to keep her here, to make her listen, but had ended up on the ground in tears as she watched her get into her car and drive off. She didn't know what else to say or how to explain it. What she had done was unforgivable, but it was done and couldn't be changed. Now she had to tell Abby before someone else did.

Jillian knocked lightly before she pushed through the door and found Abby sitting on her bed, leaning against the fabric headboard and working on her homework. "I have something to tell you, and you're probably going to hate me for it." She crossed the room and sat on the bed facing her. "Doing this story isn't the only reason we're here."

Abby didn't look up from the notebook she was writing in. "I know. We're here because you wanted to get back together with Amelia."

"Well, that happened. But that's not the reason." Jillian looked at the ceiling, trying to figure out just how to tell her. "We're here because of your father."

Abby dropped her pencil into the crack of her book. "Why would Dad want you to come to Oklahoma?"

"Not Ken. Your biological father." Jillian said.

Abby stared at Jillian blankly. "What do you mean, my biological father?"

"You were just a baby when Ken met Jamie. He was head over heels in love with you both." Jillian watched Abby closely, trying to gauge her feelings.

"So, why are you telling me now?" Abby's voice was calm and even.

Jillian was surprised that Abby wasn't more upset. "Your mother told me if anything ever happened to her and Ken, she wanted you to know your roots."

"My roots are here?" Abby looked back at the book on her lap.

"Yes." Jillian put her finger under Abby's chin and made Abby look at her. "You knew that already, didn't you?"

Abby nodded. "I saw the adoption papers in my dad's desk a few years ago."

"Why didn't you ask them about it?"

"I thought they would tell me."

"But they never did." Jillian closed her eyes and blew out a breath. "Weren't you curious at all?"

Abby shook her head. "He didn't want me. So why should I want him?"

"Oh, Abby." Jillian reached for her and she flinched. "That's not what happened at all. Your mother never told your father about you because—"

"She slept around in high school and got me as punishment." Abby stared straight ahead.

"God, no. Your mother slept with one boy in high school, and she *never* thought of you as anything less than a gift." She touched Abby's cheek and looked into her eyes. "Your mother loved you very much. Understand?"

Abby nodded, slid her book to her side, and pulled her legs up to her chest.

"Your mom had been through so much. We'd lost our parents, and then we were uprooted and moved halfway across the country." Jillian shook her head. "I don't know why it happened to her. She was always the good girl. I'm the one who made the stupid choices." Jillian got up and pulled the door closed. "It didn't matter whose DNA you have. You were her little girl."

"But she's gone, and now you don't want me."

"That's not true, honey. I'm just trying to do the right thing for you. I brought you here to get to know your real father. To get to know Blake." She glanced back at the door to make sure it was closed.

Abby was quiet for a few minutes. "Does he know?" She talked into the crevice between her body and legs as her forehead rested on her knees.

"I told him and Amelia last night."

"What did he say?"

"He said he wants to be part of your life. He wants to talk to you about it, but I think you should set the pace for that."

"Are we going to stay here?"

"I don't know, honey. Amelia is pretty upset with me right now."

"Because of me?"

"No. Because of me." All she could do now was beg Amelia's forgiveness and hope she would actually consider granting it. Jillian patted Abby on the leg. "Come on. Let's go see if they need any help at the auditorium setting up for the fund-raiser."

After they got there, Jillian scanned the auditorium for Amelia but didn't see her, only Blake and the boys, who were working on the stage decorations and lighting.

"Do you want to talk to Blake now?" Jillian asked.

"I think I'll go help the guys," Abby said, giving Blake a tentative look before she ran ahead to the stage where Logan was working.

Jillian crossed the floor to Blake. "I told her, but she's not ready to talk to you about it yet."

"That's fine. I'm not sure what to say to her either," Blake said, throwing Abby a wave when she looked over her shoulder at him.

"Is Amelia here?" Jillian asked.

"I haven't seen her yet this morning. She probably doesn't want to see you right now." He pressed his lips together, just like Amelia usually did.

"I can't blame her. I've kept some pretty big secrets." She let out a sigh "I didn't know how to tell her. I didn't know how to tell either of you."

"You're done with secrets, right? There's nothing else you haven't told us?"

Jillian shook her head. "No. Nothing."

He reached over, squeezed her shoulder. "Just give her some time."

"I wish it were that simple." She didn't have time. She was due back in New York soon. "I think it's going to take a lot more than time."

"A little groveling never hurts." Blake smiled as Suzie came across the room and slipped her arm around his waist.

"I wish it was that easy."

"Maybe a little bit of jealousy." Suzie winked.

No. Jillian refused to play games with Amelia. They already had enough obstacles in their relationship. She wasn't going to purposely create them. She just wanted the love of her life back.

❖

Amelia and Julie arrived at the auditorium to make sure all the preparations for the charity event were done correctly. She'd had a restless night but had managed to capture a few hours of sleep this morning. The auditorium looked gorgeous, with stars hanging from the rafters and glittered curtains on the walls. She hadn't known if she could pull this off, but it seemed to be all coming together.

Amelia didn't see Jillian anywhere. Half of her was relieved and the other half disappointed. She spotted Blake across the room, and when he spotted Amelia, he immediately went to her and pulled her into his arms. She squeezed her eyes shut to hold back what was left of her tears. She'd shed enough the night before.

"It's gonna be okay, sis." He kissed the top of her head. "She was here earlier looking for you."

Her stomach twisted, and she shrugged out of the embrace. "Maybe I shouldn't come tonight."

"It's your fund-raiser. You have to be here," Blake said.

"Yeah. If you don't, who's going to run the silent auction?" Julie said as she yawned absently, which prompted Amelia to do the same.

"You're perfectly capable of doing that. I don't know if I'm up to auctioning off a dance with Jillian tonight."

"You could always bid on her yourself. She *is* your Cinderella."

"Jules, you'd be the best friend ever if you'd fill in for me." Amelia gave Julie a big smile and leaned into her.

"I'm already the best friend ever." Julie gave her a shove. "Plus, I've got a date for the ball, and I don't plan to work tonight."

Amelia whipped her head around. "Darcy?"

Julie nodded and then glanced over at Blake. "Is everything set up out front?"

"Yep. The boys are going to help out with the valet parking. I rented them nice red jackets to look professional. A five-dollar donation is suggested, which will go toward the fund-raiser."

"That's awesome. I hadn't thought of that," Julie said as she walked toward the stage.

"David and I have to cut out early tonight to work on his car."

Amelia tensed. "Do you have to do that tonight?"

Blake nodded. "It's the only time Steve's available to help him with the carburetor."

"You're getting to be a regular at the school, aren't you?" Amelia lifted an eyebrow. "I thought you hated to go there."

"It's not my favorite place to be, but working with Steve in the auto shop isn't bad."

Julie walked back from the stage. "Is the lighting all set up?"

"Yep. Got it covered. Everything's done here." Blake put his hand on Amelia's back and nudged her toward Julie. "Why don't you two go home and get dressed?"

"Okay. We'll see you in a few hours." Julie took Amelia by the hand and led her to the door. "Now we just have to make you look beautiful for tonight, which may take a little work." Julie winked, and Amelia bumped her in the shoulder as they left.

Jillian stood out in front of the auditorium visiting with some of the guests while also taking pictures with new arrivals. She'd dyed her hair back to its natural chestnut color and had thrown out the contact lenses. Even with the new nose, people were beginning to recognize her as they arrived. She'd been keeping an eye on the guests who entered and hadn't seen Amelia or Julie yet. She heard the roar of the Camaro engine as it pulled up to the valet. One of the boys opened the car door for Amelia, and Jillian's heartbeat quickened as she watched her exit the car. There she was, looking more gorgeous than Jillian had ever seen her. *How can I leave her?* Blake came around the car and escorted Amelia up the steps to the building. Her stomach lurched when Amelia glanced her way and then quickly looked at the doors.

"Ready to go inside?" Marcus asked. Jillian nodded and gave one last wave to the photographers before following Amelia and Blake inside.

"I should try and talk to her."

Marcus took Jillian's elbow and guided her to a table in the opposite direction of where Amelia and Blake had gone. "Not now. You both have an obligation to fulfill here, and you don't want her leaving early, do you?"

Jillian hated it when Marcus made sense. "No. This is her night. I don't want to spoil it more than I already have."

The silent auction had been uncomfortable for Jillian. She'd gotten used to being the center of attention over the years but still didn't like it. Blake had emceed the auction, and the prize had gone for much more than Jillian had anticipated. She had no idea who would pay that kind of money just to spend time with her, although she would gladly have paid ten times the amount to spend time with Amelia tonight. She stared across the room at Amelia, who was mingling with Julie and Darcy. At least she hadn't brought anyone with her. That was reassuring. Jillian watched her lips curve up into a smile and ached at the thought of never being close to her again.

"How did I break something so incredible, Marcus?" She blew the words out in a whisper. The rock sitting in her stomach had moved to her throat.

"You know how you did it." He raised his eyebrows, took a drink of his wine, and pursed his lips. She knew that look of disappointment all too well. He'd given it to her many times since he'd arrived.

She nodded. "I do." She sipped her wine and watched as the three women ventured onto the dance floor, dancing together in a group.

"So, what are you going to do to fix it?" Marcus took the wineglass from her hands. "Where's that girl who never gives up?"

She caught Amelia looking over momentarily, stealing a glance, and suddenly Jillian had hope. She breathed in and out a couple of times to still her nerves and stood. "I'm going to dance. That's what I'm going to do." She reached out and took his hand.

"There she is." He smiled broadly as he accompanied her onto the dance floor.

They danced their way across the floor close to the three women. Jillian had a hard time keeping her eyes off Amelia, and she could see Amelia was having the same problem. The jolt shot through her like lightning when their eyes met, and then Amelia danced away from her and all Jillian could see was her backside moving to the beat in perfect rhythm. The song ended, and the DJ put on a slow tune. The odds were beginning to move in her favor.

"This is what you came for." Marcus turned Jillian around and nudged her toward Amelia.

She caught Amelia by the shoulders from behind before she'd moved too far away and whispered in her ear, "Dance with me... Please?" She closed her eyes for a moment, hoping for a positive answer. Amelia stopped, didn't move, and just when Jillian thought she was going to leave her standing there all alone, she turned around and did the exact opposite. She slid her arm around Jillian's waist and pulled her close.

"What about your date?"

"Not a date. My friend, Marcus."

They danced in silence for a few minutes, just staring into each other's eyes.

"I *am* sorry," Jillian said as she enjoyed the warmth she'd missed so much.

"I know." Amelia broke eye contact, glancing around the room at everyone except Jillian. Her heart thudded as she wondered what Amelia was thinking. "Everyone's watching us. You sure you want to go public with this?"

"Do we still have a 'this'?"

Amelia took in a deep breath. "I think so."

Relief washed over Jillian, and she pulled Amelia closer. She didn't care if everyone was watching. Amelia was looking at her, talking to her, telling her they still had a chance. They danced through two slow tunes just holding each other before she heard a voice behind her.

"May I cut in?" An arctic shiver rushed Jillian as Kelly took Jillian's hand and pulled her into her arms without waiting for an answer. "I believe I paid for this dance."

The voice echoed in Jillian's ears, and her vision tunneled. All her peripheral vision faded as she focused on the figure in front of her, one she'd hoped she'd never see again. "Kelly, what are you doing here?"

"Surprise, surprise. Aren't you glad to see me, baby?" Her tone was light and cheerful, so unlike Kelly.

"Of course I'm glad to see you. I just wish you'd told me you were coming." Sweat began to form on the back of Jillian's neck. She tried to stay calm, but everything around her seemed to be moving painfully slow. The sounds of people laughing and glasses clinking were muffled, while Kelly's voice was magnified a thousand times louder. She glanced at Amelia, whose face was blank as she turned and walked slowly back to her table.

"I would have, but you didn't tell me where you were going." Kelly moved closer and squeezed Jillian so tight she gasped for breath. "I had a hard time finding you," she whispered in her ear, and Jillian felt nauseous.

Amelia went back to the table, cursing the bad timing of the auction winner. She couldn't suppress the reaction she'd had to Jillian or the thoughts exploding in her brain. No matter what she tried to tell herself, Amelia was in love with Jillian.

"Why'd you let that chick cut in?" Darcy asked, interrupting her thoughts.

"Had to. Silent bidder." Amelia picked up a glass of water and took a gulp to cool herself.

"Well, that was certainly bad timing."

"There always seems to be something."

"She certainly is stunning tonight."

"She certainly is," Amelia said with more vulnerability than she intended.

"I can't believe I didn't recognize her." Darcy sipped her wine. "I'm glad you're going to give her another shot."

"It was just a dance, Darcy. It doesn't mean everything's gonna be peachy." Amelia knew they still had many things to iron out.

"You still love her." Darcy picked up her wineglass and took a drink. "Everyone can see that."

"I do." She shook her head and turned away from the dance floor. *God help me, I do.*

Julie arrived back from the ladies' room, dropped her clutch on the table, and straightened her dress. "Why are there always a gazillion women in the bathroom?" She looked over at Amelia. "What the fuck are you doing back here? I thought you were dancing with Jillian?"

She nodded toward the dance floor. "The silent bidder is collecting her dance."

"Her dance? Funny. I thought it was going to be a guy." Julie turned around and zoomed in on the dance floor. "That's her ex-girlfriend."

"The psycho cop?" Darcy asked. "Why is Jillian smiling?"

A wave of fear shuddered through Amelia, and she headed for Jillian. "She's probably too fucking scared *not* to smile." Julie grabbed Amelia's arm, pulled her back. "What? We have to get Jillian away from her."

"We do, but we need to be smart about it." Julie held her by the shoulders and looked her straight in the eyes. "The woman's got a temper, and we don't want to set her off, do we?"

Amelia shook her head. "No. I don't want Jillian hurt."

"Okay." Julie released her. "So you and I will dance over there. I'll cut in and take the crazy cop for a spin around the dance floor while Darcy blocks her view. You dance Jillian to the steps and then rush her through the dressing rooms and out of here." Julie grabbed her keys out of her clutch and put them in Amelia's hand. "My car's out back." She stared into Amelia's eyes. "Okay?"

"Okay," Amelia said, and Julie led her to the dance floor. They hung back, watching the stilted interaction between Jillian and Kelly.

"Ready?"

Amelia nodded.

"Here we go." Julie sidled up next to the couple and smiled widely at Kelly. "A fresh face. I don't think we've had the opportunity to meet," she said in her best Oklahoma drawl. She glanced at Jillian. "Do you mind if I take your lovely dance partner for a spin?" Julie didn't wait for an answer. She slipped in between the two, focusing her attention on Jillian's obsessed admirer as Kelly craned her neck to look around her.

Jillian clung to Amelia. "Oh, my God. I don't know how she found me. I hoped she was going to leave me alone this time."

"It's okay, baby. I've got you. Let's go." She danced her out of Kelly's view before she pulled her through the dressing rooms and out the backstage door. She pushed the unlock button on the key fob, and the car chirped. "We need to get out of town. We can go by my house and pick up some clothes."

Jillian stopped as her heart tugged. "I can't leave without Abby."

"Okay. We'll go to the house and get her, but we can't stay. Jules won't be able to keep Kelly busy for long, and I'm sure she knows where you live by now."

Understanding the urgency, Jillian nodded and got in the car. "I don't know how to get rid of her."

Amelia reached over and covered Jillian's hand with hers. "We'll have to file legal action. It may get worse before it gets better. Has she done anything illegal to you?"

Jillian thought for a moment. "Not anything recent."

"Do you think she could be the one who bugged my office?"

"I wouldn't put it past her. She always seemed to know where I was and what I was doing, even when I didn't tell her. Do you still have the bugs we found?"

"Actually, I do. I put them in the safe at the office just in case any privileged information surfaced."

"We put them in water. Can we still get fingerprints from them?"

Amelia looked at her curiously. "You mean you haven't done an investigative report on that?"

"No. Not yet." She smiled, and the mood lightened momentarily.

"Well, that's something I have experience with, and the answer is yes. As long as the item wasn't in the water too long."

"You took them out right away?"

"I did, and let them air-dry before I sealed them in a bag and put them in the safe."

Jillian turned her hand and laced her fingers with Amelia's as she drove. She felt safe with Amelia, safer than she'd felt in years.

CHAPTER THIRTY-TWO

They unlocked the door and disarmed the alarm. Jillian was relieved to see that everything looked calm. She'd sent Abby a text. She was still at the movies and should be home any minute. She hadn't told her what was going on, just that she needed to come straight home after the movie was over. Getting Abby on board with leaving so quickly would be difficult without telling her the whole story, but she didn't want to scare her.

When they went upstairs, Amelia was quiet. She seemed to be formulating her thoughts. She sat on the bed and took in a deep breath. "I've done a lot of thinking in the past few days."

"About us?"

Amelia nodded as she fidgeted with the bedspread. "We could raise Abby together…here in Oklahoma."

Jillian was speechless. Everything she'd ever wanted was sitting right in front of her.

"Oh. You hadn't planned on staying."

Jillian could see the change in her eyes. "That's not it at all, Ames." She dropped to her knees in front of her. "There was a time when I never thought anything between you and me was possible."

"And now?"

"I want it to be, Ames. I honestly do. I just don't know if it can work. We have so much to consider, but I'm willing to give it a try."

"How about we take it one step at a time." Amelia took her face in her hands and kissed her gently.

"I'd like that." Jillian rubbed her hands on Amelia's thighs before getting up and pulling Amelia into her arms. "Why don't you go downstairs and find us some snacks for the road while I finish packing." Jillian hugged her lightly.

Amelia smiled that adorable smile, spun around slowly, and hooked her thumb over her shoulder as she left. "I'll be waiting."

"I'll be right there." Jillian couldn't stop the grin from spreading across her face. Amelia wanted a life with her.

She startled when Kelly pushed out of the bathroom. "You're not going anywhere with her." Kelly crossed the room and closed the bedroom door. "You're coming back with me to New York. This is my family, *not* hers."

"Kelly." Jillian's mind spun. "How did you get in here? I mean, I didn't know you were here already."

"Of course you didn't. You failed to leave word where you went when you left the party." Jillian could see blood on Kelly's arm as she raked her fingers through her short black hair. "Do you know how long it took me to find you in this little town? Then you just left me at the party with that bitch's ex." She poked her finger toward the door.

"I just had to leave in such a rush that I forgot."

"Such a rush that you forgot about the most important person in your life?" Her stare was wildly intense. If her eyes were lasers, they would've bored a hole right through Jillian.

"I'm sorry, Kelly. It was thoughtless of me. I don't know what I was thinking." She remembered what Marcus said about letting her believe she had control. *Marcus, where the hell are you?*

"It *was* thoughtless." Kelly moved swiftly across the room, startling Jillian again. "And what were you thinking when you changed your hair?" She rubbed a strand between her fingertips. "That sandy-blond color was just awful. I'm glad you fixed it, but I'm not happy you've cut it so short." Jillian watched Kelly's intensely green, red-rimmed eyes as they skittered back and forth. She was in manic mode. "You should have asked me first."

"Yes. I should have." Jillian's gaze veered to the door when she heard Abby's voice.

"Mom, I'm home. What's so important? My friends are all going to Sara's to spend the night. Can I go?" Abby asked as she pushed open the door.

Kelly moved to the door and slammed it shut behind her. "It's so nice to see you, Abigale."

"Mom?" Abby backed up next to her. "Who is that?"

"It's so cute that she calls you Mom." Kelly looked over at her. "You can call me Aunt Kelly." She grabbed a strand of Abby's hair and twirled it around her finger. "This is what your hair should look like."

She snapped her gaze back to Jillian. "Thankfully she has your eyes, not mine." She turned back to Jillian. "I want to see your beautiful blue eyes." Kelly stood quietly for a moment, gazing deep into Jillian's eyes. "Get rid of those contacts you've been wearing. I don't want you to ever wear them again."

"Okay." Jillian took Abby's hand and moved toward the bathroom.

Kelly picked up the box of contacts from the dresser. "Throw them in the trash."

Jillian noticed a kitchen knife lying next to the box. She hadn't put it there. Keeping Abby shielded behind her, Jillian trembled as she took the contacts from Kelly and threw them in the trash basket.

Abby tugged at the back of Jillian's shirt. "Mom, I'm scared."

"It's okay, honey. Kelly's not going to hurt us. Right?"

Kelly's eyes went wide, and her face broke into a crazy, delirious smile. "Of course not. I would never hurt my family."

Amelia finished packing the snacks and headed back up the stairs. Taking the steps two at a time, she bounced up quickly and pushed the door open. It slammed back in her face. "What the hell?" She touched her nose, felt the warmth of the blood spilling onto her lip. She went to the hall bathroom, grabbed a wad of toilet paper, and held it to her nose. "Jillian." She tried to turn the doorknob, but it wouldn't turn. "Jillian," she said louder. "Are you okay?"

"I'm fine. Abby and I are just having a private chat."

A private chat? What's that about? You almost broke my nose. "Okay." She drew the word out slowly. "Anything I can participate in?"

"Not really. We're talking about college. She's thinking about going into meteorology like Logan. You wouldn't know anything about that."

"But I thought—"

"Maybe Blake can help us out," Jillian shouted through the door.

Amelia heard footsteps and then a muffled voice as something slammed against the wall. *Fuck! She's here.* She rushed down the stairs, then out front. Headlights blinded her as she stumbled across the yard to see if she could catch a glimpse of them through the window.

"What's going on?" Marcus raced up the walk and stood next to her.

"I think Kelly is up there with Jillian and Abby." All she could see was the shadowy figure of someone's back.

"How the hell did she get here so fast?"

"I don't know." Amelia ran inside and called Blake. She just hoped he'd taken his phone in with him when he went to help David with his car. Adrenaline shot through Amelia when she heard his voice. "I need you now. Jillian and Abby are in trouble. Her crazy ex-girlfriend has locked them in Jillian's room upstairs."

"On my way," Blake said, and the phone went dead.

Amelia and Marcus raced back up the stairs. "Kelly, it's Marcus. Can I come in?" Marcus asked as he knocked on the door gently.

"Marcus. Sure. Why not? Come on in and join the party."

Amelia heard the lock turn and caught a glimpse of Jillian and Abby as the door opened. Marcus slipped through the small opening, and the door slammed back into place. Amelia pressed her ear against the door in an attempt to hear what was being said.

"Can you talk some sense into this girl?" Kelly said. "She colored her hair that awful blond."

"I know. I convinced her to change it back. Right, Jillian?"

"Yes. Marcus has been helping me through a lot of things since he got here."

"I'm super thirsty, aren't you? Why don't we let Abby go downstairs and get us a few bottles of cold water?" Amelia heard Marcus trying to reason with Kelly. There was no sound for a minute or two, and she heard the door unlock again. She jumped to the side to hide from view as the door pulled open and Abby came out. Amelia put her fingers to her lips and pulled her down the stairs to the first landing. "Does she have a weapon of any kind?"

Abby shook her head as tears spilled out of her eyes and streamed down her cheeks. "There's a knife on the dresser. Who is she? She's acting crazy. She's holding my mom around the waist."

"I know." Amelia could see the terror in Abby's eyes and took her into her arms. "She's someone who's fixated on Jillian. I want you to go downstairs and wait for Blake. He should be here any minute." She took Abby's hand, pressed it to her lips, and whispered, "It's going to be all right."

Abby nodded and padded down the steps slowly. Amelia headed back up the stairs but spun around when she heard the stampede of footsteps coming into the house and met Blake and Steve Wright halfway up the steps.

"Kelly has her and Marcus locked in the bedroom," Amelia whispered.

Blake looked confused. "She followed her here from New York?"

"Yes. She was at the fund-raiser. She's been stalking her."

"How did she get in the house?" Steve asked.

"I don't know. We stopped at my place before coming here, but it was just a matter of minutes."

They heard a scuffle, Jillian screamed, and Amelia's heart thundered. Then she heard a loud thud. Amelia started up the stairs, but Blake stopped her and pressed his cell phone into her palm. "Call the police," he said and sprinted upstairs.

"No! This will not happen again," Steve said, following him.

Amelia punched in 911 as she raced up the stairs behind them. "Someone's holding my girlfriend with a knife. They're locked in the bedroom upstairs."

"Are you still in the house, ma'am?"

"Yes. I'm in the house."

"Please, go outside and wait for the police to arrive."

"No. I'm not leaving here."

"Ma'am, please. You need to wait for the police outside. They're on their way."

"Tell them to hurry. Please." She ran outside and looked up at the window to Jillian's room. She dropped the phone to the grass, ran to the trellis, and started up. Pain sliced through her as the thorns from the rose bush ripped at her hands and legs. As she neared the window opening, she slowed, holding tightly against the copper piping, trying to catch some of the conversation inside. She could hear Jillian faintly. *She's still by the door.* Amelia moved up slightly to gauge their positions in the room. Kelly had her back to the window, holding a kitchen knife by her side. Marcus was on the bed, leaning against the wall. The sleeve of his pink shirt was now crimson, soaked with blood. Jillian was shaking but somehow holding it together. Her face was calm, smiling almost, as she watched Kelly. Marcus must have gotten Jillian out of her grasp somehow. When Jillian spotted Amelia, she saw the flash of alarm in her eyes. Kelly must have seen it too, because she started to turn, but someone knocked on the door. Kelly moved toward Jillian, but she circled around the bed to the other side.

"Kelly, why don't you let us in so we can talk." Blake's muffled voice came through the door. "Jillian's told me so much about you."

"This isn't going to solve anything. She's not going to let us in." Steve's voice resonated through the door, and Amelia could see something in Jillian's eyes. Panic? Fear? Terror? Amelia wasn't quite sure what it was, but Jillian wasn't looking at Kelly anymore. She was looking at the door.

Jillian heard the voice, and a memory from fifteen years ago came rushing back. She was in her parents' bedroom peering through the slats in the closet door. She heard voices arguing. Her mother's voice: "Tommy, don't. I promise. I won't see him again." Then her father's voice: "I'll make sure of that."

Jillian watched as her mother stood behind her father, her hand on his arm. Her father's arm was outstretched, his hand holding a gun pointed across the room at someone. She couldn't see who it was. "No, Tommy, please," her mother said, pulling at his wrist. They were face-to-face, the gun between them, then an earsplitting pop. Her mother slumped and fell to the floor, her shirt stained in red. She looked over at Jillian, caught her eyes through the space in the slats, and smiled, and then she went still. Feet, large feet were by her mother's side. Jillian followed them up to see her father's face, tears streaming down his cheeks. His arms hung by his side, a gun in one of his hands. She didn't understand why her father would shoot her mother.

Then she saw him, the man who went with the voice. "Tommy, give me the gun." Steve Wright, the shop teacher at the high school. Her father put the gun in his mouth. Steve tackled him to the floor, his hands wrapped around Jillian's father's hands, struggling for the gun. Then another earsplitting pop, and blood spilled out onto the floor from her father's chest. Steve got to his knees, stared at her father's lifeless body, then swiped at his face with his hands. Steve was crying too. He got up, went over to Jillian's mother, dropped to the floor, and cradled her mother in his lap. He held her for what seemed like an eternity before placing a light kiss on her forehead. Then he picked up the phone, punched a few buttons, and left the receiver on the nightstand. He was gone.

Everything had slowed to half speed for Jillian. She heard a loud banging sound and could see Kelly talking, but she couldn't understand what she was saying. She followed her gaze to the door and watched the knob turn. She could hear the tumblers as it moved—tick, tick, tick. Then in a whoosh, it was open. Everything went black.

Amelia watched Kelly hurdle the bed, grab Jillian, and pull her into the corner of the room by the closet. *Shit!* Amelia struggled to pull herself through the window opening and onto the bed where Marcus was lying half-conscious. Kelly was having trouble holding Jillian up. Her eyes were closed. She'd passed out. Kelly couldn't hold her. She let her limp body slide down in front of her, and then Steve was on her. Kelly stabbed at him with the knife, cutting him across the belly, blood splattering across the wall.

In seconds, Steve's stomach and side were soaked with blood, but that didn't stop him. He held Kelly to the wall, struggling for the knife as Blake pulled Jillian from between them. Blake motioned for Amelia to take her, dropped Jillian into her arms, then scrambled back to help Steve, who now had Kelly pinned to the floor. Amelia swayed backward onto the bed with Jillian. Her heart raced as Marcus put his fingers to her neck, checked her pulse, and nodded.

Blake was on his hands and knees now, struggling to free the knife from Kelly's grip. He slammed it against the floor, then again against the leg of the side table as their positions shifted. The knife flew from Kelly's hand, and Steve fell to the side. Blake clenched Kelly's shirt with both hands, pulled her forward, and slammed her head against the floor. Kelly blinked and stared up at him blankly. Amelia heard the smack against Kelly's face as Blake hit her and then the sickening crack of her jaw when he hit her again.

Blake continued to hammer her until Steve grabbed his arm to stop him. "That's enough."

Blake looked up at him as though in a daze, then over at Amelia and at Jillian. She could see the rage in his eyes. All the abuse from his past had been unleashed in full force.

"She's okay, just unconscious," Marcus said, and Blake hung his head.

As the sirens became more distinct, Blake pushed himself to his feet. "I'll talk to the police," he said and left the bedroom.

❖

When Jillian woke, Amelia was asleep, her head lying on the bed, her fingers intertwined with Jillian's. She brushed away the short strands of auburn hair splayed across Amelia's cheek.

"You're awake." Amelia opened her eyes and smiled.

"You're here."

She nodded. "How could I not be?"

"How did I get here?"

"Ambulance." Amelia got up and perched on the side of the bed. "You passed out."

"Are you okay?" Jillian pulled her brows together and slid her fingers across the bandage wrapped around Amelia's hand.

"I'm fine. The rosebush and I tangled a little, that's all."

"When I saw you through the window, I was so afraid you were going to—"

"Do something stupid?" She pulled her lip up to the side.

"Get hurt." Jillian pulled her down and kissed her softly. "I'm so glad you're okay."

"I'm so glad *you're* okay." Amelia pressed her cheek to Jillian's face. "You scared the daylights out of me."

"Did the police come? Did they catch Kelly?" Panic rushed through her.

"Hey, shush." Amelia took Jillian's face in her hands, looked into her eyes. "She's locked up in a secure room."

"What if she gets loose? She could—"

"She's not going anywhere. It'll take a while for her to heal. I don't even think she's conscious. Blake went after her pretty good."

"Oh, my God. Blake!" Her stomach clenched.

"Blake is fine, except for a few bruised knuckles." Amelia took her hands and held them tightly.

"What about Marcus? Kelly stabbed him."

"He won't be playing catch anytime soon, but they got him all bandaged up, and he's doing okay. He's just a couple of doors down from you, and he's not at all thrilled that his favorite shirt is ruined."

"And Steve. Where is he?"

"He's on a different floor."

"He was hurt too?"

"Yeah. He has a pretty severe gut wound, but he probably saved your life." Amelia smiled. "I'll have to thank him for that."

"I need to see him." Jillian attempted to move and winced at the pain in her shoulder. She must have fallen on it.

"The doctor said you should rest."

"No. I need to see him now." Jillian threw the blanket back.

"Uh, okay. Hang on. Let me get a wheelchair."

"I don't need a wheelchair. I'm fine." Jillian stood, pulled the blanket from the bed, and wrapped it around her shoulders.

"If you want me to take you to Steve, you'll ride in a wheelchair."

"Fine." Jillian sank back down onto the bed. "Can we hurry, please?"

By the time Amelia got back, Jillian was standing at the door waiting for her. "Marcus was worried you might have a head injury."

"There's nothing wrong with my head." Jillian slid into the wheelchair.

"I can see that. Still the same willful woman I fell in love with." Amelia chuckled, and Jillian hopped back out of the chair.

"What did you just say?"

"That you're stubborn as hell?"

"No, the love part."

Amelia moved to her and took her in her arms. "I'm still in love with you." She brushed a strand of hair from Jillian's forehead and tucked it behind her ear. "There's no getting around it. I have been since the first moment I saw you fifteen years ago."

Jillian took in a deep breath, trying to hold back the tears clouding her vision. She felt their warmth stream down her cheeks. "I didn't know if you could ever forgive me."

"I didn't know either until I almost lost you." Amelia's blue eyes shimmered, wet with tears. "Funny how a crazy woman with a knife can give life a little clarity."

"I love you, too, Ames. I never stopped." She pulled her in, held her close. Everything felt right. Then there were kisses. Soft, slow kisses, interrupted only by small sobs and moments of joyous laughter. Being in Amelia's arms was the most wonderful feeling in the world to Jillian. A feeling she thought she would never have the opportunity to experience again. She held her close, afraid she would disappear again just as she had in all of her dreams. Jillian pulled away and looked into her eyes. She didn't want to let her go, but she had to deal with her past. "I need to see Steve."

Amelia nodded. "I'll take you. Hop in." She patted the back of the chair, and Jillian sat down.

A subtle warmth spread throughout Jillian's body. She was home again, safe. She reached back, covered Amelia's hand with hers. "I'm glad you're here with me."

"Me too. I don't plan on letting you out of my sight again." Amelia kissed the top of her head.

The nurse was adjusting Steve's medication when they entered his room. A wide smile took over his face when he saw Jillian. "Glad to see you're okay."

"You saved my life."

"I did what anyone in the same situation would do."

"You're not just anyone. You tried to stop—"

"It wasn't hard. She was a little thing." He scrunched up his face.

"No. You tried to keep my dad from killing himself after he shot my mother."

Amelia dropped down in front of Jillian. "You remember?"

Jillian nodded. "I remember it all now. My mom and dad were arguing about Steve." She looked at him, his brows pulled together. "She wanted to leave, to be with you."

"I never meant for any of it to happen," Steve said, and a tear streamed down his cheek.

"My dad was going to shoot you, but my mom got between the two of you and grabbed the gun. There was a gunshot and she fell to the floor."

"Oh, my God, baby." Amelia took Jillian's hand and pressed it to her lips.

"Then my dad realized what he had done and was going to kill himself. You tried to stop him."

"But I couldn't." He swiped at the tears running down his cheeks. "I didn't know you were there until I saw it on the news. They said you couldn't remember, so I didn't see any reason to come forward and make you relive the whole thing."

"They would've blamed you." She shook her head. "And that would've been wrong. You tried to stop it." She reached over and held his hand. "And now you've saved my life."

"I loved your mother. I could never let anything happen to you."

"I know you did." Jillian remembered her mother always being happy when Steve was around, and she was grateful her mother had experienced that happiness. She looked up at Amelia and wondered if she could do the same.

CHAPTER THIRTY-THREE

Jillian watched Amelia in the early morning moonlight as she slept. They'd made love the night before, slowly, sweetly. Jillian had savored every moment as if it were the very last time. She knew it might very well be for a long while. It had been a couple of weeks since the crazy night of the fund-raiser, and Jillian would be heading back to New York in a couple of days. She wanted so much more than a few stolen weekends a month for her life. For their life, together.

"I can't believe you just let her go." Julie slapped the law book in her hands closed and paced the office.

"I had to, Jules." Amelia squeezed her eyes shut. *No matter how far away she is, she's changed me forever. Even if she lives halfway across the country, I'll still feel her gaze, looking right through this carefully constructed wall I've erected, loving all the parts of me I hate.*

"Don't even tell me you didn't ask her to stay."

Amelia shook her head. "Okay. Then I won't."

"Why the fuck not?"

"She has a career in New York. I can't ask her to give that up." Amelia wouldn't ask Jillian to give up something for which she'd worked so hard.

"Then go with her."

"I can't go with her. Who'll fight for the kids?"

"I will." Julie tossed the book onto her desk. "There are kids in New York that need fighting for too, you know."

"You make it all sound so simple."

"It is simple. You love her. She loves you. Go." Julie grabbed the sides of the desk, and her knuckles whitened.

"She didn't ask me." Amelia's heart clenched at the memory of Jillian and Abby walking into the airport.

Julie closed her eyes and blew out a breath. "Did it ever occur to you maybe she's thinking the same thing?" She took Amelia's face in her hands. "Do you want to lose her again?" Amelia felt the heat of the tears on her cheeks. "Oh, my God, this is so not you. Stop being such an insecure idiot and get on a plane and go."

"I can't."

"Yes, you can." Julie yanked the computer keyboard across the desk and pulled up Jillian's calendar. "You have court until noon tomorrow. I'm booking you the first flight out after that."

Julie left Amelia in her office feeling relieved and scared all at once. Was this the right move? Maybe Jillian *had* wanted her to follow her to New York. What if she hadn't? She would know soon enough. All she knew right now was that an hour-long Skype conversation at the end of her day watching Jillian fade into sleep wasn't enough. She had to stop thinking about her life so much and start living.

❖

Jillian had put in a week of fourteen-hour days since she'd been back in New York, and she was exhausted. She used to love the work, the discovery, the kill at the end of the investigation, but now it didn't hold the same excitement, and she couldn't remember why she'd liked her profession at all. She peeked into Abby's room, where she was lying on her bed staring at her laptop.

"Whatcha doin'?"

"Skyping my friends."

"Oh yeah? Who are you talking to?" Since they'd come back to New York, it seemed like both Abby and Jillian had more interaction with the computer than any of their local friends. Jillian wondered if she should worry, maybe monitor Abby's social-media account more closely.

"Logan." Abby turned the screen sideways, and Logan waved.

Jillian was so exhausted it didn't even register until she saw Logan on the screen. She blinked back the unexpected tears that formed in her eyes. "Hi, Logan. How is everyone there?"

"Good, I guess. Shane's at football practice and David's playing video games." He turned the laptop and she could see David. He paused his game and looked at the screen. "Hey, Jillian. Dad and I are going on a tour of Oklahoma City University tomorrow. Mrs. P got me an art scholarship there."

"I'm glad to hear that. Is that the only one?"

"No. She got one for the University of Science and Arts in Chickasha too. But Dad liked this one better."

"Which one do *you* like, David?"

He smiled, and her heart warmed. He had the same smile as both Blake and Amelia. "I like it too."

"Awesome. Let me know how it turns out."

"There'll be art shows and stuff like that. Will you come to them?"

"Sure. Just let me know when." Jillian got up and went into the living room before the tears spilled out of her eyes, but she wasn't quick enough. Abby was right behind her.

"Mom."

"Yes, honey?" She wiped her face.

"I want to go back to Oklahoma." Abby said it softly, as though she was worried about how Jillian would react.

"Really?"

"I miss Blake and Amelia, and the boys." She flopped down on the end of the couch. "My friends there are so different from everyone here. I think they honestly liked me. Don't you miss them?"

"I do." Jillian flopped back onto the couch. Could she go back to Oklahoma? Could she possibly make a life there with Amelia? Her body warmed. Yes, she could, and she wanted to more than anything. Time for a subject change. "How about pizza for dinner?"

Jillian had showered and changed clothes by the time Marcus knocked on the door. He didn't wait for her to answer before letting himself in. He put the pizza on the counter and shouted, "Pizza delivery."

Abby rushed into the kitchen, took a couple of slices, and said, "Thanks, Uncle Marc," before she went back into her room.

"You're letting her eat in her room?" Marcus took two bottles of beer from the refrigerator. The glasses clanked as he took them from the cabinet, and that was Jillian's cue to get up.

"She's talking to her friends on the computer."

"Why don't they just come over?"

"They're in Oklahoma." She took a slice from the box and bit off a piece.

"That's a new development." He poured the beers into the glasses and handed one to Jillian.

"Thanks for bringing the pizza. I hope I didn't interrupt your plans."

"No plans. I was glad you called." He leaned back against the counter and assessed her. "You look tired."

"I'm exhausted, Marcus, and I'm not happy."

"What's not to be happy about? The people of New York love you."

"Those aren't the people I want to love me."

His lips pulled into a soft smile. "I was wondering when you were going to figure that out." He took the pizza box from the counter, carried it into the living room, and sat on the couch. "Frankly, honey, I was surprised you came back. You have a gorgeous, smart woman in Oklahoma, who literally risked her life to save you."

"She did, didn't she?" Jillian sat her beer on the coffee table and flopped down on the couch next to him. "How could I leave that behind?"

"You'll have to break your contract, and it'll probably cost you a lot of money."

"I don't care about the money, Marcus. I could live by the light in her eyes."

"Okay, then. Tomorrow you talk to your agent and tell her what you want." Marcus picked up Jillian's glass and handed it to her before clinking his with it. "To finally knowing what you want."

CHAPTER THIRTY-FOUR

Amelia was totally out of her element right now. Julie had booked her afternoon flight to New York, which hadn't given her any time to make plans for her house or anything else while she was gone. Julie had agreed to water her plants, but long-term she didn't have the slightest idea of what she was going to do with the house.

Her law practice was a whole different story. Julie had researched what Amelia needed to do in order to practice law in New York. Luckily, New York was a reciprocal-jurisdiction state, and she wouldn't have to take the bar exam again. She could be granted an admission on motion but would have to submit an application for admission to the bar with the supreme court, appellate division to get her license in New York. She'd also need to study all the state laws in order to hit the ground running.

Amelia could do all that, but Jillian might not want her there. She was walking the wire without a net, and the feeling terrified her. Even with all that, it was the most invigorating feeling in the world. She was on her way to be with Jillian, and it was all worth it.

Julie had picked her up, and they had just gotten on the highway when Amelia heard the text tone on her phone. She pulled it out of her purse to see who it was from and saw it was from Blake. She read *911 at the house.*

"Shit." She held up the phone and showed Julie the message before hitting Blake's number. She held the phone to her ear. No answer. "We need to go to the house."

"You're going to miss your flight."

"I'll have to catch another one later."

"Okay, but someone had better be bleeding when we get there." Julie took the next off-ramp, circled around, and headed south.

"Let's not hope for that." Amelia hit the button on the phone again. "Still no answer."

When they pulled up in front of the house, so many thoughts were screaming in Amelia's head, she didn't know where to start. She flew up the walk and through the door. "Blake, what's going on? Are you all right? Why aren't you answering your phone?" She spotted him on the couch with Abby. Her gaze shot from Blake to Abby, then back to Blake.

"What? How?"

"She missed us." He raised his shoulders and let them drop again.

"I did too." Amelia heard the voice from behind, and her heart pounded. She spun to see the gorgeous face she'd been missing so desperately.

"I thought you had to go back to work?" She held her spot, afraid to move until she had all the facts.

"I did, but I had a long talk with my agent, and we worked out a new contract with the station." Jillian took a few steps.

"A new contract?"

"Uh-huh." A few more steps. "It's kind of like bicoastal. I'll be here some and there some."

"Oh, so you'll still live in New York?" Amelia's heart sank. She wanted her here, with her, all the time.

"No. My home will be here, with you. I hope." Jillian's gaze was tentative, questioning. She took another step. "I got back to New York and realized I don't want to be who I am without you, and I never want to settle again. You gave me new life, Ames. I want to dive headfirst into it. With you." Another step. "I love you, Ames. If you'll have me, I want to grow old with you."

Amelia closed the distance between them and pulled Jillian into her arms. "I love you too, baby." She kissed her softly, tenderly, forgetting about everyone around them. "I was on my way to the airport."

"You were?"

She nodded. "I was coming to be with you." She touched Jillian's lips lightly with hers again. "I don't want to live without you either."

"Good, because I can't see myself anywhere else but here, with you." More kisses, murmurs of love, and more kisses. Jillian pulled away, gazed into Amelia's eyes. "Besides, I'll need some input on the kids' foundation I want to set up here."

"Really?"

"Yeah. I hear you're a great advocacy attorney." Jillian's crystalline eyes sparkled, and Amelia felt the familiar swirl in her stomach.

"Ahem," Julie said with a cough to get their attention. "Why don't I take you two home, and you can tell her all about it?" She stood in the doorway waiting.

Jillian looked at Abby, then Blake.

"Go. We've got some catching up to do." He looked at his watch. "Maybe we'll go see a movie tonight." He looked at Abby and she nodded. "So we'll see you in the morning."

Amelia ran over and gave Abby a hug, then Blake. "Best brother ever," she whispered. Then she turned around, took Jillian's hand, and pulled her out the door.

EPILOGUE

Jillian's schedule had been hectic at first. Setting up the studio space in Edmond and traveling back and forth to New York was exhausting, but it was all worth it to be able to come home to Amelia. The traveling had taken some getting used to, but now that Jillian's routine had settled down, she was the happiest she'd ever been.

She and Amelia were seated on the plane in first class, headed to Italy. Jillian had planned the trip as a surprise for Amelia a few months prior. They had gotten married at the courthouse soon after she'd moved back to Oklahoma but hadn't been able to take the time to go on a honeymoon. Jillian had told her agent she'd be making the trip during the show's filming hiatus and had arranged with Julie to cover Amelia's cases during the time they'd be gone. Surprisingly, she and Julie had become good friends over the past few months.

Amelia squeezed Jillian's hand, which was tucked protectively under Amelia's on the armrest. "Business class would've been just fine, you know."

Abby's voice rang from the seat behind them. "Uh-uh. This is awesome."

"Yeah. These snacks are sick." David agreed from across the aisle as he dug into the second snack pack he'd requested from the flight attendant.

Jillian smiled and shifted in her seat to view Abby, the boys, and Blake in the seats surrounding them. *My family.* She let out a contented sigh before she touched her lips gently to Amelia's. "The world is wide open to us, baby. We're going to take full advantage of it."

About the Author

Dena Blake grew up in a small town just north of San Francisco where she learned to play softball, ride motorcycles, and grow vegetables. She eventually moved with her family to the Southwest, where she began creating vivid characters in her mind and bringing them to life on paper.

Dena currently lives in the Southwest with her partner and is constantly amazed at what she learns from her two children. She's a would-be chef, tech nerd, and occasional auto mechanic who has a weakness for dark chocolate and a good cup of coffee.

Books Available From Bold Strokes Books

Beauty and the Boss by Ali Vali. Ellis Renois is at the top of the fashion world, but she never expects her summer assistant Charlotte Hamner to tear her heart and her business apart like sharp scissors through cheap material. (978-162639-919-8)

Fury's Choice by Brey Willows. When gods walk amongst humans, can two women find a balance between love and faith? (978-162639-869-6)

Lessons in Desire by MJ Williamz. Can a summer love stand a four-month hiatus and still burn hot? (978-163555-019-1)

Lightning Chasers by Cass Sellars. For Sydney and Parker, being a couple was never what they had planned. Now they have to fight corruption, murder, and enemies hiding in plain sight just to hold on to each other. Lightning Series, Book Two. (978-162639-965-5)

Summer Fling by Jean Copeland. Still jaded from a breakup years earlier, Kate struggles to trust falling in love again when a summer fling with sexy young singer Jordan rocks her off her feet. (978-162639-981-5)

Take Me There by Julie Cannon. Adrienne and Sloan know it would be career suicide to mix business with pleasure, however tempting it is. But what's the harm? They're both consenting adults. Who would know? (978-162639-917-4)

Unchained Memories by Dena Blake. Can a woman give herself completely when she's left a piece of herself behind? (978-162639-993-8)

Walking Through Shadows by Sheri Lewis Wohl. All Molly wanted to do was go backpacking...in her own century. (978-162639-968-6)

A Lamentation of Swans by Valerie Bronwen. Ariel Montgomery returns to Sea Oats to try to save her broken marriage but soon finds herself also fighting to save her own life and catch a murderer. (978-1-62639-828-3)

Freedom to Love by Ronica Black. What happens when the woman who spent her life worrying about caring for her family finally finds the freedom to love without borders? (978-1-63555-001-6)

House of Fate by Barbara Ann Wright. Two women must throw off the lives they've known as a guardian and an assassin and save two rival houses before their secrets tear the galaxy apart. (978-1-62639-780-4)

Planning for Love by Erin Dutton. Could true love be the one thing that wedding coordinator Faith McKenna didn't plan for? (978-1-62639-954-9)

Sidebar by Carsen Taite. Judge Camille Avery and her clerk, attorney West Fallon, agree on little except their mutual attraction, but can their relationship and their careers survive a headline-grabbing case? (978-1-62639-752-1)

Sweet Boy and Wild One by T. L. Hayes. When Rachel Cole meets soulful singer Bobby Layton at an open mic, she is immediately in thrall. What she soon discovers will rock her world in ways she never imagined. (978-1-62639-963-1)

To Be Determined by Mardi Alexander and Laurie Eichler. Charlie Dickerson escapes her life in the US to rescue Australian wildlife with Pip Atkins, but can they save each other? (978-1-62639-946-4)

True Colors by Yolanda Wallace. Blogger Robby Rawlins plans to use First Daughter Taylor Crenshaw to get ahead, but she never planned on falling in love with her in the process. (978-1-62639-927-3)

Heart Stop by Radclyffe. Two women, one with a damaged body, the other a damaged spirit, challenge each other to dare to live again. (978-1-62639-899-3)

Undercover Affairs by Julie Blair. Searching for stolen documents crucial to U.S. security, CIA agent Rett Spenser confronts lies, deceit, and unexpected romance as she investigates art gallery owner Shannon Kent. (978-1-62639-905-1)

Taking Sides by Kathleen Knowles. When passion and politics collide, can love survive? (978-1-62639-876-4)

Unexpected by Jenny Frame. When Dale McGuire falls for Rebecca Harper, the mother of the son she never knew she had, will Rebecca's troubled past stop them from making the family they both truly crave? (978-1-62639-942-6)

Canvas for Love by Charlotte Greene. When ghosts from Amelia's past threaten to undermine their relationship, Chloé must navigate the greatest romance of her life without losing sight of who she is. (978-1-62639-944-0)

Repercussions by Jessica L. Webb. Someone planted information in Edie Black's brain and now they want it back, but with the protection of shy former soldier Skye Kenny, Edie has a chance at life and love. (978-1-62639-925-9)

Spark by Catherine Friend. Jamie's life is turned upside down when her consciousness travels back to 1560 and lands in the body of one of Queen Elizabeth I's ladies-in-waiting…or has she totally lost her grip on reality? (978-1-62639-930-3)

Thorns of the Past by Gun Brooke. Former cop Darcy Flynn's heart broke when her career on the force ended in disgrace, but perhaps saving Sabrina Hawk's life will mend it in more ways than one. (978-1-62639-857-3)

You Make Me Tremble by Karis Walsh. Seismologist Casey Radnor comes to the San Juan Islands to study an earthquake but finds her heart shaken by passion when she meets animal rescuer Iris Mallery. (978-1-62639-901-3)

Girls Next Door, edited by Sandy Lowe and Stacia Seaman. Best-selling romance authors tell it from the heart—sexy, romantic stories of falling for the girls next door. (978-1-62639-916-7)

Complications by MJ Williamz. Two women battle for the heart of one. (978-1-62639-769-9)

Crossing the Wide Forever by Missouri Vaun. As Cody Walsh and Lillie Ellis face the perils of the untamed West, they discover that love's uncharted frontier isn't for the weak in spirit or the faint of heart. (978-1-62639-851-1)

Fake It till You Make It by M. Ullrich. Lies will lead to trouble, but can they lead to love? (978-1-62639-923-5)

Pursuit by Jackie D. The pursuit of the most dangerous terrorist in America will crack the lines of friendship and love, and not everyone will make it out from under the weight of duty and service. (978-1-62639-903-7)

The Practitioner by Ronica Black. Sometimes love comes calling whether you're ready for it or not. (978-1-62639-948-8)

Unlikely Match by Fiona Riley. When an ambitious PR exec and her super-rich coding geek-girl client fall in love, they learn that giving something up may be the only way to have everything. (978-1-62639-891-7)

Where Love Leads by Erin McKenzie. A high school counselor and the mom of her new student bond in support of the troubled girl, never expecting deeper feelings to emerge, testing the boundaries of their relationship. (978-1-62639-991-4)

Forsaken Trust by Meredith Doench. When four women are murdered, Agent Luce Hansen must regain trust in her most valuable investigative tool—herself—to catch the killer. (978-1-62639-737-8)

Letter of the Law by Carsen Taite. Will federal prosecutor Bianca Cruz take a chance at love with horse breeder Jade Vargas, whose dark family ties threaten everything Bianca has worked to protect—including her child? (978-1-62639-750-7)

New Life by Jan Gayle. Trigena and Karrie are having a baby, but the stress of becoming a mother and the impact on their relationship might be too much for Trigena. (978-1-62639-878-8)

Soul Survivor by I. Beacham. Sam and Joey have given up on hope, but when fate brings them together it gives them a chance to change each other's life and make dreams come true. (978-1-62639-882-5)

Unbroken by Donna K. Ford. When Kayla and Jackie, two women with every reason to reject Happily Ever After, fall in love, will they have the courage to overcome their pasts and rewrite their stories? (978-1-62639-921-1)